NEBULA AWARDS 23

NEBULA AWARDS 23

SFWA's
Choices for the Best
Science Fiction & Fantasy 1987

Edited by

MICHAEL BISHOP

Harcourt Brace Jovanovich, Publishers

San Diego   New York   London

The Library of Congress has cataloged this serial as follows:

The Nebula awards. — No. 18- — New York [N.Y.]: Arbor House, c1983–
v.; 22 cm.
Annual.
Published: San Diego, Calif.: Harcourt Brace Jovanovich, 1984–
Published for: Science Fiction Writers of America, 1983–
Continues: Nebula award stories (New York, N.Y.: 1982)
ISSN 0741-5567 = The Nebula awards
1. Science fiction, American — Periodicals. I. Science Fiction Writers of America.
PS648.S3N38   83-647399
813'.0876'08 — dc19
AACR 2 MARC-S
Library of Congress [8709r84]rev
ISBN 0-15-164930-8
ISBN 0-15-665475-X (Harvest/HBJ: pbk)

Designed by G.B.D. Smith
Printed in the United States of America

First edition

A B C D E

Permissions acknowledgments appear on pages 373–374,
which constitute a continuation of the copyright page.

In Memory of

Randall Garrett 1927–1987

Lin Carter 1930–1988

Clifford D. Simak 1904–1988

Robert A. Heinlein 1907–1988

Contents

Contents

Introduction

Michael Bishop

With gratitude and enthusiasm, I assume the editorship of the annual Nebula anthology from George Zebrowski, who did much during his three-year tenure to revitalize the Nebula Awards series. He sought not only to make the anthology as attractive to readers as the popular best-of-the-year volumes edited by Terry Carr, Gardner Dozois, and Donald Wollheim, but also to augment its value as a significant record of the year's SF activity.

To this latter end, George secured columnists to record telling developments in the movie industry and noteworthy literary trends; he elicited comments about winning and nominated stories from the writers themselves; he made sure that the winner of the Nebula for Best Novel appeared in every volume with a self-contained work of fiction; he strove to find a recent story by, or to commission an essay from, each new recipient of the Grand Master Nebula Award; he reserved the right to use an insightful essay about the *writing* of science fiction; he continued the brief tradition of publishing the Rhysling Award poetry winners; and he purposely did not limit his short-fiction selections to either the final Nebula ballot or the preliminary Nebula ballot, particularly if it seemed to him that the membership of Science Fiction Writers of America (SFWA) had overlooked a story of distinctive merit.

Most important of all, perhaps, is that George's editorship—one of expert caring—gave this Nebula Award series a stability and a continuity that it had never had before. In this, of course, he was aided by the long-term commitment of the volumes' publisher, Harcourt Brace Jovanovich, and by the editorial expertise of John Radziewicz and Vicki Austin.

SFWA and Harcourt Brace Jovanovich have blessed me with the same skillful publishing team and a three-year run of my own. I intend to adhere to George's successful game plan in compiling my numbers of this showcase anthology. Readers wishing evidence of a fresh editorial presence will find it only in the new columnist I have brought aboard, the color of my headnotes, and the runner-up and off-ballot story selections I have made.

Next year, I may have more to say in my introduction. *Nebula Awards 23*, however, is a hefty book already, and the real meat—as it always should be—is in the pages that follow.

Pine Mountain, Georgia
24 May 1988

The World Renews Itself: A View on the SF and Fantasy of 1987

Ian Watson

J. G. Ballard once praised Ian Watson as "the most interesting British SF writer of ideas—or, more accurately, the *only* British SF writer of ideas." Nowadays, some might dispute that stressed *only*, but who else, British or American, has written so well and so provocatively about the evolutionary implications of language, the idiotic waste of the arms race, the human desire for transcendence, and the metaphysical promise of alternative realities?

Watson's many novels include *The Embedding*, *The Jonah Kit*, the *Martian Inca*, *Alien Embassy*, *Miracle Visitors*, *Deathhunter*, the trilogy commencing with *The Book of the River*, and a recent novel entitled *The Power* featuring not only some of the blackest humor and most searing wit to be found in the contemporary horror story, but also a cogent dramatization of the fact that nuclear weapons are the most deadly evil in the world today. Ian Watson has also published essays, criticism, and several volumes of short stories, and even though I have never met him face to face, I regard him as one of my best and closest friends, my Northamptonshire alter ego, my transatlantic conscience.

Born in 1943 and raised on Tyneside, Watson graduated from Oxford University with a First in English in 1963 and did further research in comparative literature. He lectured at universities in East Africa (1965–1967) and Japan (1967–1970), then returned to England to teach Future Studies at Birmingham Polytechnic, a post he left in 1976 to pursue his writing career.

The Embedding, his first novel, garnered laurels not only in England and the United States, but also in Europe, winning France's prestigious Prix Apollo in 1975. In fact, from the very beginning, Watson's work has wrestled imaginatively with matters of universal import against a wide variety of international backdrops; therefore, my initial response to those self-hyping proponents of cyberpunk (see below for a fuller explanation of this phenomenon) claiming to be the first science-fiction writers to approach their work from a "global perspective," to free it from the mire of "Anglo-American parochialism," was . . . well, appalled incredulity. Even Watson, fifteen years ago, would not have made that historically blinkered claim for his *own* groundbreaking novels.

But enough of that.

I asked Ian to write the following survey/summary of the SF and fantasy fields in 1987 because I thought the readers of this annual volume would benefit from the insights of an informed, British-based observer. Ian has the interest and élan to stay abreast of the field, an unswerving faith in the potential of visionary SF to revitalize the world, and both the credentials and the cheek to make unequivocal discriminations among those items on SFWA's preliminary ballot that strike him as deserving of comment. In fact, he has looked *beyond* this ballot at some items not technically eligible for 1987's trophies, and he has done so with integrity, level-headedness, and wit. Expect a return engagement in *Nebula Awards 24*.

The world, as we shall discover, renews itself.

Books, too, renew themselves, not merely by giving birth

to sequels but also by securing a second year of Nebula Award recommendations when their authors take advantage of current rules to withdraw first editions in favor of later, more visible mass-market paperbacks. Thus, for award purposes, Gene Wolfe's important *The Urth of the New Sun* ceases to be a 1987 title and becomes instead a hot contender in 1988. Similarly, titles from 1986 have mutated into books of 1987.

This withdrawal system can be a confounding coitus interruptus for the critic. Indeed, Charles Brown, editor of *Locus*, the *Wall Street Journal* of the science-fiction field, recently deplored it as a corruption of the award's original intent.* Another anomaly of the system is that books first published in Britain or Australia have no official existence until they gain an American edition—though the fact that most voting members of Science Fiction Writers of America (SFWA) reside in the United States imparts a *degree* of logic to this rule.

In this essay on the harvest of 1987, I shall limit my remarks to titles validly on the Nebula list—with the single exception of highlighting outstanding short fiction published in the British magazine *Interzone*, an innovative outlet for new talent from both sides of the Atlantic.†

The preliminary ballot for the 1987 Nebula Award comprised 81 novels, 24 novellas (usually the smallest category), 81 novelettes, and 110 short stories; it may therefore seem to verge on a list of everything science fictional and fantastic published in the United States during the year in question. Yet it isn't, not by any means, and a survey of this huge crop must inevitably be selective; I hope, though, that it will also be symptomatic.

---

* For current rates for *Locus*, write Locus Publications, Box 13305, Oakland, CA 94661.
† *Interzone* is available by subscription only, $15 sea mail or $18 air mail for four issues, from 124 Osborne Road, Brighton BN1 6LU, United Kingdom.

Not uncommonly, the questions and puzzles posed in SF novels require ever-larger answers—to the point that the intoxicated or desperate author must tackle the entire universe. Which inevitably dwarfs the author's best efforts. For, ordinarily, the answers and the methods of approach come to seem increasingly more childish the more staggering and titanic they are. Toss in everything, and you diminish the total.

In the high-tech future of David Brin's *The Uplift War*, set in the same universe as his award-winning *Startide Rising* (1983), an ingeniously invented range of squabbling aliens have all at some stage undergone evolutionary "uplift" through the intervention of other aliens. Status depends upon one's place in the pecking order of patron-and-client races. So which vanished race of Ancients inaugurated the system? Already a chicken-and-egg problem teases us, a possibility of endless recursion. And if the first Ancients were so clever, why did they disappear?

The Uplift War pits future humanity and its client neo-chimps against the avian Galactics known as Gubru. It stars a human male and a female alien, daughter of the friendly Tymbrimi ambassador, who are fundamentally adolescent. Further, it deploys a number of adolescent clichés. Its ethos of boys-will-be-boys (and girls-will-be-girls) leads to the alien female growing big boobs to please Robert. From the adolescent phase of the development of the SF genre, Brin borrows the hoary notion of the uniqueness of humanity: we human beings alone got to the stars under our own steam, we alone use metaphors, we alone aren't set in our ways, we alone never say die. And so on.

As the plot ramifies, Brin arbitrarily tosses in machine civilizations too, so that we worry at what level of overcomplication, accompanying oversimplification, and pubescent mental age the saga will finally arrive. Along the way, however, *The Uplift War* offers some effervescent, heart-plucking, even visionary effects, not the least of which is the alien female's healing descent into Robert's symbol-laden subconscious. Nor is it at all racist; in the final *Star Wars*–style awards ceremony, the furry folk get their medals too.

Frederick Pohl completed his Heechee saga with *Annals of the Heechee*, a smart and knavish explanation of the whole shebang that inadvertently demonstrates this new science fictional law: that as a novel's threat tends to the infinite, so do its characters become more kiddyish. The scary mystery of the vanished Heechee and their abandoned items of technology—the mystery that made the original *Gateway* (1977) such a masterpiece—Pohl has now onion-peeled to a point where human child and anthropomorphized Heechee child are at school together and about to become the focus of the whole cosmos. Also, the terrible, universe-altering foes from whom the Heechee hid in their black hole turn out to be no foes at all, but electromagnetic intelligences who in a deus ex machina finale decide that human beings and Heechee, given another million years or so, will also opt to become like them. *Annals* contains the best sugar-coated cosmology lesson of 1987, with highly professional pacing, but finally it is a fairy tale, ending on a note of happily ever after. . . .

The universe is not so forgiving in Greg Bear's *The Forge of God*, a fact that led John Clute in the London *Observer* to dub this novel genuinely subversive. Here, a gang of self-replicating von Neumann machines obliterates the world utterly, despite humanity's best efforts. Meanwhile, another gang scurries to save a core of human beings and gene samples with which to repopulate the newly terraformed planets of Mars and Venus. Although the thrust of this rescue mission might seem to diminish the disaster, it gives Bear a narrative vantage from which to depict this truly awesome and moving destruction of Earth.

Other braveries include his portrayal of the sheer danger posed by an American president with Revelationist beliefs; the extension of the Gaia theory—that the world is a single living organism—to embrace the idea that human beings are the Earth's seed carriers; and the conceit that diseases such as AIDS arise specifically to spur us to master our own biology so that we may become even better planetary gonads. Bear writes a functional prose that occasionally rises to eloquence, as in his description of Yosemite at world's end; and he tends to toss in an excess of notions, a syndrome to which large-scale SF is conspicuously prone.

In *Dawn*, the first volume of her *Xenogenesis* series, Octavia Butler also posits the destruction of Earth, this time by our own nuclear stupidity. The alien Oankali, humanoid medusae intent on trading desirable genes with humankind, save our survivors in order to refurbish the planet and engineer a human-alien hybrid. Butler persuasively evokes her aliens (her humans, too, for that matter), attributing to them believable genetic imperatives. Even when a young alien interacts with a human being, the Oankali remain mature adult inventions. They also remain *alien*. They don't suddenly start acting like midwesterners, growing prodigious boobs, and falling in love. Nevertheless, the novel does contain scenes of powerful emotional, and biological, intercourse.

Butler's outstanding story "The Evening and the Morning and the Night" describes a new, genetically inherited disease, the unintended by-product of a "magic bullet" cure for cancer and other ills. Its psychotic victims mutilate themselves hideously. Lynn, a carrier, has always lived with this soul-destroying threat until a treatment center run by the sick offers her a surprising new perspective, a renewed hope, which is almost more than she can cope with.

Linguistic intercourse with superior aliens is the theme of Suzette Haden Elgin's *The Judas Rose*. In its predecessor, *Native Tongue* (1984), Elgin introduced us to an intensely male-chauvinist society and a secret female language, Láadan, that liberates the perceptions of women who slave to interpret jaw-cracking alien lingos. The sequel is more broadly satiric. Its passionate feminism invites comparison with Pamela Sargent's humanistic treatment of the flip side of sexual oppression in *The Shore of Women* (about which, more below).

Implied in *The Judas Rose* is a third novel in which Láadan might yet persuade the superior alien Consortium not to euthanase Homo sapiens for its macho bigotry.

What a lot of series there are! But as Bob Shaw's *The Ragged Astronauts*, the first book of a projected trilogy, shows us, the component novels need not be fatuous clone-work. Set in a slightly alternative universe where physical law allows a planet and its moon to share the same atmosphere, permitting hot-air balloon travel between the two, Shaw's novel gracefully yokes a delightful "rubber science" notion with a lovingly imagined ecology and an equally well-detailed society; it also features real human beings about whose fate the reader comes to care deeply. One feels that a trilogy is the necessary scale for what bids fair to be Bob Shaw's finest work to date.

Whereas books by Shaw and Bear feature an outright scientific challenge, which the characters may or may not overcome, Orson Scott Card flavors his science with ethical implications. In his *Wyrms*, typically, much gonzo biology plays a central role, just as it did in his award-winning *Speaker for the Dead* (1986). This time, alien genes and even alien organisms are able to "hide" within apparently terrestrial stock on a colony planet. Card's inventions—such as the head-worms that reanimate the decapitated dead and torment them to tell the truth—are at once admirable, as fruits of the imagination, and horrible. With a "Kristos" awaited on this alien world, the novel appears to be a cunning piece of Christian proselytism, albeit one distanced by its science fictional devices (just as Gene Wolfe's *Urth of the New Sun* is an artful, trickster recension of the Bible; but hush, about that, until next year). Card is a virtuoso of the emotions, often painful ones. His characters suffer intensely from helpless bondage, loneliness, torment, loss, and grief. Admirably brave, they also experience communion, inner freedom, love, and forgiveness—but, in the reader's mind, the memory of their anguish lingers.

Nor is *Wyrms* Card's only novel employing mystic sevens last year—for if its heroine, Patience, is seven times seven times seven generations descended from the first Starship Captain, then Alvin Maker in *Seventh Son* is a seventh son of a seventh son and thus a potential redeemer in a struggle between Satan and Goodness. This time, however, the distancing devices are the fantasy elements of hexes and effective magic and the SF paraphernalia of alternative history. *Seventh Son* is the fascinating first volume of an other-history saga of the American frontier, flawed only by the inclusion of an emigré William Blake as Taleswapper. The original Blake was a zany, hectic visionary who indeed tasted the apple of knowledge. By contrast, Taleswapper seems to be a rather self-righteous Johnny Appleseed in search of magic.

Last season's flavor d'estime was cyberpunk, a variety of SF in which authors plug their human characters into computers or other high-tech prostheses in hip, designer-sleaze futures. The premier entry in the 1987 cyberpunk stakes was George Alec Effinger's *When Gravity Fails*, a harsh but vivid neo-Chandleresque thriller set in an Islamic red-light district of wired brains, false-personality modules, sex changes, and drugs galore. Marîd, Effinger's hustler hero, is notably *sympatique* (pardon my French, but he mainly speaks Arabic or French, an interesting departure from pan-English futures), and one genuinely grieves at his final loneliness.

Although Marîd does ache from the beatings he receives and his myriad brutal drug hangovers, the reader must take on trust the resiliency of his metabolism and his continuing ability to function—an area where we must suspend disbelief in William Gibsonville, too. But Effinger's buoyant venture into cyberpunkdom is vigorous, jazzy, and strangely endearing in spite of its atrocious murders—as endearing, in fact, as the title of his own short story about a future Islamic soldier and his computerized weapons system, "King of the Cyber Rifles."

Pat Cadigan's first novel, *Mindplayers*, explores the fast

track of the brain-wired consciousness industry in hard-bitten, wisecracking, cyberpunkish style. Unlike Effinger's, her future isn't alarmingly cut-throat. A bacchanalian mind-orgy may be in progress throughout, but physical violence hardly figures. Aside from various traumatic psychoses, the altered states of consciousness and lucid dreamscapes she describes are softer in mood than the cyberspace of computer cowboys jacked into machines. The thrust is therapeutic, renewing.

Another outstanding first novel, Michael Blumlein's *The Movement of Mountains*, features the oddest yet most convincing of heroes, a highly strung glutton. He becomes physician to a genetically engineered breed of giant slave-workers who are vilely exploited. Blumlein's settings and events constantly startle. His measured prose, gemmed with epigrams, alternately disconcerts and illuminates us.

SF is in a phase of ferment. Crusades, credos, commitments abound. A rapid Darwinian evolution of styles and themes is under way. But perhaps of more consequence than the *validity* of any one path is the passionate commitment to discover the new voice, the new method, the new future vision. Commercially, today's writers are up against the stale-doughnut syndrome: last year's masterpiece and last year's Young Turk are yesterday's doughnuts. Still, genuine imaginative ferment is taking place.

Scarcely had the "cyberpunk-humanist" war of the mid-1980s slacked off, with cyberpunk perhaps beginning to erase itself like a viral computer program, than Michael Swanwick's *Vacuum Flowers* looked set to trigger a new round of conflict, the Wetware Wars. This vibrant and compassionate depiction of a solar-system-wide humanity features the instant imprinting of people with new skills, behaviors, and ideologies by daubing protoplasmic programs on their faces. Was this, cried the purists, genuine wetware as defined by the artificial intelligence labs at MIT, or a bogus cosmetic exercise? At year's end, the issue was still moot, although the SF community had learned that Rudy Rucker, that magician of higher dimensions and mathematical infinities, was working on a novel entitled *Wetware*. . . .

K. W. Jeter might have founded cyberpunk a decade ago had any publisher dared to release *Dr. Adder*, which saw print only on the movement's coattails in 1984. However, Jeter did manage to preview "steam punk" in 1979 with *Morlock Night:* high-tech sleaze by gaslight. And *Morlock Night* prefigured last year's *Infernal Devices*, a hilarious and sinister pastiche of Victorian England, containing wheels within wheels, fish-men, mad machines, a plot to split the Earth with vibrations, and a berserking Paganini robot. Although SF often strives to foreguess and imitate the accents of the alien future, here Jeter shows us that it may also transfigure the past, opening up an extra universe of possibilities that reflect, as in a fun-house mirror, the present.

In *Soldier of the Mist*, Gene Wolfe swings his time pendulum from the archaic far future of his four-volume *Book of the New Sun* and its all-remembering narrator, Severian, back to ancient Greece and an amnesiac storyteller. Soldier Latro's *recherche du temps perdu*, achieved by rereading his diary scroll every morning to discover what has been happening to him, details a puzzled but vivid quest. As if in compensation for his brain damage, the gods are visible to Latro alone; his perceptions of the supernatural and the mundane intermesh. This is also the case in *The Shattered Horse*, by S. P. Somtow, an ambitious retelling of the aftermath of the Trojan War, where myth and reality are given equal interpretative weight, lending a "Heisenbergian uncertainty" to the proceedings. But, possibly, *Soldier of the Mist* is also a book of ingenious dissimulation, a metafiction, for neither Latro nor the reader may be certain what really happened to him the day before. This narrative ploy demands continual reinterpretation of the text, making Wolfe's novel a fine instance of how a science fictional device can generate a unique and cunning literary method.

John Crowley's *Aegypt*, first installment in a projected

series, moves the reader ahead to the dawning of our present Aquarian age and the revival of hermetic knowledge. Also, an unsuccessful but intuitive history professor undertakes something of a chautauqua through rural America. In Crowley's version of Robert Pirsig's *Zen and the Art of Motorcycle Maintenance*, however, the world's secret history is the professor's motorcycle, and its occult wisdom is his stand-in for Zen. *Aegypt* is another text that will surely need reinterpretation as future volumes appear, although in my view (a judgment largely unshared, it seems), it is for long stretches the worst-written masterpiece of last year. Full of knotty, involuted sentences like "He wanted above all that she not think he was not up to her," the book has the earmarks of a secret code requiring initiation, a novel for worshipers unmindful of the discomfort of sore knees. Still, to renew the world by demonstrating that the true world is other than we thought is an ambitious exercise, not unworthy of comparison to Wolfe's strategy of renewing Latro's life from one day to the next.

Similarly self-indulgent in the fantasy vein is Peter Beagle's *The Folk of the Air*. Plagued with overwritten characters uttering offbeam, disconnected gnomic comments, this homage to the Society of Creative Anachronism often reads like a literal translation from a peculiar foreign tongue. Emma Bull's debut novel, *The War for the Oaks*, also highlights music, magic, and a transfigured modern city—Minneapolis rather than Berkeley—but in a fresh and delightful way that reinvigorates these materials. Further, the growing love between Bull's contemporary female rock singer and the fairy Phouka is both literally magical and grittily realistic.

Another authentic love story, one central to its novel's plot, occurs in *The Shore of Women*, by Pamela Sargent, who limpidly and movingly presents a postholocaust world of sheltered, stagnating cities inhabited only by women. In the brutish wilderness outside these cities roam tribes of men exiled from technology for their failed custodianship of the planet. These men worship the women as goddesses, and their ultimate reward is a summons to a city wall to contribute their seed by an impersonal technological process and to collect any male offspring memory-wiped by the city before their expulsion. The book's rebellious, exiled heroine and a tribesman robbed of his full human heritage, as are all men, fall—slowly—in love, the first love between a man and a woman in centuries. *Shore* is a brave novel of social and sexual insight; in spite of taking place in a world whose inhabitants have denied history, it has real historic sweep, and at the book's apex is rediscovered tragic love, renewed love.

Clive Barker progressed from the fierce, visionary, razor-blade horror of his first novel, *The Damnation Game*, to epic-scale magic with horrid overtones in *Weaveworld*. The setting is modern, seedy Liverpool, where Seerkind hide themselves and their modest but glittering domain in the midst of the mundane Cuckoos (ourselves) in the pattern of a magic carpet. Meanwhile, in Arabia Deserta lurks an alien angel who would destroy Seerkind vilely. Barker excels at evoking shifting, amorphous things that, despite their solidity, defy the appalled eye to fix them. His descriptions are luminously different, and his images—"molten stone seethed between its lips and murdered the poppies"—constantly startle.

Ghosts from the Yucatán past haunt the archeologist heroine of Pat Murphy's *The Falling Woman*. Just as Wolfe's soldier of the mist meets gods, Elizabeth Butler sees and meets these ancient Mayans, for another time-cusp approaches, a Mayan cycle impinging on the modern world. Elizabeth's actual spadework into the ruined past is an apt objective correlative for her digging into her own alienated past. This quiet, sad novel seems almost mainstream in both its approach and tone.

Murphy's novelette, "Rachel in Love," rings a poignant change upon the SF theme of the backyard genius. A maverick scientist, who is researching the "electric mind" in the Arizona desert, loses his daughter in a car crash but preserves her identity in the brain of a young chimpanzee. When he dies, Rachel is taken to a sordid primate research center to be treated like any other monkey. Her escape with her chimp boyfriend Johnson and their odyssey homeward capture the hearts of the American public, and our hearts too.

Another ghost—that of a U.S. combat soldier in Southeast Asia—figures in Lucius Shepard's standout novelette "Shades." This ghost has fallen captive to Communist parapsych technologists in Vietnam, and Shepard presents both the ghost's and the astonished narrator's anguish in tough, vibrant, rainbow-hued prose. "Shades" is a tale of deadly tropical warfare intensified by the addition of shamanistic mysteries. Reminiscent, though less lavishly written, is F. Paul Wilson's tale "Day-Tay-Vao" about a Vietnamese healing entity that possesses a selfish slob of a U.S. army cook. Unlike "Shades," Wilson's story does not appear in the best theme anthology of the year, *In the Field of Fire*, edited by Jeanne Van Buren Dann and Jack Dann, which deftly explores the past and ongoing impact of that complex, tragic, and perhaps essentially *alien* war, a conflict still resonating in America's soul.

As the thoughtful introduction to *In the Field of Fire* points out, the U.S. military deliberately structured a tour in Vietnam as an "alienated" experience—in the false hope of smoothly recycling its teenage veterans back into "the World" again. Indeed, many American survivors felt that they had journeyed by warp-ship to a far jungle planet, inhabited by aliens called Gooks, where their world view was savagely shattered and deadly local drugs invaded their nervous systems. Or as if someone had pushed them over a borderline into a grim alternative reality. Not remarkably, then, paranormal forces often emerge as narrative hooks in SF-cum-fantasy treatments of the Vietnam War.

Hence the ESP tales in Bruce McAllister's strong, heart-rending "Dream Baby," part of a novel in progress. This story puts forward the proposition that the hothouse of combat in

Vietnam forced the flowering of a wide range of paranormal talents, which, apparently, the CIA attempted to exploit. Based on four years of interviews with Vietnam veterans who claimed that spontaneous ESP experiences saved their lives, McAllister's story declares that "the Vietnam War, even now, wasn't what it seemed. . . ."

This same perspective colors Craig Kee Strete's contribution, "The Game of Cat and Eagle." Here, an American Indian medicine man is flown to the war zone to fight a psychic battle with the power-spirit of Vietnam. This struggle to determine whether America can in fact win the war occurs on an astral mountain discoverable on no map. One cynical, scared CIA operative compares the medicine man's mission to Hitler's dalliance with astrologers; however, Strete's ending endorses a mystic reading of events: "Beneath the shadows and smoke lived another Vietnam. . . . 'The white man cannot defeat what he cannot see, cannot conquer a land he cannot find.' "

Away from Vietnam, the psychic bestiary of American Indian shamanism figures in Ursula K. Le Guin's "Buffalo Gals, Won't You Come Out Tonight." In this fluent, teasing, magical-realist story, a child survivor of a plane crash recuperates in the township of the totem animals and learns from them something crucial about both life and death. Similarly transreal but similarly illuminating is Geoff Ryman's novella "The Unconquered Country," which transports the reader back to Southeast Asia, this time to the killing fields of an alternative Cambodia. Metamorphosed by magical realism, the houses in this fictive nation are living organisms, and women rent out wombs to grow machine components—a species of vision shared by Gwyneth Jones in *Divine Endurance*, one more imaginative tale set in a transfigured, anguish-ridden Southeast Asia.

Two other noteworthy Ryman works appeared in 1987. His strange but splendid fantasy novel *The Warrior Who Carried Life* had its first U.S. publication, and *Interzone* ran a two-part serialization of another admirably different novella, "Love Sickness." This latter focuses on a future postrevolutionary London where tailored propaganda- and information-viruses continually infect and sicken the inhabitants. One might suppose this notion a magical-realist variation on cyberpunkdom's wetware, but these viruses have their grounding in contemporary science, just as Ryman's peculiar future society has its basis in history.

"Love Sickness," then, is authentically other, despite the fact that its near-future Earth stems from our present in a seamlessly believable fashion. The story is bittersweet, grotesque, comic, and moving; it contains passages of amazing beauty and a humdinger of a cosmic climax. In Ryman's work is another new order of writing and vision, one that encourages the field to reconstitute and reanimate itself as surely as do the techniques of steam punk, surrealism, magical realism, or Rudy Rucker's elusive "freestyle" approach—in which, according to Rucker, "you write like yourself, only more so."

To renew itself, the SF/fantasy world requires a supply of new writers. Aside from Clarion (those six-week total-immersion summer courses taught by various major authors), one organ of generation is the anthology series *Writers of the Future*, plus its workshops. The third volume of the series appeared in 1987, showcasing winners and runners-up in the well-funded quarterly contests sponsored by an offshoot (said to be independent) of the late L. Ron Hubbard's organization. Here we breathe controversy, which the official SF press as represented by *Locus* and *Science Fiction Chronicle* tends to shy away from.*

Vital SF should of course stir up controversy—the marketable controversy of cyberpunk wars, wetware wars, feminist concerns, and other political and/or aesthetic agendas—

---

* *SF Chronicle* is available from Andrew Porter, Box 4175, New York, NY 10163.

but perhaps there is also an Aegyptian contemporary history of the field, which surfaces only in certain fanzines or semipro magazines. The questions of whether—or not—Scientology has been extending control-tentacles into the field under the guise of its *Writers of the Future* contests and its other promotional activities engaged the attention of Chris Evans, who tackled that question from many different points of view in his fanzine, *Conspiracy Theories*. Evans's jumping-off place was the Hubbard organization's suspected "hijacking" of Conspiracy, the 1987 World Science Fiction Convention held in Brighton, England, and of its sacrosanct Hugo Awards ceremony. Meanwhile, in *The Last Deadloss Visions*, Christopher Priest was exploring another Aegyptian minefield, namely the career of Harlan Ellison's long-promised and repeatedly deferred state-of-the-art anthology, *The Last Dangerous Visions*. Priest tossed a bottle containing a pointed message— that he believed it unlikely that the anthology would ever appear—into a seemingly pacific ocean, beneath which krakens lurk.

As for the stories in *Writers of the Future, Volume III*, those by the new, or newish, names Carolyn Ives Gilman, Martha Soukup, Jean Reitz, R. V. Branham, Lori Ann White, Tawn Stokes, Paula May, and David Wolverton certainly promise well for the literary future that these contests are ostensibly all about.

Terry Carr, the SF field's premier anthologist, died in 1987. Carr's long-running *Universe* series of original, cutting-edge anthologies will survive in alternate years, edited by Robert Silverberg and Karen Haber. Meanwhile, a new original series with high literary standards, *Synergy*, began life under the guidance of George Zebrowski; its debut volume starred Frederik Pohl in vintage satiric vein with "My Life as a Born-Again Pig," a novella.

As expected, the art of short fiction was signally alive and well in the SF field in 1987. *The Magazine of Fantasy and Science Fiction* and *Issac Asimov's Science Fiction Magazine* perhaps led all others in the number of well-crafted and innovative stories. In addition, Orson Scott Card founded an ambitious new magazine, *Short Form*, expressly to review as much of our category's short-fiction output as proved humanly possible.* However, the task of loading so much baggage on board delayed the venture's takeoff, and the service may not operate to schedule owing to the sheer volume of stories published every year. For the same reason, with far less space at my disposal, I can mention only a few more notable items in *this* essay.

In Pat Cadigan's tough-minded story "Angel," an alien race exiles its pervert criminals to Earth, where they engage in eerie vampirish intercourse with human beings. This tale mixes all the fixated erotic pain of James Tiptree, Jr.'s, classic "And I Awoke and Found Me Here on the Cold Hill Side" with the chilling vampire variations of Anne Rice. Tiptree herself—a.k.a. Alice Sheldon—powerfully addresses U.S. military interference in Central America in "Yanqui Doodle," a story in which a drug-hyped private turns his homicidal skills on the politicos who put him there. "In the Midst of Life," meanwhile, was her quiet last testament in fiction before courageously taking her ailing husband's life and then her own.

In "To Meet the Alien," Andrew Weiner sends a human starship crew to the source of a seemingly revelatory alien signal only to have them find that the aliens regard actual interstellar travel as undesirably eccentric. They hold no solutions to our problems and are perfectly indifferent to any cosmic intercourse—particularly with humanity—beyond the entertainment value of the information as such. Taken down several pegs, but still not wholly abashed, the crew members live out their lives in 1950s trailer homes replicated for them by the batlike aliens: a neat, ironic story. Aliens also figure in Walter Jon Williams's unsettling "Dinosaurs," wherein the human race has evolved into a tribe of smug,

---

* For *Short Form*, write Hatrack River Publications, PO Box 18184, Greensboro, NC 27419.

stupid, specialized superbeings, beside whom the aliens that they will almost trivially wipe out represent—satirically—the only connection with what the reader understands as humanity.

Williams had another remarkable long story in the first volume of George R. R. Martin's *Wild Cards* anthology series, proving that although shared-world franchises may abound nowadays, not all the resulting commodities need be impalatable hamburgers. *Wild Cards* posits the notion that shortly after World War II an alien plague endowed certain survivors with superhuman abilities, and Williams, in "Witness," gives us the House Un-American Activities Committee impeaching a foursome of Uncle Sam's virus-augmented superheroes. Politically and historically conscious, this novella effectively juxtaposes comic-book champions and the virulent McCarthyism that degrades and destroys them.

Another curious juxtaposition takes the fascinating characters of Charles Sheffield's "Trapalanda" to the Kingdom of the Winds in Patagonia. In pursuit of an El Dorado deduced from weather-pattern anomalies by a blind man with bionic eyes, they discover this El Dorado to be—as the rich blind seeker suspected—an alien space-time tunnel, a brief walk into which turns the narrator prematurely into an old man.

Another blind man, his life threatened by spies, stands at the center of Kim Stanley Robinson's novella "The Blind Geometer." At once a thriller, a philosophical discourse, and an exploration of the shape of fiction, this story asks a variety of questions: What is the relationship between geometry and the real world? How may an abstract "explanation" of reality project for us a full sensory plenum? How does the idea of a story body forth a living biosphere of emotion and incident? Treating the world as a text, Robinson ingeniously fuses theme and narrative, his musically complex equation only slightly clotted by brackets.

Grammatical analysis of human behavior—culture and conduct as syntax—is of course the stock in trade of semiotics, the science of signs; and Neil Ferguson, a new *Interzone* voice, explores this science in "The Second Third of C," where "C" denotes not the speed of light but the letter in the dictionary. Ferguson's story teams Kafka and Borges with Len Deighton in a semiotic thriller that shows how a writer can be consciously clever while still delivering the emotional, political, and narrative goods.

In a contrasting hilarious mood, Robinson's other major novella of the year, "Mother Goddess of the World," grants an encore to his Himalayan climber-adventurers who liberated a Yeti in "Escape from Kathmandu" (1986). Now these crazies conquer Everest, as if by accident, and encounter some of the weirder shamanistic wonders of Lamaism. If the complex high seriousness of "The Blind Geometer" echoes that of Robinson's *The Memory of Whiteness* (1985), "Mother Goddess of the World" reveals a talent for sprightly comedy. In the Nepalese wonderland, Robinson renews himself.

Meantime, in the chilly and evocative "He-We-Await," the unique Howard Waldrop (if Waldrop did not exist, it would be difficult to invent him) dramatizes a different sort of renewal. The members of a multithousand-year-old Egyptian mystery cult reincarnate a doddery pharoah beside Central Park; his neurotic, gene-regenerated son murders him; and the last days of the world are ushered in. Although Norman Mailer's *Ancient Evenings* is a hard act to follow, Waldrop shows how fresh a variation upon a theme can be in science fiction—fresher, in fact, than allegiance to wanton state-of-the-moment novelty, whose adherents may create only a sort of consensus chorus.

For example? Two flashy, street-wise cyberclones, Eric Brown's "Krash-Bangg Joe and the Pineal-Zen Equation" and Charles Stross's "The Boys," debut stories in *Interzone*. Both are laudably vigorous and inventive, and the field needs new energy gushers for renewal. But how many drug-fixed, hot-wired brains and bodies, which in the real world would be helpless wrecks, can we reasonably believe in? And is it conceptually flexible—or simply daft—to project any loony cocktail of creeds into the future? (How about Heavy-Metal Jesuit

Structuralists, black robes fluttering from their space armor and rock liturgies resounding through their aural implants?) Eric Brown's second story, "The Girl Who Died for Art, and Lived," does more than dazzle with its flash-sleaze world; it manages to move us, having a little more discipline and far fewer gratuitous pyrotechnics. "Goodbye, Houston Street," by neosurrealist Richard Kadrey, is ebullient, witty, and colorful, but can one reasonably buy even as satire the nuking of Manhattan as an ultimate artistic statement? Rebellion and fervor are fine responses to an exploitive, deadening, bourgeois world, but if the apparently anarchist narratives of cyberpunk and neosurrealism embody potent metaphors for late-phase capitalism, these same narratives can also be its toys. Still, the old surrealist program of imaginatively deranging the world in order to renew it remains the subtext.

A well-disciplined story quietly depicting substantive change is John Barnes's "Digressions from the Second Person Future," a poignant address to a future hunter-mammal living in a world after Homo sapiens has vanished, although some broken artifacts still linger. No other hangovers from the human species impinge on the consciousness of this freshly evolved inheritor of the Earth, a circumstance that puts us neatly in our long-term place. Here, indeed, is one possible outcome of the chaotic present—extinction rather than a rococo exfoliation of human subspecies and machine interfaces. An unusual, destabilizing story, detailing the narrator's relationship with his father and his remembered pet mouse, while simultaneously presenting a metaphoric but persuasive future in which humanity has no part.

In "Flowers in Edo," Bruce Sterling shows us another world on the brink of drastic change, this time with rich comic effect. Written especially for a Japanese SF magazine, this authentic pastiche of Meiji era Tokyo tells of the electrification of that city, whose citizens still believe in demons. Sterling captures the spirit of turn-of-the-century classics such as Soseki Natsume's *I Am a Cat*, and engages in Edison punk—a double coup.

In the projective geometries of SF stories, writers often seek to map one pattern atop another: the human condition atop the alien condition, a technology, or a scientific theory. The search is for an objective correlative that fuses idea and feeling in a single living narrative of strangeness that nevertheless reveals to us the familiar.

In "Schwarzschild Radius," for example, Connie Willis tellingly parallels black-hole theory with the suction to death and the slow divorce from communication suffered by soldiers trapped at the event horizon of the trenches during the First World War. And in "Glass Cloud," for another example, James Patrick Kelly deploys a mobile megasculpture to express the loneliness of an artist's dreams, his alienation. Just as Kelly's architect produces a huge, flexible, seemingly meteorological art machine, so the author creates a machine of organic narrative with which to explore emotion and character.

In "Forever Yours, Anna," Kate Wilhelm constructs a most unusual detective story, with clues located in the present, but the answer—well, elsewhen. Her handwriting-expert hero falls in love with the vanished author of certain letters. In solving the mystery, he revives, wonderfully, his own life.

Finally, to conclude on one more note of renewal, a nod to Ken Grimwood's impressive novel *Replay*. What if one could relive one's life from an earlier year with one's memory of the future intact? Grimwood renews the protagonist of this fascinating idea-adventure in just that way, and then renews him again, and yet again. *Replay* is perhaps the most affecting novel of the Nebula year, a story of multiple possibilities, love, and tragedy. Moreover, the novel has an entirely unexpected outcome that compels one to think, and think again, and yet again.

Which, ideally, is what all science fiction should do: make us think, and by thinking, feel, and by feeling, change. This is the way of self-renewal, and by self-renewal, we may also renew—to no insignificant extent—the world.

In Memoriam: Alfred Bester 1913 1987

Isaac Asimov

Isaac Asimov, designated the eighth Grand Master of the Science Fiction Writers of America in 1986, here memorializes the ninth, Alfred Bester. Asimov is the indefatigable author of nearly four hundred books, including a clutch of classic science-fiction titles and a number of nonfiction guides—to the sciences, the Bible, the plays of Shakespeare, and so on. For most readers of these *Nebula Award* volumes, he genuinely requires no introduction.

Therefore, let me write briefly of Alfred Bester.

Bester's reputation today owes its enviable sheen to two witty, colorful, and pyrotechnic novels, *The Demolished Man* (1953) and *The Stars My Destination* (1956), as well as to a dozen or more indescribably dazzling and original pieces of short fiction, among them my own favorite, "Fondly Fahrenheit" (1954), which deservedly appeared in the anthology *Science Fiction Hall of Fame*, published in 1970 to showcase landmark stories that had appeared before the founding of SFWA and the inception of the Nebula Awards in 1965.

"Fondly Fahrenheit" seems a pizzazzingly paced, far-future riff on Faulkner's "Dry September"—but it isn't. It's that, and an interplanetary psychological thriller about confused identities, the master-slave relationship, and lots more besides. Whatever the story is, its elements mesh in kaleidoscopic ways that propel and unsettle. "The thermometer in the power plant registered 100.9° murderously

Fahrenheit. All reet! All reet!" No way to explain. You'll have to read this one for yourself.

My first encounter with Bester's work came with a reading of *The Stars My Destination*, a vivid, space-age recension of Victor Hugo's *The Count of Monte Cristo* and a kind of prose forerunner—if not the actual inspiration—of the psychedelic "through-the-stargate" sequence in the Kubrick/Clarke film *2001: A Space Odyssey*. I have wanted to jaunte ever since, and I can never think of Bester without thinking of imaginative flash, intellectual nimbleness, and an inborn feel for character that always alchemized these first two gifts from mere gimmicks into powerful reflections of distinctive genius.

Two later novels, *The Computer Connection* (1974) and *Golem 100* (1980), were disappointing fallings-away from the apex of Bester's early achievement, and we must forgive Bester if he did in fact—according to Charles Platt in a recent reminiscence in the British magazine *Interzone*—come to view *Golem 100* as "beyond any doubt" his "best book." Writers always want to think their latest novel is their most nearly perfect, and, both proverbially and provably, they are often self-deluding judges of their own output.

So it apparently was with Bester, that outgoing gadfly with the omnivorous "magpie mind." His last years were reportedly not the happiest, but his knowledge that he had won the Grand Master Award may have afforded some solace. And, too, he had to have realized that his influence on the field has been not only far-reaching but revivifying. Indeed, his work seems to have had a strong impact on the new wave Samuel R. Delany avatar who wrote *Nova* (1968) as well as on the William Gibson computer demon who hard-copied *Neuromancer* (1984) into the annals of the Mirrorshades Mob.

Not long ago, in fact, K. W. Jeter, who has himself been touted as a cyberpunk on the basis of his novels *Dr. Adder* and *The Glass Hammer*, told an interviewer, "What's being labeled as cyberpunk is just the usual rediscovery of Alfred Bester that happens every two or three years in the SF field.

Almost everything labeled as cyberpunk, just as with almost any supposedly new thing in SF, really resembles nothing so much as Alfred Bester's closet. Or his wastebasket."

Jeter here indulges in hyperbole, of course, but by no means gross or indefensible hyperbole—for the simple reason that Alfred Bester *was* an original. Unquestionably, he was the most energetic, vivid, and imitation-inspiring stylistic and structural pathfinder among the nine fine writers upon whom SFWA has so far bestowed its Grand Master Award. His innovations will necessarily continue to crop up in the work of new writers. Ironically, however, some of these new writers may have only the dimmest notion from whom—at several diluted removes—they are cribbing.

As Peter Nicholls observed in *The Science Fiction Encyclopedia* (1979), "[Alfred Bester] is one of the very few genre SF writers to have bridged, unconsciously, the chasm between the old and the new wave, by becoming a hero figure for both; perhaps because in his images he conjures up, almost in one breath, both outer and inner space."

Alfred Bester died on September 30, 1987, aged seventy-three. He did not receive an obituary in the *New York Times*.

I know that because I have reached the age where I read the obituary page carefully. I am a quasi-celebrity myself and therefore have accumulated, with the years, a number of friends who are worthy of obituaries and who have also reached the age where such sad bottom lines become increasingly likely. I read the pages, wincing with apprehension, but I dare not miss the smallest notice.

Yet I did not know of Alfred Bester's death till I phoned Harlan Ellison on another subject entirely and he told me of the event several days after the fact. "Another good guy gone," he said.

Alfie (I never heard him referred to by his friends in any other way) was an old-timer, of course. His first story, "The Broken Axiom," appeared only three months after my first story, and that's old-timish enough for anyone.

He was never what *I* would call prolific, but prolific just means *a lot*. It has nothing to say about quality, and as far as Alfie was concerned, the word was quality. He published such early classics as "Adam and No Eve" and "Fondly Fahrenheit." He published a fantasy novella, "Hell Is Forever." He worked with comic magazines and travel magazines; he wrote radio scripts and sat in an editor's chair.

Most of all, he wrote a few great novels. His best (and one that knocked me for a loop when it appeared—a loop which, I realized even at the time, had a strong component of envy in it) was *The Demolished Man*, which appeared in 1953, and which had the well-deserved honor of being the first novel to win a Hugo. It is, with scarcely any argument, I imagine, the best novel about a telepathic society ever written. It is the only one I could thoroughly believe. It seemed to me that if a telepathic society existed it would have to be as Alfie described it. *The Stars My Destination* published three years later was even more flamboyant and scarcely lagged in quality.

But the *New York Times* did not give him an obituary. He was mentioned only in the "ad department" at the bottom of the page for which people pay.

Frankly, I was furious. Any two-bit writer who did not write science fiction would have been memorialized. Any musician, serious, popular, or jazz, would have made it. Any vice-president of any obscure business firm would have been favored with a headline. Upon what meat does a great science fiction writer feed that he is grown so ignorable?

It is a source of great satisfaction to me that the Science Fiction Writers of America (we guys!) did *not* ignore him. He was chosen to receive the Grand Master Award in 1988 (the ninth), and he knew about it. He was told. Nor will his death abrogate the decision, for it makes him no less worthy. At the next Nebula Awards banquet, the Grand Master Award will be given him posthumously.

And it means, sadly, that in the dozen-year history (so far) of the awards, he will have been the first Grand Master to break ranks and pass on to the Grand Perpetual Convention in the Sky.

Alfie was always a cheerful and amazingly extroverted fellow. He made me seem shy and bashful. Of course, he used to take an occasional drink, whereas I remained a teetotaling sobersides. That may well have made a difference.

In any case, he always gave me the biggest hello it was possible to hand out. I use the term figuratively, because what he gave me more than once (lots more than once, especially if he saw me before I saw him) was more than a verbal greeting. He enclosed me in a bear hug and kissed me on the cheek. And, occasionally, if I had my back to him, he did not hesitate to goose me.

This discomfited me in two ways. First, it was a direct physical discomfiture. I am not used to being immobilized by a hug and then kissed, and I am certainly not used to being goosed.

A more indirect discomfiture and a much worse one was my realization that just as I approached Alfie very warily when I saw him before he saw me, it might be possible that young women approached me just as warily, for I will not deny to you that I have long acted on the supposition that hugging, kissing, and goosing was a male prerogative, provided young women (not aging males) were the target. You have no idea how it spoiled things to me when I couldn't manage to forget that the young women might be edging away.

I wonder if Alfie did it on purpose in order to widen my understanding of human nature and to reform me. No, I don't think so. It was just his natural ebullience.

He was a lot more serious when he called me up. Of all my friends, he and Harlan were most likely to call me up to ask me questions for which they needed answers they couldn't readily find in what reference books were available. I must say that Alfie's questions were hard ones, and I could rarely come up with satisfactory answers. Generally, I would be reduced to saying, "Just make something up, Alfie. That's what *I* do." However, whereas a prolific writer such as myself is *forced* to make something up as otherwise the steady patter of the typewriter keys is interrupted, Alfie, whose hallmark was quality, could not manage that escape. He had to keep worrying the Universe till he got his answer.

Alfie had a queer and highly lopsided view of the Universe even when he wasn't writing science fiction. He interviewed me for *Publishers Weekly* about fifteen years ago. We spent a couple of hours together, while he managed to maneuver me into odd corners of my life. It finally turned out that I was very fond of soppy old ballads I had heard when I was quite young and that I would occasionally sing them. He encouraged me (I am quite a naive fellow) and so I sang for him, with a wealth of emotion, "The Boulevard of Broken Dreams."

The interview was published, and there on the printed page of the superrespectable *Publishers Weekly* was a description of me singing:

> *I walk along the street of sorrow,*
> *The Boulevard of Broken Dreams,*
> *Where gigolo and gigolette*
> *Wake up to find their cheeks are wet*
> *With tears that come of shattered schemes*
> (and so on)

It's the only place and the only time where this foul secret addiction of mine was uncovered.

Farewell, Alfie, my friend, with your gaiety and your gooses, your madness and your genius, until I come to join you in that Grand Perpetual Convention—if they let me in.

Forever Yours, Anna

Kate Wilhelm

A few years ago, I wrote an introduction to another story by Kate Wilhelm for an anthology entitled *Light Years and Dark*. Let me quote myself, then, both quoting Wilhelm and commenting on the individuality of her method:

"Kate Wilhelm has defined speculative fiction as 'the exploration of worlds that probably will never exist, that I don't believe in as real, that I don't expect the reader to accept as real, but that are realistically handled in order to investigate them, because for one reason or another they are the worlds we most dread or yearn for.'

"Altogether gracefully, then, Wilhelm walks a tightrope between the elucidation of genre concerns—cloning, say, or the quest for immortality—and the heavy emphasis on style and characterization typical of good 'realistic' fiction. Fine examples of her approach at novel length are *Where Late the Sweet Birds Sang, Juniper Time,* and *Welcome Chaos.*"

Last year, Wilhelm won a Nebula for her novelette "The Girl Who Fell into the Sky." Her most recent novels are *Huysman's Pets* and *Smart House,* and a new collection of her short fiction, *Children of the Wind,* will appear in fall 1989. Of this year's Nebula-winning story, she tells us: "I always have a hard time trying to find something to say about a story or any other piece of fiction I've written. I seem to feel that the work has to stand alone and speak for itself, and what I should talk about is the new recipe I just came across, or find out how deeply you plant your peas, or something like that.

" 'Forever Yours, Anna' is the result of being fascinated with obsessed people. One of my characters is obsessed with his work—you never meet him in the story. A woman is obsessed with a man she has fallen hopelessly in love with, and you get a glimpse of her at the very end. And my protagonist is obsessed with the letter *A* and what it stands for. Oh dear.

"I planted my last peas about an inch deep, but the most recent rain uncovered some of them and I'm thinking that an inch and a half would be better. . . ."

Anna entered his life on a spring afternoon, not invited, not even wanted. Gordon opened his office door that day to a client who was expected, and found a second man also in the hallway. The second man brought him Anna, although Gordon did not yet know this. At the moment, he simply said, "Yes?"

"Gordon Sills? I don't have an appointment, but . . . May I wait?"

"Afraid I don't have a waiting room."

"Out here's fine."

He was about fifty, and he was prosperous. It showed in his charcoal-colored suit, a discreet blue-gray silk tie, a silk shirtfront. Gordon assumed the rest of the shirt was also silk. He also assumed the stone on his finger was a real emerald of at least three carats. Ostentatious touch, that.

"Sure," Gordon said and ushered his client inside. They passed through a foyer to his office-workroom. The office section was partitioned from the rest of the room by three rice-paper screens with beautiful Chinese calligraphy. In the office area was his desk and two chairs for visitors, his chair, and an overwhelmed bookcase, with books on the floor in front of it.

Their business only took half an hour; when the client left, the hall was empty. Gordon shrugged and returned to his office. He pulled his telephone across the desk and dialed his former wife's number, let it ring a dozen times, hung up.

He leaned back in his chair and rubbed his eyes. Late-afternoon sunlight streamed through the slats in the venetian blinds, zebra light. He should go away for a while, he thought. Just close shop and walk away from it all until he started getting overdraft notices. Three weeks, he told himself, that was about as long as it would take.

Gordon Sills was thirty-five, a foremost expert in graphology, and could have been rich, his former wife had reminded him quite often. If you don't make it before forty, she had also said, too often, you simply won't make it, and he did not care, simply did not care about money, security, the future, the children's future . . .

Abruptly he pushed himself away from the desk and left the office, went into his living room. Like the office, it was messy, with several days' worth of newspapers, half a dozen books, magazines scattered haphazardly. To his eyes it was comfortable-looking, comfort-giving; he distrusted neatness in homes. Karen had most of the furniture; he had picked up only a chair, a couch, a single lamp, a scarred oak coffee table that he could put his feet on, a card table and several chairs for the kitchen. And a very good radio. It was sufficient. Some fine Japanese landscapes were on the walls.

The buzzer sounded. When he opened the door, the prosperous, uninvited client was there. He was carrying a brushed suede briefcase.

"Hi," Gordon said. "I thought you'd left."

"I did, and came back."

Gordon admitted him and led him through the foyer into the office, where he motioned toward a chair and went behind his desk and sat down. The sunlight was gone, eclipsed by the building across Amsterdam.

"I apologize for not making an appointment," his visitor said. He withdrew a wallet from his breast pocket, took out a card, and slid it across the desk. "I'm Avery Roda. On behalf of my company I should like to consult with you regarding some correspondence in our possession."

"That's my business," Gordon said. "And what is your company, Mr. Roda?"

"Draper Fawcett."

Gordon nodded slowly. "And your position?"

Roda looked unhappy. "I am vice-president in charge of research and development, but right now I am in charge of an investigation we have undertaken. My first duty in connection with this was to find someone with your expertise. You come very highly recommended, Mr. Sills."

"Before we go on any further," Gordon said, "I should tell you that there are a number of areas where I'm not interested in working. I don't do paternity suits, for example. Or employer-employee pilferage cases."

Roda flushed.

"Or blackmail," Gordon finished equably. "That's why I'm not rich, but that's how it is."

"The matter I want to discuss is none of the above," Roda snapped. "Did you read about the explosion we had at our plant on Long Island two months ago?" He did not wait for Gordon's response. "We lost a very good scientist, one of the best in the country. And we cannot locate some of his paperwork, his notes. He was involved with a woman who may have them in her possession. We want to find her, recover them."

Gordon shook his head. "You need the police then, private detectives, your own security force."

"Mr. Sills, don't underestimate our resolve or our resources. We have set all that in operation, and no one has been able to locate the woman. Last week we had a conference during which we decided to try this route. What we want from you is as complete an analysis of the woman as you can give us, based on her handwriting. That may prove fruitful." His tone said he doubted it very much.

"I assume the text has not helped."

"You assume correctly," Roda said with some bitterness. He opened his briefcase and withdrew a sheaf of papers and laid it on the desk.

From the other side Gordon could see that they were not the originals, but photocopies. He let his gaze roam over the

31

upside-down letters and then shook his head. "I have to have the actual letters to work with."

"That's impossible. They are being kept under lock and key."

"Would you offer a wine taster colored water?" Gordon's voice was bland, but he could not stop his gaze. He reached across the desk and turned the top letter right side up to study the signature. Anna. Beautifully written; even in the heavy black copy it was delicate, as artful as any of the Chinese calligraphy on his screens. He looked up to find Roda watching him intently. "I can tell you a few things from just this, but I have to have the originals. Let me show you my security system."

He led the way to the other side of the room. Here he had a long worktable, an oversized light table, a copy camera, enlarger, files. There was a computer and printer on a second desk. It was all fastidiously neat and clean.

"The files are fireproof," he said dryly, "and the safe is also. Mr. Roda, if you've investigated me, you know I've handled some priceless documents. And I've kept them right here in the shop. Leave the copies. I can start with them, but tomorrow I'll want the originals."

"Where's the safe?"

Gordon shrugged and went to the computer, keyed in his code, and then moved to the wall behind the worktable and pushed aside a panel to reveal a safe front. "I don't intend to open it for you. You can see enough without that."

"Computer security?"

"Yes."

"Very well. Tomorrow I'll send you the originals. You said you can already tell us something."

They returned to the office space. "First you," Gordon said, pointing to the top letter. "Who censored them?"

The letters had been cut off just above the greeting, and there were rectangles of white throughout.

"That's how they were when we found them," Roda said

heavily. "Mercer must have done it himself. One of the detectives said the holes were cut with a razor blade."

Gordon nodded. "Curiouser and curiouser. Well, for what it's worth at this point, she's an artist more than likely. Painter would be my first guess."

"Are you sure?"

"Don't be a bloody fool. Of course I'm not sure, not with copies to work with. It's a guess. Everything I report will be a guess. Educated guesswork, Mr. Roda, that's all I can guarantee."

Roda sank down into his chair and expelled a long breath. "How long will it take?"

"How many letters?"

"Nine."

"Two, three weeks."

Very slowly Roda shook his head. "We are desperate, Mr. Sills. We will double your usual fee if you can give this your undivided attention."

"And how about your cooperation?"

"What do you mean?"

"His handwriting also. I want to see at least four pages of his writing."

Roda looked blank.

"It will help to know her if I know her correspondent."

"Very well," Roda said.

"How old was he?"

"Thirty."

"Okay. Anything else you can tell me?"

Roda seemed deep in thought, his eyes narrowed, a stillness about him that suggested concentration. With a visible start he looked up, nodded. "What you said about her could be important already. She mentions a show in one of the letters. We assumed a showgirl, a dancer, something like that. I'll put someone on it immediately. An artist. That could be right."

"Mr. Roda, can you tell me anything else? How important

are those papers? Are they salable? Would anyone outside your company have an idea of their value?"

"They are quite valuable," he said with such a lack of tone that Gordon's ears almost pricked to attention. "If we don't recover them in a relatively short time, we will have to bring in the FBI. National security may be at stake. We want to handle it ourselves, obviously." He finished in the same monotone, "The Russians would pay millions for them, I'm certain. And we will pay whatever we have to. She has them. She says so in one of the letters. We have to find that woman."

For a moment Gordon considered turning down the job. Trouble, he thought. Real trouble. He glanced at the topmost letter again, the signature *Anna*, and he said, "Okay. I have a contract I use routinely . . ."

After Roda left, he studied the one letter for several minutes, not reading it, in fact examining it upside down again, and he said softly, "Hello, Anna."

Then he gathered up all the letters and put them in a file, which he then stored in his safe. He had no intention of starting until he had the originals. But it would comfort Roda to believe he was already at work.

Roda sent the originals and a few samples of Mercer's writing before noon the next day, and for three hours Gordon studied them all. He arranged hers on the worktable under the gooseneck lamp and turned them this way and that, not yet reading them, making notes now and then. As he had suspected, her script was fine, delicate, with beautiful shading. She used a real pen with real ink, not a felt-tip or a ballpoint. Each stroke was visually satisfying, artistic in itself. One letter was three pages long, four were two pages, the others were single sheets. None of them had a date, an address, a complete name. He cursed the person who had mutilated them. One by one he turned them over to examine the backs and jotted: "Pressure—light to medium." His other notes were equally brief: "Fluid, rapid, not conventional; proportions, 1:5." That was European and he did not think she was, but it would bear close examination. Each note was simply a direction marker, a first impression. He was whistling tunelessly as he worked and was startled when the telephone rang.

It was Karen, finally returning his many calls. The children would arrive by six, and he must return them by seven Sunday night. Her voice was cool, as if she were giving orders about laundry. He said okay and hung up, surprised at how little he felt about the matter. Before, it had given him a wrench each time they talked; he had asked questions: How was she? Was she working? Was the house all right? She had the house on Long Island, and that was fine with him, he had spent more and more time in town anyway over the past few years; but still, they had bought it together, he had repaired this and that, put up screens, taken them down, struggled with plumbing.

That night he took the two children to a Greek restaurant. Buster, eight years old, said it was yucky; Dana, ten, called him a baby and Gordon headed off the fight by saying he had bought a new Monopoly game. Dana said Buster was into winning. Dana looked very much like her mother, but Buster was her true genetic heir. Karen was into winning too.

They went to the Cloisters and fantasized medieval scenarios; they played Monopoly again, and on Sunday he took them to a puppet show at the Met and then drove them home. He was exhausted. When he got back he looked about, deeply depressed. There were dirty dishes in the sink, on the table, in the living room. Buster had slept on the couch and his bedclothes and covers were draped over it. Karen said they were getting too old to share a room any longer. Dana's bedroom was also a mess. She had left her pajamas and slippers. Swiftly he gathered up the bedding from the living room and tossed it all onto the bed in Dana's room and closed the door. He overfilled the dishwasher and turned it on, and finally went into his workroom and opened the safe.

"Hello, Anna," he said softly, and tension seeped from

him; the ache that had settled in behind his eyes vanished; he forgot the traffic jams coming home from Long Island, forgot the bickering his children seemed unable to stop.

He took the letters to the living room and sat down to read them through for the first time.

Love letters, passionate letters, humorous in places, perceptive, intelligent. Without dates it was hard to put them in chronological order, but the story emerged. She had met Mercer in the city; they had walked and talked and he had left. He had come back and this time they were together for a weekend and became lovers. She sent her letters to a post office box; he did not write to her, although he left papers covered with incomprehensible scribbles in her care. She was married to someone whose name had been cut out with a razor blade every time she referred to him. Mercer knew him, visited him, apparently. They were even friends, and had long serious talks from which she was excluded. She was afraid; Mercer was involved in something very dangerous, and no one told her what it was, although her husband knew. She called Mercer her mystery man and speculated about his secret life, his family, his insane wife, or tyrannical father, or his own lapses into lycanthropy. Gordon smiled. Anna was not a whiner or a weeper, but she was hopelessly in love with Mercer and did not even know where he lived, where he worked, what danger threatened him, anything about him except that when he was with her, she was alive and happy. That was enough. Her husband understood and wanted only her happiness, and it was destroying her, knowing she was hurting him so much, but she was helpless.

He pursed his lips and reread one. "My darling, I can't stand it. I really can't stand it any longer. I dream of you, see you in every stranger on the street, hear your voice every time I answer the phone. My palms become wet and I tingle all over, thinking it's your footsteps I hear. You are my dreams. So, I told myself today, this is how it is? No way! Am I a silly schoolgirl mooning over a television star? At twenty-six? I gathered all your papers and put them in a carton and addressed it, and as I wrote the box number, I found myself giggling. You can't send a Dear John to a post office box number. What if you failed to pick it up and an inspector opened it finally? I should entertain such a person? They're all gray and desiccated, you know, those inspectors. Let them find their own entertainment! What if they could read your mysterious squiggles and discover the secret of the universe? Do any of them deserve such enlightenment? No. I put everything back in [excised] safe—" Mercer was not the mystery man, Gordon thought then; the mystery was the other man, the nameless one whose safe hid Mercer's papers. Who was he? He shook his head over the arrangement of two men and a woman, and continued to read: "—and [excised] came in and let me cry on his shoulder. Then we went to dinner. I was starved."

Gordon laughed out loud and put the letters down on the coffee table, leaned back with his hands behind his head and contemplated the ceiling. It needed paint.

For the next two weeks he worked on the letters, and the few pages of Mercer's handwriting. He photographed everything, made enlargements, and searched for signs of weakness, illness. He keystroked the letters into his computer and ran the program he had developed, looking for usages, foreign or regional combinations, anything unusual or revealing. Mercer, he decided, had been born in a test tube and never left school and the laboratory until the day he met Anna. She was from the Midwest, not a big city, somewhere around one of the Great Lakes. The name that had been consistently cut out had six letters. She had gone to an opening, and the artist's name had been cut out also. It had nine letters. Even without her testimony about the artist, it was apparent that she had been excited by his work. It showed in the writing. He measured the spaces between the words, the size of individual letters, the angle of her slant, the proportions of everything.

Every movement she made was graceful, rhythmic. Her connections were garlands, open and trusting; that meant she
was honest herself. Her threadlike connections that strung
her words together indicated her speed in writing, her intu-
ition, which she trusted.

As the work went on he made more complete notes, drawing conclusions more and more often. The picture of Anna
was becoming real.

He paid less attention to Mercer's writing after making
an initial assessment of him. A scientist, technologist, precise, angular, a genius, inhibited, excessively secretive, a
loner. He was a familiar type.

When Roda returned, Gordon felt he could tell him more
about those two people than their own mothers knew about
them.

What he could not tell was what they looked like, or
where Anna was now, or where the papers were that she had
put in her husband's safe.

He watched Roda skim through the report on Anna. Today, rain was falling in gray curtains of water; the air felt
thick and clammy.

"That's all?" Roda demanded when he finished.

"That's it."

"We checked every art show in the state," Roda said,
scowling at him. "We didn't find her. And we have proof that
Mercer couldn't have spent as much time with her as she
claimed in the letters. We've been set up. You've been set up.
You say that she's honest, ethical, and we say she's an agent
or worse. She got her hooks in him and got those papers, and
these letters are fakes, every one of them is a fake!"

Gordon shook his head. "There's not a lie in those
letters."

"Then why didn't she come forward when he died? There
was enough publicity at the time. We saw to that. I tell you
he never spent any real time with her. We found him in a
talent hunt when he was a graduate student, and he stayed
in that damn lab ever since, seven days a week for four years.

He never had time for a relationship of the sort she talks about. It's a lie through and through. A fantasy." He slumped in his chair. Today his face was almost as gray as his very good suit. He looked years older than he had the last time he had been in the office. "They're going to win," he said in a low voice. "The woman and her partner, they're probably out of the country already. Probably left the day after the accident, with the papers, their job done. Well done. That stupid, besotted fool!" He stared at the floor for several more seconds, then straightened. His voice was hard, clipped. "I was against consulting you from the start. A waste of time and money. Voodoo crap, that's all this is. Well, we've done what we can. Send in your bill. Where are her letters?"

Silently Gordon slid a folder across the desk. Roda went through it carefully, then put it in his briefcase and stood up. "If I were you, I would not give our firm as reference in the future, Sills." He pushed Gordon's report away from him. "We can do without that. Good day."

It should have ended there, Gordon knew, but it did not end. Where are you, Anna? he thought, gazing at the world swamped in cold rain. Why hadn't she come forward, attended the funeral, turned in the papers? He had no answers. She was out there, painting, living with a man who loved her very much, enough to give her the freedom to fall in love with someone else. Take good care of her, he thought at that other man. Be gentle with her, be patient while she heals. She's very precious, you know. He leaned his head against the window, let the coolness soothe him. He said aloud, "She's very precious."

"Gordon, are you all right?" Karen asked on the phone. It was his weekend for the children again.

"Sure. Why?"

"I just wondered. You sound strange. Do you have a girlfriend?"

"What do you want, Karen?"

The ice returned to her voice, and they made arrangements for the children's arrival, when he was to return them. Library books, he thought distantly. Just like library books.

When he hung up he looked at the apartment and was dismayed by the dinginess, the disregard for the barest amenities. Another lamp, he thought. He needed a second lamp, at the very least. Maybe even two. Anna loved light. A girlfriend? He wanted to laugh, and to cry also. He had a signature, some love letters written to another man, a woman who came to his dreams and spoke to him in the phrases from her letters. A girlfriend! He closed his eyes and saw the name: Anna. The capital *A* was a flaring volcano, high up into the stratosphere, then the even, graceful *n*'s, the funny little final *a* that had trouble staying on the baseline, that wanted to fly away. And a beautiful sweeping line that flew out from it, circled above the entire name, came down to cross the first letter, turn it into an *A*, and in doing so formed a perfect palette. A graphic representation of Anna, soaring into the heavens, painting, creating art with every breath, every motion. Forever yours, Anna. Forever yours.

He took a deep breath and tried to make plans for the children's weekend, for the rest of the month, the summer, the rest of his life.

The next day he bought a lamp, and on his way home stopped in a florist shop and bought half a dozen flowering plants. She had written that the sunlight turned the flowers on the sill into jewels. He put them on the sill and raised the blind; the sunlight turned the blooms into jewels. His hands were clenched; abruptly he turned away.

He went back to work; spring became summer, hot and humid as only New York could be, and he found himself going from one art show to another. He mocked himself, and cursed himself for it, but he attended openings, examined new artists' work, signatures, again and again and again. If the investigators trained in this couldn't find her, he told himself firmly, and if the FBI couldn't find her, he was a fool to think he had even a remote chance. But he went to the shows. He was lonely, he told himself, and tried to become

interested in other women, any other woman, and continued
to attend openings.

In the fall he went to the opening of yet another new
artist, out of an art school, a teacher. And he cursed himself
for not thinking of that before. She could be an art teacher.
He made a list of schools and started down the list, perfecting
a story as he worked down it one by one. He was collecting
signatures of artists for an article he planned to write. It was
a passable story. It got him nothing.

She might be ugly, he told himself. What kind of woman
would have fallen in love with Mercer? He had been inhibited,
constricted, without grace, brilliant, eccentric, and full of
wonder. It was the wonder that she had sensed, he knew. She
had been attracted to that in Mercer, and had got through his
many defenses, had found a boy-man who was truly appeal-
ing. And he had adored her. That was apparent from her letters; it had been mutual. Why had he lied to her? Why hadn't
he simply told her who he was, what he was doing? The other
man in her life had not been an obstacle, that had been made
clear also. The two men had liked each other, and both loved
her. Gordon brooded about her, about Mercer, the other man,
and he haunted openings, became a recognized figure at the
various studios and schools where he collected signatures. It
was an obsession, he told himself, unhealthy, maybe even a
sign of neurosis—or worse. It was insane to fall in love with
someone's signature, love letters to another man.

And he could be wrong, he told himself. Maybe Roda had
been right, after all. The doubts were always short-lived.

The cold October rains had come. Karen was engaged to
a wealthy man. The children's visits had become easier because he no longer was trying to entertain them every minute;
he had given in and bought a television and video games for
them. He dropped by the Art Academy to meet Rick Hen-
derson, who had become a friend over the past few months.
Rick taught watercolors.

Gordon was in his office waiting for him to finish with a
class critique session when he saw the *A*, Anna's capital *A*.

He felt his arms prickle and sweat form on his hands, and a tightening in the pit of his stomach as he stared at an envelope on Rick's desk. Almost fearfully he turned it around to study the handwriting. The *A*'s in Art Academy were like volcanoes, reaching up into the stratosphere, crossed with a quirky, insouciant line, like a sombrero at a rakish angle. Anna's *A*. It did not soar and make a palette, but it wouldn't, not in an address. That was her personal sign.

He let himself sink into Rick's chair and drew in a deep breath. He did not touch the envelope again. When Rick finally joined him, he nodded toward it.

"Would you mind telling me who wrote that?" His voice sounded hoarse, but Rick seemed not to notice. He opened the envelope and scanned a note, then handed it over. Her handwriting. Not exactly the same, but it was hers. He was certain it was hers, even with the changes. The way the writing was positioned on the page, the sweep of the letters, the fluid grace . . . But it was not the same. The *A* in her name, Anna, was different. He felt bewildered by the differences, and knew it was hers in spite of them. Finally, he actually read the words. She would be out of class for a few days. It was dated four days ago.

"Just a kid," Rick said. "Fresh in from Ohio, thinks she has to be excused from class. I'm surprised it's not signed by her mother."

"Can I meet her?"

Now Rick looked interested. "Why?"

"I want her signature."

Rick laughed. "You're a real nut, you know. Sure. She's in the studio, making up for time off. Come on."

He stopped at the doorway and gazed at the young woman painting. She was no more than twenty, almost painfully thin, hungry looking. She wore scruffy sneakers, very old, faded blue jeans, a man's plaid shirt. Not the Anna of the letters. Not yet.

Gordon felt dizzy and held on to the door frame for a

moment, and he knew what it was that Mercer had worked on, what he had discovered. He felt as if he had slipped out of time himself as his thoughts raced, explanations formed, his next few years shaped themselves in his mind. Understanding came the way a memory comes, a gestalt of the entire event or series of events, all accessible at once. Mercer's notes had shown him to be brilliant, obsessional, obsessed with time, secretive. Roda had assumed Mercer failed because he had blown himself up. Everyone must have assumed that. But he had not failed. He had gone forward five years, six at the most, to the time when Anna would be twenty-six. He had slipped out of time to the future.

Gordon knew with certainty that it was his own name that had been excised from Anna's letters. Phrases from her letters tumbled through his mind. She had mentioned a Japanese bridge, from his painting, the flowers on the sill, even the way the sun failed when it sank behind the building across the street. He thought of Roda and the hordes of agents searching for the papers that were to be hidden, had been hidden in the safest place in the world—the future. The safe Anna would put the papers in would be his, Gordon's, safe. He closed his eyes hard, already feeling the pain he knew would come when Mercer realized that he was to die, that he had died. For Mercer there could not be a love strong enough to make him abandon his work.

Gordon knew he would be with Anna, watch her mature, become the Anna of the letters, watch her soar into the stratosphere, and when Mercer walked through his time door, Gordon would still love her, and wait for her, help her heal afterward.

Rick cleared his throat and Gordon released his grasp of the door frame, took the next step into the studio. Anna's concentration was broken; she looked up at him. Her eyes were dark blue.

Hello, Anna.

Flowers of Edo

Bruce Sterling

"Critics, myself included," wrote Bruce Sterling in his preface to *Mirrorshades: The Cyberpunk Anthology* (1986), "persist in label-mongering, despite all warnings; we must, because it's a valid source of insight—as well as great fun."

Others have so often labeled Sterling "the chief ideologue of the cyberpunk movement" that I must do so too. In this capacity, he has shown himself to be opinionated, impatient with dissenters, impossible to silence, and unshakably confident not only of the rightness but also of the final necessity of his and his cohorts' political and aesthetic agenda. His pronouncements have therefore provoked either hearty "Amens!" or offended raspberries. But the ultimate truth—and by no means a cheap one—is that Sterling, who has always acknowledged his debt to his literary forebears, has been good for the field, a noisy force for renewal.

Sterling's novels include *Involution Ocean; The Artificial Kid;* the exhilarating *Schismatrix*, a Nebula finalist in 1985; and, most recently, *Islands in the Net*. With his movement alter-ego William Gibson, Sterling is now at work on a novel, *The Difference Engine*, about Charles Babbage and his invention during the Victorian period of . . . well, a steam-driven computer.

About the following novelette Sterling writes: " '*Edo no Hana*' was first published in Hayakawa's *SF Magazine* of Tokyo, in October 1986. The English-language version, 'Flowers of Edo' [published in May 1987 in *Isaac Asimov's Science Fiction Magazine*], is the secondary text. Presumably there is a certain flavor in a good translation that cannot be captured with the original. My thanks go once again to my Japanese translator and advisor, Takashi Ogawa, and to the staff of *SF*."

Why write for first publication in a Japanese market?
"First, I got to know my Japanese translator [i.e., the Japanese translator of Sterling's novels], Yoshio Kobayashi, through SF fanzine circles. Meeting Yoshio convinced me that Japanese SF professionals were, and are, a very hip and dedicated crowd. Due to senseless cultural and economic barriers, though, almost all we Americans see of Japanese SF is awful crap like *Godzilla* and *Astroboy*. But there's a lot of sophisticated action in Tokyo. They are cosmopolitan—far more so than we Americans. They know a great deal about our SF scene—while we know almost nothing about them. . . .

"Hayakawa's *SF* had been publishing my short work, in translation, for some time. Naturally, I looked favorably on *SF*, just as I do on Britain's *Interzone* or my favorite American markets. I resolved to try to place an original story there—something that would show my Japanese readers that I recognized their importance and cared about them.

"With Yoshio's help, I then fully assumed my alternate incarnation as 'Brus Stur-ring,' Japanese SF author. The challenge, the fun, was to write actual *Japanese* SF, with Japanese characters, in a Japanese setting. As it happens, I have a longtime interest in Japanese *ukiyo-e*, a demented popular art-form, much like science fiction. And it strikes me that in some profound way, the whole world is now like 19th-century Japan—disturbed, future-shocked, full of former certainties now half-dissolved.

"So I rounded up the usual sources and wrote the story."

Autumn. A full moon floated over old Edo, behind the thinnest haze of high cloud. It shone like a geisha's night-lamp through an old mosquito net. The sky was antique browned silk.

Two sweating runners hauled an iron-wheeled rickshaw south, toward the Ginza. This was Kabukiza District, its streets bordered by low, tile-roofed wooden shops. These were modest places: coopers, tobacconists, cheap fabric shops where the acid reek of dye wafted through reed blinds and paper windows. Behind the stores lurked a maze of alleys, crammed with townsmen's wooden hovels, the walls festooned with morning glories, the tinder-dry thatched roofs alive with fleas.

It was late. Kabukiza was not a geisha district, and honest workmen were asleep. The muddy streets were unlit, except for moonlight and the rare upstairs lamp. The runners carried their own lantern, which swayed precariously from the rickshaw's drawing-pole. They trotted rapidly, dodging the worst of the potholes and puddles. But with every lurching dip, the rickshaw's strings of brass bells jumped and rang.

Suddenly the iron wheels grated on smooth red pavement. They had reached the New Ginza. Here, the air held the fresh alien smell of mortar and brick.

The amazing New Ginza had buried its old predecessor. The Flowers of Edo had killed the Old Ginza. To date, this huge disaster had been the worst, and most exciting, fire of the Meiji era. Edo had always been proud of its fires, and the Old Ginza's fire had been a real marvel. It had raged for three days and carried right down to the river.

Once they had mourned the dead, the Edokko were ready to rebuild. They were always ready. Fires, even earthquakes, were nothing new to them. It was a rare building in Low City that escaped the Flowers of Edo for as long as twenty years.

But this was Imperial Tokyo now, and not the shogun's old Edo any more. The governor had come down from High City in his horse-drawn coach and looked over the smoldering ruins of Ginza. Low City townsmen still talked about it, how the governor had folded his arms—like this—with his wrists sticking out of his Western frock coat. And how he had frowned a mighty frown. The Edo townsmen were getting used to those unsettling frowns by now. Hard, no-nonsense, modern frowns, with the brows drawn low over cold eyes that glittered with Civilization and Enlightenment.

So the governor, with a mighty wave of his modern, frock-coated arm, sent for his foreign architects. And the Englishmen had besieged the district with their charts and clanking engines and tubs full of bricks and mortar. The very heavens had rained bricks upon the black and flattened ruins. Great red hills of brick sprang up—were they houses, people wondered, were they buildings at all? Stories spread about the foreigners and their peculiar homes. The long noses, of course—necessary to suck air through the stifling brick walls. The pale skin—because bricks, it was said, drained the life and color out of a man. . . .

The rickshaw drew up short with a final brass jingle. The older rickshawman spoke, panting. "Far enough, gov?"

"Yeah, this'll do," said one passenger, piling out. His name was Encho Sanyutei. He was the son and successor of a famous vaudeville comedian and, at thirty-five, was now a well-known performer in his own right. He had been telling his companion about the Ginza Bricktown, and his folded arms and jutting underlip had cruelly mimicked Tokyo's governor.

Encho, who had been drinking, generously handed the older runner a pocketful of jingling copper sen. "Here, pal," he said. "Do something about that cough, will ya?" The runners bowed, not bothering to overdo it. They trotted off toward the nearby Ginza crowd, hunting another fare.

Parts of Tokyo never slept. The Yoshiwara District, the famous Nightless City of geishas and rakes, was one of them. The travelers had just come from Asakusa District, another sleepless place: a brawling, vibrant playground of bars, Kabuki theaters, and vaudeville joints.

The Ginza Bricktown never slept either. But the air here was different. It lacked that earthy Low City workingman's glow of sex and entertainment. Something else, something new and strange and powerful, drew the Edokko into the Ginza's iron-hard streets.

Gaslights. They stood hissing on their black foreign pillars, blasting a pitiless moon-drowning glare over the crowd. There were eighty-five of the appalling wonders, stretching arrow-straight across the Ginza, from Shiba all the way to Kyobashi.

The Edokko crowd beneath the lights was curiously silent. Drugged with pitiless enlightenment, they meandered down the hard, gritty street, in their high wooden clogs or low leather shoes. Some wore hakama skirts and jinbibaori coats; others, modern pipe-legged trousers, with top hats and bowlers.

The comedian Encho and his big companion staggered drunkenly toward the lights, their polished leather shoes squeaking merrily. To the Tokyo modernist, squeaking was half the fun of these foreign-style shoes. Both men wore inserts of "singing leather" to heighten the effect.

"I don't like their attitudes," growled Encho's companion. His name was Onogawa and, until the Emperor's Restoration, he had been a samurai. But imperial decree had abolished the wearing of swords, and Onogawa now had a post in a trading company. He frowned and dabbed at his nose, which had recently been bloodied and was now clotting. "It's all too free-and-easy with these modern rickshaws. Did you see those two runners? They looked right into our faces, just as bold as tomcats."

"Relax, will you?" said Encho. "They were just a couple of street runners. Who cares what they think? The way you act, you'd think they were shogun's overseers." Encho laughed freely and dusted off his hands with a quick, theatrical gesture. Those grim, spying overseers, with their merciless canons of Confucian law, were just a bad dream now. Like the shogun, they were out of business.

"But your face is known all over town," Onogawa complained. "What if they gossip about us? Everyone will know what happened back there."

"It's the least I could do for a devoted fan," Encho said airily.

Onogawa had sobered up a bit since his street fight in Asakusa. A scuffle had broken out in the crowd after Encho's performance—a scuffle centered on Onogawa, who had old acquaintances he would have preferred not to meet. But Encho, appearing suddenly in the crowd, had distracted Onogawa's persecutors and gotten Onogawa away.

It was not a happy situation for Onogawa, who put much stock in his own dignity, and tended to brood. He had been born in Satsuma, a province of radical samurai with stern, unbending standards. But ten years in the capital had changed Onogawa and given him an Edokko's notorious love for spectacle. Somewhat shamefully, Onogawa had become completely addicted to Encho's side-splitting skits and impersonations.

In fact, Onogawa had been slumming in Asakusa vaudeville joints at least twice each week for months. He had a wife and small son in a modest place in Nihombashi, a rather straitlaced High City district full of earnest young bankers and civil servants on their way up in life. Thanks to old friends from his radical days, Onogawa was an officer in a prosperous trading company. He would have preferred to be in the army, of course, but the army was quite small these days, and appointments were hard to get.

This was a major disappointment in Onogawa's life, and it had driven him to behave strangely. Onogawa's long-suffering in-laws had always warned him that his slumming would come to no good. But tonight's event wasn't even a geisha scandal, the kind men winked at or even admired. Instead, he had been in a squalid punch-up with low-class commoners.

And he had been rescued by a famous commoner, which was worse. Onogawa couldn't bring himself to compound his loss of face with gratitude. He glared at Encho from under the brim of his bowler hat. "So where's this fellow with the foreign booze you promised?"

"Patience," Encho said absently. "My friend's got a little

place here in Bricktown. It's private, away from the street."
They wandered down the Ginza, Encho pulling his silk top
hat low over his eyes, so he wouldn't be recognized.

He slowed as they passed a group of four young women
who were gathered before the modern glass window of a Ginza
fabric shop. The store was closed, but the women were ad-
miring the tailor's dummies. Like the dummies, the women
were dressed with daring modernity, sporting small Western
parasols, cutaway riding coats in brilliant purple, and sweeping foreign skirts over large, jutting bustles. "How about that,
eh?" said Encho as they drew nearer. "Those foreigners sure
like a rump on a woman, don't they?"

"Women will wear anything," Onogawa said, struggling
to loosen one pinched foot inside its squeaking shoe. "Plain
kimono and obi are far superior."

"Easier to get into, anyway," Encho mused. He stopped
suddenly by the prettiest of the women, a girl who had let
her natural eyebrows grow out, and whose teeth, unstained
with old-fashioned tooth blacking, gleamed like ivory in the
gaslight.

"Madame, forgive my boldness," Encho said. "But I think
I saw a small kitten run under your skirt."

"I beg your pardon?" the girl said in a flat Low City accent.
Encho pursed his lips. Plaintive mewing came from the
pavement. The girl looked down, startled, and raised her skirt
quickly almost to the knee. "Let me help," said Encho, bending down for a better look. "I see the kitten! It's climbing up
inside the skirt!" He turned. "You'd better help me, older
brother! Have a look up in there."

Onogawa, abashed, hesitated. More mewing came. Encho
stuck his entire head under the woman's skirt. "There it goes!
It wants to hide in her false rump!" The kitten squealed
wildly. "I've got it!" the comedian cried. He pulled out his
doubled hands, holding them before him. "There's the rascal
now, on the wall!" In the harsh gaslight, Encho's knotted
hands cast the shadowed figure of a kitten's head against the
brick.

Onogawa burst into convulsive laughter. He doubled over against the wall, struggling for breath. The women stood shocked for a moment. Then they all ran away, giggling hysterically. Except for the victim of Encho's joke, who burst into tears as she ran.

"Wah," Encho said alertly. "Her husband." He ducked his head, then jammed the side of his hand against his lips and blew. The street rang with a sudden trumpet blast. It sounded so exactly like the trumpet of a Tokyo omnibus that Onogawa himself was taken in for a moment. He glanced wildly up and down the Ginza prospect, expecting to see the omnibus driver, horn to his lips, reining up his team of horses.

Encho grabbed Onogawa's coat sleeve and hauled him up the street before the rest of the puzzled crowd could recover. "This way!" They pounded drunkenly up an ill-lit street into the depths of Bricktown. Onogawa was breathless with laughter. They covered a block, then Onogawa pulled up, gasping. "No more," he wheezed, wiping tears of hilarity. "Can't take another . . . ha, ha, ha . . . *step!*"

"All right," Encho said reasonably, "but not here." He pointed up. "Don't you know better than to stand under those things?" Black telegraph wires swayed gently overhead.

Onogawa, who had not noticed the wires, moved hastily out from under them. "Kuwabara, kuwabara," he muttered— a quick spell to avert lightning. The sinister magic wires were all over the Bricktown, looping past and around the thick, smelly buildings.

Everyone knew why the foreigners put their telegraph wires high up on poles. It was so the demon messengers inside could not escape to wreak havoc amongst decent folk. These ghostly, invisible spirits flew along the wires as fast as swallows, it was said, carrying their secret spells of Christian black magic. Merely standing under such a baleful influence was inviting disaster.

Encho grinned at Onogawa. "There's no danger as long as we keep moving," he said confidently. "A little exposure is harmless. Don't worry about it."

Onogawa drew himself up. "Worried? Not a bit of it." He followed Encho down the street.

The stonelike buildings seemed brutal and featureless. There were no homey reed blinds or awnings in those outsized windows, whose sheets of foreign glass gleamed like an animal's eyeballs. No cozy porches, no bamboo wind chimes or cricket cages. Not even a climbing tendril of Edo morning glory, which adorned even the worst and cheapest city hovels. The buildings just sat there, as mute and threatening as cannonballs. Most were deserted. Despite their fireproof qualities and the great cost of their construction, they were proving hard to rent out. Word on the street said those red bricks would suck the life out of a man—give him beriberi, maybe even consumption.

Bricks paved the street beneath their shoes. Bricks on the right of them, bricks on their left, bricks in front of them, bricks in back. Hundreds of them, thousands of them. Onogawa muttered to the smaller man. "Say. What *are* bricks, exactly? I mean, what are they made of?"

"Foreigners make 'em," Encho said, shrugging. "I think they're a kind of pottery."

"Aren't they unhealthy?"

"People say that," Encho said, "but foreigners live in them and I haven't noticed any shortage of foreigners lately." He drew up short. "Oh, here's my friend's place. We'll go around the front. He lives upstairs."

They circled the two-story building and looked up. Honest, old-fashioned light, from an oil lamp, glowed against the curtains of an upstairs window. "Looks like your friend's still awake," Onogawa said, his voice more cheery now.

Encho nodded. "Taiso Yoshitoshi doesn't sleep much. He's a little high-strung. I mean, peculiar." Encho walked up to the heavy, ornate front door, hung foreign-style on large brass hinges. He yanked a bellpull.

"Peculiar," Onogawa said. "No wonder, if he lives in a place like this." They waited.

The door opened inwards with a loud squeal of hinges. A man's disheveled head peered around it. Their host raised a candle in a cheap tin holder. "Who is it?"

"Come on, Taiso," Encho said impatiently. He pursed his lips again. Ducks quacked around their feet.

"Oh! It's Encho-san, Encho Sanyutei. My old friend. Come in, do."

They stepped inside into a dark landing. The two visitors stopped and unlaced their leather shoes. In the first-floor workshop, beyond the landing, the guests could dimly see bound bales of paper, a litter of tool chests and shallow trays. An apprentice was snoring behind a shrouded woodblock press. The damp air smelled of ink and cherrywood shavings.

"This is Mr. Onogawa Azusa," Encho said. "He's a fan of mine, down from High City. Mr. Onogawa, this is Taiso Yoshitoshi. The popular artist, one of Edo's finest."

"Oh, Yoshitoshi the artist!" said Onogawa, recognizing the name for the first time. "Of course! The woodblock print peddler. Why, I bought a whole series of yours once. *Twenty-Eight Infamous Murders with Accompanying Verses.*"

"Oh," said Yoshitoshi. "How kind of you to remember my squalid early efforts." The ukiyo-e print artist was a slight, somewhat pudgy man, with stooped, rounded shoulders. The flesh around his eyes looked puffy and discolored. He had close-cropped hair parted in the middle and wide, fleshy lips. He wore a printed cotton house robe, with faded bluish sunbursts, or maybe daisies, against a white background. "Shall we go upstairs, gentlemen? My apprentice needs his sleep."

They creaked up the wooden stairs to a studio lit by cheap pottery oil lamps. The walls were covered with hanging prints, while dozens more lay rolled, or stacked in corners, or piled on battered bookshelves. The windows were heavily draped and tightly shut. The naked brick walls seemed to sweat, and a vague reek of mildew and stale tobacco hung in the damp, close air.

The window against the far wall had a secondhand set of

exterior shutters nailed to its inner sill. The shutters were bolted. "Telegraph wires outside," Yoshitoshi explained, noticing the glances of his guests. The artist gestured vaguely at a couple of bedraggled floor cushions. "Please."

The two visitors sat, struggling politely to squeeze some comfort from the mashed and threadbare cushions. Yoshitoshi knelt on a thicker cushion beside his worktable, a low bench of plain pine with ink stick, grinder, and water cup. A bamboo tool jar on the table's corner bristled with assorted brushes, as well as compass and ruler. Yoshitoshi had been working; a sheet of translucent rice paper was pinned to the table, lightly and precisely streaked with ink.

"So," Encho said, smiling and waving one hand at the artist's penurious den. "I heard you'd been doing pretty well lately. This place has certainly improved since I last saw it. You've got real bookshelves again. I bet you'll have your books back in no time."

Yoshitoshi smiled sweetly. "Oh—I have so many debts . . . the books come last. But yes, things are much better for me now. I have my health again. And a studio. And one apprentice, Toshimitsu, came back to me. He's not the best of the ones I lost, but he's honest at least."

Encho pulled a short foreign briar-pipe from his coat. He opened the ornate tobacco bag on his belt, an embroidered pouch that was the pride of every Edo man-about-town. He glanced up casually, stuffing his pipe. "Did that Kabuki gig ever come to anything?"

"Oh yes," said Yoshitoshi, sitting up straighter. "I painted bloodstains on the armor of Onoe Kikugoro the Fifth. For his role in *Kawanakajima Island*. I'm very grateful to you for arranging that."

"Wait, I saw that play," said Onogawa, surprised and pleased. "Say, those were wonderful bloodstains. Even better than the ones in that murder print, 'Kasamori Osen Carved Alive by Her Stepfather.' You did that print too, am I right?" Onogawa had been studying the prints on the wall, and the familiar style had jogged his memory. "A young girl yanked backwards by a maniac with a knife, big bloody handprints all over her neck and legs . . . "

Yoshitoshi smiled. "You liked that one, Mr. Onogawa?"

"Well," Onogawa said, "it was certainly a fine effort for what it was." It wasn't easy for a man in Onogawa's position to confess a liking for mere commoner art from Low City. He dropped his voice a little. "Actually, I had quite a few of your pictures, in my younger days. Ten years ago, just before the Restoration." He smiled, remembering. "I had the *Twenty-Eight Murders*, of course. And some of the *One Hundred Ghost Stories*. And a few of the special editions, now that I think of it. Like Tamigoro blowing his head off with a rifle. Especially good sprays of blood in that one."

"Oh, I remember that one," Encho volunteered. "That was back in the old days, when they used to sprinkle the bloody scarlet ink with powdered mica. For that deluxe bloody gleaming effect!"

"Too expensive now," Yoshitoshi said sadly.

Encho shrugged. "Remember 'Naosuke Gombei Murders His Master'? With the maniac servant standing on his employer's chest, ripping the man's face off with his hands alone?" The comedian cleverly mimed the murderer's pinching and wrenching, along with loud sucking and shredding sounds.

"Oh, yes!" said Onogawa. "I wonder whatever happened to my copy of it?" He shook himself. "Well, it's not the sort of thing you can keep in the house, with my age and position. It might give the children nightmares. Or the servants ideas." He laughed.

Encho had stuffed his short pipe; he lit it from a lamp. Onogawa, preparing to follow suit, dragged his long iron-bound pipe from within his coat sleeve. "How wretched," he cried. "I've cracked my good pipe in the scuffle with those hooligans. Look, it's ruined."

"Oh, is that a smoking-pipe?" said Encho. "From the way

you used it on your attackers, I thought it was a simple bludgeon."

"I certainly would not go into the Low City without self-defense of some kind," Onogawa said stiffly. "And since the new government has seen fit to take our swords away, I'm forced to make do. A pipe is an ignoble weapon. But as you saw tonight, not without its uses."

"Oh, no offense meant, sir," said Encho hastily. "There's no need to be formal here among friends! If I'm a bit harsh of tongue I hope you'll forgive me, as it's my livelihood! So! Why don't we all have a drink and relax, eh?"

Yoshitoshi's eye had been snagged by the incomplete picture on his drawing table. He stared at it raptly for a few more seconds, then came to with a start. "A drink! Oh!" He straightened up. "Why, come to think of it, I have something very special, for gentlemen like yourselves. It came from Yokohama, from the foreign trade zone." Yoshitoshi crawled rapidly across the floor, his knees skidding inside the cotton robe, and threw open a dented wooden chest. He unwrapped a tall glass bottle from a wad of tissue and brought it back to his seat, along with three dusty sake cups.

The bottle had the flawless symmetrical ugliness of foreign manufacture. It was full of amber liquid, and corked. A paper label showed the grotesquely bearded face of an American man, framed by blocky foreign letters.

"Who's that?" Onogawa asked, intrigued. "Their king?"

"No, it's the face of the merchant who brewed it," Yoshitoshi said with assurance. "In America, merchants are famous. And a man of the merchant class can even become a soldier. Or a farmer, or priest, or anything he likes."

"Hmmph," said Onogawa, who had gone through a similar transition himself and was not at all happy about it. "Let me see." He examined the printed label closely. "Look how this foreigner's eyes bug out. He looks like a raving lunatic!"

Yoshitoshi stiffened at the term. An awkward moment of frozen silence seeped over the room. Onogawa's gaffe floated in midair among them, until its nature became clear to everyone. Yoshitoshi had recovered his health recently, but his illness had not been a physical one. No one had to say anything, but the truth slowly oozed its way into everyone's bones and liver. At length, Onogawa cleared his throat. "I mean, of course, that there's no accounting for the strange looks of foreigners."

Yoshitoshi licked his fleshy lips, and the sudden gleam of desperation slowly faded from his eyes. He spoke quietly. "Well, my friends in the Liberal Party have told me all about it. Several of them have been to America and back, and they speak the language, and can even read it. If you want to know more, you can read their national newspaper, the *Lamp of Liberty*, for which I am doing illustrations."

Onogawa glanced quickly at Encho. Onogawa, who was not a reading man, had only vague notions as to what a "liberal party" or a "national newspaper" might be. He wondered if Encho knew better. Apparently the comedian did, for Encho looked suddenly grave.

Yoshitoshi rattled on. "One of my political friends gave me this bottle, which he bought in Yokohama, from Americans. The Americans have many such bottles there—a whole warehouse. Because the American shogun, Generalissimo Guranto, will be arriving next year to pay homage to our emperor. And the Guranto, the 'puresidento,' is especially fond of this kind of drink! Which is called borubona, from the American prefecture of Kentukki."

Yoshitoshi twisted the cork loose and dribbled bourbon into all three cups. "Shouldn't we heat it first?" Encho said.

"This isn't sake, my friend. Sometimes they even put ice in it!"

Onogawa sipped carefully and gasped. "What a bite this has! It burns the tongue like Chinese peppers." He hesitated. "Interesting, though."

"It's good!" said Encho, surprised. "If sake were like an old stone lantern, then this borybona would be gaslight! Hot and fierce!" He tossed back the rest of his cup. "It's a pity there's no pretty girl to serve us our second round."

Yoshitoshi did the honors, filling their cups again. "This serving girl," Onogawa said. "She would have to be hot and fierce too—like a tigress."

Encho lifted his brows. "You surprise me. I thought you were a family man, my friend."

A warm knot of bourbon in Onogawa's stomach was reawakening an evening's worth of sake. "Oh, I suppose I seem settled enough now. But you should have known me ten years ago, before the Restoration. I was quite the tough young radical in those days. You know, we really thought we could change the world. And perhaps we did!"

Encho grinned, amused. "So! You were a shishi?"

Onogawa had another sip. "Oh, yes!" He touched the middle of his back. "I had hair down to here, and I never washed! Touch money? Not a one of us! We'd have died first! No, we lived in rags and ate plain brown rice from wooden bowls. We just went to our kendo schools, practiced swordsmanship, decided what old fool we should try to kill next. . . ." Onogawa shook his head ruefully. The other two were listening with grave attention.

The bourbon and the reminiscing had thawed Onogawa out. The lost ideals of the Restoration rose up within him irresistibly. "I was the despair of my family," he confided. "I abandoned my clan and my daimyo. We shishi radicals, you know, we believed only in our swords and the emperor. *Sonno joi!* Remember that slogan?" Onogawa grinned, the tears of *mono no aware*, the pathos of lost things, coming to his eyes.

"*Sonno joi!* The very streets used to ring with it. 'Revere the emperor, destroy the foreigners!' We wanted the emperor restored to full and unconditional power! We demanded it in the streets! Because the shogun's men were acting like frightened old women. Frightened of the black ships, the American black warships with their steam and cannon. Admiral Perry's ships."

"It's pronounced 'Peruri,' " Encho corrected gently.

"Peruri, then . . . I admit, we shishi went a bit far. We had some bad habits. Like threatening to commit hara-kiri unless the townsfolk gave us food. That's one of the problems we faced because we refused to touch money. Some of the shopkeepers still resent the way we shishi used to push them around. In fact, that was the cause of tonight's incident after your performance, Encho. Some rude fellows with long memories."

"So that was it," Encho said. "I wondered."

"Those were special times," Onogawa said. "They changed me, they changed everything. I suppose everyone of this generation knows where they were, and what they were doing, when the foreigners arrived in Edo Bay."

"I remember," said Yoshitoshi. "I was fourteen and an apprentice at Kuniyoshi's studio. And I'd just done my first print. 'The Heike Clan Sink to Their Horrible Doom in the Sea.' "

"I saw them dance once," Encho said. "The American sailors, I mean."

"Really?" said Onogawa.

Encho cast a storyteller's mood with an irresistible gesture. "Yes, my father, Entaro, took me. The performance was restricted to the shogun's court officials and their friends, but we managed to sneak in. The foreigners painted their faces and hands quite black. They seemed ashamed of their usual pinkish color, for they also painted broad white lines around their lips. Then they all sat on chairs together in a row, and one at a time they would stand up and shout dialogue. A second foreigner would answer, and they would all laugh. Later two of them strummed on strange round-bodied samisens, with long, thin necks. And they sang mournful songs, very badly. Then they played faster songs and capered and danced, kicking out their legs in the oddest way, and flinging each other about. Some of the shogun's counselors danced with them." Encho shrugged. "It was all very odd. To this day I wonder what it meant."

"Well," said Onogawa. "Clearly they were trying to

change their appearance and shape, like foxes or badgers. That seems clear enough."

"That's as much as saying they're magicians," Encho said, shaking his head. "Just because they have long noses doesn't mean they're mountain goblins. They're men—they eat, they sleep, they want a woman. Ask the geishas in Yokohama if that's not so." Encho smirked. "Their real power is in the spirits of copper wires and black iron and burning coal. Like our own Tokyo-Yokohama Railway, that the hired English built for us. You've ridden it, of course?"

"Of course!" Onogawa said proudly. "I'm a modern sort of fellow."

"That's the sort of power we need today. Civilization and Enlightenment. When you rode the train, did you see how the backward villagers in Omori come out to pour water on the engine? To cool it off, as if the railway engine were a tired horse!" Encho shook his head in contempt.

Onogawa accepted another small cup of bourbon. "So they pour water," he said judiciously. "Well, I can't see that it does any harm."

"It's rank superstition!" said Encho. "Don't you see, we have to learn to deal with those machine-spirits, just as the foreigners do. Treating them as horses can only insult them. Isn't that so, Taiso?"

Yoshitoshi looked up guilty from his absent-minded study of his latest drawing. "I'm sorry, Encho-san, you were saying?"

"What's that you're working on? May I see?" Encho crept nearer.

Yoshitoshi hastily plucked out pins and rolled up his paper. "Oh no, no, you wouldn't want to see this one just yet. It's not ready. But I can show you another recent one. . . ." He reached to a nearby stack and dexterously plucked a printed sheet from the unsteady pile. "I'm calling this series *Beauties of the Seven Nights*."

Encho courteously held up the print so that both he and

Onogawa could see it. It showed a woman in her under-robe; she had thrown her scarlet-lined outer kimono over a nearby screen. She had both natural and artificial eyebrows, lending a double seductiveness to her high forehead. Her mane of jet-black hair had a killing little wispy fringe at the back of the neck; it seemed to cry out to be bitten. She stood at some lucky man's doorway, bending to blow out the light of a lantern in the hall. And her tiny but piercingly red mouth was clamped down over a roll of paper towels.

"I get it!" Onogawa said. "That beautiful whore is blowing out the light so she can creep into some fellow's bed in the dark! And she's taking those handy paper towels in her teeth to mop up with, after they're through playing mortar-and-pestle."

Encho examined the print more closely. "Wait a minute," he said. "This caption reads 'Her Ladyship Yanagihara Aiko.' This is an imperial lady-in-waiting!"

"Some of my newspaper friends gave me the idea," Yoshitoshi said, nodding. "Why should prints always be of tiresome, stale old actors and warriors and geishas? This is the modern age!"

"But this print, Taiso . . . it clearly implies that the emperor sleeps with his ladies-in-waiting."

"No, just with Lady Yanagihara Aiko," Yoshitoshi said reasonably. "After all, everyone knows she's his special favorite. The rest of the Seven Beauties of the Imperial Court are drawn, oh, putting on their makeup, arranging flowers, and so forth." He smiled. "I expect big sales from this series. It's very topical, don't you think?"

Onogawa was shocked. "But this is rank scandal-mongering! What happened to the good old days, with the nice gouts of blood and so on?"

"No one buys those any more!" Yoshitoshi protested. "Believe me, I've tried everything! I did *A Yoshitoshi Miscellany of Figures from Literature*. Very edifying, beautifully drawn classical figures, the best. It died on the stands. Then

I did *Raving Beauties at Tokyo Restaurants*. Really hot girls, but old-fashioned geishas done in the old style. Another total waste of time. We were dead broke, not a copper piece to our names! I had to pull up the floorboards of my house for fuel! I had to work on fabric designs—two yen for a week's work! My wife left me! My apprentices walked out! And then my health . . . my brain began to . . . I had nothing to eat . . . nothing. . . . But . . . but that's all over now."

Yoshitoshi shook himself, dabbed sweat from his pasty upper lip, and poured another cup of bourbon with a steady hand. "I changed with the times, that's all. It was a hard lesson, but I learned it. I call myself Taiso now, Taiso, meaning 'Great Rebirth.' Newspapers! That's where the excitement is today! *Tokyo Illustrated News* pays plenty for political cartoons and murder illustrations. They do ten thousand impressions at a stroke. My work goes everywhere—not just Edo, the whole nation. The nation, gentlemen!" He raised his cup and drank. "And that's just the beginning. The *Lamp of Liberty* is knocking them dead! The Liberal Party committee has promised me a raise next year, and my own rickshaw."

"But I like the old pictures," Onogawa said.

"Maybe you do, but you don't buy them," Yoshitoshi insisted. "Modern people want to see what's happening now! Take an old theme picture—Yorimitsu chopping an ogre's arm off, for instance. Draw a thing like that today and it gets you nowhere. People's tastes are more refined today. They want to see real cannonballs blowing off real arms. Like my eyewitness illustrations of the Battle of Ueno. A sensation! People don't want print peddlers any more. 'Journalist illustrator'—that's what they call me now."

"Don't laugh," said Encho, nodding in drunken profundity. "You should hear what they say about me. I mean the modern writer fellows, down from the university. They come in with their French novels under their arms, and their spectacles and slicked-down hair, and all sit in the front row together. So I tell them a vaudeville tale or two. Am I 'spinning a good yarn'? Not anymore. They tell me I'm 'creating naturalistic prose in a vigorous popular vernacular.' They want to publish me in a book." He sighed and had another drink. "This stuff's poison, Taiso. My head's spinning."

"Mine, too," Onogawa said. An autumn wind had sprung up outside. They sat in doped silence for a moment. They were all much drunker than they had realized. The foreign liquor seemed to bubble in their stomachs like tofu fermenting in a tub.

The foreign spirits had crept up on them. The very room itself seemed drunk. Wind sang through the telegraph wires outside Yoshitoshi's shuttered window. A low, eerie moan.

The moan built in intensity. It seemed to creep into the room with them. The walls hummed with it. Hair rose on their arms.

"Stop that!" Yoshitoshi said suddenly. Encho stopped his ventriloqual moaning and giggled. "He's trying to scare us," Yoshitoshi said. "He loves ghost stories."

Onogawa lurched to his feet. "Demon in the wires," he said thickly. "I heard it moaning at us." He blinked, red faced, and staggered to the shuttered window. He fumbled loudly at the lock, ignoring Yoshitoshi's protests, and flung it open.

Moonlit wire clustered at the top of a wooden pole, in plain sight, a few feet away. It was a junction of cables, and leftover coils of wire dangled from the pole's cross-arm like thin black guts. Onogawa flung up the casement with a bang. A chilling gust of fresh air entered the stale room, and the prints danced on the walls. "Hey, you foreign demon!" Onogawa shouted. "Leave honest men in peace!"

The artist and entertainer exchanged unhappy glances. "We drank too much," Encho said. He lurched to his knees and onto one unsteady foot. "Leave off, big fellow. What we need now . . ." He belched. "Women, that's what."

But the air outside the window seemed to have roused Onogawa. "We didn't ask for you!" he shouted. "We don't need you! Things were fine before you came, demon! You and your foreign servants . . ." He turned half-round, looking red eyed into the room. "Where's my pipe? I've a mind to give these wires a good thrashing."

He spotted the pipe again, stumbled into the room, and picked it up. He lost his balance for a moment, then brandished the pipe threateningly. "Don't do it," Encho said, getting to his feet. "Be reasonable. I know some girls in Asakusa, they have a piano. . . ." He reached out.

Onogawa shoved him aside. "I've had enough!" he announced. "When my blood's up, I'm a different man! Cut them down before they attack first, that's my motto! *Sonno joi!*"

He lurched across the room toward the open window. Before he could reach it there was a sudden hiss of steam, like the breath of a locomotive. The demon, its patience exhausted by Onogawa's taunts, gushed from its wire. It puffed through the window, a gray, gaseous thing, its lumpy, misshapen head glaring furiously. It gave a steam-whistle roar, and its great lantern eyes glowed.

All three men screeched aloud. The armless, legless monster, like a gray cloud on a tether, rolled its glassy eyes at all of them. Its steel teeth gnashed, and sparks showed down its throat. It whistled again and made a sudden gnashing lurch at Onogawa.

But Onogawa's old sword-training had soaked deep into his bones. He leapt aside reflexively, with only a trace of stagger, and gave the thing a smart overhead riposte with his pipe. The demon's head bonged like an iron kettle. It began chattering angrily, and hot steam curled from its nose. Onogawa hit it again. Its head dented. It winced, then glared at the other men.

The townsmen quickly scrambled into line behind their champion. "Get him!" Encho shrieked. Onogawa dodged a halfhearted snap of teeth and bashed the monster across the eye. Glass cracked, and the bowl flew from Onogawa's pipe.

But the demon had had enough. With a grumble and crunch like dying gear-works, it retreated back towards its wires, sucking itself back within them, like an octopus into its hole. It vanished, but hissing sparks continued to drip from the wire.

"You humiliated it!" Encho said, his voice filled with awe and admiration. "That was amazing!"

"Had enough, eh!" shouted Onogawa furiously, leaning on the sill. "Easy enough mumbling your dirty spells behind our backs! But try an imperial warrior face to face, and it's a different story! Hah!"

"What a feat of arms!" said Yoshitoshi, his pudgy face glowing. "I'll do a picture. 'Onogawa Humiliates a Ghoul.' Wonderful!"

The sparks began to travel down the wire, away from the window. "It's getting away!" Onogawa shouted. "Follow me!"

He shoved himself from the window and ran headlong from the studio. He tripped at the top of the stairs but did an inspired shoulder-roll and landed on his feet at the door. He yanked it open.

Encho followed him headlong. They had no time to lace on their leather shoes, so they kicked on the wooden clogs of Yoshitoshi and his apprentice and dashed out. Soon they stood under the wires, where the little nest of sparks still clung. "Come down here, you rascal," Onogawa demanded. "Show some fighting honor, you skulking wretch!"

The thing moved back and forth, hissing, on the wire. More sparks dripped. It dodged back and forth, like a cornered rat in an alley. Then it made a sudden run for it.

"It's heading south!" said Onogawa. "Follow me!"

They ran in hot pursuit, Encho bringing up the rear, for he had slipped his feet into the apprentice's clogs, which were too big for him.

They pursued the thing across the Ginza. It had settled down to headlong running now and dropped fewer sparks.

"I wonder what message it carries," panted Encho.

"Nothing good, I'll warrant," said Onogawa grimly. They had to struggle to match the thing's pace. They burst from the southern edge of the Ginza Bricktown and into the darkness of unpaved streets. This was Shiba District, home of the thieves' market and the great Zojoji Temple. They followed the wires. "Aha!" cried Onogawa. "It's heading for Shinbashi Railway Station and its friends the locomotives!"

With a determined burst of speed, Onogawa outdistanced the thing and stood beneath the path of the wire, waving his broken pipe frantically. "Whoa! Go back!"

The thing slowed briefly, well over his head. Stinking flakes of ash and sparks poured from it, raining down harmlessly on the ex-samurai. Onogawa leapt aside in disgust, brushing the filth from his derby and frock coat. "Phew!"

The thing rolled on. Encho caught up with the larger man. "Not the locomotives," the comedian gasped. "We can't face those."

Onogawa drew himself up. He tried to dust more streaks of filthy ash from his soiled coat. "Well, I think we taught the nasty thing a lesson, anyway."

"No doubt," said Encho, breathing hard. He went green suddenly, then leaned against a nearby wooden fence, clustered with tall autumn grass. He was loudly sick.

They looked about themselves. Autumn. Darkness. And the moon. A pair of cats squabbled loudly in a nearby alley.

Onogawa suddenly realized that he was brandishing not a sword but a splintered stick of iron-bound bamboo. He began to tremble. Then he flung the thing away with a cry of disgust. "They took our swords away," he said. "Let them give us honest soldiers our swords back. We'd make short work of such foreign foulness. Look what it did to my coat, the filthy creature. It defiled me."

"No, no," Encho said, wiping his mouth. "You were incredible! A regular Shoki the Demon Queller."

"Shoki," Onogawa said. He dusted his hat against his

knee. "I've seen drawings of Shoki. He's the warrior demigod, with a red face and a big sword. Always hunting demons, isn't he? But he doesn't know there's a little demon hiding on top of his own head."

"Well, a regular Yoshitsune, then," said Encho, hastily grasping for a better compliment. Yoshitsune was a legendary master of swordsmanship. A national hero without parallel.

Unfortunately, the valorous Yoshitsune had ended up riddled with arrows by the agents of his treacherous half-brother, who had gone on to rule Japan. While Yoshitsune and his high ideals had to put up with a shadow existence in folklore. Neither Encho nor Onogawa had to mention this aloud, but the melancholy associated with the old tale seeped into their moods. Their world became heroic and fatal. Naturally, all the bourbon helped.

"We'd better go back to Bricktown for our shoes," Onogawa said.

"All right," Encho said. Their feet had blistered in the commandeered clogs, and they walked back slowly and carefully.

Yoshitoshi met them in his downstairs landing. "Did you catch it?"

"It made a run for the railroads," Encho said. "We couldn't stop it; it was way above our heads." He hesitated. "Say. You don't suppose it will come back here, do you?"

"Probably," Yoshitoshi said. "It lives in that knot of cables outside the window. That's why I put the shutters there."

"You mean you've seen it before?"

"Sure I've seen it," Yoshitoshi muttered. "In fact, I've seen lots of things. It's my business to see things. No matter what people say about me."

The others looked at him, stricken. Yoshitoshi shrugged irritably. "The place has atmosphere. It's quiet and no one bothers me here. Besides, it's cheap."

"Aren't you afraid of the demon's vengeance?" Onogawa said.

"I get along fine with that demon," Yoshitoshi said. "We have an understanding. Like neighbors anywhere."

"Oh," Encho said. He cleared his throat. "Well, ah, we'll be moving on, Taiso. It was good of you to give us the borubona." He and Onogawa stuffed their feet hastily into their squeaking shoes. "You keep up the good work, pal, and don't let those political fellows put anything over on you. Their ideas are weird, frankly. I don't think the government's going to put up with that kind of talk."

"Someday they'll have to," Yoshitoshi said.

"Let's go," Onogawa said, with a sidelong glance at Yoshitoshi. The two men left.

Onogawa waited until they were well out of earshot. He kept a wary eye on the wires overhead. "Your friend certainly is a weird one," he told the comedian. "What a night!"

Encho frowned. "He's gonna get in trouble with that visionary stuff. The nail that sticks up gets hammered down, you know." They walked into the blaze of artificial gaslight. The Ginza crowd had thinned out considerably.

"Didn't you say you knew some girls with a piano?" Onogawa said.

"Oh, right!" Encho said. He whistled shrilly and waved at a distant two-man rickshaw. "A piano. You won't believe the thing; it makes amazing sounds. And what a great change after those dreary geisha samisen routines. So whiny and thin and wailing and sad! It's always, 'Oh, How Piteous Is a Courtesan's Lot,' and 'Let's Stab Each Other to Prove You Really Love Me.' Who needs that old-fashioned stuff? Wait till you hear these gals pound out some 'opera' and 'waltzes' on their new machine."

The rickshaw pulled up with a rattle and a chime of bells. "Where to, gentlemen?"

"Asakusa," said Encho, climbing in.

"It's getting late," Onogawa said reluctantly. "I really ought to be getting back to the wife."

"Come on," said Encho, rolling his eyes. "Live a little.

It's not like you're just cheating on the little woman. These are high-class modern girls. It's a cultural experience."

"Well, all right," said Onogawa. "If it's cultural."

"You'll learn a lot," Encho promised.

But they had barely covered a block when they heard the sudden frantic ringing of alarm bells, far to the south.

"A fire!" Encho yelled in glee. "Hey, runners, stop! Fifty sen if you get us there while it's still spreading!"

The runners wheeled in place and set out with a will. The rickshaw rocked on its axle and jangled wildly. "This is great!" Onogawa said, clutching his hat. "You're a good fellow to know, Encho. It's nothing but excitement with you!"

"That's the modern life!" Encho shouted. "One wild thing after another."

They bounced and slammed their way through the darkened streets until the sky was lit with fire. A massive crowd had gathered beside the Shinagawa Railroad Line. They were mostly low-class townsmen, many half-dressed. It was a working-class neighborhood in Shiba District, east of Atago Hill. The fire was leaping merrily from one thatched roof to another.

The two men jumped from their rickshaw. Encho shouldered his way immediately through the crowd. Onogawa carefully counted out the fare. "But he said fifty sen," the older rickshawman complained. Onogawa clenched his fist and the men fell silent.

The firemen had reacted with their usual quick skill. Three companies of them had surrounded the neighborhood. They swarmed like ants over the roofs of the undamaged houses nearest the flames. As usual, they did not attempt to fight the flames directly. That was a hopeless task in any case, for the weathered, graying wood, paper shutters, and reed blinds flared up like tinder, in great blossoming gouts.

Instead, they sensibly relied on firebreaks. Their hammers, axes, and crowbars flew as they destroyed every house in the path of the flames. Their skill came naturally to them, for, like all Edo firemen, they were also carpenters. Special banner-men stood on the naked ridgepoles of the disintegrating houses, holding their company's ensigns as close as possible to the flames. This was more than bravado; it was good business. Their reputations, and their rewards from a grateful neighborhood, depended on this show of spirit and nerve.

Some of the crowd, those whose homes were being devoured, were weeping and counting their children. But most of the crowd was in a fine holiday mood, cheering for their favorite fire teams and laying bets.

Onogawa spotted Encho's silk hat and plowed after him. Encho ducked and elbowed through the press, Onogawa close behind. They crept to the crowd's inner edge, where the fierce blaze of heat and the occasional falling wad of flaming straw had established a boundary.

A fireman stood nearby. He wore a knee-length padded fireproof coat with a pattern of printed blocks. A thick protective headdress fell stiffly over his shoulders, and long padded gauntlets shielded his forearms to the knuckles. An apprentice in similar garb was soaking him down with a pencil-thin gush of water from a bamboo hand-pump. "Stand back, stand back," the fireman said automatically, then looked up. "Say, aren't you Encho the comedian? I saw you last week."

"That's me," Encho shouted cheerfully over the roar of flame. "Good to see you fellows performing for once."

The fireman examined Onogawa's ash-streaked frock coat. "You live around here, big fella? Point out your house for me, we'll do what we can."

Onogawa frowned. Encho broke in hastily. "My friend's from uptown! A High City company man!"

"Oh," said the fireman, rolling his eyes.

Onogawa pointed at a merchant's tile-roofed warehouse, a little closer to the tracks. "Why aren't you doing anything about that place? The fire's headed right for it!"

"That's one of merchant Shinichi's," the fireman said, narrowing his eyes. "We saved a place of his out in Kanda District last month! And he gave us only five yen."

"What a shame for him," Encho said, grinning.

"It's full of cotton cloth, too," the fireman said with satisfaction. "It's gonna go up like a rocket."

"How did it start?" Encho said.

"Lightning, I hear," the fireman said. "Some kind of fireball jumped off the telegraph lines."

"Really?" Encho said in a small voice.

"That's what they say," shrugged the fireman. "You know how these things are. Always tall stories. Probably some drunk knocked over his sake kettle, then claimed to see something. No one wants the blame."

"Right," Onogawa said carefully.

The fire teams had made good progress. There was not much left to do now except admire the destruction. "Kind of beautiful, isn't it?" the fireman said. "Look how that smoke obscures the autumn moon." He sighed happily. "Good for business, too. I mean the carpentry business, of course." He waved his gauntleted arm at the leaping flames. "We'll get this worn-out trash out of here and build something worthy of a modern city. Something big and expensive with long-term construction contracts."

"Is that why you have bricks printed on your coat?" Onogawa asked.

The fireman looked down at the block printing on his dripping cotton armor. "They do look like bricks, don't they?" He laughed. "That's a good one. Wait'll I tell the crew."

Dawn rose above old Edo. With red-rimmed eyes, the artist Yoshitoshi stared, sighing, through his open window. Past the telegraph wires, billowing smudge rose beyond the Bricktown rooftops. Another Flower of Edo reaching the end of its evanescent life.

The telegraph wires hummed. The demon had returned

71

to its tangled nest outside the window. "Don't tell, Yoshitoshi," it burbled in its deep, humming voice.

"Not me," Yoshitoshi said. "You think I want them to
lock me up again?"

"I keep the presses running," the demon whined. "Just
you deal with me. I'll make you famous, I'll make you rich.
There'll be no more slow dark shadows where townmen have
to creep with their heads down. Everything's brightness and
speed with me, Yoshitoshi. I can change things."

"Burn them down, you mean," Yoshitoshi said.

"There's power in burning," the demon hummed.
"There's beauty in the flames. When you give up trying to
save the old ways, you'll see the beauty. I want you to serve
me, you Japanese. You'll do it better than the clumsy foreigners, once you accept me as your own. I'll make you all
rich. Edo will be the greatest city in the world. You'll have
light and music at a finger's touch. You'll step across oceans.
You'll be as gods."

"And if we don't accept you?"

"You will! You must! I'll burn you until you do. I told
you that, Yoshitoshi. When I'm stronger, I'll do better than
these little flowers of Edo. I'll open seeds of hell above your
cities. Hell-flowers taller than mountains! Red blooms that
eat a city in a moment."

Yoshitoshi lifted his latest print and unrolled it before
the window. He had worked on it all night; it was done at
last. It was a landscape of pure madness. Beams of frantic
light pierced a smoldering sky. Winged locomotives, their
bellies fattened with the eggs of white-hot death, floated like
maddened blowflies above a corpse-white city. "Like this,"
he said.

The demon gave a gloating whir. "Yes! Just as I told you.
Now show it to them. Make them understand that they can't
defeat me. Show them all!"

"I'll think about it," Yoshitoshi said. "Leave me now."
He closed the heavy shutters.

He rolled the drawing carefully into a tube. He sat at his worktable again and pulled an oil lamp closer. Dawn was coming. It was time to get some sleep.

He held the end of the paper tube above the lamp's little flame. It browned at first, slowly, the brand-new paper turning the rich antique tinge of an old print, a print from the old days when things were simpler. Then a cigar-ring of smoldering red encircled its rim, and blue flame blossomed. Yoshitoshi held the paper up, and flame ate slowly down its length, throwing smoky shadows.

Yoshitoshi blew and watched his work flare up, cherry-blossom white and red. It hurt to watch it go, and it felt good. He savored the two feelings for as long as he could. Then he dropped the last flaming inch of paper in an ashtray. He watched it flare and smolder until the last of the paper became a ghost-curl of gray.

"It'd never sell," he said. Absently, knowing he would need them tomorrow, he cleaned his brushes. Then he emptied the ink-stained water over the crisp dark ashes.

Schwarzschild Radius

Connie Willis

Connie Willis has won several awards for her writing, including two Nebulas. In 1980, she received a grant from the National Endowment for the Humanities. Her books include the short-story collection *Fire Watch* and the novel *Lincoln Dreams*, and she is now at work on another novel, *The Doomsday Book*. Her science fiction occasionally proceeds from a striking metaphorical equation between some awesome physical phenomenon and the psychological state of the people affected by it, as in her early story "Daisy, in the Sun," and also in the powerful novelette showcased here.

About "Schwarzschild Radius," originally written for the Byron Preiss Visual Publications anthology *The Universe*, Willis tells us: "Science doesn't inspire many of my stories. (This will hardly come as a shock to anybody, since my work is not only classed as soft science fiction but downright mushy.) I find most of science interesting (except for flatworms and Avogadro's number) and some of it fascinating (like mitochondria), but it only rarely forms what Nabokov calls 'the secret nerves' of my stories.

"That's because it lacks affect; until you put science into human terms it doesn't inspire much of an emotional response, and one of the things I like best about science fiction is how it dramatizes the implications of scientific fact and makes me care about single-celled animals and Jupiter's red spot and even Avogadro's number.

" 'Schwarzschild Radius' is different. Nobody had to explain the implications of the black hole to me. I recognized them immediately. This was it: the nightmare we can't wake up from, the closing coffin, the trap from which there is no escape because we passed the point of no return before we even knew it was there, and there's no way out, and they can't even hear our cries for help."

Here, then, a legitimate science-fiction story that brilliantly conflates the seemingly incongruous phenomena of late-20th-century black-hole theory and the profound psychological horror of duty in the trenches during the First World War.

*"W*hen a star collapses, it sort of falls in on itself." Travers curved his hand into a semicircle and then brought the fingers in, "and sometimes it reaches a kind of point of no return where the gravity pulling in on it is stronger than the nuclear and electric forces, and when it reaches that point nothing can stop it from collapsing, and it becomes a black hole." He closed his hand into a fist. "And that critical diameter, that point where there's no turning back, is called the Schwarzschild radius." Travers paused, waiting for me to say something.

He had come to see me every day for a week, sitting stiffly on one of my chairs in an unaccustomed shirt and tie, and talked to me about black holes and relativity, even though I taught biology at the university before my retirement, not physics. Someone had told him I knew Schwarzschild, of course.

"The Schwarzschild radius?" I said in my quavery, old man's voice, as if I could not remember ever hearing the phrase before, and Travers looked disgusted. He wanted me to say, "The Schwarzschild radius! Ah, yes, I served with Karl Schwarzschild on the Russian front in World War I!" and tell him all about how he had formulated his theory of black holes while serving with the artillery, but I had not decided yet what to tell him. "The event horizon," I said.

"Yeah. It was named after Schwarzschild because he was the one who worked out the theory," Travers said. He reminded me of Muller with his talk of theories. He was the same age as Muller, with the same shock of stiff yellow hair and the same insatiable curiosity, and perhaps that was why I let him come every day to talk to me, though it was dangerous to let him get so close.

"I have drawn up a theory of the stars," Muller says while we warm our hands over the Primus stove so that they will get enough feeling in them to be able to hold the liquid barretter without dropping it. "They are not balls of fire, as the scientists say. They are frozen."

"How can we see them if they are frozen?" I say. Muller is insulted if I do not argue with him. The arguing is part of the theory.

"Look at the wireless!" he says, pointing to it sitting disemboweled on the table. We have the back off the wireless again, and in the barretter's glass tube is a red reflection of the stove's flame. "The light is a reflection off the ice of the star."

"A reflection of what?"

"Of the shells, of course."

I do not say that there were stars before there was this war, because Muller will not have an answer to this, and I have no desire to destroy his theory, and besides, I do not really believe there was a time when this war did not exist. The star shells have always exploded over the snow-covered craters of No Man's Land, shattering in a spray of white and red, and perhaps Muller's theory is true.

"At that point," Travers said, "at the event horizon, no more information can be transmitted out of the black hole because gravity has become so strong, and so the collapse appears frozen at the Schwarzschild radius."

"Frozen," I said, thinking of Muller.

"Yeah. As a matter of fact, the Russians call black holes 'frozen stars.' You were at the Russian front, weren't you?"

"What?"

"In World War I."

"But the star doesn't really freeze," I said. "It goes on collapsing."

"Yeah, sure," Travers said. "It keeps collapsing in on itself until even the atoms are stripped of their electrons and there's nothing left except what they call a naked singularity, but we can't see past the Schwarzschild radius, and nobody inside a black hole can tell us what it's like in there because they can't get messages out, so nobody can ever know what it's like inside a black hole."

"I know," I said, but he didn't hear me.

He leaned forward. "What was it like at the front?"

It is so cold we can only work on the wireless a few minutes at a time before our hands stiffen and grow clumsy, and we are afraid of dropping the liquid barretter. Muller holds his gloves over the Primus stove and then puts them on. I jam my hands in my ice-stiff pockets.

We are fixing the wireless set. Eisner, who had been delivering messages between the sectors, got sent up to the front when he could not fix his motorcycle. If we cannot fix the wireless we will cease to be telegraphists and become soldiers, and we will be sent to the front lines.

We are already nearly there. If it were not snowing we could see the barbed wire and pitted snow of No Man's Land, and the big Russian coal boxes that sometimes land in the communication trenches. A shell hit our wireless hut two weeks ago. We are ahead of our own artillery lines, and some of the shells from our guns fall on us, too, because the muzzles are worn out. But it is not the front, and we guard the liquid barretter with our lives.

"Eisner's unit was sent up on wiring fatigue last night," Muller says, "and they have not come back. I have a theory about what happened to them."

"Has the mail come?" I say, rubbing my sore eyes and

then putting my cold hands immediately back in my pockets. I must get some new gloves, but the quartermaster has none to issue. I have written my mother three times to knit me a pair, but she has not sent them yet.

"I have a theory about Eisner's unit," he says doggedly. "The Russians have a magnet that has pulled them into the front."

"Magnets pull iron, not people," I say.

I have a theory about Muller's theories. Littering the communications trenches are things that the soldiers going up to the front have discarded: water bottles and haversacks and bayonets. Hans and I sometimes tried to puzzle out why they would discard such important things.

"Perhaps they were too heavy," I would say, though that did not explain the bayonets or the boots.

"Perhaps they know they are going to die," Hans would say, picking up a helmet.

I would try to cheer him up. "My gloves fell out of my pocket yesterday when I went to the quartermaster's. I never found them. They are in this trench somewhere."

"Yes," he would say, turning the helmet round and round in his hands, "perhaps as they near the front, these things simply drop away from them."

My theory is that what happens to the water bottles and helmets and bayonets is what has happened to Muller. He was a student in university before the war, but his knowledge of science and his intelligence have fallen away from him, and now we are so close to the front, all he has left are his theories. And his curiosity, which is a dangerous thing to have kept.

"Exactly. Magnets pull iron, but *they* were carrying barbed wire!" he says triumphantly, "and so they were pulled in to the magnet."

I put my hands practically into the Primus flame and rub them together, trying to get rid of the numbness. "We had better get the barretter in the wireless again or this magnet of yours will suck it in too."

I go back to the wireless. Muller stays by the stove, thinking about his magnet. The door bangs open. It is not a real door, only an iron humpie tied to the beam that reinforces the dugout and held with a wedge, and when someone pushes against it, it flies inward, bringing the snow with it.

Snow swirls in, and light, and the sound from the front, a low rumble like a dog growling. I clutch the liquid barretter to my chest and Muller flings himself over the wireless as if it were a wounded comrade. Someone bundled in a wool coat and mittens, with a wool cap pulled over his ears, stands silhouetted against the reddish light in the doorway, blinking at us.

"Is Private Rottschieben here? I have come to see him about his eyes," he says, and I see it is Dr. Funkenheld.

"Come in and shut the door," I say, still carefully protecting the liquid barretter, but Muller has already jammed the metal back against the beam.

"Do you have news?" Muller says to the doctor, eager for new facts to spin his theories from. "Has the wiring fatigue come back? Is there going to be a bombardment tonight?"

Dr. Funkenheld takes off his mittens. "I have come to examine your eyes," he says to me. His voice frightens me. All through the war he has kept his quiet bedside voice, speaking to the wounded in the dressing station and at the stretcher bearers's posts as if they were in his surgery in Stuttgart, but now he sounds agitated and I am afraid it means a bombardment is coming and he will need me at the front.

When I went to the dressing station for medicine for my eyes, I foolishly told him I had studied medicine with Dr. Zuschauer in Jena. Now I am afraid he will ask me to assist him, which will mean going up to the front. "Do your eyes still hurt?" he says.

I hand the barretter to Muller and go over to stand by the lantern that hangs from a nail in the beam.

"I think he should be invalided home, Herr Doktor," Muller says. He knows it is impossible, of course. He was at the wireless the day the message came through that no one was to be invalided out for frostbite or "other noncontagious diseases."

"Can you find me a better light?" the doctor says to him.

Muller's curiosity is so strong that he cannot bear to leave any place where something interesting is happening. If he went up to the front I do not think he would be able to pull himself away, and now I expect him to make some excuse to stay, but I have forgotten that he is even more curious about the wiring fatigue. "I will go see what has happened to Eisner's unit," he says, and opens the door. Snow flies in, as if it had been beating against the door to get in, and the doctor and I have to push against the door to get it shut again.

"My eyes have been hurting," I say while we are still pushing the metal into place, so that he cannot ask me to assist him. "They feel like sand has gotten into them."

"I have a patient with a disease I do not recognize," he says. I am relieved, though disease can kill us as easily as a trench mortar. Soldiers die of pneumonia and dysentery and blood poisoning every day in the dressing station, but we do not fear it the way we fear the front.

"The patient has fever, excoriated lesions, and suppurating bullae," Dr. Funkenheld says.

"Could it be boils?" I say, though of course he would recognize something so simple as boils, but he is not listening to me, and I realize that it is not a diagnosis from me that he has come for.

"The man is a scientist, a Jew named Schwarzschild, attached to the artillery," he says, and because the artillery are even farther back from the front lines than we are, I volunteer to go and look at the patient, but he does not want that either.

"I must talk to the medical headquarters in Bialystok," he says.

"Our wireless is broken," I say, because I do not want to have to tell him why it is impossible for me to send a message for him. We are allowed to send only military messages, and they must be sent in code, tapped out on the telegraph key. It would take hours to send his message, even if it were possible. I hold up the dangling wire. "At any rate, you must clear it with the commandant," but he is already writing out the name and address on a piece of paper, as if this were a telegraph office.

"You can send the message when you get the wireless fixed. I have written out the symptoms."

I put the back on the wireless. Muller comes in, kicking the door open, and snow flies everywhere, picking up Dr. Funkenheld's message and sending it circling around the dugout. I catch it before it spirals into the flame of the Primus stove.

"The wiring fatigue was pinned down all night," Muller says, setting down a hand lamp. He must have gotten it from the dressing station. "Five of them frozen to death, the other eight have frostbite. The commandant thinks there may be a bombardment tonight." He does not mention Eisner, and he does not say what has happened to the rest of the thirty men in Eisner's unit, though I know. The front has gotten them. I wait, holding the message in my stiff fingers, hoping Dr. Funkenheld will say, "I must go attend to their frostbite."

"Let me examine your eyes," the doctor says, and shows Muller how to hold the lamp. Both of them peer into my eyes. "I have an ointment for you to use twice daily," he says, getting a flat jar out of his bag. "It will burn a little."

"I will rub it on my hands then. It will warm them," I say, thinking of Eisner frozen at the front, still holding the roll of barbed wire, perhaps.

He pulls my bottom eyelid down and rubs the ointment on with his little finger. It does not sting, but when I have blinked it into my eye, everything has a reddish tinge. "Will you have the wireless fixed by tomorrow?" he says.

"I don't know. Perhaps."

Muller has not put down the hand lamp. I can see by its light that he has forgotten all about the wiring fatigue and the Russian magnet and is wondering what the doctor wants with the wireless.

The doctor puts on his mittens and picks up his bag. I

realize too late I should have told him I would send the message in exchange for them. "I will come check your eyes tomorrow," he says and opens the door to the snow. The sound of the front is very close.

As soon as he is gone, I tell Muller about Schwarzschild and the message the doctor wants to send. He will not let me rest until I have told him, and we do not have time for his curiosity. We must fix the wireless.

"If you were on the wireless, you must have sent messages for Schwarzschild," Travers said eagerly. "Did you ever send a message to Einstein? They've got the letter Einstein sent to him after he wrote him his theory, but if Schwarzschild sent him some kind of message too, that would be great. It would make my paper."

"You said that no message can escape a black hole?" I said. "But they could escape a collapsing star. Is that not so?"

"Okay," Travers said impatiently and made his fingers into a semicircle again. "Suppose you have a fixed observer over here." He pulled his curved hand back and held the forefinger of his other hand up to represent the fixed observer, "and you have somebody in the star. Say when the star starts to collapse, the person in it shines a light at the fixed observer. If the star hasn't reached the Schwarzschild radius, the fixed observer will be able to see the light, but it will take longer to reach him because the gravity of the black hole is pulling on the light, so it will seem as if time on the star has slowed down and the wavelengths will have been lengthened, so the light will be redder. Of course that's just a thought problem. There couldn't really be anybody in a collapsing star to send the messages."

"We sent messages," I said. "I wrote my mother asking her to knit me a pair of gloves."

There is still something wrong with the wireless. We have received only one message in two weeks. It said, "Russian opposition collapsing," and there was so much static we could not make out the rest of it. We have taken the wireless apart twice. The first time we found a loose wire, but the second time we could not find anything. If Hans were here he would be able to find the trouble immediately.

"I have a theory about the wireless," Muller says. He has had ten theories in as many days: The magnet of the Russians is pulling our signals in to it; the northern lights, which have been shifting uneasily on the horizon, make a curtain the wireless signals cannot get through; the Russian opposition is not collapsing at all. They are drawing us deeper and deeper into a trap.

I say, "I am going to try again. Perhaps the trouble has cleared up," and put the headphones on so I do not have to listen to his new theory. I can hear nothing but a rumbling roar that sounds like the front.

I take out the folded piece of paper Dr. Funkenheld gave me and lay it on the wireless. He comes nearly every night to see if I have gotten an answer to his message, and I take off the headphones and let him listen to the static. I tell him that we cannot get through, but even though that is true, it is not the real reason I have not sent the message. I am afraid of the commandant finding out. I am afraid of being sent to the front.

I have compromised by writing a letter to the professor that I studied medicine with in Jena, but I have not gotten an answer from him yet, and so I must go on pretending to the doctor.

"You don't have to do that," Muller says. He sits on the wireless, swinging his leg. He picks up the paper with the symptoms on it and holds it to the flame of the Primus stove. I grab for it, but it is already burning redly. "I have sent the message for you."

"I don't believe you. Nothing has been getting out."

"Didn't you notice the northern lights did not appear last night?"

I have not noticed. The ointment the doctor gave to me makes everything look red at night, and I do not believe in Muller's theories. "Nothing is getting out now," I say, and hold the headphones out to him so he can hear the static. He listens, still swinging his leg. "You will get us both in trouble. Why did you do it?"

"I was curious about it." If we are sent up to the front, his curiosity will kill us. He will take apart a land mine to see how it works. "We cannot get in trouble for sending military messages. I said the commandant was afraid it was a poisonous gas the Russians were using." He swings his leg and grins because now I am the curious one.

"Well, did you get an answer?"

"Yes," he says maddeningly and puts the headphones on. "It is not a poisonous gas."

I shrug as if I do not care whether I get an answer or not. I put on my cap and the muffler my mother knitted for me and open the door. "I am going out to see if the mail has come. Perhaps there will be a letter there from my professor."

"Nature of disease unknown," Muller shouts against the sudden force of the snow. "Possibly impetigo or glandular disorder."

I grin back at him and say, "If there is a package from my mother I will give you half of what is in it."

"Even if it is your gloves?"

"No, not if it is my gloves," I say, and go to find the doctor.

At the dressing station they tell me he has gone to see Schwarzschild and give me directions to the artillery staff's headquarters. It is not very far, but it is snowing and my hands are already cold. I go to the quartermaster's and ask him if the mail has come in.

There is a new recruit there, trying to fix Eisner's motorcycle. He has parts spread out on the ground all around him in a circle. He points to a burlap sack and says, "That is all the mail there is. Look through it yourself."

Snow has gotten into the sack and melted. The ink on the envelopes has run, and I squint at them, trying to make out the names. My eyes begin to hurt. There is not a package from my mother or a letter from my professor, but there is a letter for Lieutenant Schwarzschild. The return address says "Doctor." Perhaps he has written to a doctor himself.

"I am delivering a message to the artillery headquarters," I say, showing the letter to the recruit. "I will take this up too." The recruit nods and goes on working.

It has gotten dark while I was inside, and it is snowing harder. I jam my hands in the ice-stiff pockets of my coat and start to the artillery headquarters in the rear. It is pitch-dark in the communication trenches, and the wind twists the snow and funnels it howling along them. I take off my muffler and wrap it around my hands like a girl's muff.

A band of red shifts uneasily all along the horizon, but I do not know if it is the front or Muller's northern lights, and there is no shelling to guide me. We are running out of shells, so we do not usually begin shelling until nine o'clock. The Russians start even later. Sometimes I hear machine-gun fire, but it is distorted by the wind and the snow, and I cannot tell what direction it is coming from.

The communication trench seems narrower and deeper than I remember it from when Hans and I first brought the wireless up. It takes me longer than I think it should to get to the branching that will lead north to the headquarters. The front has been contracting, the ammunition dumps and officers' billets and clearing stations moving up closer and closer behind us. The artillery headquarters has been moved up from the village to a dugout near the artillery line, not half a mile behind us. The nightly firing is starting. I hear a low rumble, like thunder.

The roar seems to be ahead of me, and I stop and look around, wondering if I can have gotten somehow turned around, though I have not left the trenches. I start again, and almost immediately I see the branching and the headquarters.

It has no door, only a blanket across the opening, and I pull my hands free of the muffler and duck through it into a tiny space like a rabbit hole, the timber balks of the earthen ceiling so low I have to stoop. Now that I am out of the roar of the snow, the sound of the front separates itself into the individual crack of a four-pounder, the whine of a star shell, and under it the almost continuous rattle of machine guns. The trenches must not be as deep here. Muller and I can hardly hear the front at all in our wireless hut.

A man is sitting at an uneven table spread with papers and books. There is a candle on the table with a red glass chimney, or perhaps it only looks that way to me. Everything in the dugout, even the man, looks faintly red. He is wearing a uniform but no coat, and gloves with the finger ends cut off, even though there is no stove here. My hands are already cold.

A trench mortar roars, and clods of frozen dirt clatter from the roof onto the table. The man brushes the dirt from the papers and looks up.

"I am looking for Dr. Funkenheld," I say.

"He is not here." He stands up and comes around the table, moving stiffly, like an old man, though he does not look older than forty. He has a moustache, and his face looks dirty in the red light.

"I have a message for him."

An eight-pounder roars, and more dirt falls on us. The man raises his arm to brush the dirt off his shoulder. The sleeve of his uniform has been slit into ribbons. All along the back of his raised hand and the side of his arm are red sores running with pus. I look back at his face. The sores in his moustache and around his nose and mouth have dried and are covered with a crust. Excoriated lesions. Suppurating bullae. The gun roars again, and the dirt rains down on his raw hands.

"I have a message for him," I say, backing away from him. I reach in the pocket of my coat to show him the message, but I pull out the letter instead. "There was a letter for you, Lieutenant Schwarzschild." I hold it out to him by one corner so he will not touch me when he takes it.

He comes toward me to take the letter, the muscles in his jaw tightening, and I think in horror that the sores must be on his legs as well. "Who is it from?" he says. "Ah, Herr Professor Einstein. Good," and turns it over. He puts his finger on the flap to open the letter, and cries out in pain. He drops the letter.

"Would you read it to me?" he says and sinks down into the chair, cradling his hand against his chest. I can see there are sores in his fingernails.

I do not have any feeling in my hands. I pick the envelope up by its corners and turn it over. The skin of his finger is still on the flap. I back away from the table. "I must find the doctor. It is an emergency."

"You would not be able to find him," he says. Blood oozes out of the tip of his finger and down over the blister in his fingernail. "He has gone up to the front."

"What?" I say, backing and backing until I run into the blanket. "I cannot understand you."

"He has gone up to the front," he says, more slowly, and this time I can puzzle out the words, but they make no sense. How can the doctor be at the front? This is the front.

He pushes the candle toward me. "I order you to read me the letter."

I do not have any feeling in my fingers. I open it from the top, tearing the letter almost in two. It is a long letter, full of equations and numbers, but the words are warped and blurred. " 'My Esteemed Colleague! I have read your paper with the greatest interest. I had not expected that one could formulate the exact solution of the problem so simply. The analytical treatment of the problem appears to me splendid. Next Thursday I will present the work, with several explanatory words, to the Academy!' "

"Formulated so simply," Schwarzschild says, as if he is

in pain. "That is enough. Put the letter down. I will read the rest of it."

I lay the letter on the table in front of him, and then I am running down the trench in the dark with the sound of the front all around me, roaring and shaking the ground. At the first turning, Muller grabs my arm and stops me. "What are you doing here?" I shout. "Go back! Go back!"

"Go back?" he says. "The front's that way." He points in the direction he came from. But the front is not that way. It is behind me, in the artillery headquarters. "I told you there would be a bombardment tonight. Did you see the doctor? Did you give him the message? What did he say?"

"So you actually held the letter from Einstein?" Travers said. "How exciting that must have been! Only two months after Einstein had published his theory of general relativity. And years before they realized black holes really existed. When was this exactly?" He took out a notebook and began to scribble notes. "My esteemed colleague . . ." he muttered to himself. "Formulated so simply. This is great stuff. I mean, I've been trying to find out stuff on Schwarzschild for my paper for months, but there's hardly any information on him. I guess because of the war."

"No information can get out of a black hole once the Schwarzschild radius has been passed," I said.

"Hey, that's great!" he said, scribbling. "Can I use that in my paper?"

Now I am the one who sits endlessly in front of the wireless sending out messages to the Red Cross, to my professor in Jena, to Dr. Einstein. I have frostbitten the forefinger and thumb of my right hand and have to tap out the letters with my left. But nothing is getting out, and I must get a message out. I must find someone to tell me the name of Schwarzschild's disease.

"I have a theory," Muller says. "The Jews have seized

power and have signed a treaty with the Russians. We are completely cut off."

"I am going to see if the mail has come," I say, so that I do not have to listen to any more of his theories, but the doctor stops me on my way out the hut.

I tell him what the message said. "Impetigo!" the doctor shouts. "You saw him! Did that look like impetigo to you?"

I shake my head, unable to tell him what I think it looks like.

"What are his symptoms?" Muller asks, burning with curiosity. I have not told him about Schwarzschild. I am afraid that if I tell him, he will only become more curious and will insist on going up to the front to see Schwarzschild himself.

"Let me see your eyes," the doctor says in his beautiful calm voice. I wish he would ask Muller to go for a hand lamp again so that I could ask him how Schwarzschild is, but he has brought a candle with him. He holds it so close to my face that I cannot see anything but the red flame.

"Is Lieutenant Schwarzschild worse? What are his symptoms?" Muller says, leaning forward.

His symptoms are craters and shell holes, I think. I am sorry I have not told Muller, for it has only made him more curious. Until now I have told him everything, even how Hans died when the wireless hut was hit, how he laid the liquid barretter carefully down on top of the wireless before he tried to cough up what was left of his chest and catch it in his hands. But I cannot tell him this.

"What symptoms does he have?" Muller says again, his nose almost in the candle's flame, but the doctor turns from him as if he cannot hear him and blows the candle out. The doctor unwraps the dressing and looks at my fingers. They are swollen and red. Muller leans over the doctor's shoulder. "I have a theory about Lieutenant Schwarzschild's disease," he says.

"Shut up," I say. "I don't want to hear any more of your stupid theories," and do not even care about the wounded look on Muller's face or the way he goes and sits by the wireless. For now I have a theory, and it is more horrible than anything Muller could have dreamt of.

We are all of us—Muller, and the recruit who is trying to put together Eisner's motorcycle, and perhaps even the doctor with his steady bedside voice—afraid of the front. But our fear is not complete, because unspoken in it is our belief that the front is something separate from us, something we can keep away from by keeping the wireless or the motorcycle fixed, something we can survive by flattening our faces into the frozen earth, something we can escape altogether by being invalided out.

But the front is not separate. It is inside Schwarzschild, and the symptoms I have been sending out, suppurative bullae and excoriated lesions, are not what is wrong with him at all. The lesions on his skins are only the barbed wire and shell holes and connecting trenches of a front that is somewhere farther in.

The doctor puts a new dressing of crepe paper on my hand. "I have tried to invalid Schwarzschild out," the doctor says, and Muller looks at him, astounded. "The supply lines are blocked with snow."

"Schwarzschild cannot be invalided out," I say. "The front is inside him."

The doctor puts the roll of crepe paper back in his kit and closes it. "When the roads open again, I will invalid you out for frostbite. And Muller too."

Muller is so surprised he blurts, "I do not have frostbite."

But the doctor is no longer listening. "You must both escape," he says—and I am not sure he is even listening to himself—"while you can."

"I have a theory about why you have not told me what is wrong with Schwarzschild," Muller says as soon as the doctor is gone.

"I am going for the mail."

"There will not be any mail," Muller shouts after me.

"The supply lines are blocked," but the mail is there, scattered among the motorcycle parts. There are only a few parts left. As soon as the roads are cleared, the recruit will be able to climb on the motorcycle and ride away.

I gather up the letters and take them over to the lantern to try to read them, but my eyes are so bad I cannot see anything but a red blur. "I am taking them back to the wireless hut," I say, and the recruit nods without looking up.

It is starting to snow. Muller meets me at the door, but I brush past him and turn the flame of the Primus stove up as high as it will go and hold the letters up behind it.

"I will read them for you," Muller says eagerly, looking through the envelopes I have discarded. "Look, here is a letter from your mother. Perhaps she has sent your gloves."

I squint at the letters one by one while he tears open my mother's letter to me. Even though I hold them so close to the flame that the paper scorches, I cannot make out the names.

" 'Dear son,' " Muller reads, " 'I have not heard from you in three months. Are you hurt? Are you ill? Do you need anything?' "

The last letter is from Professor Zuschauer in Jena. I can see his name quite clearly in the corner of the envelope, though mine is blurred beyond recognition. I tear it open. There is nothing written on the red paper.

I thrust it at Muller. "Read this," I say.

"I have not finished with your mother's letter yet," Muller says, but he takes the letter and reads: " 'Dear Herr Rottschieben, I received your letter yesterday. I could hardly decipher your writing. Do you not have decent pens at the front? The disease you describe is called Neumann's disease or pemphigus—' "

I snatch the letter out of Muller's hands and run out the door. "Let me come with you!" Muller shouts.

"You must stay and watch the wireless!" I say joyously, running along the communication trench. Schwarzschild does not have the front inside him. He has pemphigus, he has Neumann's disease, and now he can be invalided home to hospital.

I go down and think I have tripped over a discarded helmet or a tin of beef, but there is a crash, and dirt and revetting fall all around me. I hear the low buzz of a daisy cutter and flatten myself into the trench, but the buzz does not become a whine. It stops, and there is another crash and the trench caves in.

I scramble out of the trench before it can suffocate me and crawl along the edge toward Schwarzschild's dugout, but the trench has caved in all along its length, and when I crawl up and over the loose dirt, I lose it in the swirling snow.

I cannot tell which way the front lies, but I know it is very close. The sound comes at me from all directions, a deafening roar in which no individual sounds can be distinguished. The snow is so thick I cannot see the burst of flame from the muzzles as the guns fire, and no part of the horizon looks redder than any other. It is all red, even the snow.

I crawl in what I think is the direction of the trench, but as soon as I do, I am in barbed wire. I stop, breathing hard, my face and hands pressed into the snow. I have come the wrong way. I am at the front. I hear a sound out of the barrage of sound, the sound of tires on the snow, and I think it is a tank and cannot breathe at all. The sound comes closer, and in spite of myself I look up and it is the recruit who was at the quartermaster's.

He is a long way away, behind a coiled line of barbed wire, but I can see him quite clearly in spite of the snow. He has the motorcycle fixed, and as I watch, he flings his leg over it and presses his foot down. "Go!" I shout. "Get out!" The motorcycle jumps forward. "Go!"

The motorcycle comes toward me, picking up speed. It rears up, and I think it is going to jump the barbed wire, but it falls instead, the motorcycle first and then the recruit, spiraling slowly down into the iron spikes. The ground heaves, and I fall too.

I have fallen into Schwarzschild's dugout. Half of it has caved in, the timber balks sticking out at angles from the heap of dirt and snow, but the blanket is still over the door, and Schwarzschild is propped in a chair. The doctor is bending over him. Schwarzschild has his shirt off. His chest looks like Hans's did.

The front roars and more of the roof crumbles. "It's all right. It's a disease!" I shout over it. "I have brought you a letter to prove it," and hand him the letter which I have been clutching in my unfeeling hand.

The doctor grabs the letter from me. Snow whirls down through the ruined roof, but Schwarzschild does not put on his shirt. He watches uninterestedly as the doctor reads the letter.

" 'The symptoms you describe are almost certainly those of Neumann's disease, or pemphigus vulgaris. I have treated two patients with the disease, both Jews. It is a disease of the mucous membranes and is not contagious. Its cause is unknown. It always ends in death.' " Dr. Funkenheld crumples up the paper. "You came all this way in the middle of a bombardment to tell me there is no hope?" he shouts in a voice I do not even recognize, it is so unlike his steady doctor's voice. "You should have tried to get away. You should have—" and then he is gone under a crashing of dirt and splintered timbers.

I struggle toward Schwarzschild through the maelstrom of red dust and snow. "Put your shirt on!" I shout at him. "We must get out of here!" I crawl to the door to see if we can get out through the communication trench.

Muller bursts through the blanket. He is carrying, impossibly, the wireless. The headphones trail behind him in the snow. "I came to see what had happened to you. I thought you were dead. The communication trenches are shot to pieces."

It is as I had feared. His curiosity has got the best of him, and now he is trapped too, though he seems not to know it. He hoists the wireless onto the table without looking at it.

His eyes are on Schwarzschild, who leans against the remaining wall of the dugout, his shirt in his hands.

"Your shirt!" I shout and come around to help Schwarzschild put it on over the craters and shell holes of his blasted skin. The air screams and the mouth of the dugout blows in. I grab at Schwarzschild's arm, and the skin of it comes off in my hands. He falls against the table, and the wireless goes over. I can hear the splintering tinkle of the liquid barretter breaking, and then the whole dugout is caving in and we are under the table. I cannot see anything.

"Muller!" I shout. "Where are you?"

"I'm hit," he says.

I try to find him in the darkness, but I am crushed against Schwarzschild. I cannot move. "Where are you hit?"

"In the arm," he says, and I hear him try to move it. The movement dislodges more dirt, and it falls around us, shutting out all sound of the front. I can hear the creak of wood as the table legs give way.

"Schwarzschild?" I say. He doesn't answer, but I know he is not dead. His body is as hot as the Primus stove flame. My hand is underneath his body, and I try to shift it, but I cannot. The dirt falls like snow, piling up around us. The darkness is red for a while, and then I cannot see even that.

"I have a theory," Muller says in a voice so close and so devoid of curiosity it might be mine. "It is the end of the world."

"Was that when Schwarzschild was sent home on sick leave?" Travers said. "Or validated, or whatever you Germans call it? Well, yeah, it had to be, because he died in March. What happened to Muller?"

I had hoped he would go away as soon as I had told him what had happened to Schwarzschild, but he made no move to get up. "Muller was invalided out with a broken arm. He became a scientist."

"The way you did." He opened his notebook again. "Did you see Schwarzschild after that?"

The question makes no sense.

"After you got out? Before he died?"

It seems to take a long time for his words to get to me. The message bends and curves, shifting into the red, and I can hardly make it out. "No," I say, though that is a lie.

Travers scribbles. "I really do appreciate this, Dr. Rottschieben. I've always been curious about Schwarzschild, and now that you've told me all this stuff I'm even more interested," Travers says, or seems to say. Messages coming in are warped by the gravitational blizzard into something that no longer resembles speech. "If you'd be willing to help me, I'd like to write my thesis on him."

Go. Get out. "It was a lie," I say. "I never knew Schwarzschild. I saw him once, from a distance—your fixed observer."

Travers looks up expectantly from his notes as if he is still waiting for me to answer him.

"Schwarzschild was never even in Russia," I lie. "He spent the whole winter in hospital in Göttingen. I lied to you. It was nothing but a thought problem."

He waits, pencil ready.

"You can't stay here!" I shout. "You have to get away. There is no safe distance from which a fixed observer can watch without being drawn in, and once you are inside the Schwarzschild radius you can't get out. Don't you understand? We are still there!"

We are still there, trapped in the trenches of the Russian front, while the dying star burns itself out, spiraling down into that center where time ceases to exist, where everything ceases to exist except the naked singularity that is somehow Schwarzschild.

Muller tries to dig the wireless out with his crushed arm so he can send a message that nobody can hear—"Help us! Help us!"—and I struggle to free the hands that in spite of

Schwarzschild's warmth are now so cold I cannot feel them, and in the very center Schwarzschild burns himself out, the black hole at his center imploding him cell by cell, carrying him down into darkness, and us with him.

"It is a trap!" I shout at Travers from the center, and the message struggles to escape and then falls back.

"I wonder how he figured it out?" Travers says, and now I can hear him clearly. "I mean, can you imagine trying to figure out something like the theory of black holes in the middle of a war and while you are suffering from a fatal disease? And just think, when he came up with the theory, he didn't have any idea that black holes even existed."

Witness

Walter Jon Williams

Born in Minnesota in 1953, Walter Jon Williams has already done a great deal to distinguish himself from a somewhat older science-fiction writer, William Jon Watkins, with whom a few aficionados have occasionally worrisomely confused him.

His first novel, *Knight Moves*, was a finalist for the Philip K. Dick Award for best paperback original; his second book, *Hardwired*, identified him for many as another vigorous proponent of cyberpunk (see Ian Watson's "The World Renews Itself"); and his third, *Voice of the Whirlwind*— along with stories like "Dinosaurs" and "Witness"—proved that he has the talent to transcend superficially accurate categorizations. Meanwhile, his most recent novel, *Angel Station*, focuses tellingly on "the interaction between inhuman aliens and posthuman exiles."

The novella "Witness" appeared in 1987 in the first volume of the *Wild Cards* original paperback anthology series edited by George R. R. Martin. To appreciate "Witness," all one must know about the series is (1) that it raises a comic-book premise to the level of serious extrapolation and (2) that it is set in an alternative time-line in which an alien called Dr. Tachyon has created a gene-warping virus that causes in its victims either death, disease, disfigurement, or, in a few entirely random cases, superhuman powers. Terrorists unload this virus over Manhattan in 1946, and Jetboy, a famous American World War II ace, dies in his valiant, last-ditch attempt to stymie them. "Witness" begins only moments after Jetboy's death, as these unpredictable viral spores drift down into the city.

Says Williams, now a resident of Albuquerque, New Mexico, about this fast-paced but thought-provoking novella:

"The writing of 'Witness' led me into considerable research on one of the most depressing periods in American history. Even more depressing was hearing from young readers who thought I'd invented the McCarthy period for this alternative-worlds novella, that the whole thing never really could have happened. It *did* happen, of course, and in the story I was careful to have members of the House Un-American Activities Committee, popularly known as HUAC, speak in their own voices—I paraphrased only lightly, and sometimes not at all.

"I can only hope that the disbelief on the part of these young readers is a measure of how far we have come since the days of HUAC, that it really can't happen again, rather than an indication of the type of political naiveté that allowed it all to occur in the first place."

When Jetboy died I was watching a matinee of *The Jolson Story*. I wanted to see Larry Parks's performance, which everyone said was so remarkable. I studied it carefully and made mental notes.

Young actors do things like that.

The picture ended, but I was feeling comfortable and had no plans for the next few hours, and I wanted to see Larry Parks again. I watched the movie a second time. Halfway through, I fell asleep, and when I woke the titles were scrolling up. I was alone in the theater.

When I stepped into the lobby the usherettes were gone and the doors were locked. They'd run for it and forgotten to tell the projectionist. I let myself out into a bright, pleasant autumn afternoon and saw that Second Avenue was empty.

Second Avenue is never empty.

The newsstands were closed. The few cars I could see were parked. The theater marquee had been turned off. I could hear angry auto horns some distance off, and over it the rumble of high-powered airplane engines. There was a bad smell from somewhere.

New York had the eerie feeling that towns sometimes got during an air raid, deserted and waiting and nervous. I'd been in air raids during the war, usually on the receiving end, and I didn't like the feeling at all. I began walking for my apartment, just a block and a half away.

In the first hundred feet I saw what had been making the bad smell. It came from a reddish-pink puddle that looked like several gallons of oddly colored ice cream melting on the sidewalk and oozing down the gutter.

I looked closer. There were a few bones inside the puddle. A human jawbone, part of a tibia, an eye socket. They were dissolving into a light pink froth.

There were clothes beneath the puddle. An usherette's uniform. Her flashlight had rolled into the gutter and the metal parts of it were dissolving along with her bones.

My stomach turned over as adrenaline slammed into my system. I started to run.

By the time I got to my apartment I figured there had to be some kind of emergency going on, and I turned on the radio to get information. While I was waiting for the Philco to warm up I went to check the canned food in the cupboard— a couple cans of Campbell's was all I could find. My hands were shaking so much I knocked one of the cans out of the cupboard, and it rolled off the sideboard behind the icebox. I pushed against the side of the icebox to get at the can, and suddenly it seemed like there was a shift in the light and the icebox flew halfway across the room and damn near went through the wall. The pan I had underneath to catch the ice-melt slopped over onto the floor.

I got the can of soup. My hands were still trembling. I moved the icebox back, and it was light as a feather. The light kept doing weird shifts. I could pick up the box with one hand.

The radio warmed finally and I learned about the virus.

People who felt sick were to report to emergency tent hospitals set up by the National Guard all over the city. There was one in Washington Square Park, near where I was living.

I didn't feel sick, but on the other hand I could juggle the icebox, which was not exactly normal behavior. I walked to Washington Square Park. There were casualties everywhere —some were just lying in the street. I couldn't look at a lot of it. It was worse than anything I'd seen in the war. I knew that as long as I was healthy and mobile the doctors would put me low on the list for treatment, and it would be days before I'd get any help, so I walked up to someone in charge, told him I used to be in the army, and asked what I could do to help. I figured if I started to die I'd at least be near the hospital.

The doctors asked me to help set up a kitchen. People were screaming and dying and changing before the doctors' eyes, and the medics couldn't do anything about it. Feeding the casualties was all they could think to do.

I went to a National Guard deuce-and-a-half and started picking up crates of food. Each weighed about fifty pounds, and I stacked six of them on top of each other and carried them off the truck in one arm. My perception of the light kept changing in odd ways. I emptied the truck in about two minutes. Another truck had gotten bogged down in the mud when it tried to cross the park, so I picked up the whole truck and carried it to where it was supposed to be, and then I unloaded it and asked the doctors if they needed me for anything else.

I had this strange glow around me. People told me that when I did one of my stunts I glowed, that a bright golden aura surrounded my body. My looking at the world through my own radiance made the light appear to change.

I didn't think much about it. The scene around me was overwhelming, and it went on for days. People were drawing the black queen or the joker, turning into monsters, dying, transforming. Martial law had slammed down on the city—

it was just like wartime. After the first riots on the bridges there were no disturbances. The city had lived with blackouts and curfews and patrols for four years, and the people just slipped back into wartime patterns. The rumors were insane—a Martian attack, accidental release of poison gas, bacteria released by Nazis or by Stalin. To top it all off, several thousand people swore they saw Jetboy's ghost flying, without his plane, over the streets of Manhattan. I went on working at the hospital, moving heavy loads. That's where I met Tachyon.

He came by to deliver some experimental serum he was hoping might be able to relieve some symptoms, and at first I thought, Oh, Christ, here's some fruitbar got past the guards with a potion his Aunt Nelly gave him. He was a weedy guy with long metallic red hair past his shoulders, and I knew it couldn't be a natural color. He dressed as if he got his clothes from a Salvation Army in the theater district, wearing a bright-orange jacket like a bandleader might wear, a red Harvard sweater, a Robin Hood hat with a feather, plus-fours with argyle socks, and two-tone shoes that would have looked out of place on a pimp. He was moving from bed to bed with a tray full of hypos, observing each patient and sticking thc needles in people's arms. I put down the X-ray machine I was carrying and ran to stop him before he could do any harm.

And then I noticed that the people following him included a three-star general, the National Guard bird colonel who ran the hospital, and Mr. Archibald Holmes, who was one of FDR's old crowd at Agriculture, and whom I recognized right away. He'd been in charge of a big relief agency in Europe following the war, but Truman had sent him to New York as soon as the plague hit. I sidled up behind one the nurses and asked her what was going on.

"That's a new kind of treatment," she said. "That Dr. Tack-something brought it."

"It's *his* treatment?" I askcd.

"Yeah." She looked at him with a frown. "He's from another planet."

I looked at the plus-fours and Robin Hood hat. "No kidding," I said.

"No. Really. He is."

Closer up, you could see the dark circles under his weird purple eyes, the strain that showed on his face. He'd been pushing himself hard since the catastrophe, like all the doctors here—like everyone except me. I felt full of energy in spite of only getting a few hours' sleep each night.

The bird colonel from the National Guard looked at me. "Here's another case," he said. "This is Jack Braun."

Tachyon looked up at me. "Your symptoms?" he asked. He had a deep voice, a vaguely mid-European accent.

"I'm strong. I can pick up trucks. I glow gold when I do it."

He seemed excited. "A biological force field. Interesting. I'd like to examine you later. After the"—an expression of distaste crossed his face—"present crisis is over."

"Sure, Doc. Whatever you like."

He moved on to the next bed. Mr. Holmes, the relief man, didn't follow. He just stayed and watched me, fiddling with his cigarette holder.

I stuck my thumbs in my belt and tried to look useful. "Can I help you with something, Mr. Holmes?" I asked.

He seemed mildly surprised. "You know my name?" he said.

"I remember you coming to Fayette, North Dakota, back in '33," I said. "Just after the New Deal came in. You were at Agriculture then."

A long time ago. What are you doing in New York, Mr. Braun?"

"I was an actor till the theaters shut down."

"Ah." He nodded. "We'll have the theaters running again soon. Dr. Tachyon tells us the virus isn't contagious."

"That'll ease some minds."

He glanced at the entrance to the tent. "Let's go outside and have a smoke."

"Suits me." After I followed him out I dusted off my hands and accepted a custom-blended cigarette from his silver case. He lit our cigarettes and looked at me over the match.

"After the emergency's over, I'd like to run some more tests with you," he said. "Just see what it is that you can do."

I shrugged. "Sure, Mr. Holmes," I said. "Any particular reason?"

"Maybe I can give you a job," he said. "On the world stage."

Something passed between me and the sun. I looked up, and a cold finger touched my neck.

The ghost of Jetboy was flying black against the sky, his white pilot's scarf fluttering in the wind.

I'd grown up in North Dakota. I was born in 1924, into hard times. There was trouble with the banks, trouble with the farm surpluses that were keeping prices down. When the Depression hit, things went from bad to worse. Grain prices were so low that some farmers literally had to pay people to haul the stuff away. Farm auctions were held almost every week at the courthouse—farms worth fifty thousand dollars were selling for a few hundred. Half Main Street was boarded up.

Those were the days of the Farm Holidays, the farmers withholding grain to make the prices rise. I'd get up in the middle of the night to bring coffee and food to my father and cousins, who were patrolling the roads to make sure nobody sold grain behind their backs. If someone came by with grain, they'd seize the truck and dump it; if a cattle truck came by, they'd shoot the cattle and toss them on the roadside to rot. Some of the local bigwigs who were making a fortune buying underpriced wheat sent the American Legion to break the farm strike, carrying axe handles and wearing their little hats—and the whole district rose, gave the legionnaires the beating of their lives, and sent them scampering back to the city.

Suddenly a bunch of conservative German farmers were talking and acting like radicals. FDR was the first Democrat my family ever voted for.

I was eleven years old when I first saw Archibald Holmes. He was working as a troubleshooter for Mr. Henry Wallace in the Department of Agriculture, and he came to Fayette to consult with the farmers about something or other—price control or production control, probably, or conservation, the New Deal agenda that kept our farm off the auction block. He gave a little speech on the courthouse steps on his arrival, and for some reason I didn't forget it.

He was an impressive man even then. Well dressed, gray haired even though he wasn't yet forty, smoked a cigarette in a holder like FDR. He had a Tidewater way of talking, which sounded strange to my ear, as if there was something slightly vulgar about pronouncing one's R's. Soon after his visit, things started getting better.

Years later, after I got to know him well, he was always Mr. Holmes. I never could see myself calling him by his first name.

Maybe I can trace my wanderlust to Mr. Holmes's visit. I felt there had to be something outside Fayette, something outside the North Dakota way of looking at things. The way my family saw it, I was going to get my own farm, marry a local girl, produce lots of kids, and spend my Sundays listening to the parson talk about hell and my weekdays working in the fields for the benefit of the bank.

I resented the notion that this was all there was. I knew, perhaps only by instinct, that there was another kind of existence out there, and I wanted to get my share of it.

I grew up tall and broad shouldered and blond, with big hands that were comfortable around a football and what my publicity agent later called "rugged good looks." I played football and played it well, dozed through school, and during the long, dark winters I played in community theater and pageants. There was quite a circuit for amateur theater in both English and German, and I did both. I played mainly Victorian melodramas and historical spectaculars, and I got good notices, too.

Girls liked me. I was good-looking and a regular guy and they all thought I'd be just the farmer for them. I was careful never to have anyone special. I carried rubbers in my watch pocket and tried to keep at least three or four girls in the air at once. I wasn't falling into the trap that all my elders seemed to have planned for me.

We all grew up patriotic. It was a natural thing in that part of the world: There is a strong love of country that comes with punishing climates. It wasn't anything to make a fuss over; patriotism was just there, part of everything else.

The local football team did well, and I began to see a way out of North Dakota. At the end of my senior season, I was offered a scholarship to the University of Minnesota.

I never made it. Instead, the day after graduation in May of 1942, I marched to the recruiter and volunteered for the infantry.

No big deal. Every boy in my class marched with me.

I ended up with the Fifth Division in Italy and had an awful infantryman's war. It rained all the time, there was never proper shelter, every move we made was in full view of invisible Germans sitting on the next hill with Zeiss binoculars glued to their eyes, to be followed inevitably by that horrific zooming sound of an 88 coming down. . . . I was scared all the time, and I was a hero some of the time, but most of the time I was hiding with my mouth in the dirt while the shells came whizzing down, and after a few months of it I knew I wasn't coming back in one piece, and chances were I wasn't coming back at all. There were no tours, like there would be in Vietnam; a rifleman just stayed on the line until the war was over, or until he died, or until he was so shot up he couldn't go back. I accepted these facts and went on with what I had to do. I got promoted to master sergeant and eventually got a Bronze Star and three Purple Hearts, but the medals and promotions never meant as much to me as where the next pair of dry socks was coming from.

One of my buddies was a man named Martin Kozokowski, whose father was a minor theatrical producer in New York. One evening we were sharing a bottle of awful red wine and a cigarette—smoking was something else the army taught me—and I mentioned my acting career back in North Dakota, and in a gush of inebriated goodwill he said, "Hell, come to New York after the war, and me and my dad will put you on the stage." It was a pointless fantasy, since at that point none of us really thought we were coming back, but it stuck, and we talked about it afterward, and by and by, as some dreams have a way of doing, it came true.

After V-E Day I went to New York and Kozokowski the elder got me a few parts while I worked an assortment of part-time jobs, all of which were easy compared with farming and the war. Theater circles were full of intense, intellectual girls who didn't wear lipstick—not wearing lipstick was supposed to be sort of daring—and who would take you home with them if you listened to them talk about Anouilh or Pirandello or their psychoanalysis, and the best thing about them was they didn't want to get married and make little farmers. Peacetime reflexes began to come back. North Dakota started to fade away, and after a while I began to wonder if maybe the war didn't have its consolations after all.

An illusion, of course. Because some nights I'd still wake up with the 88s whistling in my ears, terror squirming in my guts, the old wound in my calf throbbing, and I'd remember lying on my back in a shell hole with mud creeping down my neck, waiting for the morphine to hit while I looked up into the sky to see a flight of silver Thunderbolts with the sun gleaming off their stubby wings, the planes hopping the mountains with more ease than I could hop out of a jeep.

And I'd remember what it was like to lie there furious with jealousy that the fighter jocks were in their untroubled sky while I bled into my field dressing and waited for morphine and plasma, and I'd think, If I ever catch one of those bastards on the ground, I'm going to make him pay for this. . . .

When Mr. Holmes started his tests he proved exactly how strong I was, which was stronger than anyone had ever seen, or even imagined. Provided I was braced well enough, I could lift up to forty tons. Machine-gun slugs would flatten themselves on my chest. Armor-piercing 20-mm cannon shells would knock me down with their transferred energy, but I'd jump back up undamaged.

They were scared to try anything bigger than a 20-mm on their tests. So was I. If I were hit with a *real* cannon, instead of just a big machine gun, I'd probably be oatmeal.

I had my limits. After a few hours of it I'd begin to get tired. I would weaken. Bullets began to hurt. I'd have to go off and rest.

Tachyon had guessed right when he talked about a biological force field. When I was in action it surrounded me like a golden halo. I didn't exactly control it—if someone shot a bullet into my back by surprise, the force field would turn on all by itself. When I started to get tired the glow would begin to fade.

I never got tired enough for it to fade entirely, not when I wanted it on. I was scared of what would happen then, and I always took care to make sure I got my rest when I needed it.

When the test results came in, Mr. Holmes called me to his apartment on Park Avenue South. It was a big place, the entire fifth floor, but a lot of the rooms had that unused smell to them. His wife had died of pancreatic cancer back in '40, and since then he'd given up most of his social life. His daughter was off at school.

Mr. Holmes gave me a drink and a cigarette and asked

me what I thought about fascism, and what I thought I could do about it. I remembered all those stiff-necked SS officers and Luftwaffe paratroops and considered what I could do about them now that I was the strongest thing on the planet.

"I imagine that now I'd make a pretty good soldier," I said.

He gave me a thin smile. "Would you *like* to be a soldier again, Mr. Braun?"

I saw right away what he was driving at. There was an emergency going on. Evil lived in the world. It was possible I could do something about it. And here was a man who had sat at the right hand of Franklin Delano Roosevelt, who in turn sat at the right hand of God, as far as I was concerned, and he was *asking* me to do something about it.

Of *course* I volunteered. It probably took me all of three seconds.

Mr. Holmes shook my hand. Then he asked me another question. "How do you feel about working with a colored man?"

I shrugged.

He smiled. "Good," he said. "In that case, I'll have to introduce you to Jetboy's ghost."

I must have stared. His smile broadened. "Actually, his name is Earl Sanderson. He's quite a fellow."

Oddly enough, I knew the name. "The Sanderson who used to play ball for Rutgers? Hell of an athlete."

Mr. Holmes seemed startled. Maybe he didn't follow sports. "Oh," he said. "I think you'll find he's a little more than that."

Earl Sanderson, Jr., was born into a life far different from mine, in Harlem, New York City. He was eleven years older than I, and maybe I never caught up to him.

Earl, Sr., was a railway car porter, a smart man, self-educated, an admirer of Fredrick Douglas and Du Bois. He was a charter member of the Niagara Movement—which became the NAACP—and later of the Brotherhood of Sleeping Car Porters. A tough, smart man, thoroughly at home in the combustive Harlem of the time.

Earl, Jr., was a brilliant youth, and his father urged him not to waste it. In high school he was outstanding as a scholar and athlete, and when he followed Paul Robeson's footsteps to Rutgers in 1930 he had his choice of scholarships.

Two years into college, he joined the Communist party. When I knew him later, he made it sound like the only reasonable choice.

"The Depression was only getting worse," he told me. "The cops were shooting union organizers all over the country, and white people were finding out what it was like to be as poor as the colored. All we got out of Russia at the time were pictures of factories working at full capacity, and here in the States the factories were closed and the workers were starving. I thought it was only a matter of time before the revolution. The CP were the only people working for the unions who were also working for equality. They had a slogan, 'Black and white, unite and fight,' and that sounded right to me. They didn't give a damn about the color bar—they'd look you in the eye and call you comrade. Which was more than I ever got from anyone else."

He had all the good reasons in the world for joining the CP in 1931. Later all those good reasons would rise up and wreck us all.

I'm not sure why Earl Sanderson married Lillian, but I understand well enough why Lillian chased Earl for all those years. "Jack," she told me, "he just *glowed*."

Lillian Abbott met Earl when he was a junior in high school. After that first meeting, she spent every spare minute with him. Bought his newspapers, paid his way into the theaters with her pocket change, attended radical meetings. Cheered him at sporting events. She joined the CP a month after he did. And a few weeks after he left Rutgers, summa cum laude, she married him.

"I didn't give Earl any choice," she said. "The only way he'd ever get me to be quiet about it was to marry me."

Neither of them knew what they were getting into, of course. Earl was wrapped up in issues that were larger than himself, in the revolution he thought was coming, and maybe he thought Lillian deserved a little happiness in this time of bitterness. It didn't cost him anything to say yes.

It cost Lillian just about everything.

Two months after his marriage Earl was on a boat to the Soviet Union, to study at Lenin University for a year, learning to be a proper agent of the Comintern. Lillian stayed at home, working in her mother's shop, attending party meetings that seemed a little lackluster without Earl. Learning, without any great enthusiasm for the task, how to be a revolutionary's wife.

After a year in Russia, Earl went to Columbia for his law degree. Lillian supported him until he graduated and went to work as counsel for A. Philip Randolph and the Brotherhood of Sleeping Car Porters, one of the most radical unions in America. Earl, Sr., must have been proud.

As the Depression eased, Earl's commitment to the CP waned—maybe the revolution wasn't coming, after all. The GM strike had been solved in favor of the CIO when Earl was learning to be a revolutionary in Russia. The Brotherhood won its recognition from the Pullman Company in 1938, and Randolph finally started drawing a salary—he'd worked all those years for free. The union and Randolph were taking up a lot of Earl's time, and his attendance at party meetings began to slide.

When the Nazi-Soviet pact was signed, Earl resigned from the CP in anger. Accommodation with the fascists was not his style.

Earl told me that after Pearl Harbor, the Depression ended for white people when the hiring at defense plants started, but few blacks were given jobs. Randolph and his people finally had enough. Randolph threatened a railway strike—

right in the middle of wartime—that was to be combined with a march on Washington. FDR sent his troubleshooter, Archibald Holmes, to work out a settlement. It resulted in Executive Order 8802, in which government contractors were forbidden to discriminate on account of race. It was one of the landmark pieces of legislation in the history of civil rights, and one of the greatest successes in Earl's career. Earl always spoke of it as one of his proudest accomplishments.

The week after Order 8802, Earl's draft classification was changed to 1-A. His work with the rail union wasn't going to protect him. The government was taking its revenge.

Earl decided to volunteer for the air corps. He'd always wanted to fly.

Earl was old for a pilot, but he was still an athlete and his conditioning got him past the physical. His record was labeled PAF, meaning Premature Anti-Fascist, which was the official designation for anyone who was unreliable enough not to like Hitler prior to 1941.

He was assigned to the 332nd Fighter Group, an all-black unit. The screening process for the black fliers was so severe that the unit ended up full of professors, ministers, doctors, lawyers—and all these bright people demonstrated first-rate pilot's reflexes as well. Because none of the air groups overseas wanted black pilots, the group remained at Tuskegee for months and months of training. Eventually they received three times as much training as the average group, and when they were finally moved, to bases in Italy, the group known as the Lonely Eagles exploded over the European theater.

They flew their Thunderbolts over Germany and the Balkan countries, including the toughest targets. They flew over fifteen thousand sorties, and during that time *not a single escorted bomber* was lost to the Luftwaffe. After word got out, bomber groups began asking specifically for the 332nd to escort their planes.

One of their top fliers was Earl Sanderson, who ended the war with fifty-three "unconfirmed" kills. The kills were unconfirmed because records were not kept for the black squadrons—the military was afraid the black pilots might get larger totals than the whites. Their fear was justified: That number put Earl above every American pilot but Jetboy, who was another powerful exception to a lot of rules.

On the day Jetboy died, Earl had come home from work with what he thought was a bad case of flu, and the next day he woke up a black ace.

He could fly, apparently by an act of will, up to five hundred miles per hour. Tachyon called it "projection telekinesis."

Earl was pretty tough, too, though not as tough as I was —like me, bullets bounced off him. But cannon rounds could hurt him, and I know he dreaded the possibility of midair collision with a plane.

And he could project a wall of force in front of him, a kind of traveling shock wave that could sweep anything out of his path. Men, vehicles, walls. A sound like a clap of thunder and they'd be thrown a hundred feet.

Earl spent a couple weeks testing his talents before letting the world know about them, flying over the city in his pilot's helmet, black leather flying jacket, and boots. When he finally let people know, Mr. Holmes was one of the first to call.

I met Earl the day after I'd signed on with Mr. Holmes. By then I'd moved into one of Mr. Holmes's spare rooms and had been given a key to the apartment. I was moving up in the world.

I recognized him right away. "Earl Sanderson," I said, before Mr. Holmes could introduce us. I shook his hand. "I remember reading about you when you played for Rutgers."

Earl took that in stride. "You have a good memory," he said.

We sat down, and Mr. Holmes explained formally what he wanted with us, and with others he hoped to recruit later. Earl felt strongly about the term *ace*, meaning someone with useful abilities, as opposed to *joker*, meaning someone who was badly disfigured by the virus—Earl felt the terms imposed a class system on those who got the wild card, and he didn't want to set us at the top of some kind of social pyramid. Mr. Holmes officially named our team the Exotics for Democracy. We were to become visible symbols of American postwar ideals, to lend credit to the American attempt to rebuild Europe and Asia, to continue the fight against fascism and intolerance.

The U.S. was going to create a postwar Golden Age, and was going to share it with the rest of the world. We were going to be its symbol.

It sounded great. I wanted in.

With Earl the decision came a little harder. Holmes had talked to him before and had asked him to make the same kind of deal that Branch Rickey later asked of Jackie Robinson: Earl had to stay out of domestic politics. He had to announce that he'd broken with Stalin and Marxism, that he was committed to peaceful change. He was asked to keep his temper under control, to absorb the inevitable anger, racism, and condescension, and to do it without retaliation.

Earl told me later how he struggled with himself. He knew his powers by then, and he knew he could change things simply by being present where important things were going on. Southern cops wouldn't be able to smash up integration meetings if someone present could flatten whole companies of state troopers. Strike breakers would go flying before his wave of force. If he decided to integrate somebody's restaurant, the entire Marine Corps couldn't throw him out—not without destroying the building, anyway.

But Mr. Holmes had pointed out that if he used his powers in that way, it wouldn't be Earl Sanderson who would pay the penalty. If Earl Sanderson were seen reacting violently to provocation, innocent blacks would be strung from oak limbs throughout the country.

Earl gave Mr. Holmes the assurance he wanted. Starting

the very next day, the two of us went on to make a lot of history.

The EFD was never a part of the U.S. government. Mr. Holmes consulted with the State Department, but he paid Earl and me out of his own pocket and I lived in his apartment.

The first thing was to deal with Perón. He'd gotten himself elected president of Argentina in a rigged election and was in the process of turning himself into a South American version of Mussolini and Argentina into a refuge for fascists and war criminals. The Exotics for Democracy flew south to see what we could do about it.

Looking back on things, I'm amazed at our assumptions. We were bent on overthrowing the constitutional government of a large foreign nation, and we didn't think anything about it. . . . Even Earl went along without a second thought. We'd just spent years fighting fascists in Europe, and we didn't see anything remarkably different in moving south and smashing them up there.

When we left, we had another man with us. David Harstein just seemed to talk himself aboard the plane. Here he was, a Jewish chess hustler from Brooklyn, one of those fast-talking curly-haired young guys that you saw all over New York selling flood insurance or used auto tires or custom suits made of some new miracle fiber that was just as good as cashmere, and suddenly he was a member of EFD and calling a lot of the shots. You couldn't help but like him. You couldn't help but agree with him.

He was an exotic, all right. He exuded pheromones that made you feel friendly with him and with the world, that created an atmosphere of bonhomie and suggestibility. He could talk an Albanian Stalinist into standing on his head and singing "The Star-Spangled Banner"—at least, as long as he and his pheromones were in the room. Afterward, when our Albanian Stalinist returned to his senses, he'd promptly denounce himself and have himself shot.

We decided to keep David's powers a secret. We spread a story that he was some kind of sneaky superman, like The Shadow on radio, and that he was our scout. Actually, he'd just get into conferences with people and make them agree with us. It worked pretty well.

Perón hadn't consolidated his power yet, having only been in office four months. It took us two weeks to organize the coup that got rid of him. Harstein and Mr. Holmes would go into meetings with army officers, and before they were done the colonels would be swearing to have Perón's head on a plate, and even after they began to think better of things, their sense of honor wouldn't let them back down on their promises.

On the morning before the coup, I found out some of my limitations. I'd read the comics when I was in the army, and I'd seen how, when the bad guys were trying to speed away in their cars, Superman would jump in front of the car, and the car would bounce off him.

I tried that in Argentina. There was a Perónist major who had to be kept from getting to his command post, and I jumped in front of his Mercedes and got knocked two hundred feet into a statue of Juan P. himself.

The problem was, I wasn't heavier than the car. When things collide, it's the object with the least momentum that gives way, and weight is a component of momentum. It doesn't matter how *strong* the lighter object is.

I got smarter after that. I knocked the statue of Perón off its perch and threw it at the car. That took care of things.

There are a few other things about the ace business that you can't learn from reading comic books. I remember comic aces grabbing the barrels of tank guns and turning them into pretzels.

It is in fact possible to do that, but you have to have the leverage to do it. You've got to plant your feet on something solid in order to have something to push against. It was far easier for me to dive under the tank and knock it off its treads.

Then I'd run around to the other side and put my arms around the gun barrel, with my shoulder under the barrel, and then yank down. I'd use my shoulder as the fulcrum of a lever and bend the barrel around myself.

That's what I'd do if I was in a hurry. If I had time, I'd punch my way through the bottom of the tank and rip it apart from the inside.

But I digress. Back to Perón.

There were a couple of critical things that had to be done. Some loyal Perónists couldn't be gotten to, and one of them was the head of an armored battalion quartered in a walled compound on the outskirts of Buenos Aires. On the night of the coup, I picked up one of the tanks and dropped it on its side in front of the gate, and then I just braced my shoulder against it and held it in place while the other tanks battered themselves into junk trying to move it.

Earl immobilized Perón's air force. He just flew behind the planes on the runway and tore off the stabilizers.

Democracy was victorious. Perón and his blond hooker took off for Portugal.

I gave myself a few hours off. While triumphant middle-class mobs poured into the street to celebrate, I was in a hotel room with the daughter of the French ambassador. Listening to the chanting mob through the window, the taste of champagne and Nicolette on my tongue, I concluded this was better than flying.

Our image got fashioned in that campaign. I was wearing old army fatigues most of the time, and that's the view of me most people remember. Earl was wearing tan Air Force officer's fatigues with the insignia taken off, boots, helmet, goggles, scarf, and his old leather flying jacket with the 332nd patch on the shoulder. When he wasn't flying he'd take the helmet off and put on an old black beret he kept in his hip pocket. Often, when we were asked to make personal appearances, Earl and I were asked to dress in our fatigues so everyone would know us. The public never seemed to realize that most of the time we wore suits and ties, just like everyone else.

When Earl and I were together, it was often in a combat situation, and for that reason we became best friends . . . people in combat become close very quickly. I talked about my life, my war, about women. He was a little more guarded—maybe he wasn't sure how I'd take hearing his exploits with white girls—but eventually, one night when we were in northern Italy looking for Bormann, I heard all about Orlena Goldoni.

"I used to have to paint her stockings on in the morning," Earl said. "I'd have to make up her legs so it would look like she had silk stockings. And I'd have to paint the seam down the back in eyeliner." He smiled. "That was a paint job I always enjoyed doing."

"Why didn't you just give her some stockings?" I asked. They were easy enough to come by. GIs wrote to their friends and relatives in the States to send them.

"I gave her lots of pairs," Earl shrugged, "but Lena'd give 'em away to the comrades."

Earl hadn't kept a picture of Lena, not where Lillian could find it, but I saw her in the pictures later, when she was billed as Europe's answer to Veronica Lake. Tousled blond hair, broad shoulders, a husky voice. Lake's screen persona was cool, but Goldoni's was hot. The silk stockings were real in the pictures, but so were the legs under them, and the picture celebrated Lena's legs as often as the director thought he could get away with it. I remember thinking how much fun Earl must have had painting her.

She was a cabaret singer in Naples when they met, in one of the few clubs where black soldiers were allowed. She was eighteen and a black-marketeer and a former courier for the Italian Communists. Earl took one look at her and threw caution to the winds. It was maybe the one time in his entire life that he indulged himself. He started taking chances. Slipping off the field at night, dodging MP patrols to be with her, sneaking back early in the morning and being on the flight line ready to take off for Bucharest or Ploeşti . . .

"We knew it wasn't forever," Earl said. "We knew the war would end sooner or later." There was a kind of distance in his eyes, the memory of a hurt, and I could see how much leaving Lena had cost him. "We were grownups about it." A long sigh. "So we said good-bye. I got discharged and went back to work for the union. And we haven't seen each other since." He shook his head. "Now she's in the pictures. I haven't seen any of them."

The next day, we got Bormann. I held him by his monk's cowl and shook him till his teeth rattled. We turned him over to the representative of the Allied War Crimes Tribunal and gave ourselves a few days' leave.

Earl seemed more nervous than I'd ever seen him. He kept disappearing to make phone calls. The press always followed us around, and Earl jumped every time a camera bulb went off. The first night, he disappeared from our hotel room, and I didn't see him for three days.

Usually I was the one exhibiting this kind of behavior, always sneaking off to spend some time with a woman. Earl's doing it caught me by surprise.

He'd spent the weekend with Lena, in a little hotel north of Rome. I saw their pictures together in the Italian papers on Monday morning—somehow the press found out about it. I wondered whether Lillian had heard, what she was thinking. Earl showed up, scowling, around noon on Monday, just in time for his flight to India: He was going to Calcutta to see Gandhi. Earl wound up stepping between the Mahatma and the bullets that some fanatic fired at him on the steps of the temple—and all of a sudden the papers were full of India, with what had just happened in Italy forgotten. I don't know how Earl explained it to Lillian.

Whatever it was he said, I suppose Lillian believed him. She always did.

Glory years, these. With the fascist escape route to South America cut, the Nazis were forced to stay in Europe, where it was easier to find them. After Earl and I dug Bormann out of his monastery, we plucked Mengele from a farm attic in Bavaria, and we got so close to Eichmann in Austria that he panicked and ran out into the arms of a Soviet patrol, and the Russians shot him out of hand. David Harstein walked into the Escorial on a diplomatic passport and talked Franco into making a live radio address in which he resigned and called for elections, and then David stayed with him on the plane all the way to Switzerland. Portugal called for elections right afterward, and Perón had to find a new home in Nanking, where he became a military adviser to the generalissimo. Nazis were bailing out of Iberia by the dozen, and the Nazi hunters caught a lot of them.

I was making a lot of money. Mr. Holmes wasn't paying me much in the way of wages, but I got a lot for making the Chesterfield endorsement and for selling my story to *Life*, and I had a lot of paid speaking engagements—Mr. Holmes hired me a speechwriter. My half of the Park Avenue apartment was free, and I never had to pay for a meal if I didn't want to. I got large sums for articles that were written over my name, things like "Why I Believe in Tolerance" and "What America Means to Me," and "Why We Need the U.N." Hollywood scouts were making incredible offers for long-term contracts, but I wasn't interested just yet. I was seeing the world.

So many girls were visiting me in my room that the tenants' association talked about installing a revolving door.

The papers started calling Earl "the Black Eagle," from the 332nd's nickname, "the Lonely Eagles." He didn't like the name much. David Harstein, by those few who knew of his talent, was "the Envoy." I was "Golden Boy," of course. I didn't mind.

EFD got another member in Blythe Stanhope van Renssaeler, whom the papers started calling "Brain Trust." She was a petite, proper upper-crust Boston lady, high-strung as a Thoroughbred, married to a scumbag New York congressman by whom she'd had three kids. She had the kind of beauty that took a while for you to notice, and then you wondered why you hadn't seen it before. I don't think she ever knew how lovely she really was.

She could absorb minds. Memories, abilities, everything.

Blythe was older than me by about ten years, but that didn't bother me, and before long I started flirting with her. I had plenty of other female companionship, and everyone knew that, so if she knew anything about me at all—and maybe she didn't, because my mind wasn't important enough to absorb—she didn't take me seriously.

Eventually her awful husband, Henry, threw her out, and she came by our apartment to look for a place to stay. Mr. Holmes was gone, and I was feeling no pain after a few shots of his twenty-year-old brandy, and I offered her a bed to stay in—mine, in fact. She blew up at me, which I deserved, and stormed out.

Hell, I hadn't intended her to take the offer as a permanent one. She should have known better.

So, for that matter, should I. Back in '47, most people would rather marry than burn. I was an exception. And Blythe was too high-strung to fool with—she was on the edge of nervous collapse half the time, with all the knowledge in her head, and one thing she didn't need was a Dakota farm boy pawing at her on the night her marriage ended.

Soon Blythe and Tachyon were together. It didn't do my self-esteem any good to be turned down for a being from another planet, but I'd gotten to know Tachyon fairly well, and I'd decided he was okay in spite of his liking for brocade and satin. If he made Blythe happy, that was fine with me. I figured he had to have something right with him to persuade a blue-stocking like Blythe to actually live in sin.

The term *ace* caught on just after Blythe joined the EFD,

so suddenly we were the Four Aces. Mr. Holmes was Democracy's Ace in the Hole, or the Fifth Ace. We were good guys, and everyone knew it.

It was amazing, the amount of adulation we received. The public simply wouldn't *allow* us to do anything wrong. Even die-hard bigots referred to Earl Sanderson as "our colored flyboy." When he spoke out on segregation, or Mr. Holmes on populism, people listened.

Earl was consciously manipulating his image, I think. He was smart, and he knew how the machinery of the press worked. The promise he'd given with such struggle to Mr. Holmes was fully justified by events. He was consciously molding himself into a black hero, an untarnished figure of aspiration. Athlete, scholar, union leader, war hero, faithful husband, ace. He was the first black man on the cover of *Time*, the first on *Life*. He had replaced Robeson as the foremost black ideal, as Robeson wryly acknowledged when he said, "I can't fly, but then Earl Sanderson can't sing."

Robeson was wrong, by the way.

Earl was flying higher than he ever had. He hadn't realized what happens to idols when people find out about their feet of clay.

The Four Aces' failures came the next year, in '48. When the Communists were on the verge of taking over in Czechoslovakia we flew to Germany in a big rush, and then the whole thing was called off. Someone at the State Department had decided the situation was too complicated for us to fix, and he'd asked Mr. Holmes not to intervene. I heard a rumor later that the government had been recruiting some ace talents of their own for covert work, and that they'd been sent in and made a bungle of it. I don't know if that's true or not.

Then, two months after the Czechoslovakian fiasco, we were sent into China to save a billion-odd people for democracy.

It was not apparent at the time, but our side had already

lost. On paper, things seemed retrievable—the generalissimo's Kuomintang still held all the major cities, their armies were well equipped, compared to Mao and his forces, and it was well known that the generalissimo was a genius. If he weren't, why had Mr. Luce made him *Time*'s Man of the Year twice?

On the other hand, the Communists were marching south at a steady rate of twenty-three point five miles per day, rain or shine, summer or winter, redistributing land as they went. Nothing could stop them—certainly not the generalissimo.

By the time we were called in, the generalissimo had resigned—he did that from time to time, just to prove to everyone that he was indispensable. So the Four Aces met with the new KMT president, a man named Chen who was always looking over his shoulder lest he be replaced once the Great Man decided to make another dramatic entrance to save the country.

The U.S. position, by then, was prepared to concede north China and Manchuria, which the KMT had already lost barring the big cities. The idea was to save the south for the generalissimo by partitioning the country. The Kuomintang would get a chance to establish itself in the south while it organized for an eventual reconquest, and the Communists would get the northern cities without having to fight for them.

We were all there, the Four Aces and Holmes—Blythe was included as a scientific adviser and ended up giving little speeches about sanitation, irrigation, and inoculation. Mao was there, and Zhou En-lai, and President Chen. The generalissimo was off in Canton sulking in his tent, and the People's Liberation Army was laying siege to Mukden in Manchuria and otherwise marching steadily south, twenty-three point five miles per day, under Lin Biao.

Earl and I didn't have much to do. We were observers, and mostly what we observed were the delegates. The KMT people were astonishingly polite, they dressed well, they had uniformed servants who scuttled about on their errands. Their interaction with one another looked like a minuet.

The PLA people looked like soldiers. They were smart, proud, military in the way that real soldiers are military, without all the white-glove prissy formality of the KMT. The PLA had been to war, and they weren't used to losing. I could tell that at a glance.

It was a shock. All I knew about China was what I'd read in Pearl Buck. That, and the certified genius of the generalissimo.

"*These* guys are fighting *those* guys?" I asked Earl.

"*Those* guys"—Earl was indicating the KMT crowd—"aren't fighting anyone. They're ducking for cover and running away. That's part of the problem."

"I don't like the looks of this," I said.

Earl seemed a little sad. "I don't, either," he said. He spat. "The KMT officials have been stealing land from the peasants. The Communists are giving the land back, and that means they've got popular support. But once they've won the war they'll take it back, just like Stalin did."

Earl knew his history. Me, I just read the papers.

Over a period of two weeks Mr. Holmes worked out a basis for negotiation, and then David Harstein came into the room and soon Chen and Mao were grinning at each other like old school buddies at a reunion, and in a marathon negotiating session China was formally partitioned. The KMT and the PLA were ordered to be friends and lay down their arms.

It all fell apart within days. The generalissimo, who had no doubt been told of our perfidy by ex-Colonel Perón, denounced the agreement and returned to save China. Lin Biao never stopped marching south. And after a series of colossal battles, the certified genius of the generalissimo ended up on an island guarded by the U.S. fleet—along with Juan Perón and his blond hooker, who had to move again.

Mr. Holmes told me that when he flew back across the

Pacific with the partition in his pocket, while the agreement unraveled behind him and the cheering crowds in Hong Kong and Manila and Oahu and San Francisco grew ever smaller, he kept remembering Neville Chamberlain and his little piece of paper, and how Chamberlain's "peace in Europe" turned into conflagration, and Chamberlain into history's dupe, the sad example of a man who meant well but who had too much hope and trusted too much in men more experienced in treachery than he.

Mr. Holmes was no different. He didn't realize that while he'd gone on living and working for the same ideals, for democracy and liberalism and fairness and integration, the world was changing around him, and that because he didn't change with the world the world was going to hammer him into the dust.

At this point the public were still inclined to forgive us, but they remembered that we'd disappointed them. Their enthusiasm was a little lessened.

And maybe the time for the Four Aces had passed. The big war criminals had been caught, fascism was on the run, and we had discovered our limitations in Czechoslovakia and China.

When Stalin blockaded Berlin, Earl and I flew in. I was in my combat fatigues again, Earl in his leather jacket. He flew patrols over the Russian wire, and the army gave me a jeep and a driver to play with. Eventually Stalin backed down.

But our activities were shifting toward the personal. Blythe was going off to scientific conferences all over the world and spent most of the rest of her time with Tachyon. Earl was marching in civil rights demonstrations and speaking all over the country. Mr. Holmes and David Harstein went to work, in that election year, for the candidacy of Henry Wallace.

I spoke alongside Earl at Urban League meetings, and to help out Mr. Holmes I said a few nice things for Mr. Wallace, and I got paid a lot of money for driving the latest-model Chrysler and for talking about Americanism.

After the election I went to Hollywood to work for Louis Mayer. The money was more incredible than anything I'd ever dreamed, and I was getting bored kicking around Mr. Holmes's apartment. I left most of my stuff in the apartment, figuring it wouldn't be long before I'd be back.

I was pulling down ten thousand per week, and I'd acquired an agent and an accountant and a secretary to answer the phone and someone to handle my publicity; all I had to do at this point was take acting and dance lessons. I didn't actually have to work yet, because they were having script problems with my picture. They'd never had to write a screenplay around a blond superman before.

The script they eventually came up with was based loosely on our adventures in Argentina, and it was called *Golden Boy*. They paid Clifford Odets a lot of money to use that title, and considering what happened to Odets and me later, that linking had a certain irony.

When they gave the script to me, I didn't care for it. I was the hero, which was just fine with me. They actually called me John Brown. But the Harstein character had been turned into a minister's son from Montana, and the Archibald Holmes character, instead of being a politician from Virginia, had become an FBI agent. The worst part was the Earl Sanderson character—he'd become a cipher, a black flunky who was only in a few scenes, and then only to take orders from John Brown and reply with a crisp, "Yes, sir," and a salute. I called up the studio to talk about this.

"We can't put him in too many scenes," I was told. "Otherwise we can't cut him out for the southern version."

I asked my executive producer what he was talking about.

"If we release a picture in the South, we can't have colored people in it, or the exhibitors won't show it. We write the scenes so that we can release a southern version by cutting out all the scenes with niggers."

I was astonished. I never knew they did things like that. "Look," I said. "I've made speeches in front of the NAACP and Urban League. I was in *Newsweek* with Mary McLeod Bethune. I can't be seen to be a party to this."

The voice coming over the phone turned nasty. "Look at your contract, Mr. Braun. You don't have script approval."

"I don't want to approve the script. I just want a script that recognizes certain facts about my life. If I do this script, my credibility will be gone. You're fucking with my *image*, here!"

After that it turned unpleasant. I made certain threats and the executive producer made certain threats. I got a call from my accountant telling me what would happen if the ten grand per week stopped coming, and my agent told me I had no legal right to object to any of this.

Finally I called Earl and told him what was going on. "*What* did you say they were paying you?" he asked.

I told him again.

"Look," he said. "What you do in Hollywood is your business. But you're new there, and you're an unknown commodity to them. You want to stand up for the right, that's good. But if you walk, you won't do me or the Urban League any good. Stay in the business and get some clout, then use it. And if you feel guilty, the NAACP can always use some of that ten grand per week."

So there it was. My agent patched up an understanding with the studio to the effect that I was to be consulted on script changes. I succeeded in getting the FBI dropped from the script, leaving the Holmes character without any set governmental affiliation, and I tried to make the Sanderson character a little more interesting.

I watched the rushes, and they were good. I liked my acting—it was relaxed, anyway, and I even got to step in front of a speeding Mercedes and watch it bounce off my chest. It was done with special effects.

The picture went into the can, and I went from a three-martini lunch into the wrap party without stopping to sober up. Three days later I woke up in Tijuana with a splitting headache and a suspicion that I'd just done something foolish. The pretty little blonde sharing the pillow told me what it was. We'd just got married. When she was in the bath I had to look at the marriage license to find out her name was Kim Wolfe. She was a minor starlet from Georgia who'd been scuffling around Hollywood for six years.

After some aspirin and a few belts of tequila, marriage didn't seem like a half-bad idea. Maybe it was time, with my new career and all, that I settled down.

I bought Ronald Colman's old pseudo-English country house on Summit Drive in Beverly Hills, and I moved in with Kim, and our two secretaries, Kim's hairdresser, our two chauffeurs, our two live-in maids. . . . Suddenly I had all these people on salary, and I wasn't quite sure where they came from.

The next picture was *The Rickenbacker Story.* Victor Fleming was going to direct, with Fredric March as Pershing and June Allyson as the nurse I was supposed to fall in love with. Dewey Martin, of all people, was to play Richthofen, whose Teutonic breast I was going to shoot full of American lead—never mind that the real Richthofen was shot down by someone else. The picture was going to be filmed in Ireland, with an enormous budget and hundreds of extras. I insisted on learning how to fly, so I could do some of the stunts myself. I called Earl long-distance about that.

"Hey," I said. "I finally learned how to fly."

"Some farm boys," he said, "just take a while."

"Victor Fleming's gonna make me an ace."

"Jack." His voice was amused. "You're *already* an ace."

Which stopped me up short, because somehow in all the activity I'd forgotten that it wasn't MGM who made me a star. "You've got a point, there," I said.

"You should come to New York a little more often," Earl said. "Figure out what's happening in the real world."

"Yeah, I'll do that. We'll talk about flying."

"We'll do that."

I stopped by New York for three days on my way to Ireland. Kim wasn't with me—she'd gotten work, thanks to me, and had been loaned to Warner Bros. for a picture. She was very southern anyway, and the one time she'd been with Earl she'd been very uncomfortable, and so I didn't mind she wasn't there.

I was in Ireland for seven months—the weather was so bad the shooting took forever. I met Kim in London twice, for a week each time, but the rest of the time I was on my own. I was faithful, after my fashion, which meant that I didn't sleep with any one girl more than twice in a row. I became a good enough pilot so that the stunt pilots actually complimented me a few times.

When I got back to California, I spent two weeks in Palm Springs with Kim. *Golden Boy* was going to premiere in two months. On my last day at the Springs, I'd just climbed out of the swimming pool when a congressional aide, sweating in a suit and tie, walked up to me and handed me a pink slip.

It was a subpoena. I was to appear before the House Un-American Activities Committee bright and early on Tuesday. The very next day.

I was more annoyed than anything. I figured they obviously had the wrong Jack Braun. I called up Metro and talked to someone in the legal department. He surprised me by saying, "Oh, we thought you'd get the subpoena sometime soon."

"Wait a minute. How'd you know?"

There was a second's uncomfortable silence. "Our policy is to cooperate with the FBI. Look, we'll have one of our attorneys meet you in Washington. Just tell the committee what you know and you can be back in California next week."

"Hey," I said. "What's the FBI got to do with it? And why didn't you tell me this was coming? And what the hell does the committee think I know, anyway?"

"Something about China," the man said. "That was what the investigators were asking us about, anyway."

I slammed the phone down and called Mr. Holmes. He and Earl and David had gotten their subpoenas earlier in the day and had been trying to reach me ever since, but couldn't get ahold of me in Palm Springs.

"They're going to try to break the Aces, farm boy," Earl said. "You'd better get the first flight east. We've got to talk."

I made arrangements, and then Kim walked in, dressed in her tennis whites, just back from her lesson. She looked better in sweat than any woman I'd ever known.

"What's wrong?" she said. I just pointed at the pink slip.

Kim's reaction was fast, and it surprised me. "Don't do what the Ten did," she said quickly. "They consulted with each other and took a hard-line defense, and none of them have worked since." She reached for the phone. "Let me call the studio. We've got to get you a lawyer."

I watched her as she picked up the phone and began to dial. A chill hand touched the back of my neck.

"I wish I knew what was going on," I said.

But I knew. I knew even then, and my knowledge had a precision and a clarity that was terrifying. All I could think about was how I wished I couldn't see the choices quite so clearly.

To me, the Fear had come late. HUAC first went after Hollywood in '47, with the Hollywood Ten. Supposedly the committee was investigating Communist infiltration of the film industry—a ridiculous notion on the face of it, since no Communists were going to get any propaganda in the pictures without the express knowledge and permission of people like Mr. Mayer and the Brothers Warner. The Ten were all current or former Communists, and they and their lawyers agreed on a defense based on the First Amendment rights of free speech and association.

The committee rode over them like a herd of buffalo over

a bed of daisies. The Ten were given contempt-of-Congress citations for their refusal to cooperate, and after their appeals ran out years later, they ended up in prison.

The Ten had figured the First Amendment would protect them, that the contempt citations would be thrown out of court within a few weeks at the most. Instead, the appeals went on for years, and the Ten went to the slammer, and during that time none of them could find a job.

The blacklist came into existence. My old friends, the American Legion, who had learned somewhat more subtle tactics since going after the Holiday Association with axe handles, published a list of known or suspected Communists so that no one employer had any excuse for hiring anyone on the list. If he hired someone, he became suspect himself, and his name could be added to the list.

None of those called before HUAC had ever committed a crime, as defined by law, nor were they ever accused of crimes. They were not being investigated for criminal activity, but for associations. HUAC had no constitutional mandate to investigate these people, the blacklist was illegal, the evidence introduced at the committee sessions was largely hearsay and inadmissible in a court of law. . . . None of it mattered. It happened anyway.

HUAC had been silent for a while, partly because their chairman, Parnell, had gotten tossed into the slammer for padding his payroll, partly because the Hollywood Ten appeals were still going through the court. But they'd gotten hungry for all that great publicity they'd gotten when they went after Hollywood, and the public had been whipped into a frenzy with the Rosenberg trials and the Alger Hiss case, so they concluded that the time was right for another splashy investigation.

HUAC's new chairman, John S. Wood of Georgia, decided to go after the biggest game on the planet.

Us.

My MGM attorney met me at the Washington airport. "I'd advise you not to talk with Mr. Holmes or Mr. Sanderson," he said.

"Don't be ridiculous."

"They're going to try to get you to take a First or Fifth Amendment defense," the lawyer said. "The First Amendment defense won't work—it's been turned down on every appeal. The Fifth is a defense against self-incrimination, and unless you've actually done something illegal, you can't use it unless you want to *appear* guilty."

"And you won't work, Jack," Kim said. "Metro won't even release your pictures. The American Legion would picket them all over the country."

"How do I know that I'll work if I talk?" I said. "All you have to do to get on the blacklist is be *called*, for crissake."

"I've been authorized to tell you from Mr. Mayer," the lawyer said, "that you will remain in his employ if you co-operate with the committee."

I shook my head. "I'm talking with Mr. Holmes tonight." I grinned at them. "We're the Aces, for heaven's sake. If we can't beat some hick congressman from Georgia, we don't *deserve* to work."

So I met Mr. Holmes, Earl, and David at the Statler. Kim said I was being unreasonable and stayed away.

There was a disagreement right from the start. Earl said that the committee had no right to call us in the first place, and that we should simply refuse to cooperate. Mr. Holmes said that we couldn't just concede the fight then and there, that we should defend ourselves in front of the committee— that we had nothing to hide. Earl told him that a kangaroo court was no place to conduct a reasoned defense. David just wanted to give his pheromones a crack at the committee. "The hell with it," I said. "I'll take the First. Free speech and association is something every American understands."

Which I didn't believe for a second, by the way. I just felt that I had to say something optimistic.

I wasn't called that first day—I loitered with David and Earl in the lobby, pacing and gnawing my knuckles, while Mr. Holmes and his attorney played Canute and tried to keep the acid, evil tide from eating the flesh from their bones. David kept trying to talk his way past the guards, but he didn't have any luck—the guards outside were willing to let him come in, but the ones inside the committee room weren't exposed to his pheromones and kept shutting him out.

The media were allowed in, of course. HUAC liked to parade its virtue before the newsreel cameras, and the newsreels gave the circus full play.

I didn't know what was going on inside until Mr. Holmes came out. He walked like a man who had a stroke, one foot carefully in front of the other. He was gray. His hands trembled, and he leaned on the arm of his attorney. He looked as if he'd aged twenty years in just a few hours. Earl and David ran up to him, but all I could do was stare in terror as the others helped him down the corridor.

The Fear had me by the neck.

Earl and Blythe put Mr. Holmes in his car, and then Earl waited for my MGM limousine to drive up, and he got into the back with us. Kim looked pouty, squeezed into the corner so he wouldn't touch her, and refused even to say hello.

"Well, I was right," he said. "We shouldn't have cooperated with those bastards at all."

I was still stunned from what I'd seen in the corridor. "I can't figure out why the hell they're doing this."

He fixed me with an amused glance. "Farm boys," he said, a resigned comment on the universe, and then shook his head. "You've got to hit them over the head with a shovel to get them to pay attention."

Kim sniffed. Earl didn't give any indication he'd heard.

"They're power-hungry, farm boy," he said. "And they've been kept out of power by Roosevelt and Truman for a lot of years. They're going to get it back, and they're drumming up this hysteria to do it. Look at the Four Aces and what do you see? A Negro Communist, a Jewish liberal, an FDR liberal, a woman living in sin. Add Tachyon and you've got an alien who's subverting not just the country but our chromosomes. There are probably others as powerful that nobody knows about. And they've all got unearthly powers, so who knows what they're up to? And they're not controlled by the government, they're following some kind of liberal political agenda, so that threatens the power base of most of the people on the committee right there.

"The way I figure it, the government has its own ace talents by now, people we haven't heard of. That means we can be done without—we're too independent and we're politically unsound. China and Czechoslovakia and the names of the other aces—that's an excuse. The point is that if they can break us right in public, they prove they can break anybody. It'll be a reign of terror that will last a generation. Not anyone, not even the President, will be immune."

I shook my head. I heard the words, but my brain wouldn't accept them. "What can we do about it?" I asked.

Earl's gaze held my eyes. "Not a damn thing, farm boy."

I turned away.

My MGM attorney played a recording of the Holmes hearing for me that night. Mr. Holmes and his attorney, an old Virginia family friend named Cranmer, were used to the ways of Washington and the ways of law. They expected an orderly proceeding, the gentlemen of the committee asking polite questions of the gentlemen witnesses.

The plan had no relation to reality. The committee barely let Mr. Holmes talk. Instead they screamed at him, rants full of vicious innuendo and hearsay, and he was never allowed to reply.

I was given a copy of the transcript. Part of it reads like this:

MR. RANKIN: When I look at this disgusting New Deal man who sits before the committee, with his smarty-pants manners and Bond Street clothes and his effete cigarette holder, everything that is American and Christian in me revolts at the sight. The New Deal man! That damned New Deal permeates him like a cancer, and I want to scream, "You're everything that's wrong with America. Get out and go back to Red China where you belong, you New Deal socialist! In China they'll welcome you and your treachery."

CHAIRMAN: The honorable member's time has expired.

MR. RANKIN: Thank you, Mr. Chairman.

CHAIRMAN: Mr. Nixon?

MR. NIXON: What were the names of those people in the State Department who you consulted with prior to your journey to China?

WITNESS: May I remind the committee that those with whom I dealt were American public servants acting in good faith . . .

MR. NIXON: The committee is not interested in their records. Just their names.

The transcript goes on and on, eighty pages of it altogether. Mr. Holmes had, it appeared, stabbed the generalissimo in the back and lost China to the Reds. He was accused of being soft on communism, just like that parlor-pink Henry Wallace, whom he supported for the presidency. John Rankin of Mississippi—probably the weirdest voice on the committee—accused Mr. Holmes of being part of the Jewish-Red conspiracy that had crucified Our Savior. Richard Nixon of California kept asking after names—he wanted to know the people Mr. Holmes consulted with in the State Department so that he could do to them what he'd already done to Alger Hiss. Mr. Holmes didn't give any names and pleaded the First Amendment. That's when the committee really rose to its feet in righteous indignation: They mauled him for hours, and the next day they sent down an indictment for contempt of Congress. Mr. Holmes was on his way to the penitentiary.

He was going to prison, and he hadn't committed a single crime.

―――――

"Jesus Christ. I've got to talk to Earl and David."

"I've already advised you against that, Mr. Braun."

"The hell with that. We've got to make plans."

"Listen to him, honey."

"The hell with that." The sound of a bottle clinking against a glass. "There's got to be a way out of this."

When I got to Mr. Holmes's suite, he'd been given a sedative and put to bed. Earl told me that Blythe and Tachyon had gotten their subpoenas and would arrive the next day. We couldn't understand why. Blythe never had any part in the political decisions, and Tachyon hadn't had anything to do with China or American politics at all.

David was called the next morning. He was grinning as he went in. He was going to get even for all of us.

MR. RANKIN: I would like to assure the Jewish gentleman from New York that he will encounter no bias on account of his race. Any man who believes in the fundamental principles of Christianity and lives up to them, whether he is Catholic or Protestant, has my respect and confidence.

WITNESS: May I say to the committee that I object to the characterization of "Jewish gentleman."

MR. RANKIN: Do you object to being called a Jew or being called a gentleman? What are you kicking about?

After that rocky start, David's pheromones began to infiltrate the room, and though he didn't quite have the committee dancing in a circle and singing "Hava Nagila," he did have them genially agreeing to cancel the subpoenas, call off the hearings, draft a resolution praising the Aces as patriots, send a letter to Mr. Holmes apologizing for their conduct, revoke the contempt of Congress citations for the Hollywood Ten, and in general make fools out of themselves for several hours, right in front of the newsreel cameras. John Rankin called David "America's little Hebe friend," high praise from him. David waltzed out, we saw that ear-to-ear grin, and we pounded him on the back and headed back to the Statler for a celebration.

We had opened the third bottle of champagne when the hotel dick opened the door and congressional aides delivered a new round of subpoenas. We turned on the radio and heard Chairman John Wood give a live address about how David had used "mind control of the type practiced in the Pavlov Institute in Communist Russia," and that this deadly form of attack would be investigated in full.

I sat down on the bed and stared at the bubbles rising in my champagne glass.

The Fear had come again.

Blythe went in the next morning. Her hands were trembling. David was turned away by hall guards wearing gas masks.

There were trucks with chemical-warfare symbols out front. I found out later that if we tried to fight our way out, they were going to use phosgene on us.

They were constructing a glass booth in the hearing room. David would testify in isolation, through a microphone. The control of the mike was in John Wood's hands.

Apparently HUAC were as shaken as we, because their questioning was a little disjointed. They asked her about China, and since she'd gone in a scientific capacity she didn't have any answers for them about the political decisions. Then they asked her about the nature of her power, how exactly she absorbed minds and what she did with them. It was all fairly polite. Henry van Renssaeler was still a congressman, after all, and professional courtesy dictated they not suggest his wife ran his mind for him.

They sent Blythe out and called in Tachyon. He was dressed in a peach-colored coat and Hessian boots with tassels. He'd been ignoring his attorney's advice all along—he went in with the attitude of an aristocrat whose reluctant duty was to correct the misapprehensions of the mob.

He outsmarted himself completely, and the committee ripped him to shreds. They nailed him for being an illegal alien, then stomped over him for being responsible for releasing the wild-card virus, and to top it all off they demanded the names of the aces he'd treated, just in case some of them happened to be evil infiltrators influencing the minds of America at the behest of Uncle Joe Stalin. Tachyon refused.

They deported him.

Harstein went in the next day, accompanied by a file of marines dressed for chemical warfare. Once they had him in the glass booth they tore into him just as they had Mr. Holmes. John Wood held the button on the mike and would never let him talk, not even to answer when Rankin called him a slimy kike, right there in public. When he finally got his chance to speak, David denounced the committee as a bunch of Nazis. That sounded to Mr. Wood like contempt of Congress.

By the end of the hearing, David was going to prison too.

Congress adjourned for the weekend. Earl and I were going before the committee on Monday next.

We sat in Mr. Holmes's suite Friday night and listened to the radio, and it was all bad. The American Legion was organizing demonstrations in support of the committee all around the country. There were rounds of subpoenas going out to people over the country who were known to have ace abilities—no deformed jokers got called, because they'd look bad on camera. My agent had left a message telling me that Chrysler wanted their car back, and that the Chesterfield people had called and were worried.

I drank a bottle of scotch. Blythe and Tachyon were in hiding somewhere. David and Mr. Holmes were zombies, sitting in the corner, their eyes sunken, turned inward to their own personal agony. None of us had anything to say, except Earl. "I'll take the First Amendment, and damn them all," he said. "If they put me in prison, I'll fly to Switzerland."

I gazed into my drink. "I can't fly, Earl," I said.

"Sure you can, farm boy," he said. "You told me yourself."

"*I can't fly, dammit!* Leave me alone."

I couldn't stand it anymore, and took another bottle with me and went to bed. Kim wanted to talk and I just turned my back and pretended to be asleep.

"Yes, Mr. Mayer."

"Jack? This is terrible, Jack, just terrible."

"Yes, it is. These bastards, Mr. Mayer. They're going to wreck us."

"Just do what the lawyer says, Jack. You'll be fine. Do the brave thing."

"Brave?" Laughter. "*Brave?*"

"It's the right thing, Jack. You're a hero. They can't touch you. Just tell them what you know, and America will love you for it."

"You want me to be a rat."

"Jack, Jack. Don't use those kind of words. It's a patriotic thing I want you to do. The right thing. I want you to be a hero. And I want you to know there's always a place at Metro for a hero."

"How many people are gonna buy tickets to see a rat, Mr. Mayer? How many?"

"Give the phone to the lawyer, Jack. I want to talk to him. You be a good boy and do what he says."

"The hell I will."

"Jack. What can I do with you? Let me talk to the lawyer."

Earl was floating outside my window. Raindrops sparkled on the goggles perched atop his flying helmet. Kim glared at him and left the room. I got out of bed and went to the window and opened it. He flew in, dropped his boots onto the carpet, and lit a smoke.

"You don't look so good, Jack."

"I have a hangover, Earl."

He pulled a folded *Washington Star* out of his pocket. "I

have something here that'll sober you up. Have you seen the paper?"

"No. I haven't seen a damn thing."

He opened it. The headline read: "Stalin Announces Support for Aces."

I sat on the bed and reached for the bottle. "Jesus."

Earl threw the paper down. "He wants us to go down. We kept him out of Berlin, for god's sake. He has no reason to love us. He's persecuting his own wild-card talents over there."

"The bastard, the bastard." I closed my eyes. Colors throbbed on the backs of my lids. "Got a butt?" I asked. He gave me one, and a light from his wartime Zippo. I leaned back in bed and rubbed the bristles on my chin.

"The way I see it," Earl said, "we're going to have ten bad years. Maybe we'll even have to leave the country." He shook his head. "And then we'll be heroes again. It'll take at least that long."

"You sure know how to cheer a guy up."

He laughed. The cigarette tasted vile. I washed the taste away with scotch.

The smile left Earl's face, and he shook his head. "It's the people that are going to be called after us—those are the ones I'm sorry for. There's going to be a witch hunt in this country for years to come." He shook his head. "The NAACP is paying for my lawyer. I just might give him back. I don't want any organization associated with me. It'll just make it harder for them later."

"Mayer's been on the phone."

"Mayer." He grimaced. "If only those guys who run the studios had stood up when the Ten went before the committee. If they'd shown some guts none of this would ever have happened." He gave me a look. "You'd better get a new lawyer. Unless you take the Fifth." He frowned. "The Fifth is quicker. They just ask you your name, you say you won't answer, then it's over."

"What difference does the lawyer make, then?"

"You've got a point there." He gave me a ragged grin. "It really *isn't* going to make any difference, is it? Whatever we say or do. The committee will do what they want, either way."

"Yeah. It's over."

His grin turned, as he looked at me, to a soft smile. For a moment, I saw the glow that Lillian had said surrounded him. Here he was, on the verge of losing everything he'd worked for, about to be used as a weapon that would cudgel the civil rights movement and anti-fascism and anti-imperialism and labor and everything else that mattered to him, knowing that his name would be anathema, that anyone he'd ever associated with would soon be facing the same treatment . . . and he'd accepted it all somehow, saddened of course, but still solid within himself. The Fear hadn't even come close to touching him. He wasn't afraid of the committee, of disgrace, of the loss of his position and standing. He didn't regret an instant of his life, a moment's dedication to his beliefs.

"It's over?" he said. There was a fire in his eyes. "Hell, Jack," he laughed, "it's not over. One committee hearing ain't the war. We're aces. They can't take that away. Right?"

"Yeah. I guess."

"I better leave you to fix your hangover." He went to the window. "Time for my morning constitutional, anyway."

"See you later."

He gave me the thumbs-up sign as he threw a leg over the sill. "Take care, farm boy."

"You too."

I got out of bed to close the window just as the drizzle turned to downpour. I looked outside into the street. People were running for cover.

"Earl *really was a Communist*, Jack. He belonged to the party for years, he went to Moscow to study. Listen, darling"—

imploring now—*"you can't help him.* He's going to get crucified no matter what you do."

"I can show him he ain't alone on the cross."

"Swell. Just swell. I'm married to a martyr. Just tell me, how are you helping your friends by taking the Fifth? Holmes isn't coming back to public life. David's hustled himself right into prison. Tachyon's being deported. And Earl's doomed, sure as anything. You can't even carry their cross for them."

"Now who's being sarcastic?"

Screaming now. *"Will you put down that bottle and listen to me?* This is something your country wants you to do! It's the right thing!"

I couldn't stand it anymore, so I went for a walk in the cold February afternoon. I hadn't eaten all day and I had a bottle of whiskey in me, and the traffic kept hissing past as I walked, the rain drizzling in my face, soaking through my light California jacket, and I didn't notice any of it. I just thought of those faces, Wood and Rankin and Francis Case, the faces and the hateful eyes and the parade of constant insinuations, and then I started running for the Capitol. I was going to find the committee and smash them, bang heads together, make them run gabbling in fear. I'd brought democracy to Argentina, for crissake, and I could bring it to Washington the same way.

The Capitol windows were dark. Cold rain gleamed on the marble. No one was there. I prowled around looking for an open door, and then finally I bashed through a side entrance and headed straight for the committee room. I yanked the door open and stepped inside.

It was empty, of course. I don't know why I was so surprised. There were only a few spotlights on. David's glass booth gleamed in the soft light like a piece of fine crystal. Camera and radio equipment sat in its place. The chairman's gavel glowed with brass and polish. Somehow, as I stood like an imbecile in the hushed silence of the room, the anger went out of me.

I sat down in one of the chairs and tried to remember what I was doing here. It was clear the Four Aces were doomed. We were bound by the law and by decency, and the committee was not. The only way we could fight them was to break the law, to rise up in their smug faces and smash the committee room to bits, laughing as the congressmen dived for cover beneath their desks. And if we did that we'd become what we fought, an extralegal force for terror and violence. We'd become what the committee claimed we were. And that would only make things worse.

The Aces were going down, and nothing could stop it.

As I came down the Capitol steps, I felt perfectly sober. No matter how much I'd had to drink, the booze couldn't stop me from knowing what I knew, from seeing the situation in all its appalling, overwhelming clarity.

I knew, I'd known all along, and I couldn't pretend that I didn't.

I walked into the lobby next morning with Kim on one side and the lawyer on the other. Earl was in the lobby, with Lillian standing there clutching her purse.

I couldn't look at them. I walked past them, and the marines in their gas masks opened the door, and I walked into the hearing room and announced my intention to testify before the committee as a friendly witness.

Later, the committee developed a procedure for friendly witnesses. There would be a closed session first, just the witness and the committee, a sort of dress rehearsal so that everyone would know what they were going to talk about and what information was going to be developed, so things would go smoothly in public session. That procedure hadn't been developed when I testified, so everything went a little roughly.

I sweated under the spotlights, so terrified I could barely speak—all I could see were those nine sets of evil little eyes staring at me from across the room, and all I could hear were their voices, booming at me from the loudspeakers like the voice of God.

Wood started off, asking me the opening questions: who I was, where I lived, what I did for a living. Then he started going into my associations, starting with Earl. His time ran out and he turned me over to Kearney.

"Are you aware that Mr. Sanderson was once a member of the Communist party?"

I didn't even hear the question. Kearney had to repeat it.

"Huh? Oh. He told me, yes."

"Do you know if he is currently a member?"

"I believe he split with the party after the Nazi-Soviet thing."

"In 1939."

"If that's what, when, the Nazi-Soviet thing happened . . . '39. I guess." I'd forgotten every piece of stagecraft I'd never known. I was fumbling with my tie, mumbling into the mike, sweating. Trying not to look into those nine sets of eyes.

"Are you aware of any Communist affiliations maintained by Mr. Sanderson subsequent to the Nazi-Soviet pact?"

"No."

Then it came. "He has mentioned to you no names belonging to Communist or Communist-affiliated groups?"

I said the first thing that came into my head. Not even thinking. "There was some girl, I think, in Italy. That he knew during the war. I think her name was Lena Goldoni. She's an actress now."

Those sets of eyes didn't even blink. But I could see little smiles on their faces. And I could see the reporters out of the corner of my eye, bending suddenly over their notepads.

"Could you spell the name, please?"

So there was the spike in Earl's coffin. Whatever could have been said about Earl up to then, it would have at least revealed him true to his principles. The betrayal of Lillian implied other betrayals, perhaps of his country. I'd destroyed him with just a few words, and at the time I didn't even know what it was I was doing.

I babbled on. In a sweat to get it over, I said anything that came into my head. I talked about loving America, and about how I just said those nice things about Henry Wallace to please Mr. Holmes, and I'm sure it was a foolish thing to have done. I didn't want to change the southern way of life, the southern way of life was a fine way of life. I saw *Gone With the Wind* twice, a great picture. Mrs. Bethune was just a friend of Earl's I got photographed with.

Velde took over the questioning.

"Are you aware of the names of any so-called aces who may be living in this country today?"

"No. None, I mean, besides those who have already been given subpoenas by the committee."

"Do you know if Earl Sanderson knows any such names?"

"No."

"He has not confided to you in any way?"

I took a drink of water. How many times could they repeat this? "If he knows the names of any aces, he has not mentioned them in my presence."

"Do you know if Mr. Harstein knows of any such names?" On and on. "No."

"Do you believe that Dr. Tachyon knows any such names?"

They'd already dealt with this. I was just confirming what they knew. "He's treated many people afflicted by the virus. I assume he knows their names. But he has never mentioned any names to me."

"Does Mrs. van Renssaeler know of the existence of any other aces?"

I started to shake my head, then a thought hit me, and I stammered out, "No. Not in herself, no."

Velde plodded on. "Does Mr. Holmes—" he started, and then Nixon sensed something here, in the way I'd just answered the question, and he asked Velde's permission to interrupt. Nixon was the smart one, no doubt. His eager, young chipmunk face looked at me intently over his microphone.

"May I request the witness to clarify that statement?"

I was horrified. I took another drink of water and tried to think of a way out of this. I couldn't. I asked Nixon to repeat the question. He did. My answer came out before he finished.

"Mrs. van Renssaeler has absorbed the mind of Dr. Tachyon. She would know any names that he would know."

The strange thing was, they hadn't figured out about Blythe and Tachyon up till then. They had to have the big jock from Dakota come in and put the pieces together for them.

I should have just taken a gun and shot her. It would have been quicker.

Chairman Wood thanked me at the end of my testimony. When the chairman of HUAC said thank you, it meant you were okay as far as they were concerned, and other people could associate with you without fear of being branded a pariah. It meant you could have a job in the United States of America.

I walked out of the hearing room with my lawyer on one side and Kim on the other. I didn't meet the eyes of my friends. Within an hour I was on a plane back to California.

The house on Summit was full of congratulatory bouquets from friends I'd made in the picture business. There were telegrams from all over the country about how brave I'd been, about what a patriot I was. The American Legion was strongly represented.

Back in Washington, Earl was taking the Fifth.

They didn't just listen to the Fifth and then let him go. They asked him one insinuating question after another, and made him take the Fifth to each. Are you a Communist? Earl answered with the Fifth. Are you an agent of the Soviet government? The Fifth. Do you associate with Soviet spies? The Fifth. Do you know Lena Goldoni? The Fifth. Was Lena Goldoni your mistress? The Fifth. Was Lena Goldoni a Soviet agent? The Fifth.

Lillian was seated in a chair right behind. Sitting mute,

clutching her bag, as Lena's name came up again and again.

And finally Earl had had enough. He leaned forward, his face taut with anger.

"I have better things to do than incriminate myself in front of a bunch of fascists!" he barked, and they promptly ruled he'd waived the Fifth by speaking out, and they asked him the questions all over again. When, trembling with rage, he announced that he'd simply paraphrased the Fifth and would continue to refuse any answer, they cited him for contempt.

He was going to join Mr. Holmes and David in prison.

People from the NAACP met with him that night. They told him to disassociate himself from the civil rights movement. He'd set the cause back fifty years. He was to stay clear in the future.

The idol had fallen. He'd molded his image into that of a superman, a hero without flaw, and once I'd mentioned Lena the populace suddenly realized that Earl Sanderson was human. They blamed him for it, for their own naiveté in believing in him and for their own sudden loss of faith; and in olden times they might have stoned him or hanged him from the nearest apple tree, but in the end what they did was worse.

They let him live.

Earl knew he was finished, was a walking dead man, that he'd given them a weapon that was used to crush him and everything he believed in, that had destroyed the heroic image he'd so carefully crafted, that he'd crushed the hopes of everyone who'd believed in him. . . . He carried the knowledge with him to his dying day, and it paralyzed him. He was still young, but he was crippled, and he never flew as high again, or as far.

The next day HUAC called Blythe. I don't even want to think about what happened then.

———

Golden Boy opened two months after the hearings. I sat next to Kim at the premiere, and from the moment the film began I realized it had gone terribly wrong.

The Earl Sanderson character was gone, just sliced out of the film. The Archibald Holmes character wasn't FBI, but he wasn't independent either; he belonged to that new organization, the CIA. Someone had shot a lot of new footage. The fascist regime in South America had been changed to a Communist regime in Eastern Europe, all run by olive-skinned men with Spanish accents. Every time one of the characters said "Nazi," it was dubbed in "Commie," and the dubbing was loud and bad and unconvincing.

I wandered in a daze through the reception afterward. Everyone kept telling me what a great actor I was, what a great picture it was. The film poster said *Jack Braun—A Hero America Can Trust!* I wanted to vomit.

I left early and went to bed.

I went on collecting ten grand per week while the picture bombed at the box office. I was told the Rickenbacker picture was going to be a big hit, but right now they were having script problems with my next picture. The first two screenwriters had been called up before the committee and ended up on the blacklist because they wouldn't name names. It made me want to weep.

After the Hollywood Ten appeals ran out, the next actor they called was Larry Parks, the man I'd been watching when the virus hit New York. He named names, but he didn't name them willingly enough and his career was over.

I couldn't seem to get away from the thing. Some people wouldn't talk to me at parties. Sometimes I'd overhear bits of conversation. "Judas Ace." "Golden Rat." "Friendly Witness," said like it was a name, or title.

I bought a Jaguar to make myself feel better.

In the meantime, the North Koreans charged across the 38th parallel and the U.S. forces were getting crunched at

Taejŏn. I wasn't doing anything other than taking acting lessons a couple of times each week.

I called Washington direct. They gave me a lieutenant colonel's rank and flew me out on a special plane.

Metro thought it was a great publicity stunt.

I was given a special helicopter, one of those early Bells, with a pilot from the swamps of Louisiana who exhibited a decided death wish. There was a cartoon of me on the side panels, with one knee up and one arm up high, like I was Superman flying.

I'd get taken behind North Korean lines and then I'd kick ass. It was very simple.

I demolished entire tank columns. Any artillery that got spotted from our side were turned into pretzels. I made four North Korean generals prisoner and rescued General Dean from the Koreans who had captured him. I pushed entire supply convoys off the sides of mountains. I was grim and determined and angry, and I was saving American lives, and I was very good at it.

There is a picture of me that got on the cover of *Life*. It shows me with this tight Clint Eastwood smile, holding a T-34 over my head. There is a very surprised North Korean in the turret. I'm glowing like a meteor. The picture was titled *Superstar of Pusan, superstar* being a new word back then.

I was very proud of what I was doing.

Back in the States, *Rickenbacker* was a hit. Not as big a hit as everyone expected, but it was spectacular and it made quite a bit of money. Audiences seemed to be a bit ambivalent in their reactions to the star. Even with me on the cover of *Life*, there were some people who couldn't quite see me as a hero.

Metro re-released *Golden Boy*. It flopped again.

I didn't much care. I was holding the Pusan Perimeter. I was right there with the GIs, under fire half the time, sleeping in a tent, eating out of cans and looking like someone out of a Bill Mauldin cartoon. I think it was fairly unique behavior for a light colonel. The other officers hated it, but General Dean supported me—at one point he was shooting at tanks with a bazooka himself—and I was a hit with the soldiers.

They flew me to Wake Island so that Truman could give me the Medal of Honor, and MacArthur flew out on the same plane. He seemed preoccupied the whole time, didn't waste any time in conversation with me. He looked incredibly old, on his last legs. I don't think he liked me.

A week later, we broke out of Pusan and MacArthur landed X Corps at Inchon. The North Koreans ran for it.

Five days later, I was back in California. The army told me, quite curtly, that my services were no longer necessary. I'm fairly certain it was MacArthur's doing. He wanted to be the superstar of Korea, and he didn't want to share any of the honors. And there were probably other aces—nice, quiet, anonymous aces—working for the U.S. by then.

I didn't want to leave. For a while, particularly after MacArthur got crushed by the Chinese, I kept phoning Washington with new ideas about how to be useful. I could raid the airfields in Manchuria that were giving us such trouble. Or I could be the point man for a breakthrough. The authorities were very polite, but it was clear they didn't want me.

I did hear from the CIA, though. After Dien Bien Phu, they wanted to send me into Indochina to get rid of Bao Dai. The plan seemed half-assed—they had no idea who or what they wanted to put in Bao Dai's place, for one thing; just expected "native anticommunist liberal forces" to rise and take command—and the guy in charge of the operation kept using Madison Avenue jargon to disguise the fact he knew nothing about Vietnam or any of the people he was supposed to be dealing with.

I turned them down. After that, my sole involvement with the federal government was to pay my taxes every April.

While I was in Korea, the Hollywood Ten appeals ran out. David and Mr. Holmes went to prison. David served three years. Mr. Holmes served only six months and then was released on account of his health. Everyone knows what happened to Blythe.

Earl flew to Europe and appeared in Switzerland, where he renounced his U.S. citizenship and became a citizen of the world. A month later, he was living with Orlena Goldoni in her Paris apartment. She'd become a big star by then. I suppose he decided that since there was no point in concealing their relationship anymore, he'd flaunt it.

Lillian stayed in New York. Maybe Earl sent her money. I don't know.

Perón came back to Argentina in the mid 1950s, along with his peroxide chippie. The Fear moving south.

I made pictures, but somehow none of them was the success that was expected. Metro kept muttering about my image problem.

People couldn't believe I was a hero. I couldn't believe it either, and it affected my acting. In *Rickenbacker*, I'd had conviction. After that, nothing.

Kim had her career going by now. I didn't see her much. Eventually her detective got a picture of me in bed with the girl dermatologist who came over to apply her makeup every morning, and Kim got the house on Summit Drive, with the maids and gardener and chauffeurs and most of my money, and I ended up in a small beach house in Malibu with the Jaguar in the garage. Sometimes my parties would last weeks.

There were two marriages after that, and the longest lasted only eight months. They cost me the rest of the money I'd made. Metro let me go, and I worked for Warner. The pictures got worse and worse. I made the same western about six times over.

Eventually I bit the bullet. My picture career had died years before, and I was broke. I went to NBC with an idea for a televison series.

Tarzan of the Apes ran for four years. I was executive

producer, and on the screen I played second banana to a chimp. I was the first and only blond Tarzan. I had a lot of points and the series set me up for life.

After that I did what every ex-Hollywood actor does: I went into real estate. I sold actors' homes in California for a while, and then I put a company together and started building apartments and shopping centers. I always used other people's money—I wasn't taking a chance on going broke again. I put up shopping centers in half the small towns in the Midwest.

I made a fortune. Even after I didn't need the money any more, I kept at it. I didn't have much else to do.

When Nixon got elected, I felt ill. I couldn't understand how people could believe that man.

After Mr. Holmes got out of prison he went to work as editor of the *New Republic*. He died in 1955, lung cancer. His daughter inherited the family money. I suppose my clothes were still in his closets.

Two weeks after Earl flew the country, Paul Robeson and W. E. B. Du Bois joined the CPUSA, receiving their party cards in a public ceremony in Herald Square. They announced they were joining the protest of Earl's treatment before HUAC.

HUAC called a lot of blacks into their committee room. Even Jackie Robinson was summoned and appeared as a friendly witness. Unlike the white witnesses, the blacks were never asked to name names. HUAC didn't want to create any more black martyrs. Instead, the witnesses were asked to denounce the views of Sanderson, Robeson, and Du Bois. Most of them obliged.

Through the 1950s and most of the 1960s, it was difficult to get a grasp on what Earl was doing. He lived quietly with Lena Goldoni in Paris and Rome. She was a big star, active politically, but Earl wasn't seen much.

He wasn't hiding, I think. Just keeping out of sight. There's a difference.

There were rumors, though. That he was seen in Africa

during various wars for independence. That he fought in Algeria against the French and the Secret Army. When asked, Earl refused to confirm or deny his activities. He was courted by left-wing individuals and causes, but rarely committed himself publicly. I think, like me, he didn't want to be used again. But I also think he was afraid that he'd do damage to a cause by associating himself with it.

Eventually the reign of terror ended, just as Earl said it would. While I was swinging on jungle vines as Tarzan, John and Robert Kennedy killed the blacklist by marching past an American Legion picket line to see *Spartacus*, a film written by one of the Hollywood Ten.

Aces began coming out of hiding, entering public life. But now they wore masks and used made-up names, just like the comics I'd read in the war and thought were so silly. It wasn't silly now. They were taking no chances. The Fear might one day return.

Books were written about us. I declined all interviews. Sometimes the question came up in public, and I'd just turn cold and say, "I decline to talk about that at this time." My own Fifth Amendment.

In the 1960s, when the civil rights movement began to heat up in this country, Earl came to Toronto and perched on the border. He met with black leaders and journalists, talked only about civil rights.

But Earl was, by that time, irrelevant. The new generation of black leaders invoked his memory and quoted his speeches, and the Panthers copied his leather jacket, boots, and beret, but the fact of his continuing existence, as a human being rather than a symbol, was a bit disturbing. The movement would have preferred a dead martyr, whose image could have been used for any purpose, rather than a live, passionate man who said his own opinions loud and clear.

Maybe he sensed this when he was asked to come south. The immigration people would probably have allowed it. But he hesitated too long, and then Nixon was president. Earl wouldn't enter a country run by a former member of HUAC.

By the 1970s, Earl settled permanently into Lena's apartment in Paris. Panther exiles like Cleaver tried to make common cause with him and failed.

Lena died in 1975 in a train crash. She left Earl her money.

He'd give interviews from time to time. I tracked them down and read them. According to one interviewer, one of the conditions of the interview was that he wouldn't be asked about me. Maybe he wanted certain memories to die a natural death. I wanted to thank him for that.

There's a story, a legend almost, spread by those who marched on Selma in '65 during the voting rights crusade . . . that when the cops charged in with their tear gas, clubs, and dogs, and the marchers began to fall before the wave of white troopers, some of the marchers swore that they looked skyward and saw a man flying there, a straight black figure in a flying jacket and helmet, but that the man just hovered there and then was gone, unable to act, unable to decide whether the use of his powers would have aided his cause or worked against it. The magic hadn't come back, not even at such a pivotal moment, and after that there was nothing in his life but the chair in the cafe, the pipe, the paper, and the cerebral hemorrhage that finally took him into whatever it is that waits in the sky.

Every so often, I begin to wonder if it's over, if people have really forgotten. But aces are a part of life now, a part of the background, and the whole world is raised on ace mythology, on the story of the Four Aces and their betrayer. Everyone knows the Judas Ace, and what he looks like.

During one of my periods of optimism I found myself in New York on business. I went to Aces High, the restaurant in the Empire State Building where the new breed of ace hangs out. I was met at the door by Hiram, the ace who used to call himself Fatman until word of his real identity got out, and I could tell right away that he recognized me and that I was making a big mistake.

He was polite enough, I'll give him that, but his smile

cost him a certain amount of effort. He seated me in a dark corner, where people wouldn't see me. I ordered a drink and the salmon steak.

When the plate came, the steak was surrounded with a neat circle of dimes. I counted them. Thirty pieces of silver.

I got up and left. I could feel Hiram's eyes on me the whole time. I never came back.

I couldn't blame him at all.

When I was making *Tarzan*, people were calling me well preserved. After, when I was selling real estate and building developments, everyone told me how much the job must be agreeing with me. I looked so young.

If I look in the mirror now, I see the same young guy who was scuffling the New York streets going to auditions. Time hasn't added a line, hasn't changed me physically in any way. I'm fifty-five now, and I look twenty-two. Maybe I won't ever grow old.

I still feel like a rat. But I only did what my country told me.

Maybe I'll be the Judas Ace forever.

Sometimes I wonder about becoming an ace again, putting on a mask and costume so that no one will recognize me. Call myself Muscle Man or Beach Boy or Blond Giant or something. Go out and save the world, or at least a little piece of it.

But then I think, no. I had my time, and it's gone. And when I had the chance, I couldn't even save my own integrity. Or Earl. Or anybody.

I should have kept the dimes. I earned them, after all.

Judgment Call

John Kessel

John Kessel, a Nebula winner in 1982 for his novella "Another Orphan," teaches in the English department at North Carolina State University in Raleigh. With Mark Van Name, he runs the Sycamore Hill Writers Workshop every summer from that same city, and, at thirty-eight, he is already well known for writing ruthlessly literate SF. His first novel was *Freedom Beach* with James Patrick Kelly, another fine writer.

Kessel's is an intellect to reckon with, and I very much like this novelette, a down-and-dirty near-future look at our national pastime. In one of those myopic lapses typical of organizations as large as SFWA, "Judgment Call" failed to pass from the preliminary Nebula ballot to the final ballot, but no matter. Read it here, and read, too, the author's own comments about the origins of this sly, deceptive slider of a story:

" 'Judgment Call,' although not strictly about baseball, shows evidence of my lifetime love of the game (go Royals, go Red Sox). The main thing I was trying to do was to get inside Sandy Ellison's head. Trying to understand him got me thinking about winning and losing, and how destructive people's attitudes toward them can be. At some level I really believe the adage 'It's not whether you win or lose, but how you play the game' (or, 'The end does not justify the means').

"The story's set in 1999 because of the approaching millennium, which many people think will bring the Second Coming and the final Judgment Call.

"In different form, 'Judgment Call' is a chapter from my novel *Good News from Outer Space*.

"I'd like to thank the students at Clarion '86 and my friends and colleagues at Sycamore Hill that year for comments and advice."

Bottom of the first, no score, Dutch on first, Simonetti on second, two outs. In the bar afterwards, Sandy replayed it in his head.

Sandy had faced this Louisville pitcher maybe twice before. He had a decent fastball and a good curve, enough so he'd gotten Sandy out more than his share. And Sandy was in a slump (three for eighteen in the last five games) and the count was one and two; and the Louisville catcher was riding him. The ump was real quiet, but Sandy knew he was just waiting to throw his old rabbit punch to signal the big K, fist punching the air, but it might as well be Sandy's gut. It was hot. His legs felt rubbery.

Old War Memorial was quiet. There weren't more than fifteen hundred people there, tops; Louisville was leading the American Association, and the Bisons were dead last. The steel struts holding up the roof in right were ranked in the distance like the trees of the North Carolina pine forest where he grew up, lost in the haze and shadows of the top rows where nobody ever sat. The sky was overcast, and a heavy wind from the lake snapped the flag out in left center, but it was very hot for Buffalo, even for June. People were saying the climate was changing: It was the ozone layer, the Japs, the UFOs, the end of the world. Some off-duty cop or sanitation worker with a red face was ragging him from the stands. Sandy would have liked to deck him, but he had to ignore it because the pitcher was crouched over, shaking off signals. He went into his stretch.

Then something happened: Suddenly Sandy knew, he just knew, he could hit this guy. The pitcher figured he had Sandy plugged, curveball, curveball, outside corner and low, then up high and tight with the fastball to keep him from leaning, but it hit Sandy like a line drive between the eyes that he had the *pitcher* plugged, he *knew* where the next pitch was going to be. And there it was, fastball inside corner, and he turned on it and *bye-bye baby!* That sweet crack of the ash. Sandy watched it sail out over the left-field fence, saw the pitcher, head down, kick dirt from the mound—sorry guy, might could be you won't see the majors as soon as you thought—and jogged around the bases feeling so *good*. He was going to live forever. He was going to get laid every night.

That was just his first at bat. In the top of the sixth he made a shoestring catch in right center, and in the second and the seventh he threw out runners trying to go from first to third. At the plate he went four for five, bringing his average up to a tantalizing .299. And number five was an infield bouncer that Sandy was sure he'd beat out, but the wop ump at first called him out. A judgment call. The pud-knocker. But it was still the best game Sandy had ever played.

And Aronsen, the Sox's general manager, was in town to take a look at the Bisons in the hope of finding somebody they could bring up to help them after the bad start they'd had. After the game he came by in the locker room. He glanced at Sandy's postgame blood panel. Sandy played it cool: He was at least 0.6 under the limit on DMD, not even on scale for steroids. Sandy should get ready right away, Aronsen told him, to catch the morning train to Chicago. They were sending Estivez down and bringing him up. They were going to give him a chance to fill the hole in right field. Yessir, Sandy said, polite, eager.

Lordy, lordy, *yessir*, he'd thought as he walked down Best with Dutch and Leon toward the Main Street tramway—good-bye War Memorial. The hulk of the stadium, the exact color of a down-east dirt farmer's tobacco-stained teeth, loomed above them, the art-deco globes that topped its corners covered with pigeon shit. Atop the corroded limestone wall that ran along the street was a chain-link fence, rusted brown, and atop the fence glistened new coils of barbed wire. The barbed wire was supposed to keep vagrants from living in the stadium. It made the place look like a prison.

Now it was a few hours later, and Sandy was having a

drink with Dutch and Leon at the Ground Zero on Delaware. He'd already stopped by a machine and withdrawn the entire six hundred dollars in his account, had called up the rental office and told them he was leaving and they could rent the place because he wasn't coming back. Chalk up one for his side. Sandy paid for the first round. He had it figured: You paid for the first stiff one, you didn't hesitate a bit, and the others would remember that much better than how slow you were on the second or third, so if you played it right you came out ahead on drinks when the evening was done. Even when you didn't, you got the rep with the regulars at the bar for being a generous kind of guy. Sure enough, Dutch had paid for the second round and Leon for the third, and then some fans came by and got the next two. So Sandy was way ahead. His day. Only one thing was needed to make it complete.

"You lucky sonofabitch," Dutch shouted over the din of the talk and the flatscreen behind the bar. "You haven't played that well in a month. The Killer decides to go crazy on the day that Aronsen's in town."

There was more than kidding in Dutch's voice. "That's when it pays to look your best," Sandy said.

Dutch stared at the screen, where a faggot VJ with a wig and ruffles and lace cuffs was counting down the Top 100 videos of the twentieth century. Most of them were from the last two years. "Wouldn't do me any good," Dutch said. "They've got two first basemen ahead of me. I could hit .350 and I wouldn't get a shot at the majors."

"Playin' the wrong position, man," said Leon. His high eyebrows gave him a perpetually innocent expression.

Dutch didn't have the glove to play anywhere else but first. Sandy felt a little sorry for Dutch, who had wrecked his chances with HGH. At eighteen he had been a pretty hot prospect, a first basemen who could hit for average and field okay. But he didn't have any power, so he'd taken the hormone in order to beef up. He'd beefed up, all right, going to six-five, 230, but his reflexes got shot to hell in the process.

Now he could hit twenty home runs in triple-A ball, but he struck out too much and his fielding was mediocre and he was slow as an ox. And the American League had abandoned the DH rule just about the time Dutch went off the drug.

It was a sad story. But Sandy got tired of his bitching too. A real friend didn't bitch at you when you got called up. "You ought to work on the glove," he said.

A glint of hate showed in Dutch's face for a second, then he said, "I got to piss," and headed for the men's room.

"Sometimes he gets to me," Sandy said.

Leon lazily watched the women in the room, leaning his back against the bar, elbows resting on the edge, his big, gnarled catcher's hands hanging loosely from his wrists. On the screen behind him a naked girl was bouncing up and down on a pink neon pogo stick. Sandy couldn't tell if she was real or vidsynthed.

"Got to admit, Killer, you ain't been playin' that good lately," Leon said over his shoulder. They called Sandy the Killer because of the number of double plays he hit into: Killer as in rally killer. "You been clutched out. Been tryin' too hard."

Now it was Leon, too. Leon had grown up in Fayetteville, not ten miles from Sandy's dad's farm, but Sandy would not have hung around with Leon back there. Leon was ten years older, his father was a noncom at Fort Bragg, and he was the wrong color. Sandy always felt like blacks were keeping secrets that he would just as soon not know.

Sandy finished his bourbon and ordered another. "You don't win without trying."

Leon just nodded. "Look at that talent, there." He pointed his chin toward a table in the corner.

At the table, alone, sat a woman. He wondered how she had got there without him noticing her: She had microshort blond hair and a pale oval face with a pointed chin. Blue lips. Her dark eyelashes were long enough so that he could see them from the bar. But what got him was her body. Even from across the room Sandy could tell she was major-league material. She wore a tight blue dress and was drinking something pale, on the rocks.

She looked over at them, calmly locked glances with Sandy. Something strange happened then. He had a feeling of vertigo, and then was overwhelmed by a vivid memory, a flashback to something that had happened to him long before.

It's the end of the summer of your junior year of high school, and you're calling Jocelyn from the parking lot of the Dairy King out near Highway 95. Brutal heat. Tapping your car keys impatiently on the dented metal shelf below the phone. Jocelyn is going to Atlantic Beach with Sid Phillips and she hasn't even told you. Five rings, six. You had to get the news from Trudy Jackson and act like you knew all about it when it was like you'd been kneed in the groin.

An answer. "Hello?"

"Miz James, this is Sandy Ellison. Can I talk to Jocelyn?"

"Just a minute." Another wait. The sun burns the back of your neck.

"Hello." Jocelyn's voice sounds nervous.

The anger explodes in your chest. "What the fuck do you think you're doing?"

A semi blasts by, kicking up a cloud of dust and gravel. You turn your back to the road and hold your hand over your other ear.

"What are you talking about?"

"You better not fuck with me, Jocelyn. I won't take it."

"Slow down, Sandy. I—"

"If you go to the beach with him it's over." You try to make it sound like a threat instead of a plea.

At first Jocelyn doesn't answer. Then she says, "You always were a jerk." She hangs up.

You stand there with the receiver in your hand. It feels hot and greasy. The dial tone mocks you. Then Jeff Baxter and Jack Stubbs drive up in Jeff's Trans-am, and the three of you cruise out to the lake and drink three six-packs. "Bitch," you call her. "Fucking bitch."

The woman was still staring at him. She didn't look at all like Jocelyn. Sandy broke eye contact. He realized that Dutch had come back, had been back for a while while Sandy was spaced out. Fucking Jocelyn.

Sandy made a decision. "One hundred says I boost her tonight."

Leon regarded him coolly. Dutch snorted. "Gonna pull down your batting average, boy."

"Definitely a tough chance," Leon said.

"You think so? It's my day. We'll see who's trying too hard, Leon."

"You got a bet."

Sandy pulled the wad of bills out of his shirt pocket and laid two fifties on the bar. "You hold it, Dutch. I'll get it back tomorrow when I pick up my gear." Dutch stuffed the redbucks into his shirt pocket. Sandy picked up his drink and went over to the table. The woman watched him the whole way. Up close she was even more spectacular. "Hey," he said.

"Hello. It's about time. I've been waiting for you."

He pulled out a chair and sat down. "Sure you have."

"I never lie." Her smile was a dare. "How much is riding on this?"

He couldn't tell whether she was hostile or just a tease. Well, he could go with the pitch. "One hundred," Sandy said. "That's a week's pay in triple-A."

"What is triple-A?" Her husky voice had some trace of accent to it—hispanic?

"Baseball. My name is Sandy Ellison. I play for the Bisons."

She sipped her drink. Her ears were small and flat against her head. The shortness of her hair made her head seem large and her violet eyes enormous. He would die if he didn't have her that night. "Are you a good player?" she asked.

"I just got called up to the majors. Monday night I'll be starting for Chicago."

"You are a lucky man."

The way she said it made Sandy think for a moment he

was being set up: Leon and Dutch and all that talk about luck. But Dutch was too dumb to pull some elaborate practical joke. Leon was smart enough, but he wasn't mean enough. Still, it would be a good idea to stay on his guard. "Not luck; skill."

"Oh, skill. I thought you were lucky."

"How come I've never seen you here before?"

"I'm from out of town."

"I figured as much. Where?"

"Lexington."

Sandy ran his finger around the rim of his glass. "Kentucky? We just played Louisville. You follow the Cards on their road trips?"

"Road trips?"

"The game we played today was against the Louisville Cardinals. They're in town on a road trip."

"What a coincidence." Again the smile. "I'm on a road trip too. But I'm not following this baseball team. I came to Buffalo for another reason, and I'm leaving tomorrow."

"It's a good town to be leaving. You help me celebrate and I'll help you."

"That's why I'm here."

Right. Sandy glanced over at the bar. Leon and Dutch were talking to a couple of women. On the flatscreen was a news flash about the microwave deluge in Arizona. Shots of househubs at the supermarket wearing their aluminized suits. He turned back to the woman and smiled. "Run that by me again."

The woman gazed at him calmly over her high cheekbones. "Come on, Sandy. Read my lips. This is your lucky day and I'm here to celebrate it with you. A skillful man like you must understand what that means."

"Did Leon put you up to this? If he did the bet's off."

"Leon is one of those two men at the bar? I don't know him. If I were to guess I would guess that he is the black man. I'd also guess that you proposed the bet to him, not he to you. Am I right?"

"I made the bet."

"You see. My lucky guess. Well, if you made the bet with Leon then it's unlikely that Leon hired me to trick you. It is unlikely for other reasons too."

This was the weirdest pickup talk Sandy had ever heard. "Why do I get the feeling there's a proposition coming?"

"Don't tell me you didn't expect a proposition to pass between us sometime during this conversation."

"For sure. But I expected to be making it."

"Go ahead."

Sandy studied her. "You northern girls are different."

"I'm not from the North."

"Then you're from a different part of the South than I grew up in."

"It takes all kinds. May I ask you a question?"

"Sure."

"Why the bet?"

"I just wanted to make it interesting."

"I'm not interesting enough unless there's money riding on me?"

Riding on her. Sandy smiled. The woman smiled back. "I just like to raise the stakes," he said. "But the bet is between me and them, to prove a point. It has nothing to do with you."

"You're not very flattering."

"That's not what I meant."

"Yes. We can make it even more interesting. You think you can please me?"

Sandy finished his bourbon. "If you can be pleased."

"Good. So let's make it very interesting." She opened her clutch purse and tilted it toward him. She reached inside and held something so that Sandy could see it. A glint of metal. It was a straight razor.

"If you don't please me, I get to hurt you. Just a little."

Sandy stared at her. "Are you kidding?"

She stared back. Her look was steady.

"Maybe you're not as good as you tell me. Maybe you'll need to have some luck."

She had to be teasing. Sandy considered the odds. Even if she wasn't, he thought he could handle her. Sandy stood up. "It's a deal."

She didn't move. "You're sure you want to try this?"

"I know what I want when I see it."

"You already know enough to make a decision?"

He came around to her side of the table. "Let's go," he said. She closed her purse and led him toward the door. Sandy winked at Leon as they passed the bar; Leon's face looked as surprised and skeptical as ever. The girl's hips, swaying as she walked ahead of him, pulled him along the way the smell of food in the dumpster by the concession stand drew the retirees living in the cardboard boxes on Jefferson Avenue.

Once in the street he slipped an arm around her waist and nudged her over to the side of the building. Her perfume was dizzying. "What's your name?" he asked her.

"Judith," she said.

"Judith." It sounded so old-fashioned. There was a Judith in the Bible, he thought. But he had never paid attention in Bible class.

He kissed her. He had to force his tongue between her lips. Then she bit it, lightly. Her mouth was strong and wet. She moved her hips against him.

You are twelve. You're sitting in the Beulah Land Baptist Church with your mother. She must be thirty-five or so, a pretty woman with blond hair, putting on a little weight. Your father doesn't go to church. Lately your mother has been going more often and reading from the Bible after supper.

Some of your classmates, including Carrie Ford and Sue Harvey, are being baptized that Sunday. The two girls ride the bus with you, and Carrie has the biggest tits in the seventh grade.

The choir sings a hymn while the Reverend Foster takes the girls into the side room, and when the song is done the curtains in front of the baptismal font open and there stand the reverend and Carrie, waist deep in the water. Carrie is wearing a blue robe, trying nervously not to smile. Behind them is a painting of the lush green valley of the Promised Land, and the shining City on the Hill. The strong light from the spot above them makes Carrie's golden hair shine too.

The Reverend Foster puts his hand on Carrie's shoulder, lifts his other hand toward heaven and calls on the Lord.

"Do you renounce Satan and all his ways?" he asks Carrie.

"Yes," she says, looking holy. She crosses her hands at the wrists, palms in, and folds her hands over those tits, as if to hold them in.

The reverend touches the back of her neck. She jumps a bit, and you know she didn't expect that, but then lets him duck her head beneath the surface of the water. He holds her down for a long time, makes sure she knows who's boss. You like that. The reverend says the words of the baptism and pulls her up again.

Carrie gasps and sputters. She lifts her hands to push the hair away from her eyes. The robe clings to her chest. You can see everything. As she tries to catch her breath, you feel yourself getting an erection.

You put your hand on your lap, try to make it go away, but the mere contact with your pants leg makes you get even harder. You can't help it; your dick has run away with you. You turn red and shift uncomfortably in the pew, and your mother looks at you. She sees your hand on your lap.

"Sandy!" she hisses. A woman in front of you looks around.

Your mother tries to ignore you. The curtains close. You wish you were dead. At the same time you want to get up, go to the side room and watch Carrie Ford take off her wet robe and towel herself dry.

He felt the warmth of Judith's lips on his, her arms around his neck. He pushed away from her, staring. This was no time for some drug flashback. After a moment he placed his hands on either side of her head against the wall, leaned toward her. She bit her lower lip. He had an erection after all. Whether it was because of the memory or Judith he couldn't tell; he felt the embarrassment and guilt that had burned in him at the church. He felt mad. "Listen," he said. "Let's go to my place."

"Whatever you like." They walked down the block to the tram station. Sandy lived in one of the luxury condos that had been built on the Erie Basin before the market crash. He had an expensive view across the lake. It was even more high-rent now that the Sunbelters were moving north to escape the drought.

They got off downtown and walked up River Street to the apartment; he inserted his ID card and punched in the security code. The lock snapped open and Sandy ushered her in.

The place was wasted on Judith. She walked through the living room, the moon through the skylight throwing triangular shadows against the cathedral ceiling and walls, and thumbed on the bedroom light as if she had been there before. When he followed her he found her standing just inside the door. She began to unbutton his shirt. He felt hot. He tried to undress her, but she pushed his hands away, pushed him backward until he fell awkwardly onto the water bed. She stood above him. The expression on her face was very grave.

She knelt on the undulating bed and rested her hands on his chest. He fumbled on the headboard shelf for the yohimbine. She pushed his hand away, took one of the caps and broke it under his nose. His heart slammed against his ribs as if it would leap out of his chest; the air he breathed was hot and dry, and the tightness of the crotch of his jeans was agony. Eventually she helped him with that, but not before she had spent what seemed like an eternity making it worse.

The sight of her naked almost made him come right then. But she knew how to control that. She seemed to know everything in his mind before he knew it himself, responded or didn't respond as he needed, precisely, kindly. She became everything that he wanted. She took him to the brink again and again, stopped just short, brought him back. She seemed hooked into the sources of his desire: his pain, his fear, his hope all translated into the simple, slow motions of her sex and his. He forgot to worry about whether he was pleasing her. He forgot who he was. For an hour he forgot everything.

It was dark. Sandy lay just on the edge of sleep with his eyelids sliding closed and the distant sound of a siren in the air. The siren faded.

"You're beautiful, Sandy," Judith said. "I may not cut you after all."

Sandy felt so groggy he could hardly think. "Nobody cuts the killer," he mumbled, and laughed. He rolled onto his stomach. The bed undulated; he felt dizzy.

"Such a wonderful body. Such a hard dick."

She slid her hand down his backbone, and as she did all the muscles of his back relaxed, as if it were a twisted cord that she was unwinding. It was almost a dream. In the back of his mind was a tiny alarm, like the siren that had passed into another part of the city.

"Now," said Judith, "I want to tell you a story."

"Sure."

Lightly stroking his back, Judith said, "This is the story of Yancey Camera."

"Funny name." He felt so sleepy.

"It is. To begin with, Yancey Camera was a young man of great promise and undistrustful good nature. Would you believe me if I told you that he was as handsome as the leading man in a black-and-white movie? He was that handsome, and was as smart as he was handsome and was as rich as he was smart. His dick was as reliable as his credit rating. He was a lucky young man.

"But Yancey did not believe in luck. Oh, he gave lip service to luck; when people said, 'Yancey, you're a lucky boy,' he'd say, 'Yes, I guess I am.' But when he thought about it, he understood that when they told him how lucky he was they were really saying that he did not deserve his good fortune, had done nothing to earn it, and in a more rationally ordered universe he would not be handsome, smart, or rich, and his dick would be no more reliable than any other man's. Yancey came to realize that when people commented on his luck they were really expressing their envy, and he immediately suspected those people. This lack of trust enabled him to spot more than a few phonies, for there was a large degree of truth in Yancey Camera's analysis.

"The problem was that as time went on and Yancey saw how much venality was concealed by people's talk of luck, he forgot that he had not initially done anything to earn the good looks, intellect, wealth, and hard dick that he possessed. In other words, Sandy, he came to disbelieve in luck. He thought that a man of his skills could control every situation. He forgot about the second law of thermodynamics, which tells us that we all lose, and that those times when we win are merely local statistical deviations in a universal progress from a state of lower to a state of higher entropy. Yancey's own luck was just such a local deviation. As time passed and Yancey's good fortune continued, he began ultimately to think that he was beyond the reach of the second law of thermodynamics."

Forget the alarm, forget the razor. The second law of sexual dynamics. First you screw her, then she talks. Sandy thought about the instant he had hit the home run, the feel of the bat in his hands, the contact with the ball so pure and sweet he knew it was out of the park even before he had finished following through.

"This is a sin that the Fates call hubris," Judith said, "and as soon as they realized the extent of Yancey Camera's error, they set about to rectify the situation. Now, there are several ways in which such an imbalance can be restored. It can be done in stages, or it can be done in one sudden, enormous stroke.

"And here my story divides: In one version of the story, Yancey Camera marries a beautiful young woman, fathers four sons, and opens an automobile dealership. Unfortunately, because Yancey's home is built on the site of a chemical-waste dump, one of his boys is born with spina bifida and is confined to a wheelchair. This child dies at the age of twelve. One of his other boys is unable to compete in school and becomes a behavior problem. A third is brilliant but commits suicide at the age of fourteen when his girlfriend goes to the beach with another boy. Under the pressure of these disappointments Yancey's wife becomes a shrill harridan. She gets fat and drinks and embarrasses him at parties. Yancey gets fat too, and loses his hair. He is left with the consolation of his auto dealership, but then there is a war in the Middle East in which the oil fields are destroyed with atomic weapons. Suddenly there is no more oil. Yancey goes bankrupt. A number of other things happen which I will not tell you about. Suffice it to say that by the end of this version of the story Yancey has lost his good looks, his money, and finally his fine mind, which becomes unhinged by the pressures of his misfortune. In the end he loses his hard dick, too, and dies cursing his bad luck. For in the end he is certain that bad luck, and not his own behavior, is responsible for his destruction. And he is right."

"That's too bad."

"That is too bad, isn't it." Judith lifted the hair from the back of his neck with the tips of her fingers. It tickled.

"The other version of the story, Sandy, is even more interesting. Yancey Camera grows older and success follows success in his life. He marries a beautiful young woman who does not get fat and fathers four completely healthy and well-adjusted sons. He becomes a successful lawyer and enters politics. He wins every election he enters. Eventually he becomes the President of the Entire Country. As president he visits every state capital. Everywhere he goes the people of the nation gather to meet him, and when Yancey departs he leaves two groups of citizens behind. The first group goes home saying, 'What a fortunate people we are to have such a handsome, smart, and wealthy president.' Others say, 'What a smart, handsome, and wealthy people we are to have elected such a handsome, smart, and wealthy leader.' What a skilled nation, they tell themselves, they must be. Like their president, they assume that their gifts are not the result of good luck but of their inherent virtue. Therefore, all who point out this good luck must be jealous. And so the Fates, or the second law of thermodynamics, deal with Yancey's nation as they dealt with Yancey in the other version of this story. In their arrogance, Yancey Camera and his people, in the effort to maintain an oil supply for their automobiles, provoke a war which destroys all life on earth including the lives, good looks, wealth, and hard dicks of all the citizens of that country, lucky and unlucky. The end.

"What do you think of that, Sandy?"

Sandy was on the verge of sleep. "I think you're hung up on dicks," he mumbled, smiling to himself. "All you women."

"Could be," Judith whispered. Her breath was warm on his ear. He fell asleep.

He woke with a start. She was no longer lying beside him. How could he have let down his guard so easily? She could have ripped him off—or worse. Where had he put the cash from the bank? He rolled over and reached for his pants on the floor beside the bed, poked his index finger into the hip pocket. It was empty. He felt an adrenal surge, lurched out of bed, began to haul on his pants. He was hopping toward the hallway, tugging on his zipper, when he saw her through the open bathroom door.

She turned toward him. The light behind her was on. Her face was totally in shadow, and her voice, when she spoke, was even huskier than the voice he had heard before.

"Did you find it?" she asked.

He felt afraid. "Find what?"

"Your money."

Then he remembered he had stuck the crisp bills, fresh from the machine, into the button-flap pocket of his shirt. He ran back to the bed, found the shirt on the floor, and fumbled at it. The money was there.

When he turned back to her, she was standing over him. She reached down and touched his face.

You're fifteen. You are sitting at the chipped Formica table in the kitchen of the run-down farmhouse, sweating in the ninety-degree heat, eating a peanut butter sandwich and drinking a glass of sweet tea. The air is damp and hot as a fever compress. Through the patched screen door you can see the porch, the dusty, red-clay yard, and a corner of the tobacco field, vivid green, running down toward the even darker line of trees along the bend of the Cape Fear that marks the edge of the farm. The air is full of the sweet smell of the tobacco. Even the sandwich tastes of it.

You're wearing your high school baseball uniform. Your spikes and glove—a Dale Murphy autograph—rest on the broken yellow vinyl of the only other serviceable kitchen chair. You're starting in right today, at two o'clock, in the first round of the Cumberland County championships, and afterward you're going out for pizza with Jocelyn. Your heart is pulling you away from the farm, your thoughts fly through a jumble of images: Jocelyn's fine, blond hair, the green of the infield grass, the brightly painted ads on the outfield fence, the way the chalk lines glow blinding white in the summer sun, the smell of Jocelyn's shoulders when you bury your face in the nape of her neck. If you never have to suffer through another summer swamped under the sickly sweet smell of tobacco it will be all right with you.

You finish eating and are washing out the glass and plate in the sink when you hear your father's boots on the porch, and the screen door slams behind him. You ignore the old man. He comes over to the counter, opens the cupboard and takes out the bottle of sour mash bourbon and a drinking glass. Less than an inch is left in the bottom of the bottle. He curses and pours the bourbon into the glass, then drinks it off without putting down the bottle. He sighs heavily and leans against the counter.

You dry your hands quickly and get your glove and spikes.

"Where you going?" your father asks, as if the uniform and equipment are not enough.

"We got a game today."

He looks at you. His eyes are set in a network of wrinkles that come from squinting against the sun. Mr. Witt, the high school coach, has the same wrinkles around his eyes, but his are from playing outfield when he was with Atlanta. And Mr. Witt's eyes are not red.

Your father doesn't say anything. He takes off his billed cap and wipes his forearm across his brow. He turns and reaches into the sugar canister he keeps in the cupboard next to his bottles. You try to leave but are stopped by his voice again. "Where's the sugar bowl money?"

"I don't know."

His voice is heavy, slow. "There was another twelve dollars in here. What did you do with it?"

You stand in the door, helpless. "I didn't touch your money."

"Liar. What did you do with it!"

Pure hatred flares in you. "I didn't take your fucking money, you old drunk!"

You slam out the screen door and stalk over to the beat-up Maverick that you worked nights and weekends saving up to buy. You grind the gearshift into first, let the engine roar through the rotten muffler, spin the tires on the dirt in the yard. In the side mirror you see the old man standing on the porch shouting at you. But you can't hear what he's shouting, and the image shakes crazily as you bounce up the rutted drive.

Sandy flinched. He was crouched in his apartment and

the woman was standing over him. He still shook with anger at his father's accusation, still sweated from the heat; he could still smell the tobacco baking in the sun. How he had hated the old man and his suspicion. For the first time in years he felt the vivid contempt he'd had then for the small-ness that made his father that way.

He backed away from Judith, shaking. She reached out and touched him again.

You're in this same bedroom, right beside the bed where you've just gotten your ashes hauled better than you have in your entire life, in order to stick your finger into a pocket to see whether you've been robbed. On the day that you made the majors, on the day you played better than you have in your entire life, on the day you played better than, in truth, you know you are really able to play. Sticking your finger into your pants pocket like a halfwit sticking his finger up his ass because it feels so good. A pitiful loser. Just like your father.

Sandy jerked away from her. He scrambled toward the bed, suddenly terrified. His knees were so weak he couldn't pull himself into the bed.

"What's the matter, Sandy?" She stepped toward him.

"Don't touch me!"

"You don't like my touch?"

"You're going to kill me." He said it quietly, amazed, and as he spoke he realized it was true.

She moved closer. "That remains to be seen, Sandy."

"Don't touch me again! Please!"

"Why not?"

Cowering, he looked up at her, trying to make out her face in the darkness. It wasn't fair. But then something welled up in him and he knew it *was* fair, and that was almost more than he could stand. "I'm sorry," he said.

She knelt beside him, wrapped her arms around him and said nothing.

After a while he stopped crying. He wiped his eyes and

nose with the corner of the bedsheet, ashamed. He sat on the edge of the bed, back to her. "I'm sorry," he said.

"Yes," she said. Then he saw that in her other hand, the one she had not touched him with, she held the straight razor. She had been holding it all the time.

"I didn't realize I might be hurting your feelings," he said.

"You can't hurt my feelings." There was no emotion in her voice. There was nothing. Looking at her face was like looking at an empty room.

"Don't worry," she said, folding the blade back into the handle. "I won't hurt you."

It was a blind voice. Sandy shuddered. She leaned toward him. Her body was excruciatingly beautiful, yet he stumbled back from the bed, grabbing for his shirt, as if the pants weren't enough, as if it were January and he was lost on the lakefront in a blizzard.

"You don't have to be afraid," she said. "Come to bed."

He stood there, indecisive. He had to get out of there. She was insane—fuck insane, she wasn't even human. He looked into her cold face. It was not dead. It was like the real woman was in another place and this body was a receiver over which she was bringing him a message from a far distance—from another country, from across the galaxy. If he left now he would be okay, he knew. But something that might have happened to him would not happen, and in order to find out what that was he would have to take a big chance. He looked up at the moon through the skylight. The clouds passed steadily across it, making it look like it was moving. The moon didn't move that fast; it moved so slowly that you couldn't tell, except Sandy knew that in five minutes the angle of the shadows on the wall and chair and bed would be all different. The room would be changed.

She was still in the bed. Sandy came back, dropped the shirt, took off his pants, and got in beside her. Her skin was very smooth.

The clock read 8:45; he would have to hurry. He felt good. He got his bags out of the closet and began to pack. Halfway through, he stopped to get the shirt he had left on the floor. He picked it up and shoved it into his laundry bag, then remembered the cash and pulled it out again. She had left him fifteen dollars. One ten, five ones.

He pushed the shirt down into the bottom of the bag and finished packing. He called a cab and rode over to War Memorial.

On the Hitachi in the cab he watched the morning news, hoping to get the baseball scores. Nothing. The Reverend Gilray declares the Abomination of Desolation has begun, the Judgment is at hand. Reports the Israelis have used tactical nukes in the Djibouti civil war. Three teenagers spot another UFO at Chestnut Ridge.

When he got to the park, Sandy tipped the cabby a redbuck and went directly to the locker room and cleaned out his locker. He was hoping to avoid Leon or Dutch, but just as he was getting ready to leave, Dutch showed up to take some hitting before the Sunday afternoon game.

"Looks like I underrated you, sport. Just like on the field." He hauled out his wallet and began to get out the bills.

"Keep it," Sandy said.

"Huh?" Dutch, surprised, looked like a vanilla imitation of Leon's perpetual innocence.

"Leon won the bet."

Dutch snickered. "She got wise to you, huh?"

Sandy zipped his bag shut and picked up his glove and bats. He smiled. "You could say that. I got to go—cab's waiting. Wish me luck."

"Thought you didn't need luck."

"Goes to show you what I know. Say good-bye to Leon for me, okay?" He shook Dutch's hand and left.

The Glassblower's Dragon

Lucius Shepard

The peripatetic Lucius Shepard—this month in Nantucket,
next year in the Antilles—has recently been at work on
three different novels, *Kingsley's Labyrinth, Louisiana
Breakdown,* and *The End of Life As We Know It.* He won
a Nebula for his brilliant 1986 novella about a future war
in Guatemala, "R&R," later incorporated into his prestigious Bantam New Fiction novel, *Life During Wartime*
(1987). About *Wartime* (optioned in 1988 for filming by 20th
Century Fox and director James Cameron), American Book
Award winner Bob Shacochis declared, "A devastating
achievement: A giant has appeared out there on the plains
of contemporary fiction."

True. But in the early 1980s, Shepard made his literary
debut *in the science fiction field,* and no matter in which
direction he allows his formidable talent to carry him, many
would argue that it soars the highest when he applies his
hard-won wisdom and the magic of his imagination to "little"—i.e., *real*—people confronting such basic human concerns as love and war, death and renewal. Brief but by no
means superficial, "The Glassblower's Dragon" is breath-
taking evidence of Shepard's hard-bitten lyricism.

About the story, he says, "I grew up in Florida and have
lived in New York City, places that attract large numbers
of people from other parts of the country, many of whom
become enervated and disaffected by the peculiar emptiness
of life in those regions, and who seem to grope at style rather
than substance in attempting to find some reason to go on
living. I was interested in putting two of them together, in
giving them a slim chance for redemption."

On a Florida beach south of Fort Myers, in a tile-roofed bungalow set among sabal palms, there lived a glassblower named Carter McCrae, a lean, gray-haired man of fifty, whose tanned, seamed face displayed a cynicism born of two failed marriages and a number of lesser trials. In the workshop beside the bungalow, he produced pieces of marvelous delicacy that were sought after by museums throughout the world; yet he derived no spiritual satisfaction from his work, for he was of the belief that no human act—be it artistic or political or interpersonal—could be other than trivial, other than flawed. For the most part he lived alone, but from time to time women came to share the bungalow, some staying a night, some a week, some a month or two. The majority of these women were quite young, a circumstance perhaps attributable to the Electran obsession, and his current companion was a twenty-four-year-old named Sharon, a redhead with a pale complexion and a sensitive cast of feature that belied her callowness. For the past nine months, she had been traveling in Central America, an aimlessness she was utilizing—she said—to arrive at a career decision. Carter doubted such a decision would ever materialize; he foresaw that she would settle for a marriage of convenience and end up making some poor soul as miserable as his own wives had made him. Like his glassworks, she was a lovely, depthless surface.

Though her range of experience was less wide than Carter's, Sharon's disillusionment with life was equal to his and equally a product of indulgence (that is, if you subscribe to the belief that it is an indulgence to affect disillusionment from the vantage of a life of relative privilege); she was a true child of the eighties, seeing worth only in the material and espousing a trendy disaffection with spiritual values and unions based upon emotional attachment. Perhaps it was this similarity of outlook, this mating of ennui and cynicism, that had fired their mutual attraction. For a while they pretended to be in love, pretending that the age difference between them did not exist. They were both aware of each other's pretense; this awareness, in fact, led them to play games with each other, alternating counterfeits of passion with spells of indifference, and watching the results. But by the end of a month, Sharon had begun to show signs of restlessness, and, noticing these signs, Carter—who had fallen into the trap of trying to arouse her listless spirit, and therefore had succeeded in fostering a more paternal image than he would have liked—became withdrawn and silent, and spent more and more time each day in his workshop, erecting defenses against the impending breakup. He knew it would be difficult: Even the pretense of love had required of him an emotional investment that had left him vulnerable to pain.

A month after Sharon had moved in, she waked with a severe fever: one of those curious maladies that doubtless are caused by a virus, but seem in their sudden onset and departure to have been seeded by a wind that blows through us for a day or so. Carter fixed her a pallet in the shade beneath the overhang of the bungalow roof, and brought her fruit juice and magazines. Then he sat beside her, entertained her with conversation, and made sketches of her mouth; she had a slight overbite that lent her face a sexy apprehensiveness, and he thought he would try to duplicate it on the face of a glass angel he intended to create. Watching his hand swoop across the paper, having at the moment an unqualified impression of him as a good, strong man, she said dazedly, wistfully, "I wish I loved you."

He stiffened. "That's a hell of a thing to say!" he snapped, and stalked off toward his workshop; but after a few paces, he turned and came back and sat beside her in the sand. He gave her a searching look. "Why can't you?" he asked. "Because of my age?"

Sharon usually avoided intimate confrontations at all

cost, but the combination of her gratitude and her fever-provoked self-image of a helpless and possibly mordant waif had produced a thirst for honesty. "I guess so," she said. "When we're making love, I don't think about it at all. But then afterward, I . . . I just think how strange it is to have made love with someone so much older. Sometimes I say to myself, When he's a hundred, you'll be seventy-six, and it sounds reasonable. Our staying together, I mean. But then I'll think, when he's sixty, I'll only be thirty-six; and that doesn't make as much sense." She swallowed back a dryness in her throat. "I'm sorry."

He studied the frail perfection of her features: lines bracketing her mouth as fine as scratches in soapstone; eyelids so thin they appeared in certain lights to be translucent, and cheekbones so sharp they seemed about to cut through her skin. He thought that if he could render that sort of precision in glass, he would deem worthwhile all his years of work.

"Why're you looking at me like that?" she asked, concerned that he might be preparing to tell her to leave: She did not feel well enough to walk into town.

"Just thinking how pretty you are."

She shot him an angry look. "I'm not!"

"Of course you are." He chuckled. "It's amazing how many beautiful women have poor opinions of themselves. It's as if they've decided that having good looks means they don't deserve anything else. Like you. You insist on denying your potential. . . ."

"I don't have potential. I'm just a piece of ass!"

He was startled by her vehemence. "That's not true."

She laughed. "Know how I entertained myself in New York? I'd get all punked out. Wear this silver lamé dress and corpse makeup and a belted ray gun. My hair in spikes. And I'd go to the dance clubs. All of 'em. Kamikaze, the Palladium. I called myself Future Girl. The doormen like it if you have a special persona; they're more liable to let you in. So I became Future Girl. I measured my life in headlines about her. Future

Girl Gives Head in the Palladium Bathroom. Future Girl Toots Coke off a Toilet Seat While Getting Banged from the Rear by an Ad Exec. Future Girl Does a Train with Four Pale New Wave Creeps." She spat this out like a stream of bile and was annoyed that he did not appear shocked.

"Why did you do it?"

"I loved it! It was *me!*"

"If that's so, why'd you quit?"

"I ran up against a headline I couldn't deal with."

She gazed out at the Gulf, its untroubled waters a steely blue except near the horizon, where lay a lacquered crimson reflection of the setting sun. Sandpipers scooted along the brown muck of the tidal margin. He waited for her to explain, and when she remained silent, he asked how the headline had read.

"Future Girl Gets Raped." She couldn't bring herself to meet his eyes. "You're the first man I've made it with since it happened. But all that means is, I'm ready to be Future Girl again."

"It doesn't have to mean that."

"I don't understand," she said. "How can you deny what I'm saying about myself? You don't have any better opinion of yourself than I do."

"Yeah," he said after a pause. "You're right. I've done degrading things . . . though that's not what afflicts me. I've put them into perspective. My difficulty lies in what I'm afraid of becoming."

"And what's that?"

"When I was in my twenties, I did some wandering around myself. Europe, South America. And at one point I ended up in this little town in southern Mexico. San Cristóbal de las Cases. I stayed with this old man who made a habit of taking in strays. He'd been a writer, had a couple of terrible marriages, and had more or less given up on life. Every night a bunch of us would sit around his hearth and talk. And sooner or later, John—that was his name—would tell us his vision of the future. He'd gone to Jesus, and had these vivid dreams about the Apocalypse. Armies of men glowing with radio-activity fighting on dry seabeds. Things like that. He was a romantic figure. We wrote about him in our journals. That's what he was to us—a journal entry." In his mind's eye, he saw John's embittered face, and, too, he seemed to hear his doomful tones.

"You don't have visions."

"No, but I've imitated his life in every other way. And I'm younger than he was. Give me another few years, and I'll work up some kind of fantasy."

"I wish . . . I wish I could help."

"You have. Beauty always helps."

Sharon couldn't think of a response. Finally she said, "Do you want to make love?"

"Not really. You're leaving soon. We both know that."

"What's that got to do with it?"

Irritated, he got to his feet. "I don't need a pity fuck. Another one of you will come along on the next bus." He put his hand to his eyes. "I'm sorry. Look, we had some good times. Let's just let it be, all right?"

"All right . . . if that's what you want."

"I'm going to do some work. If you'd like, I'll make you a going-away gift. Any requests?"

A rush of fever swept over her, and it seemed to bear an answer up from her depths. "Make me a dragon."

"Why a dragon?"

"I don't know. . . . Maybe because they don't exist."

Carter's level of inspiration was not up to such a complicated piece as a dragon. He decided to do her something abstract. Call it "Dragon." But after he had affixed the parison—a thick-walled bubble of molten glass—to the end of the pipe, his level of inspiration declined further. He stepped out of the workshop, intending to drop the parison into the sand. The sun was almost down, a sliver of fire on the horizon, and in its last glow, Sharon's hair was flame colored; her skin was ivory reddened by firelight. Seeing her, Carter was overcome by sadness and longing, and imagining for a moment that like a musician he could produce a melody perfectly expressive of his feelings, he lifted the pipe, closed his eyes, and blew into it.

From Sharon's vantage the expanding parison was upheld against the dying sun and looked to be filled with red fire. Looked to be a winged shaped writhing, attempting to break free of the glass stem from which it developed. She blinked, thinking she must be suffering a hallucination born of the fever, because she knew such complex pieces could not be made with a simple breath. But the shape did not vanish; rather, grew more and more intricate, extruding a long serpentine neck and tail, then a narrow, reptilian head. The figure was not much larger than a cat, difficult to see due to its translucency, but she had no doubt of its nature: It was a dragon.

Even though Carter's eyes remained closed, he knew something extraordinary was happening. The breath that flowed out of him seemed endless, and it also seemed that he could feel the configuration of the shape it was producing in his throat. And when at last he did open his eyes, he was only mildly surprised to see the dragon give a sinuous twist that snapped its glass tether, and go whirling up above his head, its graceful wings rippling, fighting for altitude. Its balled eyes winked like baleful gems; its sleek belly appeared to enclose a boil of fiery gas, and every scale to hold a charge of crimson energy.

The dragon began to fly in circles above Sharon and Carter, circles that grew smaller and smaller, and they felt drawn toward each other by those dwindling orbits, like bits of flotsam being pulled into the core of a whirlpool. Finally they stood side by side, staring up at the dragon, which then flew a complicated series of loops above their heads reminiscent of the eloquent passes a magician might make with his hand above a smoking pentagram. For a second it hovered barely more than an arm's length away; it seemed to be regarding them with a contemplative eye, as if judging the merits of its work. Sharon had never seen anything so beautiful. The dragon was perfectly detailed, its glass talons tipped with the blood of the sunset, its fangs sparkling, and its clever features embodying a fierce smile that expressed an unmistakable satisfaction. She turned to Carter and perceived in his face a bedrock masculine principle whose existence she would have ridiculed a moment before; she realized that he had created this magical creature for her from a depth of emotion that she had never suspected could be directed toward her, and overwhelmed by this realization, she returned that emotion in full measure. As for Carter, he understood that Sharon had provided him the basic materials from which to create the dragon, that some quality in her had kindled inside him a spark of true feeling that his breath had fanned into life, that she had shaped with her wish, with the magical will that women invoke when they know love is wholly given.

The dragon let out a tiny hiss, wheeled up higher than palms, its glass surfaces reflecting myriad prisms. Then it arrowed straight toward the setting sun, of which a mere sliver still showed in the west. Within seconds it was lost to sight, vanishing just as the sun vanished below the horizon, signaling day's end with a pale green flash that pierced upward through low-lying clouds and held steady for the space of a breath, only to fade with the stubbornness of a powerful dream. And as if that flash were the pure form of knowledge that derives from such dreams, Sharon and Carter became aware that this magic born of the struggle between their tarnished sensibilities and their unstained hopes was not something that would last. Soon they would have to confront a world devoid of magic; soon they would have to speak, to break the spell of heated silence woven by the dragon's circling flight; and they would win at love, or they would lose.

And loss was probable, for love is an illusion with the fragility of glass and light, whose magic must constantly be renewed. But for the moment they did not allow themselves to think of these things. They were content to stare after the dragon, after the sole truth in their lives that no lie could disparage.

The moon rose, applying a sheen of silver to the dark, placid waters of the Gulf; out to sea, pale clouds like ghostly thoughts cruised across the first stars. Sharon and Carter turned to one another, and though they were afraid of all that would come, the night began without error.

Rachel in Love

Pat Murphy

In retrospect, it appears that 1987 was Pat Murphy's year, for she won the Nebula Award both for her cleanly written Mayan fantasy novel, *The Falling Woman*, and for an unconventionally formulaic (see Murphy's own comments below) novelette about a romance between a bewildered chimpanzee and a heedless research-facility janitor. Her career had been building irresistibly toward these victories for some time, from the publication of her first novel, *The Shadow Hunter*, through such fine foreshadowing tales as "On a Hot Summer Night in a Place Far Away" and her neatly ironic "In the Abode of Snows."

About *The Falling Woman*, Murphy writes: "The prevailing notion in Western culture seems to be that science is the answer—no matter what the question happens to be. I've got nothing against science, but I prefer to join people like Loren Eisley and Joseph Campbell in taking a broader view of the world.

"In *The Way of the Animal Powers*, Joseph Campbell wrote, 'Gods that are dead are simply those that no longer speak to the science or the moral order of the day. . . . Every god that is dead can be conjured again to life.' *The Falling Woman* reflects my agreement with Campbell's belief in the power of the past."

And here Murphy clarifies my "unconventionally formulaic" crack about her award-winning novelette, "Rachel in Love": "When I was a reporter for a daily newspaper, I interviewed a woman who wrote for the confession magazines—*True Confessions*, *Modern Romance*, and the like. During the course of the interview, the writer explained that the basic formula for a confessions story is 'Sin, suffer, and repent.' The heroine (always a heroine, never a hero) somehow sins, usually by falling in love with an inappropriate man; she suffers as a result; and finally she repents, seeing the error of her ways. I had this formula in mind while writing 'Rachel in Love,' and in its own peculiar way, the story follows the formula."

It does so, the reader will discover, not only peculiarly but poignantly.

It is a Sunday morning in summer, and a small, brown chimpanzee named Rachel sits on the living room floor of a remote ranch house on the edge of the Painted Desert. She is watching a Tarzan movie on television. Her hairy arms are wrapped around her knees and she rocks back and forth with suppressed excitement. She knows that her father would say that she's too old for such childish amusements, but since Aaron is still sleeping, he can't chastise her.

On the television, Tarzan has been trapped in a bamboo cage by a band of wicked Pygmies. Rachel is afraid that he won't escape in time to save Jane from the ivory smugglers who hold her captive. The movie cuts to Jane, who is tied up in the back of a jeep, and Rachel whimpers softly to herself. She knows better than to howl; she peeked into her father's bedroom earlier, and he was still in bed. Aaron doesn't like her to howl when he is sleeping.

When the movie breaks for a commercial, Rachel goes to her father's room. She is ready for breakfast and she wants him to get up. She tiptoes to the bed to see if he is awake.

His eyes are open and he is staring at nothing. His face is pale and his lips are a purplish color. Dr. Aaron Jacobs, the man Rachel calls father, is not asleep. He is dead, having died in the night of a heart attack.

When Rachel shakes him, his head rocks back and forth in time with her shaking, but his eyes do not blink and he does not breathe. She places his hand on her head, nudging him so that he will waken and stroke her. He does not move. When she leans toward him, his hand falls limply to dangle over the edge of the bed.

In the breeze from the open bedroom window, the fine wisps of gray hair that he had carefully combed over his bald spot each morning shift and flutter, exposing the naked scalp. In the other room, elephants trumpet as they stampede across the jungle to rescue Tarzan. Rachel whimpers softly, but her father does not move.

Rachel backs away from her father's body. In the living room, Tarzan is swinging across the jungle on vines, going to save Jane. Rachel ignores the television. She prowls through the house as if searching for comfort—stepping into her own small bedroom, wandering through her father's laboratory. From the cages that line the walls, white rats stare at her with hot red eyes. A rabbit hops across its cage, making a series of slow, dull thumps, like a feather pillow tumbling down a flight of stairs.

She thinks that perhaps she made a mistake. Perhaps her father is just sleeping. She returns to the bedroom, but nothing has changed. Her father lies open-eyed on the bed. For a long time, she huddles beside his body, clinging to his hand.

He is the only person she has ever known. He is her father, her teacher, her friend. She cannot leave him alone.

The afternoon sun blazes through the window, and still Aaron does not move. The room grows dark, but Rachel does not turn on the lights. She is waiting for Aaron to wake up. When the moon rises, its silver light shines through the window to cast a bright rectangle on the far wall.

Outside, somewhere in the barren, rocky land surrounding the ranch house, a coyote lifts its head to the rising moon and wails, a thin sound that is as lonely as a train whistling through an abandoned station. Rachel joins in with a desolate howl of loneliness and grief. Aaron lies still and Rachel knows that he is dead.

When Rachel was younger, she had a favorite bedtime story. *Where did I come from?* she would ask Aaron, using the abbreviated gestures of ASL, American Sign Language. *Tell me again.*

"You're too old for bedtime stories," Aaron would say.

Please, she would sign. *Tell me the story.*

In the end, he always relented and told her. "Once upon a time, there was a little girl named Rachel," he said. "She was a pretty girl, with long, golden hair like a princess in a fairy tale. She lived with her father and her mother and they were all very happy."

Rachel would snuggle contentedly beneath her blankets. The story, like any good fairy tale, had elements of tragedy. In the story, Rachel's father worked at a university, studying the workings of the brain and charting the electric fields that the nervous impulses of an active brain produced. But the other researchers at the university didn't understand Rachel's father; they distrusted his research and cut off his funding. (During this portion of the story, Aaron's voice took on a bitter edge.) So he left the university and took his wife and daughter to the desert, where he could work in peace.

He continued his research and determined that each individual brain produced its own unique pattern of fields, as characteristic as a fingerprint. (Rachel found this part of the story quite dull, but Aaron insisted on including it.) The shape of this "Electric Mind," as he called it, was determined by habitual patterns of thoughts and emotions. Record the Electric Mind, he postulated, and you could capture an individual's personality.

Then one summer day, the doctor's wife and beautiful daughter went for a drive. A truck barreling down a winding cliffside road lost its brakes and met the car head-on, killing both the girl and her mother. (Rachel clung to Aaron's hand during this part of the story, frightened by the sudden evil twist of fortune.)

But though Rachel's body had died, all was not lost. In his desert lab, the doctor had recorded the electrical patterns produced by his daughter's brain. The doctor had been experimenting with the use of external magnetic fields to impose the patterns from one animal onto the brain of another. From an animal supply house, he obtained a young chimpanzee. He used a mixture of norepinephrin-based transmitter substances to boost the speed of neural processing in the chimp's brain, and then he imposed the pattern of his daughter's mind upon the brain of this young chimp, combining the two after his own fashion, saving his daughter in his own way. In the chimp's brain was all that remained of Rachel Jacobs.

The doctor named the chimp Rachel and raised her as his own daughter. Since the limitations of the chimpanzee larynx made speech very difficult, he instructed her in ASL. He taught her to read and to write. They were good friends, the best of companions.

By this point in the story, Rachel was usually asleep. But it didn't matter—she knew the ending. The doctor, whose name was Aaron Jacobs, and the chimp named Rachel lived happily ever after.

Rachel likes fairy tales and she likes happy endings. She has the mind of a teenage girl, but the innocent heart of a young chimp.

Sometimes, when Rachel looks at her gnarled brown fingers, they seem alien, wrong, out of place. She remembers having small, pale, delicate hands. Memories lie upon memories, layers upon layers, like the sedimentary rocks of the desert buttes.

Rachel remembers a blond-haired, fair-skinned woman who smelled sweetly of perfume. On a Halloween long ago, this woman (who was, in these memories, Rachel's mother) painted Rachel's fingernails bright red because Rachel was dressed as a gypsy and gypsies liked red. Rachel remembers the woman's hands: white hands with faintly blue veins hidden just beneath the skin, neatly clipped nails painted rose pink.

But Rachel also remembers another mother and another time. Her mother was dark and hairy and smelled sweetly of overripe fruit. She and Rachel lived in a wire cage in a room filled with chimps, and she hugged Rachel to her hairy breast whenever any people came into the room. Rachel's mother groomed Rachel constantly, picking delicately through her fur in search of lice that she never found.

Memories upon memories: jumbled and confused, like random pictures clipped from magazines, a bright collage that makes no sense. Rachel remembers cages: cold wire mesh beneath her feet, the smell of fear around her. A man in a white lab coat took her from the arms of her hairy mother and pricked her with needles. She could hear her mother howling, but she could not escape from the man.

Rachel remembers a junior-high-school dance where she wore a new dress: She stood in a dark corner of the gym for hours, pretending to admire the crepe-paper decorations because she felt too shy to search among the crowd for her friends.

She remembers when she was a young chimp: She huddled with five other adolescent chimps in the stuffy freight compartment of a train, frightened by the alien smells and sounds.

She remembers gym class: gray lockers and ugly gym suits that revealed her skinny legs. The teacher made everyone play softball—even Rachel, who was unathletic and painfully shy. Rachel at bat, standing at the plate, was terrified to be the center of attention. "Easy out," said the catcher, a hard-edged girl who ran with the wrong crowd and always smelled of cigarette smoke. When Rachel swung at the ball and missed, the outfielders filled the air with malicious laughter.

Rachel's memories are as delicate and elusive as the dusty moths and butterflies that dance among the rabbit brush and sage. Memories of her girlhood never linger; they land for an instant, then take flight, leaving Rachel feeling abandoned and alone.

Rachel leaves Aaron's body where it is, but closes his eyes and pulls the sheet up over his head. She does not know what else to do. Each day she waters the garden and picks some greens for the rabbits. Each day, she cares for the rats and the rabbits, bringing them food and refilling their water bottles. The weather is cool, and Aaron's body does not smell too bad, though by the end of the week, a wide line of ants runs from the bed to the open window.

At the end of the first week, on a moonlit evening, Rachel decides to let the animals go free. She releases the rabbits one by one, climbing on a stepladder to reach down into the cage and lift each placid bunny out. She carries each one to the back door, holding it for a moment and stroking the soft, warm fur. Then she sets the animal down and nudges it in the direction of the green grass that grows around the perimeter of the fenced garden.

The rats are more difficult to deal with. She manages to wrestle the large rat cage off the shelf, but it is heavier than she thought it would be. Though she slows its fall, it lands on the floor with a crash, and the rats scurry to and fro within. She shoves the cage across the linoleum floor, sliding it down the hall, over the doorsill, and onto the back patio. When she opens the cage door, rats burst out like popcorn from a popper, white in the moonlight and dashing in all directions.

Once, while Aaron was taking a nap, Rachel walked along the dirt track that led to the main highway. She hadn't planned on going far. She just wanted to see what the highway looked like, maybe hide near the mailbox and watch a car drive past. She was curious about the outside world, and her fleeting fragmentary memories did not satisfy that curiosity.

She was halfway to the mailbox when Aaron came roaring

up in his old jeep. "Get in the car," he shouted at her. "Right now!" Rachel had never seen him so angry. She cowered in the jeep's passenger seat, covered with dust from the road, unhappy that Aaron was so upset. He didn't speak until they got back to the ranch house, and then he spoke in a low voice, filled with bitterness and suppressed rage.

"You don't want to go out there," he said. "You wouldn't like it out there. The world is filled with petty, narrow-minded, stupid people. They wouldn't understand you. And anyone they don't understand, they want to hurt. They hate anyone who's different. If they know that you're different, they punish you, hurt you. They'd lock you up and never let you go."

He looked straight ahead, staring through the dirty windshield. "It's not like the shows on TV, Rachel," he said in a softer tone. "It's not like the stories in books."

He looked at her then and she gestured frantically: *I'm sorry. I'm sorry.*

"I can't protect you out there," he said. "I can't keep you safe."

Rachel took his hand in both of hers. He relented then, stroking her head. "Never do that again," he said. "Never."

Aaron's fear was contagious. Rachel never again walked along the dirt track, and sometimes she had dreams about bad people who wanted to lock her in a cage.

Two weeks after Aaron's death, a black-and-white police car drives slowly up to the house. When the policemen knock on the door, Rachel hides behind the couch in the living room. They knock again, try the knob, then open the door, which she has left unlocked.

Suddenly frightened, Rachel bolts from behind the couch, bounding toward the back door. Behind her, she hears one man yell, "My god! It's a gorilla!"

By the time he pulls his gun, Rachel has run out the back door and away into the hills. From the hills she watches as an ambulance drives up and two men in white take Aaron's body away. Even after the ambulance and the police car drive away, Rachel is afraid to go back to the house. Only after sunset does she return.

Just before dawn the next morning, she wakens to the sound of a truck jouncing down the dirt road. She peers out the window to see a pale green pickup. Sloppily stenciled in white on the door are the words PRIMATE RESEARCH CENTER. Rachel hesitates as the truck pulls up in front of the house. By the time she has decided to flee, two men are getting out of the truck. One of them carries a rifle.

She runs out the back door and heads for the hills, but she is only halfway to hiding when she hears a sound like a sharp intake of breath and feels a painful jolt in her shoulder. Suddenly, her legs give way and she is tumbling backward down the sandy slope, dust coating her red-brown fur, her howl becoming a whimper, then fading to nothing at all. She falls into the blackness of sleep.

The sun is up. Rachel lies in a cage in the back of the pickup truck. She is partially conscious and she feels a tingling in her hands and feet. Nausea grips her stomach and bowels. Her body aches.

Rachel can blink, but otherwise she can't move. From where she lies, she can see only the wire mesh of the cage and the side of the truck. When she tries to turn her head, the burning in her skin intensifies. She lies still, wanting to cry out, but unable to make a sound. She can only blink slowly, trying to close out the pain. But the burning and nausea stay.

The truck jounces down a dirt road, then stops. It rocks as the men get out. The doors slam. Rachel hears the tailgate open.

A woman's voice: "Is that the animal the county sheriff wanted us to pick up?" A woman peers into the cage. She wears a white lab coat, and her brown hair is tied back in a single braid. Around her eyes, Rachel can see small wrinkles, etched by years of living in the desert. The woman doesn't look evil. Rachel hopes that the woman will save her from the men in the truck.

"Yeah. It should be knocked out for at least another half hour. Where do you want it?"

"Bring it into the lab where we had the rhesus monkeys. I'll keep it there until I have an empty cage in the breeding area."

Rachel's cage scrapes across the bed of the pickup. She feels each bump and jar as a new pain. The man swings the cage onto a cart, and the woman pushes the cart down a concrete corridor. Rachel watches the walls pass just a few inches from her nose.

The lab contains rows of cages in which small animals sleepily move. In the sudden stark light of the overhead fluorescent bulbs, the eyes of white rats gleam red.

With the help of one of the men from the truck, the woman manhandles Rachel onto a lab table. The metal surface is cold and hard, painful against Rachel's skin. Rachel's body is not under her control; her limbs will not respond. She is still frozen by the tranquilizer, able to watch, but that is all. She cannot protest or plead for mercy.

Rachel watches with growing terror as the woman pulls on rubber gloves and fills a hypodermic needle with a clear solution. "Mark down that I'm giving her the standard test for tuberculosis; this eyelid should be checked before she's moved in with the others. I'll add thiabendazole to her feed for the next few days to clean out any intestinal worms. And I suppose we might as well de-flea her as well," the woman says. The man grunts in response.

Expertly, the woman closes one of Rachel's eyes. With her open eye, Rachel watches the hypodermic needle approach. She feels a sharp pain in her eyelid. In her mind, she is howling, but the only sound she can manage is a breathy sigh.

The woman sets the hypodermic aside and begins methodically spraying Rachel's fur with a cold, foul-smelling liquid. A drop strikes Rachel's eye and burns. Rachel blinks, but she cannot lift a hand to rub her eye. The woman treats Rachel with casual indifference, chatting with the man as she spreads Rachel's legs and sprays her genitals. "Looks healthy enough. Good breeding stock."

Rachel moans, but neither person notices. At last, they finish their torture, put her in a cage, and leave the room. She closes her eyes, and the darkness returns.

Rachel dreams. She is back at home in the ranch house. It is night and she is alone. Outside, coyotes yip and howl. The coyote is the voice of the desert, wailing as the wind wails when it stretches itself thin to squeeze through a crack between two boulders. The people native to this land tell tales of Coyote, a god who was a trickster—unreliable, changeable, mercurial.

Rachel is restless, anxious, unnerved by the howling of the coyotes. She is looking for Aaron. In the dream, she knows he is not dead, and she searches the house for him, wandering from his cluttered bedroom to her small room to the linoleum-tiled lab.

She is in the lab when she hears something tapping: a small, dry scratching, like a windblown branch against the window, though no tree grows near the house and the night is still. Cautiously, she lifts the curtain to look out.

She looks into her own reflection: a pale oval face, long blond hair. The hand that holds the curtain aside is smooth and white with carefully clipped fingernails. But something is wrong. Superimposed on the reflection is another face peering through the glass: a pair of dark brown eyes, a chimp face with red-brown hair and jug-handle ears. She sees her own reflection and she sees the outsider; the two images merge and blur. She is afraid, but she can't drop the curtain and shut the ape face out.

She is a chimp looking in through the cold, bright windowpane; she is a girl looking out; she is a girl looking in; she is an ape looking out. She is afraid, and the coyotes are howling all around.

Rachel opens her eyes and blinks until the world comes into focus. The pain and tingling have retreated, but she still feels a little sick. Her left eye aches. When she rubs it, she feels a raised lump on the eyelid where the woman pricked her. She lies on the floor of a wire mesh cage. The room is hot and the air is thick with the smell of animals.

In the cage beside her is another chimp, an older animal with scruffy, dark-brown fur. He sits with his arms wrapped around his knees, rocking back and forth, back and forth. His head is down. As he rocks, he murmurs to himself, a meaningless cooing that goes on and on. On his scalp, Rachel can see a gleam of metal: a permanently implanted electrode protrudes from a shaven patch. Rachel makes a soft questioning sound, but the other chimp will not look up.

Rachel's own cage is just a few feet square. In one corner is a bowl of monkey pellets. A water bottle hangs on the side of the cage. Rachel ignores the food, but drinks thirstily.

Sunlight streams through the windows, sliced into small sections by the wire mesh that covers the glass. She tests her cage door, rattling it gently at first, then harder. It is securely latched. The gaps in the mesh are too small to admit her hand. She can't reach out to work the latch.

The other chimp continues to rock back and forth. When Rachel rattles the mesh of her cage and howls, he lifts his head wearily and looks at her. His red-rimmed eyes are unfocused; she can't be sure he sees her.

Hello, she gestures tentatively. *What's wrong?*

He blinks at her in the dim light. *Hurt,* he signs in ASL. He reaches up to touch the electrode, fingering skin that is already raw from repeated rubbing.

Who hurt you? she asks. He stares at her blankly and she repeats the question. *Who?*

Men, he signs.

As if on cue, there is the click of a latch, and the door to the lab opens. A bearded man in a white coat steps in, followed by a clean-shaven man in a suit. The bearded man seems to be showing the other man around the lab. "... only preliminary testing, so far," the bearded man is saying. "We've been hampered by a shortage of chimps trained in ASL." The two men stop in front of the old chimp's cage. "This old fellow is from the Oregon center. Funding for the language program was cut back, and some of the animals were dispersed to other programs." The old chimp huddles at the back of the cage, eyeing the bearded man with suspicion.

Hungry? the bearded man signs to the old chimp. He holds up an orange where the old chimp can see it.

Give orange, the old chimp gestures. He holds out his hand, but comes no nearer to the wire mesh than he must to reach the orange. With the fruit in hand, he retreats to the back of his cage.

The bearded man continues, "This project will provide us with the first solid data on neural activity during use of sign language. But we really need greater access to chimps with advanced language skills. People are so damn protective of their animals."

"Is this one of yours?" the clean-shaven man asks, pointing to Rachel. She cowers in the back of the cage, as far from the wire mesh as she can get.

"No, not mine. She was someone's household pet, apparently. The county sheriff had us pick her up." The bearded man peers into her cage. Rachel does not move; she is terrified that he will somehow guess that she knows ASL. She stares at his hands and thinks about those hands putting an electrode through her skull. "I think she'll be put in breeding stock," the man says as he turns away.

Rachel watches them go, wondering at the cruelty of these people. Aaron was right: They want to punish her, they want to put an electrode in her head.

After the men are gone, she tries to draw the old chimp

into conversation, but he will not reply. He ignores her as he eats his orange. Then he returns to his former posture, hiding his head and rocking himself back and forth.

Rachel, hungry despite herself, samples one of the food pellets. It has a strange medicinal taste, and she puts it back in the bowl. She needs to pee, but there is no toilet and she cannot escape the cage. At last, unable to hold it, she pees in one corner of the cage. The urine flows through the wire mesh to soak the litter below, and the smell of warm piss fills her cage. Humiliated, frightened, her head aching, her skin itchy from the flea spray, Rachel watches as the sunlight creeps across the room.

The day wears on. Rachel samples her food again, but rejects it, preferring hunger to the strange taste. A black man comes and cleans the cages of the rabbits and rats. Rachel cowers in her cage and watches him warily, afraid that he will hurt her too.

When night comes, she is not tired. Outside, coyotes howl. Moonlight filters in through the high windows. She draws her legs up toward her body, then rests with her arms wrapped around her knees. Her father is dead, and she is a captive in a strange place. For a time, she whimpers softly, hoping to awaken from this nightmare and find herself at home in bed. When she hears the click of a key in the door to the room, she hugs herself more tightly.

A man in green coveralls pushes a cart filled with cleaning supplies into the room. He takes a broom from the cart and begins sweeping the concrete floor. Over the rows of cages, she can see the top of his head bobbing in time with his sweeping. He works slowly and methodically, bending down to sweep carefully under each row of cages, making a neat pile of dust, dung, and food scraps in the center of the aisle.

The janitor's name is Jake. He is a middle-aged deaf man who has been employed by the Primate Research Center for the past seven years. He works the night shift. The personnel director at the Primate Research Center likes Jake because he fills the federal quota for handicapped employees, and because he has not asked for a raise in five years. There have been some complaints about Jake—his work is often sloppy—but never enough to merit firing the man.

Jake is an unambitious, somewhat slow-witted man. He likes the Primate Research Center because he works alone, which allows him to drink on the job. He is an easy-going man, and he likes the animals. Sometimes, he brings treats for them. Once, a lab assistant caught him feeding an apple to a pregnant rhesus monkey. The monkey was part of an experiment on the effect of dietary restrictions on fetal brain development, and the lab assistant warned Jake that he would be fired if he was ever caught interfering with the animals again. Jake still feeds the animals, but he is more careful about when he does it, and he has never been caught again.

As Rachel watches, the old chimp gestures to Jake. *Give banana*, the chimp signs. *Please banana*. Jakes stops sweeping for a minute and reaches down to the bottom shelf of his cleaning cart. He returns with a banana and offers it to the old chimp. The chimp accepts the banana and leans against the mesh while Jake scratches his fur.

When Jake turns back to his sweeping, he catches sight of Rachel and sees that she is watching him. Emboldened by his kindness to the old chimp, Rachel timidly gestures to him. *Help me.*

Jake hesitates, then peers at her more closely. Both his eyes are shot with a fine lacework of red. His nose displays the broken blood vessels of someone who has been friends with the bottle for too many years. He needs a shave. But when he leans close, Rachel catches the scent of whiskey and tobacco. The smells remind her of Aaron and give her courage.

Please help me, Rachel signs. *I don't belong here.*

For the last hour, Jake has been drinking steadily. His view of the world is somewhat fuzzy. He stares at her blearily. Rachel's fear that he will hurt her is replaced by the fear that he will leave her locked up and alone. Desperately she signs again. *Please please please. Help me. I don't belong here. Please help me go home.*

He watches her, considering the situation. Rachel does not move. She is afraid that any movement will make him leave. With a majestic speed dictated by his inebriation, Jake leans his broom on the row of cages behind him and steps toward Rachel's cage again. *You talk?* he signs.

I talk, she signs.

Where did you come from?

From my father's house, she signs. *Two men came and shot me and put me here. I don't know why. I don't know why they locked me in jail.*

Jake looks around, willing to be sympathetic, but puzzled by her talk of jail. *This isn't jail,* he signs. *This is a place where scientists raise monkeys.*

Rachel is indignant. *I am not a monkey,* she signs. *I am a girl.*

Jake studies her hairy body and her jug-handle ears. *You look like a monkey.*

Rachel shakes her head. *No. I am a girl.*

Rachel runs her hands back over her head, a very human gesture of annoyance and unhappiness. She signs sadly, *I don't belong here. Please let me out.*

Jake shifts his weight from foot to foot, wondering what to do. *I can't let you out. I'll get in big trouble.*

Just for a little while? Please?

Jake glances at his cart of supplies. He has to finish off this room and two corridors of offices before he can relax for the night.

Don't go, Rachel signs, guessing his thoughts.

I have work to do.

She looks at the cart, then suggests eagerly, *Let me out and I'll help you work.*

Jake frowns. *If I let you out, you will run away.*

No, I won't run. I will help. Please let me out.

You promise to go back?

Rachel nods.

Warily, he unlatches the cage. Rachel bounds out, grabs a whisk broom from the cart, and begins industriously sweeping bits of food and droppings from beneath the row of cages. *Come on*, she signs to Jake from the end of the aisle. *I will help.*

When Jake pushes the cart from the room filled with cages, Rachel follows him closely. The rubber wheels of the cleaning cart rumble softly on the linoleum floor. They pass through a metal door into a corridor where the floor is carpeted and the air smells of chalk dust and paper.

Offices let off the corridor, each one a small room furnished with a desk, bookshelves, and a blackboard. Jake shows Rachel how to empty the wastebaskets into a garbage bag. While he cleans the blackboards, she wanders from office to office, trailing the trash-filled garbage bag.

At first, Jake keeps a close eye on Rachel. But after cleaning each blackboard, he pauses to sip whiskey from a paper cup. At the end of the corridor, he stops to refill the cup from the whiskey bottle that he keeps wedged between the Saniflush and the window cleaner. By the time he is halfway through the second cup, he is treating her like an old friend, telling her to hurry up so that they can eat dinner.

Rachel works quickly, but she stops sometimes to gaze out the office windows. Outside, moonlight shines on a sandy plain, dotted here and there with scrubby clumps of rabbit brush.

At the end of the corridor is a larger room in which there are several desks and typewriters. In one of the wastebaskets, buried beneath memos and candy-bar wrappers, she finds a magazine. The title is *Love Confessions*, and the cover has a picture of a man and woman kissing. Rachel studies the cover, then takes the magazine, tucking it on the bottom shelf of the cart.

Jake pours himself another cup of whiskey and pushes

the cart to another hallway. Jake is working slower now, and as he works he makes humming noises, tuneless sounds that he feels only as pleasant vibrations. The last few blackboards are sloppily done, and Rachel, finished with the wastebaskets, cleans the places that Jake missed.

They eat dinner in the janitor's storeroom, a stuffy, windowless room furnished with an ancient, grease-stained couch, a battered black-and-white television, and shelves of cleaning supplies. From a shelf, Jake takes the paper bag that holds his lunch: a baloney sandwich, a bag of barbecued potato chips, and a box of vanilla wafers. From behind the gallon jugs of liquid cleanser, he takes a magazine. He lights a cigarette, pours himself another cup of whiskey, and settles down on the couch. After a moment's hesitation, he offers Rachel a drink, pouring a shot of whiskey into a chipped ceramic cup.

Aaron never let Rachel drink whiskey, and she samples it carefully. At first the smell makes her sneeze, but she is fascinated by the way that the drink warms her throat, and she sips some more.

As they drink, Rachel tells Jake about the men who shot her and the woman who pricked her with a needle, and he nods. *The people here are crazy*, he signs.

I know, she says, thinking of the old chimp with the electrode in his head. *You won't tell them I can talk, will you?*

Jake nods. *I won't tell them anything.*

They treat me like I'm not real, Rachel signs sadly. Then she hugs her knees, frightened at the thought of being held captive by crazy people. She considers planning her escape: She is out of the cage and she is sure she could outrun Jake. As she wonders about it, she finishes her cup of whiskey. The alcohol takes the edge off her fear. She sits close beside Jake on the couch, and the smell of his cigarette smoke reminds her of Aaron. For the first time since Aaron's death she feels warm and happy.

She shares Jake's cookies and potato chips and looks

at the *Love Confessions* magazine that she took from the trash. The first story that she reads is about a woman named Alice. The headline reads: "I Became a Go-go Dancer to Pay Off My Husband's Gambling Debts, and Now He Wants Me to Sell My Body."

Rachel sympathizes with Alice's loneliness and suffering. Alice, like Rachel, is alone and misunderstood. As Rachel slowly reads, she sips her second cup of whiskey. The story reminds her of a fairy tale: The nice man who rescues Alice from her terrible husband replaces the handsome prince who rescued the princess. Rachel glances at Jake and wonders if he will rescue her from the wicked people who locked her in the cage.

She has finished the second cup of whiskey and eaten half Jake's cookies when Jake says that she must go back to her cage. She goes reluctantly, taking the magazine with her. He promises that he will come for her again the next night, and with that she must be content. She puts the magazine in one corner of the cage and curls up to sleep.

She wakes early in the afternoon. A man in a white coat is wheeling a low cart into the lab.

Rachel's head aches with hangover and she feels sick. As she crouches in one corner of her cage, he stops the cart beside her cage and then locks the wheels. "Hold on there," he mutters to her, then slides her cage onto the cart.

The man wheels her through long corridors where the walls are cement blocks painted institutional green. Rachel huddles unhappily in the cage, wondering where she is going and whether Jake will ever be able to find her.

At the end of a long corridor, the man opens a thick metal door, and a wave of warm air strikes Rachel. It stinks of chimpanzees, excrement, and rotting food. On either side of the corridor are metal bars and wire mesh. Behind the mesh, Rachel can see dark, hairy shadows. In one cage, five adolescent chimps swing and play. In another, two females huddle together, grooming each other. The man slows as he passes a cage in which a big male is banging on the wire with his fist, making the mesh rattle and ring.

"Now, Johnson," says the man. "Cool it. Be nice. I'm bringing you a new little girlfriend."

With a series of hooks, the man links Rachel's cage with the cage next to Johnson's and opens the doors. "Go on, girl," he says. "See the nice fruit." In the new cage is a bowl of sliced apples with an attendant swarm of fruit flies.

At first, Rachel will not move into the new cage. She crouches in the cage on the cart, hoping that the man will decide to take her back to the lab. She watches him get a hose and attach it to a water faucet. But she does not understand his intention until he turns the stream of water on her. A cold blast strikes her on the back and she howls, fleeing into the new cage to avoid the cold water. Then the man closes the doors, unhooks the cage, and hurries away.

The floor is bare cement. Her cage is at one end of the corridor, and two of its walls are cement block. A doorway in one of the cement-block walls leads to an outside run. The other two walls are wire mesh: one facing the corridor; the other, Johnson's cage.

Johnson, quiet now that the man has left, is sniffing around the door in the wire mesh wall that joins their cages. Rachel watches him anxiously. Her memories of other chimps are distant, softened by time. She remembers her mother; she vaguely remembers playing with other chimps her age. But she does not know how to react to Johnson when he stares at her with great intensity and makes a loud huffing sound. She gestures to him in ASL, but he only stares harder and huffs again. Beyond Johnson, she can see other cages and other chimps, so many that the wire mesh blurs her vision and she cannot see the other end of the corridor.

To escape Johnson's scrutiny, she ducks through the door into the outside run, a wire mesh cage on a white concrete foundation. Outside there is barren ground and rabbit brush. The afternoon sun is hot, and all the other runs are deserted until Johnson appears in the run beside hers. His attention disturbs her and she goes back inside.

She retreats to the side of the cage farthest from Johnson. A crudely built wooden platform provides her with a place to sit. Wrapping her arms around her knees, she tries to relax and ignore Johnson. She dozes off for a while, but wakes to a commotion across the corridor.

In the cage across the way is a female chimp in heat. Rachel recognizes the smell from her own times in heat. Two keepers are opening the door that separates the female's cage from the adjoining cage, where a male stands, watching with great interest. Johnson is shaking the wire mesh and howling as he watches.

"Mike here is a virgin, but Susie knows what she's doing," one keeper was saying to the other. "So it should go smoothly. But keep the hose ready."

"Yeah?"

"Sometimes they fight. We only use the hose to break it up if it gets real bad. Generally, they do okay."

Mike stalks into Susie's cage. The keepers lower the cage door, trapping both chimps in the same cage. Susie seems unalarmed. She continues eating a slice of orange while Mike sniffs at her genitals with every indication of great interest. She bends over to let Mike finger her pink bottom, the sign of estrus.

Rachel finds herself standing at the wire mesh, making low moaning noises. She can see Mike's erection, hear his grunting cries. He squats on the floor of Susie's cage, gesturing to the female. Rachel's feelings are mixed: She is fascinated, fearful, confused. She keeps thinking of the description of sex in the *Love Confessions* story: When Alice feels Danny's lips on hers, she is swept away by the passion of the moment. He takes her in his arms and her skin tingles as if she were consumed by an inner fire.

Susie bends down and Mike penetrates her with a loud grunt, thrusting violently with his hips. Susie cries out shrilly and suddenly leaps up, knocking Mike away. Rachel watches, overcome with fascination. Mike, his penis now limp, follows Susie slowly to the corner of the cage, where he begins grooming her carefully. Rachel finds that the wire mesh has cut her hands where she gripped it too tightly.

It is night, and the door at the end of the corridor creaks open. Rachel is immediately alert, peering through the wire mesh and trying to see down to the end of the corridor. She bangs on the wire mesh. As Jake comes closer, she waves a greeting.

When Jake reaches for the lever that will raise the door to Rachel's cage, Johnson charges toward him, howling and waving his arms above his head. He hammers on the wire mesh with his fists, howling and grimacing at Jake. Rachel ignores Johnson and hurries after Jake.

Again Rachel helps Jake clean. In the laboratory, she greets the old chimp, but the animal is more interested in the banana that Jake has brought than in conversation. The chimp will not reply to her questions, and after several tries, she gives up.

While Jake vacuums the carpeted corridors, Rachel empties the trash, finding a magazine called *Modern Romance* in the same wastebasket that had provided *Love Confessions*.

Later, in the janitor's lounge, Jake smokes a cigarette, sips whiskey, and flips through one of his own magazines. Rachel reads love stories in *Modern Romance*.

Every once in a while, she looks over Jake's shoulder at grainy pictures of naked women with their legs spread wide apart. Jake looks for a long time at a picture of a blond woman with big breasts, red fingernails, and purple-painted eyelids. The woman lies on her back and smiles as she strokes the pinkness between her legs. The picture on the next page shows her caressing her own breasts, pinching the dark nipples. The final picture shows her looking back over her shoulder. She is in the position that Susie took when she was ready to be mounted.

Rachel looks over Jake's shoulder at the magazine, but

she does not ask questions. Jake's smell began to change as soon as he opened the magazine; the scent of nervous sweat mingles with the aromas of tobacco and whiskey. Rachel suspects that questions would not be welcome just now.

At Jake's insistence, she goes back to her cage before dawn.

Over the next week, she listens to the conversations of the men who come and go, bringing food and hosing out the cages. From the men's conversation, she learns that the Primate Research Center is primarily a breeding facility that supplies researchers with domestically bred apes and monkeys of several species. It also maintains its own research staff. In indifferent tones, the men talk of horrible things. The adolescent chimps at the end of the corridor are being fed a diet high in cholesterol to determine cholesterol's effect on the circulatory system. A group of pregnant females is being injected with male hormones to determine how that will affect the female offspring. A group of infants is being fed a low-protein diet to determine adverse effects on their brain development.

The men look through her as if she were not real, as if she were a part of the wall, as if she were no one at all. She cannot speak to them; she cannot trust them.

Each night, Jake lets her out of her cage and she helps him clean. He brings treats: barbecued potato chips, fresh fruit, chocolate bars, and cookies. He treats her fondly, as one would treat a precocious child. And he talks to her.

At night, when she is with Jake, Rachel can almost forget the terror of the cage, the anxiety of watching Johnson pace to and fro, the sense of unreality that accompanies the simplest act. She would be content to stay with Jake forever, eating snack food and reading confessions magazines. He seems to like her company. But each morning, Jake insists that she must go back to the cage and the terror. By the end of the first week, she has begun plotting her escape.

Whenever Jake falls asleep over his whiskey, something

that happens three nights out of five, Rachel prowls the center alone, surreptitiously gathering things that she will need to survive in the desert: a plastic jug filled with water, a plastic bag of food pellets, a large beach towel that will serve as a blanket on the cool desert nights, a discarded plastic shopping bag in which she can carry the other things. Her best find is a road map on which the primate center is marked in red. She knows the address of Aaron's ranch and finds it on the map. She studies the roads and plots a route home. Cross country, assuming that she does not get lost, she will have to travel about fifty miles to reach the ranch. She hides these things behind one of the shelves in the janitor's storeroom.

Her plans to run away and go home are disrupted by the idea that she is in love with Jake, a notion that comes to her slowly, fed by the stories in the confessions magazines. When Jake absent-mindedly strokes her, she is filled with a strange excitement. She longs for his company and misses him on the weekends when he is away. She is happy only when she is with him, following him through the halls of the center, sniffing the aroma of tobacco and whiskey that is his own perfume. She steals a cigarette from his pack and hides it in her cage, where she can savor the smell of it at her leisure.

She loves him, but she does not know how to make him love her back. Rachel knows little about love: She remembers a high school crush where she mooned after a boy with a locker near hers, but that came to nothing. She reads the confessions magazines and Ann Landers's column in the newspaper that Jake brings with him each night, and from these sources, she learns about romance. One night, after Jake falls asleep, she types a badly punctuated, ungrammatical letter to Ann. In the letter, she explains her situation and asks for advice on how to make Jake love her. She slips the letter into a sack labeled Outgoing Mail, and for the next week she reads Ann's column with increased interest. But her letter never appears.

Rachel searches for answers in the magazine pictures that seem to fascinate Jake. She studies the naked women, especially the big-breasted woman with the purple smudges around her eyes.

One night, in a secretary's desk, she finds a plastic case of eye shadow. She steals it and takes it back to her cage. The next evening, as soon as the center is quiet, she upturns her metal food dish and regards her reflection in the shiny bottom. Squatting, she balances the eye shadow case on one knee and examines its contents: a tiny makeup brush and three shades of eye shadow—Indian Blue, Forest Green, and Wildly Violet. Rachel chooses the shade labeled Wildly Violet.

Using one finger to hold her right eye closed, she dabs her eyelid carefully with the makeup brush, leaving a gaudy, orchid-colored smudge on her brown skin. She studies the smudge critically, then adds to it, smearing the color beyond the corner of her eyelid until it disappears in her brown fur. The color gives her eye a carnival brightness, a lunatic gaiety. Working with great care, she matches the effect on the other side, then smiles at herself in the glass, blinking coquettishly.

In the other cage, Johnson bares his teeth and shakes the mesh. She ignores him.

When Jake comes to let her out, he frowns at her eyes. *Did you hurt yourself?* he asks.

No, she says. Then, after a pause, *Don't you like it?*

Jake squats beside her and stares at her eyes. Rachel puts a hand on his knee and her heart pounds at her own boldness. *You are a very strange monkey*, he signs.

Rachel is afraid to move. Her hand on his knee closes into a fist; her face folds in on itself, puckering around the eyes.

Then, straightening up, he signs, *I liked your eyes better before.*

He likes her eyes. She nods without taking her eyes from his face. Later, she washes her face in the women's rest room, leaving dark smudges the color of bruises on a series of paper towels.

Rachel is dreaming. She is walking through the Painted Desert with her hairy brown mother, following a red rock canyon that Rachel somehow knows will lead her to the Primate Research Center. Her mother is lagging behind: She does not want to go to the center; she is afraid. In the shadow of a rock outcropping, Rachel stops to explain to her mother that they must go to the center because Jake is at the center.

Rachel's mother does not understand sign language. She watches Rachel with mournful eyes, then scrambles up the canyon wall, leaving Rachel behind. Rachel climbs after her mother, pulling herself over the edge in time to see the other chimp loping away across the windblown red cinder-rock and sand.

Rachel bounds after her mother, and as she runs she howls like an abandoned infant chimp, wailing her distress. The figure of her mother wavers in the distance, shimmering in the heat that rises from the sand. The figure changes. Running away across the red sands is a pale blond woman wearing a purple sweatsuit and jogging shoes, the sweet-smelling mother that Rachel remembers. The woman looks back and smiles at Rachel. "Don't howl like an ape, daughter," she calls. "Say Mama."

Rachel runs silently, dream running that takes her nowhere. The sand burns her feet and the sun beats down on her head. The blond woman vanishes in the distance, and Rachel is alone. She collapses on the sand, whimpering because she is alone and afraid.

She feels the gentle touch of fingers grooming her fur, and for a moment, still half asleep, she believes that her hairy mother has returned to her. In the dream, she opens her eyes and looks into a pair of dark-brown eyes, separated from her by wire mesh. Johnson. He has reached through a gap in the fence to groom her. As he sorts through her fur, he makes soft cooing sounds, gentle comforting noises.

Still half asleep, she gazes at him and wonders why she was so fearful. He does not seem so bad. He grooms her for a time, and then sits nearby, watching her through the mesh. She brings a slice of apple from her dish of food and offers it to him. With her free hand, she makes the sign for apple. When he takes it, she signs again: apple. He is not a particularly quick student, but she has time and many slices of apple.

All Rachel's preparations are done, but she cannot bring herself to leave the center. Leaving the center means leaving Jake, leaving potato chips and whiskey, leaving security. To Rachel, the thought of love is always accompanied by the warm taste of whiskey and potato chips.

Some nights, after Jake is asleep, she goes to the big glass doors that lead to the outside. She opens the doors and stands on the steps, looking down into the desert. Sometimes a jackrabbit sits on its haunches in the rectangles of light that shine through the glass doors. Sometimes she sees kangaroo rats, hopping through the moonlight like rubber balls bouncing on hard pavement. Once, a coyote trots by, casting a contemptuous glance in her direction.

The desert is a lonely place. Empty. Cold. She thinks of Jake snoring softly in the janitor's lounge. And always she closes the door and returns to him.

Rachel leads a double life: janitor's assistant by night, prisoner and teacher by day. She spends the afternoons drowsing in the sun and teaching Johnson new signs.

On a warm afternoon, Rachel sits in the outside run, basking in the sunlight. Johnson is inside, and the other chimps are quiet. She can almost imagine she is back at her father's ranch, sitting in her own yard. She naps and dreams of Jake.

She dreams that she is sitting in his lap on the battered old couch. Her hand is on his chest: a smooth pale hand with red-painted fingernails. When she looks at the dark screen of the television set, she can see her reflection. She is a thin teenager with blond hair and blue eyes. She is naked.

Jake is looking at her and smiling. He runs a hand down her back and she closes her eyes in ecstasy.

But something changes when she closes her eyes. Jake is grooming her as her mother used to groom her, sorting her hair in search of fleas. She opens her eyes and sees Johnson, his diligent fingers searching through her fur, his intent brown eyes watching her. The reflection on the television screen shows two chimps, tangled in each other's arms.

Rachel wakes to find that she is in heat for the first time since she came to the center. The skin surrounding her genitals is swollen and pink.

For the rest of the day, she is restless, pacing to and fro in her cage. On his side of the wire mesh wall, Johnson is equally restless, following her when she goes outside, sniffing long and hard at the edge of the barrier that separates him from her.

That night, Rachel goes eagerly to help Jake clean. She follows him closely, never letting him get far from her. When he is sweeping, she trots after him with the dustpan and he almost trips over her twice. She keeps waiting for him to notice her condition, but he seems oblivious.

As she works, she sips from a cup of whiskey. Excited, she drinks more than usual, finishing two full cups. The liquor leaves her a little disoriented, and she sways as she follows Jake to the janitor's lounge. She curls up close beside him on the couch. He relaxes with his arms resting on the back of the couch, his legs stretching out before him. She moves so that she presses against him.

He stretches, yawns, and rubs the back of his neck as if trying to rub away stiffness. Rachel reaches around behind him and begins to gently rub his neck, reveling in the feel of his skin, his hair against the backs of her hands. The thoughts that hop and skip through her mind are confusing. Sometimes it seems that the hair that tickles her hands is Johnson's; sometimes she knows it is Jake's. And sometimes it doesn't seem to matter. Are they really so different? They are not so different.

She rubs his neck, not knowing what to do next. In the confessions magazines, this is where the man crushes the woman in his arms. Rachel climbs into Jake's lap and hugs him, waiting for him to crush her in his arms. He blinks at her sleepily. Half asleep, he strokes her, and his moving hand brushes near her genitals. She presses herself against him, making a soft sound in her throat. She rubs her hip against his crotch, aware now of a slight change in his smell, in the tempo of his breathing. He blinks at her again, a little more awake now. She bares her teeth in a smile and tilts her head back to lick his neck. She can feel his hands on her shoulders, pushing her away, and she knows what he wants. She slides from his lap and turns, presenting him with her pink genitals, ready to be mounted, ready to have him penetrate her. She moans in anticipation, a low, inviting sound.

He does not come to her. She looks over her shoulder and he is still sitting on the couch, watching her through half-closed eyes. He reaches over and picks up a magazine filled with pictures of naked women. His other hand drops to his crotch and he is lost in his own world.

Rachel howls like an infant who has lost its mother, but he does not look up. He is staring at the picture of the blond woman.

Rachel runs down dark corridors to her cage, the only home she has. When she reaches the corridor, she is breathing hard and making small, lonely, whimpering noises. In the dimly lit corridor, she hesitates for a moment, staring into Johnson's cage. The male chimp is asleep. She remembers the touch of his hands when he groomed her.

From the corridor, she lifts the gate that leads into Johnson's cage and enters. He wakes at the sound of the door and sniffs the air. When he sees Rachel, he stalks toward her, sniffing eagerly. She lets him finger her genitals, sniff deeply of her scent. His penis is erect and he grunts in excitement. She turns and presents herself to him and he mounts her, thrusting deep inside. As he penetrates, she thinks, for a moment, of Jake and of the thin, blond teenage girl named

Rachel, but then the moment passes. Almost against her will she cries out, a shrill exclamation of welcoming and loss.

After he withdraws his penis, Johnson grooms her gently, sniffing her genitals and softly stroking her fur. She is sleepy and content, but she knows that they cannot delay.

Johnson is reluctant to leave his cage, but Rachel takes him by the hand and leads him to the janitor's lounge. His presence gives her courage. She listens at the door and hears Jake's soft breathing. Leaving Johnson in the hall, she slips into the room. Jake is lying on the couch, the magazine draped over his legs. Rachel takes the equipment that she has gathered and stands for a moment, staring at the sleeping man. His baseball cap hangs on the arm of a broken chair, and she takes that to remember him by.

Rachel leads Johnson through the empty halls. A kangaroo rat, collecting seeds in the dried grass near the glass doors, looks up curiously as Rachel leads Johnson down the steps. Rachel carries the plastic shopping bag slung over her shoulder. Somewhere in the distance, a coyote howls, a long, yapping wail. His cry is joined by others, a chorus in the moonlight.

Rachel takes Johnson by the hand and leads him into the desert.

A cocktail waitress, driving from her job in Flagstaff to her home in Winslow, sees two apes dart across the road, hurrying away from the bright beams of her headlights. After wrestling with her conscience (she does not want to be accused of drinking on the job), she notifies the county sheriff.

A local newspaper reporter, an eager young man fresh out of journalism school, picks up the story from the police report and interviews the waitress. Flattered by his enthusiasm for her story and delighted to find a receptive ear, she tells him details that she failed to mention to the police: One of the apes was wearing a baseball cap and carrying what looked like a shopping bag.

The reporter writes up a quick, humorous story for the morning edition, and begins researching a feature article to be run later in the week. He knows that the newspaper, eager for news in a slow season, will play a human-interest story up big—kind of *Lassie, Come Home* with chimps.

Just before dawn, a light rain begins to fall, the first rain of spring. Rachel searches for shelter and finds a small cave formed by three tumbled boulders. It will keep off the rain and hide them from casual observers. She shares her food and water with Johnson. He has followed her closely all night, seemingly intimidated by the darkness and the howling of distant coyotes. She feels protective toward him. At the same time, having him with her gives her courage. He knows only a few gestures in ASL, but he does not need to speak. His presence is comfort enough.

Johnson curls up in the back of the cave and falls asleep quickly. Rachel sits in the opening and watches dawnlight wash the stars from the sky. The rain rattles against the sand, a comforting sound. She thinks about Jake. The baseball cap on her head still smells of his cigarettes, but she does not miss him. Not really. She fingers the cap and wonders why she thought she loved Jake.

The rain lets up. The clouds rise like fairy castles in the distance and the rising sun tints them pink and gold and gives them flaming red banners. Rachel remembers when she was younger and Aaron read her the story of Pinnochio, the little puppet who wanted to be a real boy. At the end of his adventures, Pinnochio, who has been brave and kind, gets his wish. He becomes a real boy.

Rachel had cried at the end of the story, and when Aaron asked why, she had rubbed her eyes on the backs of her hairy hands. *I want to be a real girl*, she signed to him. *A real girl.*

"You are a real girl," Aaron had told her, but somehow she had never believed him.

The sun rises higher and illuminates the broken rock

turrets of the desert. There is a magic in this barren land of unassuming grandeur. Some cultures send their young people to the desert to seek visions and guidance, searching for true thinking spawned by the openness of the place, the loneliness, the beauty of emptiness.

Rachel drowses in the warm sun and dreams a vision that has the clarity of truth. In the dream, her father comes to her. "Rachel," he says to her, "it doesn't matter what anyone thinks of you. You're my daughter."

I want to be a real girl, she signs.

"You are real," her father says. "And you don't need some two-bit drunken janitor to prove it to you." She knows she is dreaming, but she also knows that her father speaks the truth. She is warm and happy and she doesn't need Jake at all. The sunlight warms her and a lizard watches her from a rock, scurrying for cover when she moves. She picks up a bit of loose rock that lies on the floor of the cave. Idly, she scratches on the dark red sandstone wall of the cave. A lopsided heart shape. Within it, awkwardly printed: Rachel and Johnson. Between them, a plus sign. She goes over the letters again and again, leaving scores of fine lines on the smooth rock surface. Then, late in the morning, soothed by the warmth of the day, she sleeps.

Shortly after dark, an elderly rancher in a pickup truck spots two apes in a remote corner of his ranch. They run away and lose him in the rocks, but not until he has a good look at them. He calls the police, the newspaper and the Primate Research Center.

The reporter arrives first thing the next morning, interviews the rancher, and follows the men from the Primate Research Center as they search for evidence of the chimps. They find monkey shit near the cave, confirming that the runaways were indeed nearby. The news reporter, an eager and curious young man, squirms on his belly into the cave and finds the names scratched on the cave wall. He peers at it. He might have dismissed them as the idle scratchings of kids, except that the names match the names of the missing chimps. "Hey," he calls to his photographer, "Take a look at this."

The next morning's newspaper displays Rachel's crudely scratched letters. In a brief interview, the rancher has mentioned that the chimps were carrying bags. "Looked like supplies," he said. "They looked like they were in for the long haul."

On the third day, Rachel's water runs out. She heads toward a small town, marked on the map. They reach it in the early morning—thirst forces them to travel by day. Beside an isolated ranch house, she finds a faucet. She is filling her bottle when Johnson grunts in alarm.

A dark-haired woman watches from the porch of the house. She does not move toward the apes, and Rachel continues filling the bottle. "It's all right, Rachel," the woman, who has been following the story in the papers, calls out. "Drink all you want."

Startled but still suspicious, Rachel caps the bottle and, keeping her eyes on the woman, drinks from the faucet. The woman steps back into the house. Rachel motions Johnson to do the same, to hurry and drink. She turns off the faucet when he is done.

They are turning to go when the woman emerges from the house carrying a plate of tortillas and a bowl of apples. She sets them on the edge of the porch and says, "These are for you."

The woman watches through the window as Rachel packs the food into her bag. Rachel puts away the last apple and gestures her thanks to the woman. When the woman fails to respond to the sign language, Rachel picks up a stick and writes in the sand of the yard. "Thank You," Rachel scratches, then waves good-bye and sets out across the desert. She is puzzled, but happy.

The next morning's newspaper includes an interview with the dark-haired woman. She describes how Rachel turned on the faucet and turned it off when she was through, how the chimp packed the apples neatly in her bag and wrote in the dirt with a stick.

The reporter also interviews the director of the Primate Research Center. "These are animals," the director explains angrily. "But people want to treat them like they're small, hairy people." He describes the center as "primarily a breeding center with some facilities for medical research." The reporter asks some pointed questions about their acquisition of Rachel.

But the biggest story is an investigative piece. The reporter reveals that he has tracked down Aaron Jacobs's lawyer and learned that Jacobs left a will. In this will, he has bequeathed all his possessions—including his house and surrounding land—to "Rachel, the chimp I acknowledge as my daughter."

The reporter makes friends with one of the young women in the typing pool at the research center, and she tells him the office scuttlebutt: People suspect that the chimps may have been released by a deaf and drunken janitor, who was subsequently fired for negligence. The reporter, accompanied by a friend who can communicate in sign language, finds Jake in his apartment in downtown Flagstaff.

Jake, who has been drinking steadily since he was fired, feels betrayed by Rachel, by the primate center, by the world. He complains at length about Rachel: They had been friends, and then she took his baseball cap and ran away. He just didn't understand why she had run away like that.

"You mean she could talk?" the reporter asks through his interpreter.

Of course she can talk, Jake signs impatiently. *She is a smart monkey.*

The headlines read: "Intelligent Chimp Inherits Fortune!" Of course, Aaron's bequest isn't really a fortune and she isn't just a chimp, but close enough. Animal rights activists rise up in Rachel's defense. The case is discussed on the national news. Ann Landers reports receiving a letter from a chimp named Rachel; she had thought it was a hoax perpetrated by the boys at Yale. The American Civil Liberties Union assigns a lawyer to the case.

By day, Rachel and Johnson sleep in whatever hiding places they can find: a cave; a shelter built for range cattle; the shell of an abandoned car, rusted from long years in a desert gully. Sometimes Rachel dreams of jungle darkness, and the coyotes in the distance become a part of her dreams, their howling becomes the cries of fellow apes.

The desert and the journey have changed her. She is wiser, having passed through the white-hot love of adolescence and emerged on the other side. She dreams, one day, of the ranch house. In the dream, she has long blond hair and pale white skin. Her eyes are red from crying and she wanders the house restlessly, searching for something that she has lost. When she hears coyotes howling, she looks through a window at the darkness outside. The face that looks in at her has jug-handle ears and shaggy hair. When she sees the face, she cries out in recognition and opens the window to let herself in.

By night, they travel. The rocks and sands are cool beneath Rachel's feet as she walks toward her ranch. On television, scientists and politicians discuss the ramifications of her case, describe the technology uncovered by investigation of Aaron Jacobs's files. Their debates do not affect her steady progress toward her ranch or the stars that sprinkle the sky above her.

It is night when Rachel and Johnson approach the ranch house. Rachel sniffs the wind and smells automobile exhaust and strange humans. From the hills, she can see a small camp beside a white van marked with the name of a local television station. She hesitates, considering returning to the safety of the desert. Then she takes Johnson by the hand and starts down the hill. Rachel is going home.

Rhysling Poetry Award Winners

Jonathan V. Post
John Calvin Rezmerski
W. Gregory Stewart

What are the Rhysling Awards, and why are their winners showing up in these Nebula Award collections?

Let me quote George Zebrowski's introduction to the winning poems in last year's volume: "Although there is no Nebula Award for poetry, the situation is more than remedied by the Science Fiction Poetry Association's Rhysling Award for long and short poems. The award is named after the blind poet of the spaceways who appears in 'The Green Hills of Earth,' a story written by Nebula Grand Master Robert A. Heinlein and published in 1947. It has become traditional to publish the Rhysling winners in the annual Nebula anthology."

The competition for the 1987 Rhyslings produced a tie in the short-poem category (under fifty lines) between Jonathan V. Post's "Before the Big Bang" and John Calvin Rezmerski's "A Dream of Heredity." Meanwhile, the winner in the long-poem category (over fifty lines) was "Daedalus," by W. Gregory Stewart.

A graduate of Caltech, Jonathan V. Post has earned bachelor of science degrees in both mathematics and poetry, a master's degree in artificial intelligence, and a doctorate in molecular cybernetics. He is president and CEO of Computer Futures, Inc., and Emerald City Publishing, and he does consulting work in aerospace computing for such clients as the U.S. armed services, NASA, Boeing, and Yamaha. Post has published more than a hundred fantasy or science-oriented poems, and he is working on *Cold War*

Cosmos, a sequel to his novel *The Leisure of the Theory Class*. The Hubble Large Space Telescope mentioned in the subtitle of Post's poem is a billion-dollar instrument to be launched from the space shuttle; reputedly, it will be able to see to the edge of the universe and thus back to the beginning of time.

John Calvin Rezmerski, author of "A Dream of Heredity," is a solipsist ("He wrote a will / leaving everything to himself / when he comes again") teaching English and science fiction at Gustavus Adolphus College in St. Peter, Minnesota, to which he commutes a hundred miles from his home in Minneota, Minnesota. He has published several volumes of poetry and is a contributing editor to *Tales of the Unanticipated*.

W. Gregory Stewart, a Canadian-born computer programmer for a great metropolitan phone company in California, won the long-poem Rhysling for "Daedalus." He cites as his most telling biographical fact his marriage to an artist, "Saint Helen the Patient," whose work and person he intensely admires. Stewart has published poetry in *Star*Line, Dreams and Nightmares, Amazing Stories, The Lyric*, and other small press and genre magazines. In a letter, he mentioned that "Daedalus" was written "for the crew of the *Challenger*—theirs was the last gasp of Camelot." Modestly—and, I think, sensitively—he added, "Having said this, I don't know what else to say about the poem. . . . I wouldn't want to trivialize that tragedy or have anyone raise cries of exploitation. Perhaps I'm too close to it." In my view, "Daedalus" does the opposite of trivialize, and only a cynic could regard its eloquence as opportunistic.

Jonathan V. Post

Before the Big Bang: News from the Hubble Large Space Telescope

The Astronomer was red-eyed, pale,
his face was gray with stubble;
he was 13 on a sliding scale
of 1 to 10 in trouble.

"Is Physics just a fairy tale?"
he asked, and then began to wail,
"Why DID we seek the holy grail?
Why DID we launch the Hubble?

The launch was good (relax, exhale)
the data systems did not fail,
we peered beyond the cosmic veil,
the anti-cosmic double

to back before the quarks prevail.
We digitized each dark detail
but it was all to no avail,
it burst our pretty bubble."

"WHAT did you see," I asked, "Before
Beginning's Big Bang lights?"
(I reviews and interviews. I edits and I writes.)
"Before the start of Time, before the Universe's Birth,
What DID the Hubble show, ten billion years before the Earth?"

He told me. Now I writes no more.
I drinks a bit. I edits.

"Right before the Beginning," he said,
"is when THEY roll the credits!"

John Calvin Rezmerski
A Dream of Heredity

I am walking around
   with my son on my back
   and his son sitting
      on his son's back and
      I get angry
      because they
      are getting
      a free ride
      and my
      feet are
   numb.

I look down at my feet and see
   they are not moving—
   I am sitting on my father's
   shoulders and he is
      sitting on his own
      father's—we are
         midway more or less
         in a stack of men
            that disappears way up
            into clouds
            like a tornado,
            a tornado that spins
            down to where

                    the stack rests
                 on the back of an ape who
              is not too
              bright but
               has more
                goodwill
             and loyalty
              than I have
            ever felt
              toward
              him.

All around us, a mob of women locked arm in arm
shout and argue about the whole stack of us, but
they can come face to face only with the ape.
Now and then they try to push us over, but whenever someone pushes at the front, someone else
pushes back from behind. We are a tower, im-
pregnable and unyielding. They are a fierce and
irresistible savanna. The air is full of the
sound of explosions. The smell of powder is
everywhere, and the astringent taste of stalemate. The battle is over. They cannot budge us
and we cannot get off each other's backs. We are
all paralyzed because the ape can't move. I wake
up saying, "Ease off, let the ape breathe. Let me
                                        down."

W. Gregory Stewart
Daedalus

Father, if
        you read this, I am dead,
        a waxen wrack of flesh
        and wing unfeathered. If
you read this,
        you will know that I
        have tried to touch the sun,
        and you will know that in this
I have failed.

But do not grieve,
        my father; do not grieve for me.
        We spent our closest year
        in grand and common dream.
We gathered quill
        and plume in secret, sought
        the dove for underwing
        and hawk to wrap the winds about
our farthest reach.

Finch and eagle,
        eider, too; the every barb
        aligned, reset along its
        shaft, then hidden, placed
by size and sort

        behind the doors
        behind the doors
        (against the winds
and prying eyes).

And the hives!
        Oh, father, remember the hives?
        Bees robbed for comb instead of
        honey were no less angry for that
lesser theft.
        I laid mud upon you and we laughed,
        you as much of earth that day
        as I (too briefly) have been of
the heavens.

Father, I pray
        you, shed no tears for me. Instead,
        a promise: to hold fast that dream.
        Know that it was arrogance—and accident—
but not the dream . . .
        my own damned fault perhaps, but it
        was not Apollo cast me down,
        and not the Fates:
they've never cared.

Keep your wings.
        This at the last—if only for
        my memory, cast not your wings away.
        Remember—I have seen the Heavens,
I have flown,
        and having flown would rather be
        as I am now than stricken down
        in dotage, weak and never having
known the sky.

Angel

Pat Cadigan

"Promise me you will not use the word *housewife* anywhere
in my bio material," wrote Pat Cadigan soon after I asked
to reprint "Angel" in *Nebula Awards 23*. "*Mommy,* however, is acceptable." She and her husband, Arnold Fenner,
are the parents of a son, Robert Michael, whom they often
affectionately call Bobzilla, Scourge of the Midwest.

Cadigan's short fiction has appeared in *Omni, Asimov's, Fantasy & Science Fiction, Wild Cards, Light Years
and Dark, Twilight Zone, Tropical Chill, Mirrorshades:
The Cyberpunk Anthology*, and a number of best-of-the-
year collections. Her story "Pretty Boy Crossover" was a
finalist for the 1986 Nebula. Her first novel, *Mindplayers*,
vied for the Philip K. Dick Award in 1987, and her second,
Synners, will appear sometime in 1989. All Cadigan's work
is typified by a hard-bitten but evocative prose, an understanding of the bleaker side of the human psyche, and a
wistful, undergirding compassion that never degenerates
into the maudlin.

She calls her short-story finalist "Angel" a "departure":
"I seldom write about aliens, probably because I don't really
believe in them. I don't *disbelieve* in them, I'm just agnos-
tic. However, if we ever do have even the most glancing
contact with aliens, will the contact itself be so alien that
we don't recognize it for what it is? Maybe Kurt Vonnegut
was onto something and the Great Wall of China means,
'Hang on, message coming.' Or not. As one of Arthur C.
Clarke's aliens says, SF would have us believe that our
planet is the crossroads of the galaxy.

"Maybe the only people in on it would be those who
are aliens in their own land, as it were. The native alien in
'Angel' is extreme, but not impossible and not unheard of.
Nothing is quite so alien to the bell-shaped curve that de-

termines 'normal' in our society as the sexually ambiguous; nothing would be quite so alien to that same bell-shaped curve as mating that does not involve sex (among vertebrates, that is). Not bonding, but mating, with an exchange of materials.

"If you were an alien, where would you go to hide out, and with whom—to a shiny suburb with a grouping acceptable to the cultural mainstream, or to the less desirable part of town, with someone society would just as soon not think about? (Assume you are not ALF.)"

Stand with me awhile, Angel, I said, and Angel said he'd do that. Angel was good to me that way, good to have with you on a cold night and nowhere to go. We stood on the street corner together and watched the cars going by and people and all. The streets were lit up like Christmas: streetlights, store lights, marquees over the all-night movie houses and bookstores blinking and flashing. Shank of the evening in east midtown. Angel was getting used to things here and getting used to how I did, nights. Standing outside, because what else are you going to do. He was my Angel now, had been since that other cold night when I'd been going home, because where are you going to go, and I'd found him and took him with me. It's good to have someone to take with you, someone to look after. Angel knew that. He started looking after me, too.

Like now. We were standing there awhile and I was looking around at nothing and everything, the cars cruising past, some of them stopping now and again for the hookers posing by the curb, and then I saw it, out of the corner of my eye. Stuff coming out of the Angel, shiny like sparks but flowing like liquid. Silver fireworks. I turned and looked all the way at him and it was gone. And he turned and gave a little grin like he was embarrassed I'd seen. Nobody else saw it, though;

not the short guy who paused next to the Angel before crossing the street against the light, not the skinny hype looking to sell the boom-box he was carrying on his shoulder, not the homeboy strutting past us with both his girlfriends on his arms, nobody but me.

The Angel said, Hungry?

Sure, I said. I'm hungry.

Angel looked past me. Okay, he said. I looked, too, and here they came, three leather boys, visor caps, belts, boots, key rings. On the cruise together. Scary stuff, even though you know it's not looking for you.

I said, Them? *Them?*

Angel didn't answer. One went by, then the second, and the Angel stopped the third by taking hold of his arm.

Hi.

The guy nodded. His head was shaved. I could see a little gray-black stubble under his cap. No eyebrows, disinterested eyes. The eyes were because of the Angel.

I could use a little money, the Angel said. My friend and I are hungry.

The guy put his hand in his pocket and wiggled out some bills, offering them to the Angel. The Angel selected a twenty and closed the guy's hand around the rest.

This will be enough, thank you.

The guy put his money away and waited.

I hope you have a good night, said the Angel.

The guy nodded and walked on, going across the street to where his two friends were waiting on the next corner. Nobody found anything weird about it.

Angel was grinning at me. Sometimes he was *the* Angel, when he was doing something, sometimes he was Angel, when he was just with me. Now he was Angel again. We went up the street to the luncheonette and got a seat by the front window so we could still watch the street while we ate.

Cheeseburger and fries, I said without bothering to look

at the plastic-covered menus lying on top of the napkin holder. The Angel nodded.

Thought so, he said. I'll have the same, then.

The waitress came over with a little tiny pad to take our order. I cleared my throat. It seemed like I hadn't used my voice in a hundred years. "Two cheeseburgers and two fries," I said, "and two cups of—" I looked up at her and froze. She had no face. Like, *nothing*, blank from hairline to chin, soft little dents where the eyes and nose and mouth would have been. Under the table, the Angel kicked me, but gentle.

"And two cups of coffee," I said.

She didn't say anything—how could she?—as she wrote down the order and then walked away again. All shaken up, I looked at the Angel but he was calm like always.

She's a new arrival, Angel told me and leaned back in his chair. Not enough time to grow a face.

But how can she breathe? I said.

Through her pores. She doesn't need much air yet.

Yah, but what about—like, I mean, don't other people *notice* that's she's got nothing there?

No. It's not such an extraordinary condition. The only reason you notice is because you're with me. Certain things have rubbed off on you. But no one else notices. When they look at her, they see whatever face they expect someone like her to have. And eventually, she'll have it.

But you have a face, I said. You've always had a face.

I'm different, said the Angel.

You sure are, I thought, looking at him. Angel had a beautiful face. That wasn't why I took him home that night, just because he had a beautiful face—I left all that behind a long time ago—but it was there, his beauty. The way you think of a man being beautiful: good clean lines, deep-set eyes, ageless. About the only way you could describe him—look away and you'd forget everything except that he was beautiful. But he did have a face. He *did*.

Angel shifted in the chair—these were like somebody's old kitchen chairs, you couldn't get too comfortable in them—and shook his head, because he knew I was thinking troubled thoughts. Sometimes you could think something and it wouldn't be troubled and later you'd think the same thing and it would be troubled. The Angel didn't like me to be troubled about him.

Do you have a cigarette? he asked.

I think so.

I patted my jacket and came up with most of a pack that I handed over to him. The Angel lit up and amused us both by having the smoke come out his ears and trickle out of his eyes like ghostly tears. I felt my own eyes watering for his; I wiped them and there was that *stuff* again, but from me now. I was crying silver fireworks. I flicked them on the table and watched them puff out and vanish.

Does this mean I'm getting to *be* you, now? I asked.

Angel shook his head. Smoke wafted out of his hair. Just things rubbing off on you. Because we've been together and you're—susceptible. But they're different for you.

Then the waitress brought our food and we went on to another sequence, as the Angel would say. She still had no face, but I guess she could see well enough because she put all the plates down just where you'd think they were supposed to go and left the tiny little check in the middle of the table.

Is she—I mean, did you know her, from where you—

Angel gave his head a brief little shake. No. She's from somewhere else. Not one of my—people. He pushed the cheeseburger and fries in front of him over to my side of the table. That was the way it was done; I did all the eating and somehow it worked out.

I picked up my cheeseburger and I was bringing it up to my mouth when my eyes got all funny and I saw it coming up like a whole *series* of cheeseburgers, whoom-whoom-whoom, trick photography, only for real. I closed my eyes and jammed the cheeseburger into my mouth, holding it there, waiting for all the other cheeseburgers to catch up with it.

You'll be okay, said the Angel. Steady, now.

I said with my mouth full, That was—that was *weird.* Will I ever get used to this?

I doubt it. But I'll do what I can to help you.

Yah, well, the Angel *would* know. Stuff rubbing off on me, he could feel it better than I could. He was the one it was rubbing off *from.*

I had put away my cheeseburger and half of Angel's and was working on the french fries for both of us when I noticed he was looking out the window with this hard, tight expression on his face.

Something? I asked him.

Keep eating, he said.

I kept eating but I kept watching, too. The Angel was staring at a big blue car parked at the curb right outside the diner. It was silvery blue, one of those lots-of-money models, and there was a woman kind of leaning across from the driver's side to look out the passenger window. She was beautiful in that lots-of-money way, tawny hair swept back from her face and even from here I could see she had turquoise eyes. Really beautiful woman. I almost felt like crying. I mean, jeez, how did people get that way and me too harmless to live.

But the Angel wasn't one bit glad to see her. I knew he didn't want me to say anything, but I couldn't help it.

Who is she?

Keep eating, Angel said. We need the protein, what little there is.

I ate and watched the woman and the Angel watch each other and it was getting very—I don't know, very *something* between them, even through the glass. Then a cop car pulled up next to her and I knew they were telling her to move it along. She moved it along.

Angel sagged against the back of his chair and lit another cigarette, smoking it in the regular, unremarkable way.

What are we going to do tonight? I asked the Angel as we left the restaurant.

Keep out of harm's way, Angel said, which was a new answer. Most nights we spent just kind of going around soaking everything up. The Angel soaked it up, mostly. I got some of it along with him, but not the same way he did. It was different for him. Sometimes he would use me like a kind of filter. Other times he took it direct. There'd been the big car accident one night, right at my usual corner, a big old Buick running a red light smack into somebody's nice Lincoln. The Angel had had to take it direct because I couldn't handle that kind of stuff. I didn't know how the Angel could take it but he could. It carried him for days afterward, too. I only had to eat for myself.

It's the intensity, little friend, he'd told me, as though that was supposed to explain it.

It's the intensity, not whether it's good or bad. The universe doesn't know good or bad, only less or more. Most of you have a bad time reconciling this. *You* have a bad time with it, little friend, but you get through better than other people. Maybe because of the way you are. You got squeezed out of a lot, you haven't had much of a chance at life. You're as much an exile as I am, only in your own land.

That may have been true, but at least I *belonged* here, so that part was easier for me. But I didn't say that to the Angel. I think he liked to think he could do as well or better than me at living—I mean, I couldn't just look at some leather boy and get him to cough up a twenty-dollar bill. Cough up a fist in the face or worse, was more like it.

Tonight, though, he wasn't doing so good and it was that woman in the car. She'd thrown him out of step, kind of.

Don't think about her, the Angel said, just out of nowhere. Don't think about her anymore.

Okay, I said, feeling creepy because it was creepy when the Angel got a glimpse of my head. And then, of course, I couldn't think about anything else hardly.

Do you want to go home? I asked him.

No. I can't stay in now. We'll do the best we can tonight, but I'll have to be very careful about the tricks. They take so much out of me and if we're keeping out of harm's way, I might not be able to make up for a lot of it.

It's okay, I said. I ate. I don't need anything else tonight, you don't have to do any more.

Angel got that look on his face, the one where I knew he wanted to give me things, like feelings I couldn't have any more. Generous, the Angel was. But I didn't need those feelings, not like other people seem to. For a while, it was like the Angel didn't understand that, but he let me be.

Little friend, he said, and almost touched me. The Angel didn't touch a lot. I could touch him and that would be okay but if *he* touched somebody, he couldn't help *doing* something to them, like the trade that had given us the money. That had been deliberate. If the trade had touched the Angel first, it would have been different; nothing would have happened unless the Angel touched him back. All touch meant something to the Angel that I didn't understand. There was touching without touching, too. Like things rubbing off on me. And sometimes, when I did touch the Angel, I'd get the feeling that it was maybe more his idea than mine, but I didn't mind that. How many people were going their whole lives never being able to touch an Angel?

We walked together, and all around us the street was really coming to life. It was getting colder, too. I tried to make my jacket cover more. The Angel wasn't feeling it. Most of the time hot and cold didn't mean much to him. We saw the three rough-trade guys again. The one Angel had gotten the money from was getting into a car. The other two watched it drive away and then walked on. I looked over at the Angel.

Because we took his twenty, I said.

Even if we hadn't, Angel said.

So we went along, the Angel and me, and I could feel how different it was tonight than it was all the other nights we'd walked or stood together. The Angel was kind of pulled back into himself and it seemed to be keeping a check on me, pushing us closer together. I was getting more of those fireworks out of the corners of my eyes, but when I'd turn my head to look, they'd vanish. It reminded me of the night I'd found the Angel standing on my corner all by himself in pain. The Angel told me later that was real talent, knowing he was in pain. I never thought of myself as any too talented, but the way everyone else had been just ignoring him, I guess I must have had something to see him after all.

The Angel stopped us several feet down from an all-night bookstore. Don't look, he said. Watch the traffic or stare at your feet, but don't look or it won't happen.

There wasn't anything to see right then but I didn't look anyway. That was the way it was sometimes, the Angel telling me it made a difference whether I was watching something or not, something about the other people being conscious of me being conscious of them. I didn't understand, but I knew Angel was usually right. So I was watching traffic when the guy came out of the bookstore and got his head punched.

I could almost see it out of the corner of my eye. A lot of movement, arms and legs flying and grunty noises. Other people stopped to look but I kept my eyes on the traffic, some of which was slowing up so they could check out the fight. Next to me, the Angel was stiff all over. Taking it in, what he called the expenditure of emotional kinetic energy. No right, no wrong, little friend, he'd told me. Just energy, like the rest of the universe.

So he took it in and I *felt* him taking it in and while I was feeling it, a kind of silver fog started creeping around my eyeballs and I was in two places at once. I was watching the traffic and I was in the Angel watching the fight and feeling him charge up like a big battery.

It felt like nothing I'd ever felt before. These two guys slugging it out—well, one guy doing all the slugging and the other skittering around trying to get out from under the fists and having his head punched but good and the Angel drinking it like he was sipping at an empty cup and somehow getting it to have something in it after all. Deep inside him, whatever made the Angel go was getting a little stronger.

I kind of swung back and forth between him and me, or swayed might be more like it was. I wondered about it, because the Angel wasn't touching me. I really was getting to *be* him, I thought; Angel picked that up and put the thought away to answer later. It was like I was traveling by the fog, being one of us and then the other, for a long time, it seemed, and then after a while I was more me than him again and some of the fog cleared away.

And there was that car, pointed the other way this time, and the woman was climbing out of it with this big weird smile on her face, as though she'd won something. She waved at the Angel to come to her.

Bang went the connection between us, dead, and the Angel shot past me, running away from the car. I went after him. I caught a glimpse of her jumping back into the car and yanking at the gearshift.

Angel wasn't much of a runner. Something funny about his knees. We'd gone maybe a hundred feet when he started wobbling, and I could hear him pant. He cut across a Park & Lock that was dark and mostly empty. It was back-to-back with some kind of private parking lot, and the fences for each one tried to mark off the same narrow strip of lumpy pavement. They were easy to climb, but Angel was too panicked. He just *went* through them before he even thought about it; I knew that because if he'd been thinking, he'd have wanted to save what he'd just charged up for when he really needed out bad enough.

I had to haul myself over the fences in the usual way, and when he heard me rattling on the saggy chain-link, he stopped and looked back.

Go, I told him. Don't wait on me!

He shook his head sadly. Little friend, I'm a fool. I could stand to learn from you a little more.

Don't stand, run! I got over the fences and caught up with

him. Let's go! I yanked his sleeve as I slogged past, and he
followed at a clumsy trot.

Have to hide somewhere, he said, camouflage ourselves
with people.

I shook my head, thinking we could just run maybe four
more blocks and we'd be at the freeway overpass. Below it
were the butt-ends of old roads closed off when the freeway
had been built. You could hide there the rest of your life and
no one would find you. But Angel made me turn right and
go down a block to this rundown crack-in-the-wall called
Stan's Jigger. I'd never been in there—I'd never made it a
practice to go into bars—but the Angel was pushing too hard
to argue.

Inside it was smelly and dark and not too happy. The
Angel and I went down to the end of the bar and stood under
a blood-red light while he searched his pockets for money.

Enough for one drink apiece, he said.

I don't want anything.

You can have soda or something.

The Angel ordered from the bartender, who was suspicious. This was a place for regulars and nobody else, and
certainly nobody else like me or the Angel. The Angel knew
that even stronger than I did but he just stood and pretended
to sip his drink without looking at me. He was all pulled into
himself and I was hovering around the edges. I knew he was
still pretty panicked and trying to figure out what he could
do next. As close as I was, if he had to get real far away, he
was going to have a problem and so was I. He'd have to tow
me along with him, and that wasn't the most practical thing
to do.

Maybe he was sorry now he'd let me take him home. He'd
been so weak then, and now what with all the filtering and
stuff I'd done for him, he couldn't just cut me off without a
lot of pain.

I was trying to figure out what I could do for him now
when the bartender came back and gave us a look that meant

order or get out and he'd have liked it better if we got out.
So would everyone else there. The few other people standing
at the bar weren't looking at us but they knew right where
we were, like a sore spot. It wasn't hard to figure out what
they thought about us either, maybe because of me or because
of the Angel's beautiful face.

We got to leave, I said to the Angel, but he had it in his
head this was good camouflage. There wasn't enough money
for two more drinks so he smiled at the bartender and slid
his hand across the bar and put it on top of the bartender's.
It was tricky doing it this way; bartenders and waitresses
took more persuading, because it wasn't normal for them just
to give you something.

The bartender looked at the Angel with his eyes half-
closed. He seemed to be thinking it over. But the Angel had
just blown a lot going through the fence instead of climbing
over it and the fear was scuttling his concentration and I just
knew that it wouldn't work. And maybe my knowing that
didn't help either.

The bartender's free hand dipped down below the bar and
came up with a small club. "Faggot!" he roared and caught
Angel just over the ear. Angel slammed into me and we both
crashed to the floor. Plenty of emotional kinetic energy in
here, I thought dimly as the guys standing at the bar fell on
us, and I didn't think anything more as I curled up into a ball
under their fists and boots.

We were lucky they didn't much feel like killing anyone.
Angel went out the door first, and they tossed me out on top
of him. As soon as I landed on him, I knew we were both in
trouble; something was broken inside him. So much for keeping out of harm's way. I rolled off him and lay on the pavement, staring at the sky and trying to catch my breath. There
was blood in my mouth and my nose, and my back was on
fire.

Angel? I said, after a bit.

He didn't answer. I felt my mind get kind of all loose and

runny, like my brains were leaking out my ears. I thought about the trade we'd taken the money from and how I'd been scared of him and his friends and how silly that had been. But then, I was too harmless to live.

The stars were raining silver fireworks down on me. It didn't help.

Angel? I said again.

I rolled over onto my side to reach for him and there she was. The car was parked at the curb and she had Angel under the armpits, dragging him toward the open passenger door. I couldn't tell if he was conscious or not, and that scared me. I sat up.

She paused, still holding the Angel. We looked into each other's eyes and I started to understand.

"Help me get him into the car," she said at last. Her voice sounded hard and flat and unnatural. "Then you can get in too. In the *backseat*."

I was in no shape to take her out. It couldn't have been better for her than if she'd set it up herself. I got up, the pain flaring in me so bad that I almost fell down again, and I took the Angel's ankles. His ankles were so delicate, almost like a woman's, like *hers*. I didn't really help much except to guide his feet in as she sat him on the seat and strapped him in with the shoulder harness. I got in the back as she ran around to the other side of the car, her steps real light and peppy, like she'd found a million dollars lying there on the sidewalk.

We were out on the freeway before the Angel stirred in the shoulder harness. His head lolled from side to side on the back of the seat. I reached up and touched his hair lightly, hoping she couldn't see me do it.

Where are you taking me, the Angel said.

"For a ride," said the woman. "For the moment."

Why does she talk out loud like that? I asked the Angel. Because she knows it bothers me.

"You know I can focus my thoughts better if I say things

out loud," she said. "I'm not just like one of your little push-overs." She glanced at me in the rearview mirror. "Just *what* have you gotten yourself into since you left, darling? Is that a boy or a girl?"

I pretended I didn't care about what she said or that I was too harmless to live or any of that stuff, but the way she said it, she meant it to sting.

Friends can be either, Angel said. It doesn't matter which. Where are you taking us?

Now it was *us.* In spite of everything, I almost could have smiled.

"Us? You mean, you and me? Or are you really referring to your little pet back there?"

My friend and I are together. You and I are *not.*

The way the Angel said it made me think he meant more than not together; like he'd been with her once the way he was with me now. The Angel let me know I was right. Silver fireworks started flowing slowly off his head down the back of the seat, and I knew there was something wrong about it. There was too much all at once.

"Why can't you talk out loud to me, darling?" the woman said with fakey-sounding petulance. "Just say a few words and make me happy. You have a lovely voice when you use it."

That was true, but the Angel never spoke out loud unless he couldn't get out of it, like when he'd ordered from the bartender. Which had probably helped the bartender decide about what he thought we were, but it was useless to think about that.

"All right," said Angel, and I knew the strain was awful for him. "I've said a few words. Are you happy?" He sagged in the shoulder harness.

"Ecstatic. But it won't make me let you go. I'll drop your pet at the nearest hospital and then we'll go home." She glanced at the Angel as she drove. "I've missed you so much. I can't *stand* it without you, without you making things happen. Doing your little miracles. You knew I'd get addicted to it, all the things you could do to people. And then you just took off, I didn't know what had happened to you. And it *hurt.*" Her voice turned kind of pitiful, like a little kid's. "I was in real *pain.* You must have been, too. Weren't you? Well, *weren't you?*"

Yes, the Angel said. I was in pain too.

I remembered him standing on my corner where I'd hung out all that time by myself until he came. Standing there in pain. I didn't know why or from what then; I just took him home, and after a little while the pain went away. When he decided we were together, I guess.

The silvery flow over the back of the car seat thickened. I cupped my hands under it, and it was like my brain was lighting up with pictures. I saw the Angel before he was my Angel in this really nice house, the woman's house, and how she'd take him places, restaurants or stores or parties, thinking at him real hard so that he was all filled up with her and had to do what she wanted him to. Steal sometimes; other times, weird stuff, make people do silly things like suddenly start singing or taking their clothes off. That was mostly at the parties, though she made a waiter she didn't like burn himself with a pot of coffee. She'd get men, too, through the Angel, and they'd think it was the greatest idea in the world to go to bed with her. Then she'd make the Angel show her the others, the ones that had been sent here the way he had for crimes nobody could have understood, like the waitress with no face. She'd look at them, sometimes try to do things to them to make them uncomfortable or unhappy. But mostly she'd just stare.

It wasn't like that in the very beginning, the Angel said weakly, and I knew he was ashamed.

It's okay, I told him. People can be nice at first, I know that. Then they find out about you.

The woman laughed. "You two are *so* sweet and pathetic. Like a couple of little children. I guess that's what you were looking for, wasn't it, darling? Except children can be cruel, too, can't they? So you got this—*creature* for yourself." She looked at me in the rearview mirror again as she slowed down a little, and for a moment I was afraid she'd seen what I was doing with the silvery stuff still pouring out of the Angel. It was starting to slow now. There wasn't much time left. I wanted to scream, but the Angel was calming me for what was coming next. "What happened to you, anyway?"

Tell her, said the Angel. To stall for time, I knew; keep her occupied.

I was born funny, I said. I had both sexes.

"A hermaphrodite!" she exclaimed with real delight.

She loves freaks, the Angel said, but she didn't pay any attention.

There was an operation, but things went wrong. They kept trying to fix it as I got older, but my body didn't have the right kind of chemistry or something. My parents were ashamed. I left after a while.

"You poor thing," she said, not meaning anything like that. "You were *just* what darling here needed, weren't you? Just a little nothing, no demands, no desires. For anything." Her voice got all hard. "They could probably fix you up now, you know."

I don't want it. I left all that behind a long time ago, I don't need it.

"*Just* the sort of little pet that would be perfect for you," she said to the Angel. "Sorry I have to tear you away. But I can't get along without you now. Life is so boring. And empty. And—" She sounded puzzled. "And like there's nothing more to live for since you left me."

That's not me, said the Angel. That's you.

"No, it's a lot of you, too, and you know it. You know you're addictive to human beings, you knew that when you came here—when they *sent* you here. Hey, you, *pet*, do you know what his crime was, why they sent him to this little backwater penal colony of a planet?"

Yeah, I know, I said. I really didn't, but I wasn't going to tell her that.

"What do you think about *that*, little pet neuter?" she said gleefully, hitting the accelerator pedal and speeding up. "What do you think of the crime of refusing to mate?"

The Angel made a sort of an out-loud groan and lunged at the steering wheel. The car swerved wildly and I fell backwards, the silvery stuff from the Angel going all over me. I tried to keep scooping it into my mouth the way I'd been doing, but it was flying all over the place now. I heard the crunch as the tires left the road and went onto the shoulder. Something struck the side of the car, probably the guardrail, and made it fishtail, throwing me down on the floor. Up front the woman was screaming and cursing and the Angel wasn't making a sound, but in my head I could hear him sort of keening. Whatever happened, this would be it. The Angel had told me all that time ago after I'd taken him home that they didn't last long after they got here, the exiles from his world and other worlds. Things tended to *happen* to them, even if they latched on to someone like me or the woman. They'd be in accidents or the people here would kill them. Like antibodies in a human rejecting something or fighting a disease. At least I belonged here, but it looked like I was going to die in a car accident with the Angel and the woman both. I didn't care.

The car swerved back onto the highway for a few seconds and then pitched to the right again. Suddenly there was nothing under us and then we thumped down on something, not road but dirt or grass or something, bombing madly up and down. I pulled myself up on the back of the seat just in time to see the sign coming at us at an angle. The corner of it started to go through the windshield on the woman's side and then all I saw for a long time was the biggest display of silver fireworks ever.

It was hard to be gentle with him. Every move hurt, but I didn't want to leave him sitting in the car next to *her*, even if she was dead. Being in the backseat had kept most of the glass from flying into me, but I was still shaking some out of my hair and the impact hadn't done much for my back.

I laid the Angel out on the lumpy grass a little ways from the car and looked around. We were maybe a hundred yards from the highway, near a road that ran parallel to it. It was dark, but I could still read the sign that had come through the windshield and split the woman's head in half. It said Construction Ahead, Reduce Speed. Far off on the other road, I could see a flashing yellow light, and at first I was afraid it was the police or something, but it stayed where it was and I realized that must be the construction.

"Friend," whispered the Angel, startling me. He'd never spoken aloud to me, not directly.

Don't talk, I said, bending over him, trying to figure out some way I could touch him, just for comfort. There wasn't anything else I could do now.

"I have to," he said, still whispering. "It's almost all gone. Did you get it?"

Mostly, I said. Not all.

"I meant for you to have it."

I know.

"I don't know that it will really do you any good." His breath kind of bubbled in his throat. I could see something wet and shiny on his mouth, but it wasn't silver fireworks. "But it's yours. You can do as you like with it. Live on it the way I did. Get what you need when you need it. But you can live as a human, too. Eat. Work. However, whatever."

I'm not human, I said. I'm not any more human than you, even if I do belong here.

"Yes you are, little friend. I haven't made you any less human," he said, and coughed some. "I'm not sorry I wouldn't mate. I couldn't mate with my own. It was too . . . I don't know . . . too little of me, too much of them—something. I couldn't bond; it would have been nothing but emptiness. The Great Sin: to be unable to give, because the universe knows only less or more, and I insisted that it would be good or bad. So they sent me here. But in the end, you know, they got their way, little friend." I felt his hand on me for a moment before it fell away. "I did it, after all. Even if it wasn't with my own."

The bubbling in his throat stopped. I sat next to him for a while in the dark. Finally I felt it, the Angel stuff. It was kind of fluttery-churny, like too much coffee on an empty stomach. I closed my eyes and lay down on the grass, shivering. Maybe some of it was shock, but I don't think so. The silver fireworks started, in my head this time, and with them came a lot of pictures I couldn't understand. Stuff about the Angel and where he'd come from and the way they mated. It was a lot like how we'd been together, the Angel and me. They looked a lot like us but there were a lot of differences, too, things I couldn't make out. I couldn't make out how they'd sent him here, either—by *light*, in, like, little bundles or something. It didn't make any sense to me, but I guessed an Angel could be light. Silver fireworks.

I must have passed out or something, because when I opened my eyes, it felt like I'd been lying there a long time. It was still dark, though. I sat up and reached for the Angel, thinking I ought to hide his body.

He was gone. There was just a sort of wet sandy patch where he'd been.

I looked at the car and her. All that was still there. Somebody was going to see it soon. I didn't want to be around for that.

Everything still hurt, but I managed to get to the other road and start walking back toward the city. It was like I could *feel* it now, the way the Angel must have, as though it were vibrating like a drum or ringing like a bell with all kinds of stuff, people laughing and crying and loving and hating and being afraid and everything else that happens to people. The stuff that the Angel took in, energy, that I could take in now if I wanted.

And I knew that taking it in that way, it would be bigger than anything all those people had, bigger than anything I could have had if things hadn't gone wrong with me all those years ago.

I wasn't so sure I wanted it. Like the Angel, refusing to mate back where he'd come from. He wouldn't, there, and I couldn't, here. Except now I could do something else.

I wasn't so sure I wanted it. But I didn't think I'd be able to stop it, either, any more than I could stop my heart from beating. Maybe it wasn't really such a good thing or a right thing. But it was like the Angel said: The universe doesn't know good or bad, only less or more.

Yeah. I heard *that*.

I thought about the waitress with no face. I could find them all now, all the ones from the other places, other worlds that sent them away for some kind of alien crimes nobody would have understood. I could find them all. They threw away their outcasts, I'd tell them, but here we *kept* ours. And here's how. Here's how you live in a universe that only knows less or more.

I kept walking toward the city.

Freezeframe

Gregory Benford

Gregory Benford, author of one of my favorite recent SF novels, *Timescape*, a Nebula Award winner in 1980, is working through a long series of connected novels: *In the Ocean of Night, Across the Sea of Suns, Great Sky River,* and *Tides of Light.* In addition, he has recently published a paper on a new model of the galactic center in *Astrophysical Journal*—for, in his first career, Benford is professor of physics at the University of California, Irvine, where he spends most of his time researching turbulent plasmas and astrophysical matters.

George Zebrowksi included Benford's novella "Newton Sleep" in last year's *Nebula Awards* volume. I have selected the much shorter "Freezeframe" (which went largely unnoticed last year by Benford's peers) for a reason not unlike Zebrowksi's when he selected "Newton Sleep"—namely, that Benford always brings a fresh and insightful point of view to topics done to hackneyed death by less intuitively analytical writers.

Notes Benford, the physicist: "My fiction is usually grounded in my experience of the realm of research. . . . But occasionally, I abandon the somewhat austere byways of science and write about more cozy subjects. I have two children, and my wife and I have cocked a wry eyebrow at the way children are reared in California, particularly among fast-lane achievers. So I speculated on how this would eventually work itself out. Would it give us parenting as convenient as those quick-frozen packets you dump into boiling water and—presto—duckling l' orange for two, with wild rice?"

In Benford's witty speculation, maybe so, maybe so.

Well, Jason, it'll take some explaining. Got a minute? Great.

Here's the invitation. It's for the weekend, and it's not just the kid's birthday party, no. You and me, we've been out of touch the last couple years, so let me run through a little flashback, okay?

Teri and me, we're world-gobblers. You've known that since you and me were roomies, right? Remember the time I took a final, went skiing all afternoon, had a heavy date, was back next day for another final—and aced them both? Yeah, you got it, fella, aced the date, too. Those were the days, huh?

Anyway, my Teri's the same—girl's got real fire in her. No Type A or anything, just *alive*. And like sheet lightning in bed.

We grab life with both hands. Always have. If you work in city government, like me, you got to keep ahead of the oppo. Otherwise you see yourself hung out to dry on the six o'clock news and the next day nobody can remember your name.

Goes double for Teri. She's in liability and claims, a real shark reef. Pressureville. So many lawyers around these days, half of them bred in those barracuda farms, those upgraded speed-curricula things. So we've got to watch our ass.

Right, watching Teri's is no trouble, I'll take all I can get. That woman really sends me. We're both in challenging careers, but she finds the time to make my day, every day, get it? Our relationship is stage center with us, even though we're putting in ten-hour days.

That's what started us thinking. We need the time to work on our marriage, really firm it up when the old schedule starts to fray us around the edges. We've been through those stress management retreats, the whole thing, and we *use* it.

So we're happy. But still, about a year ago we started to feel something was *missing*.

Yeah, you got it. The old cliché—a kid. Teri's been hearing the old bio clock tick off the years. We got the condo, two sharp cars, time-share in Maui, portfolio thick as your wrist—but it's not enough.

Teri brought it up carefully, not sure I'd like the idea of sharing all this wonderful bounty with a cranky little brat. I heard her through, real quality listening, and just between you and me, old buddy, I didn't zoom in on the idea right away.

I mean, we're fast-lane folks. Teri's happy poring over legal programs, looking for a precedent-busting angle, zipping off to an amped workout at the gym, and then catching one of those black-and-white foreign films with the hard-to-read subtitles. Not much room in her schedule to pencil in a feeding or the mumps. I had real trouble conceptualizing how she—much less *I*—could cope.

But she *wanted* this, I could tell from the soft, watery look her eyes get. She's a real woman, y'know?

But the flip side was, no way she'd go for months of waddling around looking and feeling like a cow. Getting behind in her briefs because of morning sickness? Taking time off for the whole number? Not Teri's kind of thing.

What? Oh, sure, adoption.

Well, we did the research on that.

Let me put it this way. We both think the other's pretty damn special. Unique. And our feeling was, why raise a kid that's running on somebody else's genetic program? We're talented people, great bodies, not too hard on the eyes—why not give our kids those advantages?

You got to look at it from his point of view. He should have parents who provide the very best in everything, including genes. So he had to be ours—all ours.

So you can see our problem. Balancing the trade-offs, and nothing looks like a winner. We'd hit a roadblock.

That's where my contacts came in handy. Guy at work told me about this company, GeneInc.

The corporation was looking for a franchise backer, and the city was getting involved because of all the legal hassles. Red tape had to be cut with the AMA, the local hospitals, the usual stuff. No big deal, just takes time.

I did a little angling on the variances they needed, and in return they were real nice. We got invited to a few great parties up in the hills. Glitzy affairs, some big media people flown in to spice things up. And that's when we got the word.

Their secret is, they speed up the whole thing. It's entirely natural, no funny chemicals or anything. Purely electrical and a little hormone tinkering, straight goods.

What they do is, they take a little genetic material from Teri and me, they put it in a blender or something, they mix it and match it and batch it. There's this thing called inculcated growth pattern. Just jargon to me, but what it means is, they can *tune* the process, see. Nature does it slow and easy, but GeneInc can put the pedal to the metal. Go through the prelim stages, all in the lab.

Yeah, you got it fella, you can't see Teri pushing around a basketball belly, can you? That's why it's like GeneInc was tight-wrapped for lives like ours—lives on the go.

So she goes in one Friday, right after a big staff meeting, and with me holding her hand she has the implantation. She overnights in the clinic, watching a first-run movie. Next day she's home. We have dinner at that great new restaurant, T. S. Eliot's, you really got to try the blackened redfish there, and all she's got to do is take these pills every four hours.

Three weeks like that, she's growing by the minute. Eats like a horse. I tell you, we had a running tab at every pasta joint within five blocks of the apartment.

She's into the clinic every forty-eight hours for the treatments, smooth as a press release. Teri's clicking right along, the kid's growing ten times the normal rate.

Before I can get around to buying cigars, zip, here's a seven-pound wonder. Great little guy. Perfect—my eyes, her smile, wants to eat everything in sight. Grabs for the milk supply like a real ladies' man.

And no effects from the GeneInc speedup, not a square inch less than A-max quality. You hear all kinds of scare talk about gene-diddling, how you might end up with a kid from Zit City. Well, the Chicken Littles were wrong-o, in spades.

We figure we'd handle things from there. Maybe send out the diapers, hire a live-in if we could find a nice quiet illegal— Teri could handle the Spanish.

We had the right vector, but we were a tad short on follow-through. Teri started getting cluster headaches. Big ones, in technicolor.

So I filled in for her. Read some books on fathering, really got into it. And I'm telling you, it jigsawed my days beyond belief.

Face it, we had high-impact lives. I gave up my daily racquetball match—and you know how much of a sacrifice that was for a diehard jock like me, high school football and all. But I did it for the kid.

Next, Teri had to drop out of her extra course in fast-lane brokering, too, which was a real trauma. I mean, we'd practically spent the projected income from that training. Factored it into our estimated taxes, even. I'd already sunk some extra cash into a honey of a limited partnership. It had some sweetheart underwriting features and we just couldn't resist it.

Man, crisis time. If she didn't get her broker's license on schedule, we'd be stretched so thin you could see through us.

She couldn't link into the course on home computer, either. Software mismatch or something, and by the time she got it down-wired she was too far behind in the course.

See what I mean? Bleaksville.

But we were committed parents. We believe in total frankness, up-front living.

So we went back to GeneInc and had a talk with one of their counselors. Wonderful woman. She takes us into a beautiful room—soft lighting, quality leather couch, and some of that classy baroque trumpet music in the background. Just the right touch. Tasteful. Reassuring.

She listens to us and nods a lot and knows just what we're talking about. We trust her, almost like it was therapy. Which I guess it was.

And we let it all spill. The irritations. Man, I never knew a little package could scream so much. Feeding. No grandparents closer than three thousand miles, and they're keeping their distance. Got their retirement condo, walls all around it, a rule that you can't bring a kid in for longer than twenty-four hours. Not exactly Norman Rockwell, huh? So no quick fix there.

And the kid, he's always awake and wanting to play just when we're stumbling home, zombies. So you cram things in. We had trouble synching our schedules. Lost touch with friends *and* business contacts.

See, I spend a lot of time on the horn, keeping up with people I know I'll need sometime. Or just feeling out the gossip shops for what's hot. Can't do that with a squall-bomb on my knee.

Teri had it even worse. She'd bought all the traditional mother package and was trying to pack that into her own flat-out style. Doesn't work.

Now, the usual way to handle this would be for somebody to lose big, right?

Teri drops back and punts, maybe. Stops humping so hard, lets up. So maybe a year downstream, some younger, beady-eyed type shoulders her aside. She ends up targeted on perpetual middle-management. The desert. Oblivion. Perpetual Poughkeepsie.

Or else I lower *my* revs. Shy off the background briefings, drop off the party committee, don't sniff around for possible corners to get tight with. You know how it is.

What? No, ol' buddy, you're dead on—not my scene.

But listen, my real concern wasn't my job, it was our relationship. We really work at it. Total communication takes time. We really get into each other. That's just us.

So the lady at GeneInc listens, nods, and introduces us

to their top-drawer product line. Exclusive. *Very* high tech. It blew us away.

Freezeframe, they call it.

Look, the kid's going to be sleeping ten, twelve hours a day anyway, right? GeneInc just packs all that time into our workweek. Rearranges the kid's schedule, is basically what it is.

Simple electronic stimulus to the lower centers. Basic stuff, they told me; can't damage anything. And totally under our control.

When we want him, the kid's on call. Boost his voltage, allow some warm-up . . .

Sure, Jason. See, he's running at low temperature during the workday. Helps the process. So we come dragging home, have some Chardonnay to unwind, catch the news. When we're ready for him we hit a few buttons, warm him up, and there he is, bright and agreeable 'cause he had a ton of extra sack time. Can't get tired and pesky.

I mean, the kid's at his best and we're at peak too. Relaxed, ready for some A-plus parenting.

Well, we took the Zen pause on the idea, sure. Thought it over. Teri talked it out with her analyst. Worked on the problem, got her doubts under control.

And we went for it. Little shakedown trouble, but nothing big. GeneInc, they've got a fix for everything.

We boost him up for weekends, when we've got space. Quality time, that's what the kid gets. We've set up a regular schedule. Weekdays for us, weeknights and weekends for him.

Now GeneInc's got an add-on you wouldn't believe: Downtime Education, they call it. While he's sleeping through our days, Downtime Ed brings him up to speed on verbals, math, sensory holism, the works. Better than a real teacher, in many ways.

So we feel that—oh yeah, the invitation.

It's for his big blast. Combo first birthday party and graduation from third grade. We put him on the inside track, and he's burning it up. We couldn't be happier. Our kind of kid, for sure.

Pretty soon we'll integrate him into the GeneInc school for accelerated cases, others like him. There's a whole community of these great kids springing up, y'know. They're either in Downtime, learning up a storm, or getting on-line, first-class attention in Freezeframe weekends.

I tell you, Jason, these kids are going to be the best. They'll slice and dice any Normkid competition they run into.

And us—it's like a new beginning. We get to have it all *and* we know the kid's not suffering. He'll have a high school diploma by the time he's ten. He'll be a savvy littly guy. And we'll load on all the extras, too. Emotional support, travel, the works.

We'll have him on tap when we want him. That'll stretch out his physical childhood, of course, but speed up his mental growth. Better all around, really, 'cause Teri and I totally like him.

See, we want to spread him over more of our lives, keep him for maybe thirty years. Why not have one really top-of-the-line kid, enjoy him most of your life? Efficient.

So look, I got to trot. Map's on the back of the invitation, come and enjoy. No need for a present unless you want to. Teri'll love seeing you again.

And while you're there, I can show you the GeneInc equipment. Beautiful gear, sharp lines. Brochures, too. I've got a kind of little franchise agreement with them, getting in on the ground floor of this thing.

What? Well, that's not the way I'd put it, Jason. This is a class product line.

Calling it a Tupperware party—hey, that's way out of line. We're talking quality here.

You'll see. Just drop on by. No obligation. Oh, yeah, and I got some great Cabernet you should try, something I picked up on the wine futures market.

My God, look at the time. See you, ol' buddy.

Have a nice day.

The Blind Geometer

Kim Stanley Robinson

Kim Stanley Robinson's first professional short-story sale
—barring an earlier one about which I may be ignorant—
was to Damon Knight's *Orbit 18*, which appeared in 1976.
In the years since then, he has established himself as one
of the most original and literate voices in contemporary SF.
His novels include *The Wild Shore, Icehenge, The Memory
of Whiteness,* and *The Gold Coast,* while his short fiction
comprises such admirably diverse titles as "Black Air,"
"The Lucky Strike," "Green Mars" (recently paired in a Tor
hardcover with a long story by Arthur C. Clarke), and two
comic novellas set in the Himalayas. His collection *The
Planet on the Table* gathers eight of his stories and provides
a good overview of his concerns and approaches.

Although he has several previous nominations to his
credit (and although "Black Air" earned him a World Fantasy Award), "The Blind Geometer" marks Robinson's first
Nebula Award.

About his award-winning novella—a more accessible
study of how blindness must feel *from the inside* than James
Dickey's demanding novel *Alnilam*—Robinson wants to
say nothing, preferring to allow the work to speak for itself.
However, he thanks Jim Gammon and Ward Newmeyer for
lessons about blindness and the disabled; Carter Scholz for
introducing him to modern music; Ernest Bramah and
T. D. Cutsforth "for their writing about blindness"; and
Patrick Ledden "for his geometry classes at UCSD."

"The Blind Geometer" first appeared in 1986 in a lovely
limited edition from Cheap Street. *Isaac Asimov's Science
Fiction Magazine* reprinted it, slightly revised, in 1987.

When you are born blind, your development is different from that of sighted infants. (I was born blind. I know.) The reasons for this difference are fairly obvious. Much normal early infant development, both physical and mental, is linked to vision, which coordinates all sense and action. Without vision, reality is . . . (it's hard to describe) a sort of void, in which transitory things come to existence when grasped and mouthed and heard; then, when the things fall silent or are dropped, they melt away, they *cease to exist*. (I wonder if I have not kept a bit of that feeling with me always.) It can be shown that this sense of object permanence must be learned by sighted infants as well—move a toy behind a screen, and very young babies will assume the toy has ceased to exist—but vision (seeing part of a toy [or a person] behind the screen) makes their construction of a sense of object permanence fairly rapid and easy. With the blind child, it is a much harder task; it takes months, sometimes years. And with no sense of an object world, there can be no complementary concept of *self*; without this concept, all phenomena can be experienced as part of an extended "body." (Haptic space [or tactile space, the space of the body] expanding to fill visual space . . .) Every blind infant is in danger of autism.

> But we also have, and know that we have, the capacity
> of complete freedom to transform, in thought and phantasy,
> our human historical existence. . . .
> Edmund Husserl, *The Origin of Geometry*

My first memories are of the Christmas morning when I was some three and a half years old, when one of my gifts was a bag of marbles. I was fascinated by the way the handfuls of marbles felt: heavy, glassy spheres, all so smooth and clickety, all so much the same. . . . I was equally impressed by the leather bag that had contained them. It was so pliable, had such a baggy shape, could be drawn up by such a leathery drawstring. (I must tell you, from the viewpoint of tactual aesthetics, there is nothing quite so beautiful as well-oiled leather. My favorite toy was my father's boot). Anyway, I was rolling on my belly over the marbles spread on the floor (more contact) when I came against the Christmas tree, all prickly and piney. Reaching up to break off some needles to rub between my fingers, I touched an ornament that felt to me, in my excitement, like a lost marble. I yanked on it (and on the branch, no doubt) and—down came the tree.

The alarum afterward is only a blur in my memory, as if it all were on tape, and parts of it forever fast-forwarded to squeaks and trills. Little unspliced snippets of tape: my memory. (My story.)

How often have I searched for snippets before that one, from the long years of my coming to consciousness? How did I first discover the world beyond my body, beyond my searching hands? It was one of my greatest intellectual feats—perhaps the greatest—and yet it is lost to me.

So I read, and learn how other blind infants have accomplished the task. My own life, known to me through words —the world become a text—this happens to me all the time. It is what T. D. Cutsforth called entering the world of "verbal unreality," and it is part of the fate of the curious blind person.

I never did like Jeremy Blasingame. He was a colleague for a few years, and his office was six doors down from mine. It seemed to me that he was one of those people who are fundamentally uncomfortable around the blind; and it's always the blind person's job to put these people at their ease, which gets to be a pain in the ass. (In fact, I usually ignore the problem.) Jeremy always watched me closely (you can tell this by voice), and it was clear that he found it hard to believe that I was one of the co-editors of *Topological Geometry*, a journal he submitted to occasionally. But he was a good mathematician and a fair topologist, and we published most of his submissions, so that he and I remained superficially friendly.

Still, he was always probing, always picking my brains. At this time I was working hard on the geometry of n-dimensional manifolds, and some of the latest results from CERN and SLAC and the big new cyclotron on Oahu were fitting into the work in an interesting way: It appeared that certain subatomic particles were moving as if in a multidimensional manifold, and I had Sullivan and Wu and some of the other physicists from these places asking me questions. With them I was happy to talk, but with Jeremy I couldn't see the point. Certain speculations I once made in conversation with him later showed up in one of his papers, and it just seemed to me that he was looking for help without actually saying so.

And there was the matter of his image. In the sun I perceived him as a shifting, flecked brightness. It's unusual I can see people at all, and as I couldn't really account for this (was it vision, or something else?) it made me uncomfortable.

But no doubt in retrospect I have somewhat exaggerated this uneasiness.

The first event of my life that I recall that has any emotion attached to it (the earlier ones being mere snips of tape that could have come from anyone's life, given how much feeling is associated with them) comes from my eighth year, and has to do, emblematically enough, with math. I was adding columns with my Braille punch, and, excited at my new power, I took the bumpy sheet of figures to show my father. He puzzled over it for a while. "Hmm," he said. "Here, you have to make very sure that the columns are in straight, vertical rows." His long fingers guided mine down a column. "Twenty-two is off to the left, feel that? You have to keep them all straight."

Impatiently I pulled my hand away, and the flood of frustration began its tidal wash through me (most familiar of sensations, felt scores of times a day); my voice tightened to a high whine: "But *why?* It doesn't *matter—*"

"Yeah it does." My father wasn't one for unnecessary neatness, as I already knew well from tripping over his misplaced briefcase, ice skates, shoes. . . . "Let's see." He had my fingers again. "You know how numbers work. Here's twenty-two. Now what that means is two twos and two tens. This two marks the twenty, this two marks the two, even though they're both just two characters, right? Well, when you're adding, the column to the far right is the column of ones. Next over is the column of tens, and next over is the column of hundreds. Here you've got three hundreds, right? Now if you have the twenty-two over to the left too far, you'll add the twenty in the hundreds column, as if the number were two hundred twenty rather than twenty-two. And that'll be wrong. So you have to keep the columns really straight—"

Understanding, ringing me as if I were a big old church bell, and it the clapper. It's the first time I remember feeling that sensation that has remained one of the enduring joys of my life: *to understand.*

And understanding mathematical concepts quickly led to power (and how I craved that!), power not only in the abstract world of math, but in the real world of father and school. I remember jumping up and down, my dad laughing cheerily, me dashing to my room to stamp out columns as straight as the ruler's edge, to add column after column of figures.

Oh, yes: Carlos Oleg Nevsky, here. Mother Mexican, father Russian (military advisor). Born in Mexico City in 2018, three months premature, after my mother suffered a bout of German measles during the pregnancy. Result: almost total blindness (I can tell dark from [bright] light). Lived in Mexico City until father was transferred to Soviet embassy in Washington, D.C., when I was five. Lived in Washington almost continuously since then; my parents divorced when I was fifteen. Mathematics professor at George Washington University since 2043.

One cold spring afternoon I encountered Jeremy Blasingame in the faculty lounge as I went to get a coffee refill—in the lounge, where nobody ever hangs out. "Hello, Carlos, how's it going?"

"Fine," I said, reaching about the table for the sugar. "And you?"

"Pretty good. I've got a kind of an interesting problem over at my consulting job, though. It's giving me fits."

Jeremy worked for the Pentagon in military intelligence or something, but he seldom talked about what he did there, and I certainly never asked. "Oh, yes?" I said, as I found the sugar and spooned some in.

"Yes. They've got a coding problem that I bet would interest you."

"I'm not much for cryptography." Spy games—the math involved is really very limited. Sweet smell of sugar, dissolving in the lounge's bad coffee.

"Yes, I know," Jeremy said. "But"—an edge of frustration in his voice; it's hard to tell when I'm paying attention, I know (a form of control)—"but this may be a geometer's code. We have a subject, you see, drawing diagrams."

A *subject*. "Hmph," I said. Some poor spy scribbling away in a cell somewhere . . .

"So—I've got one of the drawings here. It reminds me of the theorem in your last article. Some projection, perhaps."

"Yes?" Now what spy would draw something like that?

"Yeah, and it seems to have something to do with her speech, too. Her verbal sequencing is all dislocated—words in strange order, sometimes."

"Yes? What happened to her?"

"Well . . . here, check out the drawing."

I put out a hand. "I'll take a look."

"And next time you want coffee, come ask me. I do a proper job of it in my office."

"All right."

I suppose I have wondered all my life what it would be like to see. And all my work, no doubt, is an effort to envision things in the inward theater. "I see it *feelingly*." In language, in music, most of all in the laws of geometry, I find the best ways I can to see: by analogy to touch, and to sound, and to abstractions. Understand: To know the geometries fully is to comprehend exactly the physical world that light reveals; in a way one is then perceiving something like the Platonic ideal forms underlying the visible phenomena of the world. Sometime the great ringing of comprehension fills me so entirely that I feel I *must* be seeing; what more could it be? I believe that I see.

Then comes the problem of crossing the street, of finding my misplaced keys. Geometry is little help; it's back to the hands and ears as eyes, at that point. And then I know that I do not see at all.

Let me put it another way. Projective geometry began in the Renaissance, as an aid to painters newly interested in perspective, in the problems of representing the three-dimensional world on a canvas; it quickly became a mathematics of great power and elegance. The basic procedure can be described quickly: When a geometrical figure is *projected* from one plane to another (as light, they tell me, projects the image on a slide onto a wall), certain properties of the figure are changed (lengths of sides, measures of angles), while other properties are not—points are still points, lines lines, and certain proportions still hold, among other things.

Now imagine that the visual world is a geometrical figure, which in a way it is. But then imagine that it has been projected inward onto something different, not onto a plane, but onto a Möbius strip or a Klein bottle, say, or onto a manifold actually much more complex and strange than those (you'd be surprised). Certain features of the figure are gone for good (color, for instance), but other essential features remain. And projective geometry is the art of finding what features or qualities survive the transformations of projection. . . .

Do you understand me?

A geometry for the self—non-Euclidean, of course; in fact, strictly Nevskyan, as it has to be to help me, as I make my projections from visual space to auditive space, to haptic space.

The next time I met Blasingame he was anxious to hear what I thought of his diagram. (There could be an acoustics of emotion—thus a mathematics of emotion; meanwhile, the ears of the blind do these calculations every day.)

"One drawing isn't much to go on, Jeremy. I mean, you're right, it looks like a simple projective drawing, but with some odd lines crossing it. Who knows what they mean? The whole thing might be something scribbled by a kid."

"She's not that young. Want to see more?"

"Well . . ." This woman he kept mentioning, some sort of Mata Hari prisoner in the Pentagon, drawing geometrical figures and refusing to speak except in riddles . . . naturally I was intrigued.

"Here, take these anyway. There seems to be a sort of progression."

"It would help if I could talk to this *subject* who's doing all these."

"Actually, I don't think so . . . but"—seeing my irritation—"I can bring her by, I think, if these interest you."

"I'll check them out."

"Good, good." Peculiar edge of excitement in his voice, tension, anticipation of . . . Frowning, I took the papers from him.

That afternoon I shuffled them into my special Xerox machine, and the stiff reproductions rolled out of it heavily ridged. I ran my hands over the raised lines and letters slowly.

Here I must confess to you that most geometrical drawings are almost useless to me. If you consider it, you will quickly see why: Most drawings are two-dimensional representations of what a three-dimensional construction *looks* like. This does me no good and in fact is extremely confusing. Say I feel a trapezoid on the page; is that meant to be a trapezoid, or is it rather a representation of a rectangle not coterminous with the page it lies on? Or the conventional representation of a plane? Only a *description* of the drawing will tell me that. Without a description I can only deduce what the figure *appears* to mean. Much easier to have 3-D models to explore with my hands.

But in this case, not possible. So I swept over the mishmash of ridges with both hands, redrew it with my ridging pen several times over, located the two triangles in it, and the lines connecting the two triangles' corners, and the lines made by extending the triangles' sides in one direction. I tried to make from my Taylor collection a 3-D model that accounted for the drawing—try that sometime, and understand how difficult this kind of intellectual feat can be! Projective imagination . . .

Certainly it seemed to be a rough sketch of Desargues' theorem.

Desargues' theorem was one of the first theorems clearly concerned with projective geometry; it was proposed by Girard Desargues in the mid-seventeenth century, in between his architectural and engineering efforts, his books on music, etc. It is a relatively simple theorem, showing that two triangles that are projections of each other generate a group of points off to one side that lie on a single line. Its chief interest is in showing the kind of elegant connections that projection so often creates.

(It is also true that this theorem is reciprocal; that is, if you postulate two triangles whose extensions of the sides meet at three collinear points, then it is possible to show that the triangles are projections of each other. As they say in the textbooks, I leave the proof of this as an exercise for the reader.)

But so what? I mean, it is a beautiful theorem, with the sort of purity characteristic of Renaissance math—but what was it doing in a drawing made by some poor prisoner of the Pentagon?

I considered this as I walked to my health club, Warren's Spa (considered it secondarily, anyway, and no doubt subconsciously; my primary concerns were the streets and the traffic. Washington's streets bear a certain resemblance to one of those confusing geometrical diagrams I described [the state streets crossing diagonally the regular gridwork, creating a variety of intersections]; happily, one doesn't have to comprehend all the city at once to walk in it. But it is easy to become lost. So as I walked I concentrated on distances, on the sounds of the streets that tended to remain constant, on smells [the dirt of the park at M and New Hampshire, the hot dog vendor on 21st and K]; meanwhile, my cane established the world directly before my feet, my sonar shades whistled rising or falling notes as objects approached or receded. . . . It takes some work just to get from point A to point B without getting disoriented [at which point one has to grind one's teeth and ask for directions] but it can be done, it is one of those small tasks/accomplishments [one chooses which, every time] that the blind cannot escape)—still, I did consider the matter of the drawing as I walked.

On 21st and H, I was pleased to smell the pretzel cart of my friend Ramon, who is also blind. His cart is the only one where the hot plate hasn't roasted several pretzels to that metallic burnt odor that all the other carts put off; Ramon prefers the clean smell of freshly baked dough, and he claims it brings him more customers, which I certainly believe. "Change only, please," he was saying to someone briskly, "there's a change machine on the other side of the cart for your convenience, thanks. Hot pretzels! Hot pretzels, one dollar!"

"Hey there, Superblink!" I called as I approached him.

"Hey yourself, Professor Superblink," he replied. (*Superblink* is a mildly derogatory name used by irritated sighted social service people to describe those of their blind colleagues who are aggressively or ostentatiously competent in getting around, etc., who make a *display* of their competence. Naturally, we have appropriated the term for our own use; sometimes it means the same thing for us—when used in the third person, usually—but in the second person, it's a term of affection.) "Want a pretzel?"

"Sure."

"You off to the gym?"

"Yeah, I'm going to throw. Next time we play you're in trouble."

"That'll be the day, when my main mark starts beating me!"

I put four quarters in his callused hand, and he gave me a pretzel. "Here's a puzzle for you," I said. "Why would someone try to convey a message by geometrical diagram?"

He laughed. "Don't ask me, that's your department!"

"But the message isn't for me."

"Are you sure about that?"

I frowned.

At the health club I greeted Warren and Amanda at the front desk. They were laughing over a headline in the tabloid newspaper Amanda was shaking; they devoured those things and pasted the best headlines all over the gym.

"What's the gem of the day?" I asked.

"How about 'Gay Bigfoot Molests Young Boys'?" Warren suggested.

"Or 'Woman Found Guilty of Turning Husband into Bank President,' " Amanda said, giggling. "She drugged him and did 'bemod' to him until he went from teller to president."

Warren said, "I'll have to do that for you, eh, Amanda?"

"Make me something better than a bank president."

Warren clicked his tongue. "Entirely too many designer drugs, these days. Come on, Carlos, I'll get the range turned on." I went to the locker room and changed, and when I got to the target room Warren was just done setting it up. "Ready to go," he said cheerily as he rolled past me.

I stepped in, closed the door, and walked out to the center of the room, where a waist-high wire column was filled with baseballs. I pulled out a baseball, hefted it, felt the stitching. A baseball is a beautiful object: nicely flared curves of the seams over the surface of a perfect sphere, exactly the right weight for throwing.

I turned on the range with a flick of a switch and stepped away from the feeder, a ball in each hand. Now it was quite silent, only the slightest whirr faintly breathing through the soundproofed walls. I did what I could to reduce the sound of my own breathing, heard my heartbeat in my ears.

Then a *beep* behind me to my left, and low; I whirled and threw. Dull thud. "Right . . . low," said the machine voice from above, softly. *Beep*—I threw again: "Right . . . high," it said louder, meaning I had missed by more. "Shit," I said as I got another two balls. "Bad start."

Beep—a hard throw to my left—*clang!* "Yeah!" There is very little in life more satisfying than the bell-like clanging of the target circle when hit square. It rings at about middle C with several overtones, like a small, thick church bell hit with a hammer. The sound of success.

Seven more throws, four more hits. "Five for ten," the machine voice said. "Average strike time, one point three five seconds. Fastest strike time, point eight four seconds."

Ramon sometimes hit the target in half a second or less, but I needed to hear the full beep to keep my average up. I set up for another round, pushed the button, got quiet; *beep* throw, *beep* throw, working to shift my feet faster, to follow through, to use the information from my misses to correct for the next time the target was near the floor, or the ceiling, or behind me (my weakness is the low ones; I can't seem to throw down accurately). And as I warmed up I threw harder and harder . . . just throwing a baseball as hard as you can is a joy in itself. And then to set that bell ringing! *Clang!* It chimes every cell of you.

But when I quit and took a shower, and stood before my locker and reached in to free my shirt from a snag on the top of the door, my fingers brushed a small metal wire stuck to an upper inside corner, where the door would usually conceal it from both me and my sighted companions; it came away when I pulled on it. Fingering the short length I couldn't be certain what it was, but I had my suspicions, so I took it to my friend James Gold, who works in acoustics in the engineering department, and had him take a confidential look at it.

"It's a little remote microphone, all right," he said, and then joked, "Who's bugging you, Carlos?"

He got serious when I asked him where I could get a system like that for myself.

John Metcalf — "Blind Jack of Knaresborough" — (1717–1810). At six he lost his sight through smallpox, at nine he could get on pretty well unaided, at fourteen he announced his intention of disregarding his affliction thenceforward and of behaving in every respect as a normal human being. It is true that immediately on this brave resolve he fell into a gravel pit and received a serious hurt while escaping, under pursuit, from an orchard he was robbing . . . fortunately this did not affect his self-reliance. At twenty he had made a reputation as a pugilist.(!)

> Ernest Bramah, Introduction,
> *The Eyes of Max Carrados*

When I was young I loved to read Bramah's stories about Max Carrados, the blind detective. Carrados could hear, smell, and feel with incredible sensitivity, and his ingenious deductions were never short of brilliant; he was fearless in a pinch; also, he was rich and had a mansion, and a secretary, manservant, and chauffeur who acted as his eyes. All great stuff for the imaginative young reader, as certainly I was. I read every book I could get my hands on; the voice of my reading machine was more familiar to me than any human voice that I knew. Between that reading and my mathematical work, I could have easily withdrawn from the world of my own experience into Cutsforth's "verbal unreality," and babbled on like Helen Keller about the shapes of clouds and the colors of flowers and the like. The world become nothing but a series of texts; sounds kind of like deconstructionism, doesn't it? And of course at an older age I was enamored of the deconstructionists of the last century. The world as text: Husserl's *The Origin of Geometry* is 22 pages long, Derrida's *Introduction to the Origin of Geometry* is 153 pages long; you can see why it would have appealed to me. If, as the deconstructionists seemed to say, the world is nothing but a collection of texts, and I can read, then I am not missing anything by being blind, am I?

The young can be very stubborn, very stupid.

"All right, Jeremy," I said. "Let me meet this mysterious *subject* of yours who draws all this stuff."

"You want to?" he said, trying to conceal his excitement.

"Sure," I replied. "I'm not going to find out any more about all this until I do." My own subtext, yes; but I am better at hiding such things than Jeremy is.

"What have you found out? Do the diagrams mean anything to you?"

"Not much. You know me, Jeremy, drawings are my weakness. I'd rather have her do it in models, or writing, or verbally. You'll have to bring her by if you want me to continue."

"Well, okay. I'll see what I can do. She's not much help, though. You'll find out." But he was pleased.

———

One time in high school I was walking out of the gym after P.E., and I heard one of my coaches (one of the best teachers I have ever had) in his office, speaking to someone (he must have had his back to me)—he said, "You know, it's not the physical handicaps that will be the problem for most of these kids. It's the emotional problems that tend to come with the handicaps that will be the real burden."

I was in my office listening to my reading machine. Its flat, uninflected mechanical voice (almost unintelligible to some of my colleagues) had over the years become a sort of helpless, stupid friend. I called it George, and was always programming into it another pronunciation rule to try to aid its poor speech, but to no avail; George always found new ways to butcher the language. I put the book facedown on the glass; "Finding first line," croaked George, as the scanner inside the machine thumped around. Then it read from Roberto Torretti, quoting and discussing Ernst Mach. (Hear this spoken in the most stilted, awkward, syllable-by-syllable mispronunciation that you can imagine.)

" 'Our notions of space are rooted in our *physiological* constitution' " (George raises his voice in pitch to indicate italics, which also slow him down considerably). " 'Geometric concepts are the product of the idealization of *physical* experiences of space.' Physiological space is quite different from the infinite, isotropic, metric space of classical geometry and physics. It can, at most, be structured as a topological space. When viewed in this way, it naturally falls into several components: visual or optic space, tactile or haptic space, auditive space, etc. Optic space is anisotropic, finite, limited. Haptic space or 'the space of our skin corresponds to a two-dimensional, finite, unlimited (closed) Riemannian space.' This is nonsense, for R-spaces are metric, while haptic space is not. I take it that Mach means to say that the latter can naturally be regarded as a two-dimensional compact connected topological space. Mach does not emphasize enough the disconnectedness of haptic from optic space—"

There came four quick knocks at my door. I pressed the button on George that stopped him and said, "Come in!"

The door opened. "Carlos!"

"Jeremy," I said. "How are you?"

"Fine. I've brought Mary Unser with me—you know, the one who drew—"

I stood, feeling/hearing the presence of the other in the room. And there are times (like this one) when you *know* the other is in some odd, undefinable way, *different*, or . . . (Our language is not made for the experience of the blind.) "I'm glad to meet you."

I have said that I can tell dark from light, and I can, though it is seldom very useful information. In this case, however, I was startled to have my attention drawn to my "sight"—for this woman was darker than other people, she was a sort of bundle of darkness in the room, her face distinctly lighter than the rest of her (or was that her face, exactly?).

A long pause. Then: "On border stand we n-dimensional space the," she said. Coming just after George's reading, I was struck by a certain similarity: The mechanical lilt from word to word; the basic incomprehension of a reading machine. . . . Goose bumps rose on my forearms.

Her voice itself, on the other hand, had George beat hands down. Fundamentally vibrant under the odd intonation, it was a voice with a very thick timbre, a bassoon or a hurdy-gurdy of a voice, with the buzz of someone who habitually speaks partly through the sinuses; this combined with over-relaxed vocal cords, what speech pathologists call glottal fry. Usually nasal voices are not pleasant, but pitch them low enough . . .

She spoke again, more slowly (definitely glottal fry): "We stand on the border of n-dimensional space."

"Hey," Jeremy said. "Pretty good!" He explained: "Her word order isn't usually as . . . ordinary as that."

"So I gathered," I said. "Mary, what do you mean by that?"

"I—*oh*—" A kazoo squeak of distress, pain. I approached her, put out a hand. She took it as if to shake: a hand about the size of mine, narrow, strong fat muscle at base of thumb; trembling distinctly.

"I work on the geometries of topologically complex spaces," I said. "I am more likely than most to understand what you say."

"Are within never see we points us." ·

"That's true." But there was something wrong here, something I didn't like, though I couldn't tell exactly what it was. Had she spoken toward Jeremy? Speaking to me while she looked at him? Bundle of darkness in the dark . . . "But why are your sentences so disordered, Mary? Your words don't come out in the order you thought them. You must know that, since you understand us."

"Folded—*oh!*—" Again the double-reed squeak, and suddenly she was weeping, trembling hard; we sat her down on my visitor's couch, and Jeremy got her a glass of water while she quaked in my hands. I stroked her hair (short, loosely curled, wild) and took the opportunity for a quick phrenological check: skull regular and, as far as I could tell, undamaged; temples wide, distinct; same for eye sockets; nose a fairly ordinary pyramidal segment, no bridge to speak of; narrow cheeks, wet with tears. She reached up and took my right hand, squeezed it hard, three times fast, three times slow, all the time sobbing and sort of hiccupping words: "Pain it, station. I, oh, fold end, bright, light, space fold, oh, ohhh . . ."

Well, the direct question is not always the best way. Jeremy returned with a glass of water, and drinking some seemed to calm her. Jeremy said, "Perhaps we could try again later. Although . . ." He didn't seem very surprised.

"Sure," I said. "Listen, Mary, I'll talk to you again when you're feeling better."

———

After Jeremy got her out of the office and disposed of her (how? with whom?) he returned to the seventh floor.

"So what the hell happened to her?" I asked angrily. "Why is she like that?"

"We aren't completely sure," he said slowly. "Here's why. She was one of the scientists staffing Tsiolkovsky Base Five, up in the mountains on the back side of the moon, you know. She's an astronomer and cosmologist. Well—I have to ask you to keep this quiet—one day Base Five stopped all broadcasting, and when they went over to see what was wrong, they found only her, alone in the station in a sort of catatonic state. No sign of the other scientists or station crew—eighteen people gone without a trace. And nothing much different to explain what had happened, either."

I *hmphed*. "What do they think happened?"

"They're still not sure. Apparently, no one else was in the area, or could have been, et cetera. It's been suggested by the Russians, who had ten people there, that this could be first contact—you know, that aliens took the missing ones, and somehow disarranged Mary's thought processes, leaving her behind as a messenger that isn't working. Her brain scans are bizarre. I mean, it doesn't sound very likely . . ."

"No."

"But it's the only theory that explains everything they found there. Some of which they won't tell me about. So, we're doing what we can to get Mary's testimony, but as you can see, it's hard. She seems most comfortable drawing diagrams."

"Next time we'll start with that."

"Okay. Any other ideas?"

"No," I lied. "When can you bring her back again?"

As if because I was blind I couldn't tell I was being duped! I struck fist into palm angrily. Oh, they were making a mistake, all right. They didn't know how much the voice reveals. The voice's secret expressivity reveals *so much!*—the language really is not adequate to tell it; we need that mathematics of emotion. . . . In the high school for the blind that I briefly attended for some of my classes, it often happened that a new teacher was instantly disliked, for some falseness in his or her voice, some quality of condescension or pity or self-congratulation that the teacher (and his or her superiors) thought completely concealed, if they knew of it at all. But it was entirely obvious to the students, because the voice (if what I have heard is true) is much more revealing than facial expressions; certainly it is less under our control. This is what makes most acting performances so unsatisfactory to me; the vocal qualities are so stylized, so removed from those of real life. . . .

And here, I thought, I was witnessing a performance.

There is a moment in Olivier Messiaen's *Visions de l'Amen* when one piano is playing a progression of major chords, very traditionally harmonic, while on another piano high pairs of notes plonk down across the other's chords, ruining their harmony, crying out, Something's wrong! Something's wrong!

I sat at my desk and swayed side to side, living just such a moment. Something was wrong.

When I collected myself I called the department secretary, who had a view of the hall to the elevator. "Delphina, did Jeremy just leave?"

"Yes, Carlos. Do you want me to try and catch him?"

"No, I only need a book he left in his office. Can I borrow the master key and get it?"

"Okay."

I got the key, entered Jeremy's office, closed the door. One of the tiny pickups that James Gold had gotten for me fit right under the snap-in plug of the telephone cord. Then a microphone under the desk, behind a drawer. And out. (I have to be bold every day, you see, just to get by. But they didn't know that.)

Back in my office I closed and locked the door, and began

273

to search. My office is big: two couches, several tall bookcases, my desk, a file cabinet, a coffee table. . . . When the partitions on the seventh floor of the Gelman Library were moved around to make more room, Delphina and George Hampton, who was chairman that year, had approached me nervously: "Carlos, you wouldn't mind an office with no windows, would you?"

I laughed. All of the full professors had offices on the outer perimeter of the floor, with windows.

"You see," George said, "since none of the windows in the building opens anyway, you won't be missing out on any breezes. And if you take this room in the inner core of the building, then we'll have enough space for a good faculty lounge."

"Fine," I said, not mentioning that I could see sunlight, distinguish light and dark. It made me angry that they hadn't remembered that, hadn't thought to ask. So I nicknamed my office the Vault, and I had a lot of room, but no windows. The halls had no windows either, so I was really without sun, but I didn't complain.

Now I got down on hands and knees and continued searching, feeling like it was hopeless. But I found one, on the bottom of the couch. And there was another in the phone. Bugged. I left them in position and went home.

Home was a small top-floor apartment up near 21st and N streets, and I supposed it was bugged too. I turned up Stockhausen's *Telemusik* as loud as I could stand it, hoping to drive my listeners into a suicidal fugal state, or at least give them a headache. Then I slapped together a sandwich, downed it angrily.

I imagined I was captain of a naval sailing ship (like Horatio Hornblower), and that because of my sharp awareness of the wind I was the best captain afloat. They had had to evacuate the city, and all the people I knew were aboard, depending on me. But we were caught against a lee shore by two large ships of the line, and in the ensuing broadsides (roar of cannon, smell of gunpowder and blood, screams of wounded like shrieking seagulls), everyone I knew fell— chopped in half, speared by giant splinters, heads removed by cannonball, you name it. Then when they were all corpses on the sand-strewn, splintered decking, I felt a final broadside discharge, every ball converging on me as if I were point 0 at the tip of a cone. Instant dissolution and death.

I came out of it feeling faintly disgusted with myself. But because it actively defends the ego by eradicating those who attack its self-esteem, Cutsforth calls this type of fantasy in the blind subject healthy. (At least in fourteen-year-olds.) So be it. Here's to health. Fuck all of you.

Geometry is a language, with a vocabulary and syntax as clear and precise as humans can make them. In many cases, definitions of terms and operations are explicitly spelled out, to help achieve this clarity. For instance, one could say:

Let (parentheses) designate corollaries.
Let [brackets] designate causes.
Let {braces} designate . . .

But would it be true, in this other language of the heart?

Next afternoon I played beepball with my team. Sun hot on my face and arms, spring smell of pollen and wet grass. Ramon got six runs in the at-bat before mine (beepball is a sort of cricket/softball mix, played with softball equipment ["It proves you can play cricket blind" one Anglophobe {she was Irish} said to me once]), and when I got up I scratched out two and then struck out. Swinging *too* hard. I decided I liked outfield better. The beepball off in the distance, lofted up in a short arc, smack of bat, follow the ball up and up— out toward me!—drift in its direction, the rush of fear, glove before face as it approaches, stab for it, off after it as it rolls by—pick it up—Ramon's voice calling clearly, "Right here! Right here!" and letting loose with a throw—really putting everything into it—and then, sometimes, hearing that beep-ball lance off into the distance and smack into Ramon's glove. It was great. Nothing like outfield.

And next inning I hit one *hard*, and that's great too. That feeling goes right up your arms and all through you.

Walking home I brooded over Max Carrados, blind detective, and over Horatio Hornblower, sighted naval captain. Over Thomas Gore, the blind senator from Oklahoma. As a boy his fantasy was to become a senator. He read the *Congressional Record*, joined the debate team, organized his whole life around the project. And he became senator. I knew that sort of fantasy as well as I knew the vengeful adolescent daydreams: All through my youth I dreamed of being a mathematician. And here I was. So one could do it. One could imagine doing something, and then do it.

But that meant that one had, by definition, imagined something *possible*. And one couldn't always say ahead of the attempt whether one had imagined the possible or the impossible. And even if one had imagined something possible, that didn't guarantee a successful execution of the plan.

The team we had played was called Helen Keller Jokes (there are some good ones, too [they come {of course} from Australia] but I won't go into that). It's sad that such an intelligent woman was so miseducated—not so much by Sullivan as by her whole era: all that treacly Victorian sentimentality poured into her: "The fishing villages of Cornwall are very picturesque, seen either from the beaches or the hilltops, with all their boats riding to their moorings or sailing about in the harbor. When the moon, large and serene, floats up the sky, leaving in the water a long track of brightness like a plow breaking up a soil of silver, I can only sigh my ecstasy"—come on, Helen. Now *that* is living in a world of texts.

But didn't I live most (all?) of my life in texts as least as unreal to me as moonlight on water was to Helen Keller? These n-dimensional manifolds . . . I suppose the basis for my abilities in them was the lived reality of haptic space, but still, it was many removes from my actual experience. And so was the situation I found myself confronted with now, Jeremy and Mary acting out some drama I did not comprehend . . . and so was my plan to deal with it. Verbalism . . . words versus reality.

I caressed my glove, refelt the knock of bat against beepball. Brooded over my plan.

The next time Jeremy brought Mary Unser by my office, I said very little. I got out my "visitor's supply" of paper and pencils and set her down at the coffee table. I brought over my models: subatomic particles breaking up in a spray of wire lines, like water out of a showerhead; strawlike Taylor sticks for model making; polyhedric blocks of every kind. And I sat down with the ridged sheets made from her earlier drawings, as well as the models I had attempted to make of them, and I started asking very limited questions. "What does this line mean? Does it go before or behind? Is this R or R'? Have I got this right?"

And she would honk a sort of laugh, or say, "No, no, no, no" (no problem with sequencing there), and draw furiously. I took the pages as she finished them and put them in my Xerox, took out the ridged, bumpy sheets and had her guide my fingers over them. Even so they were difficult, and with a squeak of frustration she went to the straw models, clicking together triangles, parallels, etc. This was easier, but eventually she reached a limit here too. "Need drawing beyond," she said.

"Fine. Write down whatever you want."

She wrote and then read aloud to me, or I put it through the Xerox machine marked *translation to Braille*. And we forged on, with Jeremy looking over our shoulders the whole time.

And eventually we came very close to the edge of my work, following subatomic particles down into the microdimensions where they appeared to make their "jumps." I had proposed an n-dimensional topological manifold, where $1<n<$ infinity, so that the continuum being mapped fluctuated between one and some finite number of dimensions, going from a curving line to a sort of n-dimensional Swiss cheese, if you like, depending on the amounts of energy displayed in the area, in any of the four "forms" of electromagnetism, gravity, or the strong and weak interactions. The geometry for this manifold-pattern (so close to the experience of haptic space) had, as I have said, attracted the attention of physicists at CERN and SLAC—but there were still unexplained data, as far as I could tell, and the truth was, *I had not published this work.*

So here I was "conversing" with a young woman who in ordinary conversations could not order her words correctly—who in this realm spoke with perfect coherence—who was in fact speaking about (inquiring about?) the edges of my own private work.

The kind of work that Jeremy Blasingame used to ask me about so curiously.

I sighed. We had been going on for two or three hours, and I sat back on the couch. My hand was taken up in Mary's, given a reassuring squeeze. I didn't know what to make of it. "I'm tired."

"I feel better," she said. "Easier to talk way—this way."

"Ah," I said. I took up the model of a positron hitting a "stationary" muon: a wire tree, trunk suddenly bursting into a mass of curling branches. . . . So it was here: one set of events, a whole scattering of explanations. Still, the bulk of the particles shot out in a single general direction (the truths of haptic space).

She let go of my hand to make one last diagram. Then she Xeroxed it for me, and guided my hands over the ridged copy.

Once again it was Desargues' theorem.

———

At this point Mary said, "Mr. Blasingame, I need a drink of water." He went out to the hall water dispenser, and she quickly took my forefinger between her finger and thumb (pads flattening with an inappropriate pressure, until my finger ached)—squeezed twice, and jabbed my finger first onto her leg, then onto the diagram, tracing out one of the triangles. She repeated the movements, then poked my leg and traced out the other triangle. Then she traced down the line off to the side, the one generated by the projection of the two triangles, over and over. What did she mean?

Jeremy returned, and she let my hand go. Then in a while, after the amenities (hard handshake, quivering hand), Jeremy whisked her off.

When he returned, I said, "Jeremy, is there any chance I can talk to her alone? I think she's made nervous by your presence—the associations, you know. She really does have an interesting perspective on the n-dimensional manifold, but she gets confused when she stops and interacts with you. I'd just like to take her for a walk, you know—down by the canal, or the Tidal Basin, perhaps, and talk things over with her. It might get the results you want."

"I'll see what they say," Jeremy said in an expressionless voice.

That night I put on a pair of earplugs and played the tape of Jeremy's phone conversations. In one when the phone was picked up he said, "He wants to talk with her alone now."

"Fine," said a tenor voice. "She's prepared for that."

"This weekend?"

"If he agrees." Click.

I listen to music. I listen to twentieth-century composers the most, because many of them made their music out of the sounds of the world we live in now, the world of jets and sirens and industrial machinery, as well as bird song and woodblock and the human voice. Messiaen, Partch, Reich, Glass, Shapiro, Subotnik, Ligeti, Penderecki—these first explorers away from the orchestra and the classical tradition remain for me the voices of our age; they speak to me. In fact, they speak for me; in their dissonance and confusion and anger I hear myself being expressed. And so I listen to their difficult, complex music because I understand it, which gives me pleasure, and because while doing so I am participating fully, I am excelling, no one can bring more to the act than I. I am *in control*.

I listened to music.

You see, these *n*-dimensional manifolds . . . if we understand them well enough to manipulate them, to tap their energy . . . well, there is a tremendous amount of energy contained in those particles. That kind of energy means power, and power . . . draws the powerful. Or those seeking power, fighting for it. I began to feel the extent of the danger.

She was quiet as we walked across the Mall toward the Lincoln Memorial. I think she would have stopped me if I had spoken about anything important. But I knew enough to say nothing, and I think she guessed I knew she was bugged. I held the back of her upper arm loosely in my left hand and let her guide us. A sunny, windy day, with occasional clouds obscuring the sun for a minute or two. Down by the Mall's lake the slightly stagnant smell of wet algae tinged all the other scents: grass, dust, the double strand of lighter fluid and cooking meat. . . . The sink of darkness swirling around the Vietnam Memorial. Pigeons cooed their weird, larger-than-life coos and flapped away noisily as we walked through their affairs. We sat on grass that had been recently cut, and I brushed a hand over the stiff blades.

A curious procedure, this conversation. No visuals, for me; and perhaps we were being watched, as well. (Such a common anxiety of the blind, the fear of being watched—and here it was true.) And we couldn't talk freely, even though at the same time we had to say something, to keep Blasingame and friends from thinking I was aware of anything wrong. "Nice day." "Yeah, I'd love to be out on the water on a day like this." "Really?" "Yeah."

And all the while, two fingers held one finger. My hands are my eyes, and always have been. Now they were as expressive as voice, as receptive as ever touch can be, and into haptic space we projected a conversation of rare urgency. Are you okay? I'm okay. Do you know what's going on? Not entirely, can't explain.

"Let's walk down to the paddle boats and go out on the basin, then."

I said, "Your speech is much better today."

She squeezed my hand thrice, hard. False information? "I . . . had . . . electroshock." Her voice slid, slurred; it wasn't entirely under control.

"It seems to have helped."

"Yes. Sometimes."

"And the ordering of your mathematical thought?"

Buzzing laugh, hurdy-gurdy voice. "I don't know— more disarranged, perhaps—complementary procedure? You'll have to tell me."

"As a cosmologist did you work in this area?"

"The topology of the microdimensions apparently determines both gravity and the weak interaction, wouldn't you agree?"

"I couldn't say. I'm not much of a physicist."

Three squeezes again. "But you must have an idea or two about it?"

"Not really. You?"

"Perhaps . . . once. But it seems to me your work is directly concerned with it."

"Not that I know of."

Stalemate. Was that right? I was becoming more and more curious about this woman, whose signals to me were so mixed. . . . Once again she seemed a bundling of darkness in the day, a whirlpool where all lightness disappeared, except for around her head. (I suppose I imagine all that I "see," I suppose they are always haptic visions.)

"Are you wearing dark clothes?"

"Not really. Red, beige . . ."

As we walked I held her arm more tightly. She was about my height. Her arm muscles were distinct, and her lats pushed out from her ribs. "You must swim."

"Weight lifting, I'm afraid. They made us on Luna."

"On Luna," I repeated.

"Yes," and she fell silent.

This was really impossible. I didn't think she was completely an ally—in fact I thought she was lying—but I felt an underlying sympathy from her, and a sense of conspiracy with her, that grew more powerful the longer we were together. The problem was, what did that feeling mean? Without the ability to converse freely, I was stymied in my attempts to learn more; pushed this way and that in the cross-currents of her behavior, I could only wonder what she was thinking. And what our listeners made of this mostly silent day in the sun.

So we paddled out onto the Tidal Basin and talked from time to time about the scene around us. I loved the feel of being on water—the gentle rocking over other boats' wakes, the wet stale smell. "Are the cherry trees blossoming still?"

"Oh, yes. Not quite at the peak, but just past. It's beautiful. Here"—she leaned out—"here's one about to drown." She put it in my hand. I sniffed at it. "Do they smell?"

"No, not much," I said. "The prettier people say flowers are, the less scent they seem to have. Did you ever notice that?"

"I guess. I like the scent of roses."

"It's faint, though. These blossoms must be very beautiful—they smell hardly at all."

"En masse they are lovely. I wish you could see them."

I shrugged. "And I wish you could touch their petals, or feel us bouncing about as I do. I have enough sense data to keep entertained."

"Yes . . . I suppose you do." She left her hand covering mine. "I suppose we're out quite a ways," I said. So that we couldn't be seen well from the shore, I meant.

"From the dock, anyway. We're actually almost across the basin."

I moved my hand from under hers and held her shoulder. Deep hollow behind her collarbone. This contact, this conversation of touch . . . it was most expressive hand to hand, and so I took her hand again, and our fingers made random entanglements, explorations. Children shouting, then laughing in boats to our left, voices charged with excitement. How to speak in this language of touch?

Well, we all know that. Fingertips, brushing lines of the palm; ruffling the fine hair at the back of the wrist; fingers pressing each other back: These are sentences, certainly. And it is a difficult language to lie in. That catlike, sensuous stretch, under my stroking fingertips . . .

"We've got a clear run ahead of us," she said after a time, voice charged with humming overtones.

"Stoke the furnaces," I cried. "Damn the torpedoes!" And with a gurgling *clug-clug-clug-clug* we paddle-wheeled over the basin into the fresh wet wind, sun on our faces, laughing at the release from tension (bassoon and baritone), crying out, "Mark Twain!" or "Snag dead ahead!" in jocular tones, entwined hands crushing the other as we pedaled harder and harder. . . . "Down the Potomac!" "Across the sea!" "Through the gates of Hercules!" "On to the Golden Fleece!" Spray cold on the breeze—

She stopped pedaling, and we swerved left.

"We're almost back," she said quietly.

We let the boat drift in, without a word.

My bugs told me that my office had been broken into, by two, possibly three, people, only one of whom spoke—a man, in an undertone: "Try the file cabinet." The cabinet drawers were rolled out (familiar clicking of the runners over the ball bearings), and the desk drawers too, and then there was the sound of paper shuffling, of things being knocked about.

I also got an interesting phone conversation over Jeremy's phone. The call was incoming; Jeremy said, "Yes?" and a male voice—the same one Jeremy had called earlier—said, "She says he's unwilling to go into any detail."

"That doesn't surprise me," Jeremy said. "But I'm sure he's got—"

"Yes, I know. Go ahead and try what we discussed."

The break-in, I supposed.

"Okay." Click.

No doubt it never even occurred to them that I might turn the tables on them, or act against them in any way, or even figure out that something was strange. It made me furious.

At the same time I was frightened. You feel the lines of force, living in Washington, D.C.; feel the struggle for power among the shadowy groups surrounding the official government; read of the unsolved murders, of shadowy people whose jobs are not made clear. . . . As a blind person, one feels apart from the nebulous world of intrigue and hidden force, on the edge by reason of disability. ("No one harms a blind man.") Now I knew I was part of it, pulled in and on my own. It was frightening.

One night I was immersed in Harry Partch's *Cloud Chamber Music*, floating in those big glassy notes, when my doorbell rang. I picked up the phone. "Hello?"

"It's Mary Unser. May I come up?"

"Sure." I pushed the button and walked onto the landing.

She came up the stairs alone. "Sorry to bother you at home," she buzzed, out of breath. Such a voice. "I looked up your address in the phone book. I'm not supposed . . ."

She stood before me, touched my right arm. I lifted my hand and held her elbow. "Yes?"

Nervous, resonant laugh. "I'm not supposed to be here."

Then you'll soon be in trouble, I wanted to say. But surely

she knew my apartment would be bugged? Surely she *was* supposed to be here? She was trembling violently, enough so that I put up my other hand and held her by the shoulders. "Are you all right?"

"Yes. No." Falling oboe tones, laugh that was not a laugh . . . She seemed frightened, very frightened. I thought, if she is acting she is *very* good.

"Come on in," I said, and led her inside. I went to the stereo and turned down the Partch—then reconsidered, and turned it back up. "Have a seat—the couch is nice." I was nervous myself. "Would you like something to drink?" Quite suddenly it all seemed unreal, a dream, one of my fantasies. Phantasmagoric cloud chamber ringing to things, how did I know what was real?

"No. Or yes." She laughed again, that laugh that was not a laugh.

"I've got some beer." I went to the refrigerator, got a couple of bottles, opened them.

"So what's going on?" I said as I sat down beside her. As she spoke I drank from my beer, and she stopped from time to time to take long swallows.

"Well, I feel that the more I understand what you're saying about the transfer of energies between n-dimensional manifolds, the better I understand what . . . happened to me." But now there was a different sound to her voice—an overtone was gone, it was less resonant, less nasal.

I said, "I don't know what I can tell you. It's not something I can talk about, or even write down. What I can express, I have, you know. In papers." This a bit louder, for the benefit of our audience. (If there was one.)

"Well . . ." and her hand, under mine, began to tremble again.

We sat there for a very long time, and all during that time we conversed through those two hands, saying things I can scarcely recall now, because we have no language for that sort of thing. But they were important things nevertheless, and after a while I said, "Here. Come with me. I'm on the top floor, so I have a sort of porch on the roof. Finish your beer. It's a pleasant night out, you'll feel better outside." I led her through the kitchen to the pantry, where the door to the backstairs was. "Go on up." I went back to the stereo and put on Jarrett's *Köln Concert*, loud enough so we'd be able to hear it. Then I went up the stairs onto the roof, and crunched over the tarred gravel.

This was one of my favorite places. The sides of the building came up to the chest around the edge of the roof, and on two sides large willows draped their branches over it, making it a sort of haven. I had set a big old wreck of a couch out there, and on certain nights when the wind was up and the air was cool, I would lie back on it with a bumpy Braille planisphere in my hands, listening to Scholz's *Starcharts* and feeling that with those projections I knew what it was to see the night sky.

"This is nice," she said.

"Isn't it?" I pulled the plastic sheet from the couch, and we sat.

"Carlos?"

"Yes?"

"I—I—" that double-reed squeak.

I put an arm around her. "Please," I said, suddenly upset myself. "Not now. Not now. Just relax. Please." And she turned into me, her head rested on my shoulder; she trembled. I dug my fingers into her hair and slowly pulled them through the tangles. Shoulder length, no more. I cupped her ears, stroked her neck. She calmed.

Time passed, and I only caressed. No other thought, no other perception. How long this went on I couldn't say—perhaps a half-hour? Perhaps longer? She made a sort of purring kazoo sound, and I leaned forward and kissed her. Jarrett's voice, crying out briefly over a fluid run of piano notes. She pulled me to her; her breath caught, rushed out of her. The kiss became intense, tongues dancing together in a whole intercourse of their own, which I felt all through me in that *chakra* way, neck, spine, belly, groin, nothing but kiss. And without the slightest bit of either intention or resistance, I fell into it.

I remember a college friend once asked me, hesitantly, if I didn't have trouble with my love life. "Isn't it hard to tell when they . . . want to?" I had laughed. The whole process, I had wanted to say, was amazingly easy. The blinds' dependence on touch puts them in an advance position, so to speak: Using hands to see faces, being led by the hand (being dependent), one has already crossed what Russ calls the border between the world of not-sex and the world of sex; once over that border (with an other feeling protective) . . .

My hands explored her body, discovering it then and there for the first time—as intensely exciting a moment as there is, in the whole process. I suppose I expect narrow-cheeked people to be narrow hipped (it's mostly true, you'll find), but it wasn't so, in this case—her hips flared in those feminine curves that one can only hold, without ever getting used to (without ever [the otherness of the other] quite believing). On their own my fingers slipped under clothes, between buttons, as adroit as little mice, clever, lusty little creatures, unbuttoning blouse, reaching behind to undo bra with a twist. She shrugged out of them both and I felt the softness of her breasts while she tugged at my belt. I shifted, rolled, put my ear to her hard sternum, kissing the inside of one breast as it pressed against my face, feeling that quick heartbeat speak to me. . . . She moved me back, got me unzipped, we paused for a speedy moment and got the rest of our clothes off, fumbling at our own and each other's until they were clear. Then it was flesh to flesh, skin to skin, in a single haptic space jumping with energy, with the insistent *yes* of caresses, mouth to mouth, four hands full, body to body, with breasts and erect penis crushed, as it were, between two pulsing walls of muscle.

The skin is the ultimate voice.

So we made love. As we did (my feet jabbing the end of the couch, which was quite broad enough, but a little too short) I arched up and let in the breeze between us (cool on our sweat), leaned down and sucked on first one nipple and then the other—

(thus becoming helpless in a sense, a needy infant, utterly dependent [because for the blind from birth, mother love is even more crucial than for the rest of us; the blind depend on their mothers for almost *everything*, for the sense of object permanence, for the education that makes the distinction between self and world, for the beginning of language, and also for the establishment of a private language that compensates for the lack of sight {if your mother doesn't know that a sweeping hand means *"I want"!*} and bridges the way to the common tongue—without all that, which only a mother can give, the blind infant is lost; without mother love beyond mother love, the blind child will very likely go mad] so that to suck on a lover's nipple brings back that primal world of trust and need, I am sure of it)

—I was sure of it even then, as I made love to this strange other Mary Unser, a woman as unknown to me as any I had ever spoken with. At least until now. Now with each plunge into her (cylinder capped by cone, sliding through cylinder into rough sphere, neuron to neuron, millions of them fusing across, so that I could not tell where I stopped and she began) I learned more about her, the shape of her, her rhythms, her whole nerve-reality, spoken to me in movement and touch (spread hands holding my back, flanks, bottom) and in those broken bassoon tones that were like someone humming, briefly, involuntarily. "Ah," I said happily at all this sensation, all this new knowledge, feeling all my skin and all my nerves swirl up like a gust of wind into my spine, the back of my balls, to pitch into her all my self—

When we were done (oboe squeaks) I slid down, bending my knees so my feet stuck up in the air. I wiggled my toes in the breeze. Faint traffic noises played a sort of city music to accompany the piano in the apartment. From the airshaft came the sound of a chorus of pigeons, sounding like monkeys with their jaws wired shut, trying to chatter. Mary's skin was damp and I licked it, loving the salt. Patch of darkness in my blur of vision, darkness bundling in it . . . She rolled onto her side and my hands played over her. Her biceps made a smooth, hard bulge. There were several moles on her back, like little raisins half buried in her skin. I pushed them down, fingered the knobs of her spine. The muscles of her back put her spine in a deep trough of flesh.

I remembered a day my blind science class was taken to a museum, where we were allowed to feel a skeleton. All those hard bones, in just the right places; it made perfect sense, it was exactly as if felt under skin, really—there were no big surprises. But I remember being so upset by the experience of feeling the skeleton that I had to go outside and sit down on the museum steps. I don't know to this day exactly why I was so shaken, but I suppose (all those hard things left behind) it was something like this: It was frightening to know how *real* we were!

Now I tugged at her, gently. "Who are you, then?"

"Not now." And as I started to speak again she put a finger to my mouth (scent of us): "A friend." Buzzing nasal whisper, like a tuning fork, like a voice I was beginning (and this scared me, for I knew I did not know her) to love: "A friend . . ."

At a certain point in geometrical thinking, vision becomes only an obstruction. Those used to visualizing theorems (as in Euclidean geometry) reach a point, in the n-dimensional manifolds or elsewhere, where the concepts simply *can't* be visualized; and the attempt to do so only leads to confusion and misunderstanding. Beyond that point an interior geometry, a haptic geometry, guided by a kinetic esthetics, is probably the best sensory analogy we have; and so I have my advantage.

But in the real world, in the geometries of the heart, do I ever have any comparable advantage? Are there things we feel that can never be seen?

The central problem for everyone concerned with the relationship between geometry and the real world is the question of how one moves from the incommunicable impressions of the sensory world (vague fields of force, of danger), to the generally agreed-upon abstractions of the math (the explanation). Or, as Edmund Husserl puts it in *The Origin of Geometry* (and on this particular morning George was enunciating this passage for me with the utmost awkwardness): "How does geometrical ideality (just like that of all the sciences) proceed from its primary intrapersonal origin, where it is a structure within the conscious space of the first inventor's soul, to its ideal objectivity?"

At this point Jeremy knocked at my door: four quick raps. "Come in, Jeremy," I said, my pulse quickening.

He opened the door and looked in. "I have a pot of coffee just ready to go," he said. "Come on down and have some."

So I joined him in his office, which smelled wonderfully of strong French roast. I sat in one of the plush armchairs that circled Jeremy's desk, accepted a small glazed cup, sipped from it. Jeremy moved about the room restlessly as he chattered about one minor matter after another, obviously avoiding the topic of Mary and all that she represented. The coffee sent a warm flush through me—even the flesh of my feet buzzed with heat, though in the blast of air-conditioned air from the ceiling vent I didn't start to sweat. At first it was a comfortable, even pleasant sensation. The bitter, murky taste of the coffee washed over my palate, through the roof of my mouth into my sinuses, from there up behind my eyes, through my brain, all the way down my throat, into my lungs: I breathed coffee, my blood singing with warmth.

. . . I had been talking about something. Jeremy's voice came from directly above and before me, and it had a crackly, tinny quality to it, as if made by an old carbon microphone: "And what would happen if the Q energy from this manifold were directed through these vectored dimensions into the macrodimensional manifold?"

Happily I babbled, "Well, provide each point P of an n-dimensional differentiable manifold M with the analogue of a tangent plane, an n-dimensional vector space Tp(M), called the tangent space at P. Now we can define a *path* in manifold M as a differentiable mapping of an open interval of R into M. And along this path we can fit the *whole* of the forces defining K the submanifold of M, a lot of energy to be sure," and I was writing it down, when the somatic effect of the drug caught up with the mental effect, and I recognized what was happening. ("Entirely too many new designer drugs these days . . .") Jeremy's breathing snagged as he looked up to see what had stopped me; meanwhile, I struggled with a slight wave of nausea, caused more by the realization that I had been drugged than by the chemicals themselves, which had very little "noise." What had I told him? And why, for God's sake, did it matter so much?

"Sorry," I muttered through the roar of the ventilator. "Bit of a headache."

"Sorry to hear that," Jeremy said, in a voice exactly like George's. "You look a little pale."

"Yes," I said, trying to conceal my anger. (Later, listening to the tape of the conversation, I thought I only sounded confused.) (And I hadn't said much about my work, either— mostly definitions.) "Sorry to run out on you, but it really is bothering me."

I stood, and for a moment I panicked; the location of the room's door—the most fundamental point of orientation, remembered without effort in every circumstance—wouldn't come to me. I was damned if I would ask Jeremy Blasingame about such a thing, or stumble about in front of him. I consciously fought to remember: desk faces door, chair faces desk, door therefore behind you. . . .

"Let me walk you to your office," Jeremy said, taking me by the arm. "Listen, maybe I can give you a lift home?"

"That's all right," I said, shrugging him off. I found the door by accident, it seemed, and left him. Down to my office, wondering if I would get the right door. My blood was hot Turkish coffee. My head spun. The key worked, so I had found the right door. Locked in, I went to my couch and lay down. I was as dizzy there as standing, but found I couldn't move again. I spun in place helplessly. I had read that the designer drugs used for such purposes had almost no somatic effect, but perhaps this was true only for subjects less sensitive to their kinetic reality—otherwise, why was I reacting so? Fear. Or Jeremy had put something beyond the truth drug in me. A warning? Against? Suddenly I was aware of the tight boundaries of my comprehension, beyond it the wide manifold of action I did not understand—and the latter threatened to completely flood the former, so that there would be left nothing at all that I understood about this matter. Such a prospect terrified me.

Some time later—perhaps as much as an hour—I felt I had to get home. Physically I felt much better, and it was only when I got outside in the wind that I realized that the psychological effects of the drug were still having their way with me. Rare, heavy waft of diesel exhaust, a person wearing clothes rank with old sweat: These smells overwhelmed any chance I had of locating Ramon's cart by nose. My cane felt unusually long, and the rising and falling whistles of my sonar glasses made a musical composition like something out of Messiaen's *Catalogue d'Oiseaux*. I stood entranced by the effect. Cars zoomed past with their electric whirrs, the wind made more sound than I could process. I couldn't find Ramon and decided to give up trying; it would be bad to get him mixed up in any of this anyway. Ramon was my best friend. All those hours at Warren's throwing together, and when we played beeper ping-pong at his apartment we sometimes got to laughing so hard we couldn't stand—what else is friendship than that, after all?

Distracted by thoughts such as these, and by the bizarre music of wind and traffic, I lost track of which street I was crossing. The *whoosh* of a car nearly brushing me as I stepped up from a curb. Lost! "Excuse me, is this Pennsylvania or K?" Fuckyouverymuch. Threading my way fearfully between broken bottles, punji-stick nails poking up out of boards on the sidewalk, low-hanging wires holding up tree branch or street sign, dog shit on the curb waiting like banana peel to skid me into the street under a bus, speeding cars with completely silent electric motors careening around the corner, muggers who didn't care if I was blind or paraplegic or whatever, manholes left open in the crosswalks, rabid dogs with their toothy jaws stuck out between the rails of a fence, ready to bite . . . Oh, yes, I fought off all these dangers and more, and I must have looked mad tiptoeing down the sidewalk, whapping my cane about like a man beating off devils.

By the time I got into my apartment I was shaking with fury. I turned on Steve Reich's *Come Out* (in which the phrase "Come out to show them" is looped countless times) as loud as I could stand it, and barged around my place alternately cursing and crying (that stinging of the eyes), all under the sound of the music. I formulated a hundred impossible plans of revenge against Jeremy Blasingame and his shadowy employers. I brushed my teeth for fifteen minutes to get the taste of coffee out of my mouth.

By the next morning I had a workable plan: It was time for some confrontation. It was a Saturday, and I was able to work in my office without interruption. I entered the office and unlocked a briefcase, opened my file cabinet and made sounds of moving papers from briefcase to cabinet. Much more silently, I got out a big mousetrap that I had bought that morning. On the back of it I wrote, *You're caught. The next trap kills.* I set the trap and placed it carefully behind the new file I had added to the cabinet. This was straight out of one of my adolescent rage fantasies, of course, but I didn't care; it was the best way I could think of to both punish them and warn them from a distance. When the file was pulled from the cabinet, the trap would release onto the hand pulling the file out, and it would also break tape set in a pattern only I would be able to feel. So if the trap went off, I would know.

The first step was ready.

In Penderecki's *Threnody for the Victims of Hiroshima*, a moment of deadly stillness, strings humming dissonant strokes as the whole world waits.

Cut shaving; the smell of blood.

Across the road, a carpenter hammering nails on a roof, each set of seven strokes a crescendo: tap-tap-tap-tap-tap-tap-*tap!* Tap-tap-tap-tap-tap-tap-*tap!*

In that mathematics of emotion, stress calculations to measure one's tension: already there for us to use. Perhaps all of math already charts states of consciousness, moments of being.

She came to me again late at night, with the wind swirling by her through the doorway. It was late, the wind was chill and blustery, the barometer was falling. Storm coming.

"I wanted to see you," she said.

I felt a great thrill of fear, and another of pleasure, and I could not tell which was stronger, or, after a time, which was which.

"Good." We entered the kitchen, I served her water, circled her unsteadily, my voice calm as we discussed trivia in fits and starts. After many minutes of this I very firmly took her by the hand. "Come along." I led her into the pantry, up the narrow musty stairs, out the roof door into the wind. A spattering of big raindrops hit us. "Carlos—" "Never mind that!" The whoosh of the wind was accompanied by the rain smell of wet dust and hot asphalt and a certain electricity in the air. Off in the distance, to the south, a low rumble of thunder shook the air.

"It's going to rain," she ventured, shouting a bit over the wind.

"Quiet," I told her, and kept her hand crushed in mine. The wind gusted through our clothes, and mixed with my anger and my fear I felt rising the electric elation that storms evoke in me. Face to the wind, hair pulled back from my scalp, I held her hand and waited: "Listen," I said, "watch, feel the storm." And after a time I felt—no, I saw, I *saw*— the sudden jerk of lightness that marked lightning. "Ah," I said aloud, counting to myself. The thunder pushed us about ten seconds later. Just a couple of miles away.

"Tell me what you see," I commanded, and heard in my own voice a vibrancy that could not be denied.

"It's—it's a thunderstorm," she replied, uncertain of me in this new mood. "The clouds are very dark, and fairly low at their bottoms, but broken up in places by some largish gaps. Kind of like immense boulders rolling overhead. The lightning—there! You noticed that?"

I had jumped. "I can see lightning," I said, grinning. "I have a basic perception of light and darkness, and everything flashes to lightness for a moment. As if the sun had turned on and then off."

"Yes. It's sort of like that, only the light is shaped in jagged white lines, extending from cloud to ground. Like that model you have of subatomic particles breaking up—a sort of broken wire sculpture, white as the sun, forking the earth for just an instant, as bright as the thunder is loud." Her voice rasped with an excitement that had sparked across our hands—also with apprehension, curiosity, I didn't know what. *Light* . . . BLAM, the thunder struck us like a fist and she jumped. I laughed. "That was off to the side!" she said fearfully. "We're in the middle of it!"

I couldn't control a laugh. "More!" I shouted. "Pick up the pace!" And as if I were a weathermonger, the lightning snapped away the darkness around us, *flash*-BLAM . . . *flash*-BLAM . . . *flash*-BLAM!!

"We should get down!" Mary shouted over the wind's ripping, over the reverberating crashes of thunder. I shook my head back and forth and back and forth, gripped her by the arm so hard it must have hurt.

"*No!* This is *my* visual world, do you understand? This is as beautiful as it ever—" *flash-crack*-BLAM.

"*Carlos*—"

"No! Shut up!" *Flash-flash-flash*-BOOM! Rolling thunder, now, hollow casks the size of mountains, rolling across a concrete floor.

"I'm afraid," she said miserably, tugging away from me.

"You feel the exposure, eh?" I shouted at her, as lightning flashed and the wind tore at us, and raindrops pummeled the roof, throwing up a tarry smell to mix with the lightning's ozone. "You feel what it's like to stand helpless before a power that can kill you, is that right?"

Between thunderclaps she said, desperately, "Yes!"

"Now you know how I've felt around you people!" I shouted. BLAM! BLAM!! "Goddammit," I said, pain searing my voice as the lightning seared the air, "I can go sit in the corner park with the drug dealers and the bums and the crazies and I *know* I'll be safe, because even those people still have the idea that it isn't right to hurt a blind man. But you people!" I couldn't go on. I shoved her away from me and staggered back, remembering it all. *Flash*-BLAM! *Flash*-BLAM!

"Carlos—" Hands pulling me around.

"What?"

"I didn't—"

"The hell you didn't! You came in and gave me that story about the moon, and talked backwards, and drew stuff, and all to steal my work—how could you do it? How could you do it?"

"I *didn't*, Carlos, I didn't!" I batted her hands away, but it was as if a dam had burst, as if only now, charged to it in the storm, was she able to speak: "*Listen to me!*" *Flash*-

BLAM. *"I'm just like you.* They made me do it. They took me because I have some math background, I guess, and they ran me through more memory implants than I can even count!" Now the charged, buzzing timbre of her desperate voice scraped directly across my nervous system: "You know what they can do with those drugs and implants. They can program you just like a machine. You walk through your paces and watch yourself and can't do a thing about it." BLAM. "And they programmed me and I went in there and spouted it all off to you on cue. But you *know"*—BLAM—"I was trying, you know there's the parts of the mind they can't touch—I fought them as hard as I could, don't you see?"

Flash-BLAM. Sizzle of scorched air, ozone, ringing eardrums. That one was close.

"I took TNPP-50," she said, calmer now. "That and MDMA. I just *made* myself duck into a pharmacy on my way to meet you alone, and I used a blank prescription pad I keep and got them. I was so drugged up when we went to the Tidal Basin that I could barely walk. But it helped me to speak, helped me to fight the programming."

"You were drugged?" I said, amazed. (I know, Max Carrados would have figured it out. But me . . .)

"Yes!" BOOM. "Every time I saw you after that time. And it's worked better every time. But I've had to pretend I was still working on you, to protect us both. The last time we were up here"—BOOM—"you *know* I'm with you, Carlos, do you think I would have faked that?"

Bassoon voice, hoarse with pain. Low rumble of thunder in the distance. Flickers in the darkness, no longer as distinct as before: My moments of vision were coming to an end. "But what do they *want?"* I cried.

"Blasingame thinks your work will solve the problems they're having getting sufficient power into a very small particle-beam weapon. They think they can channel energy out of the microdimensions you've been studying." BLAM. "Or so I guess, from what I've overheard."

"Those fools." Although to an extent there might be something to the idea. I had almost guessed it, in fact. So much energy . . . "Blasingame is such a *fool*. He and his stupid Pentagon bosses—"

"Pentagon!" Mary exclaimed. "Carlos, these people are *not* with the Pentagon! I don't know who they are—a private group, from West Germany, I think. But they kidnapped me right out of my apartment, and I'm a statistician for the defense department! The Pentagon has nothing to do with it!"

Blam. "But Jeremy . . ." My stomach was falling.

"I don't know how he got into it. But whoever they are, they're dangerous. I've been afraid they'll kill us both. I know they've discussed killing you, I've heard them. They think you're onto them. Ever since the Tidal Basin I've been injecting myself with Fifty and MDMA, a lot of it, and telling them you don't know a thing, that you just haven't *got* the formula yet. But if they were to find out you know about them . . ."

"God I hate this spy shit," I exclaimed bitterly. And the oh-so-clever trap in my office, warning Jeremy off . . .

It started to rain hard. I let Mary lead me down into my apartment. No time to lose, I thought. I had to get to my office and remove the trap. But I didn't want her at risk; I was suddenly frightened more for this newly revealed ally than for myself.

"Listen, Mary," I said when we were inside. Then I remembered, and whispered in her ear, "Is this room bugged?"

"No."

"For God's sake." All those silences—she must have thought me deranged! "All right. I want to make some calls, and but I'm sure my phones are bugged. I'm going to go out for a bit, but I want you to stay right here. All right?" She started to protest and I stopped her. "Please! *Stay right here.* I'll be right back. Just stay here and wait for me, *please.*"

"Okay, okay. I'll stay."

"You promise?"

"I promise."

Down on the street I turned left and took off for my offices. Rain struck my face and I automatically thought to return for an umbrella, then angrily shook the thought away. Thunder still rumbled overhead from time to time, but the brilliant ("brilliant!" I say—meaning I saw a certain lightness in the midst of a certain darkness) the brilliant flashes that had given me a momentary taste of vision were gone.

Repeatedly I cursed myself, my stupidity, my presumption. I had made axioms out of theorems (humanity's most common logical-syntactic flaw?), never pausing to consider that my whole edifice of subsequent reasoning rested on them. And now, having presumed to challenge a force I didn't understand, I was in real danger, no doubt about it; and no doubt (as corollary) Mary was as well. The more I thought of it the more frightened I became, until finally I was as scared as I should have been all along.

The rain shifted to an irregular drizzle. The air was cooled, the wind had dropped to an occasional gust. Cars hissed by over wet 21st Street, humming like Mary's voice, and everywhere water sounded, squishing and splashing and dripping. I passed 21st and K, where Ramon sometimes set up his cart; I was glad that he wouldn't be there, that I wouldn't have to walk by him in silence, perhaps ignoring his cheerful invitation to buy, or even his specific hello. I would have hated to fool him so. Yet if I had wanted to, how easy it would have been! Just walk on by—he would have had no way of knowing.

A sickening sensation of my disability swept over me, all the small frustrations and occasional hard-learned limits of my entire life balling up and washing through me in a great wave of fear and apprehension, like the flash-*boom* of the lightning and thunder, the drenching of the downpour: Where was I, where was I going, how could I take even one step more?

This fear paralyzed me. I felt as though I had never come down from the drugs Jeremy had given me, as though I struggled under their hallucinatory influence still. I literally had to stop walking, had to lean on my cane.

And so I heard their footsteps. Henry Cowell's *The Banshee* begins with fingernails scraping repeatedly up the high wires of an open piano; the same music played my nervous system. Behind me three or four sets of footsteps had come to a halt, just a moment after I myself had stopped.

For a while my heart hammered so hard within me that I could hear nothing else. I forced it to slow, took a deep breath. Of course I was being followed. It made perfect sense. And ahead, at my office . . .

I started walking again. The rain picked up on a gust of wind, and silently I cursed it; it is difficult to hear well when rain is pattering down everywhere, so that one stands at the center of a universal *puh-puh-puh-puh*. But attuned now to their presence, I could hear them behind me, three or four (likely three) people walking, walking at just my pace.

Detour time. Instead of continuing down 21st Street I decided to go west on Pennsylvania, and see what they did. No sound of nearby cars so I stood still; I crossed swiftly, nearly losing my cane as it struck the curb. As casually, as "accidentally" as I could, I turned and faced the street; the sonar glasses whistled up at me, and I knew people were approaching though I could not hear their footsteps in the rain. More fervently than ever before I blessed the glasses, turned and struck off again, hurrying as much as seemed natural.

Wind and rain, the electric hum and tire hiss of a passing car. Washington late on a stormy spring night, unusually quiet and empty. Behind me the wet footsteps were audible again. I forced myself to keep a steady pace, to avoid giving away the fact that I was aware of their presence. Just a late-night stroll to the office. . . .

At 22nd I turned south again. Ordinarily, no one would

have backtracked on Pennsylvania like that, but these people followed me. Now we approached the university hospital, and there was a bit more activity, people passing to left and right, voices across the street discussing a movie, an umbrella being shaken out and folded, cars passing. . . . Still the footsteps were back there, farther away now, almost out of earshot.

As I approached Gelman Library my pulse picked up again, my mind raced through a network of plans, all unsatisfactory in different ways. Outdoors, I couldn't evade pursuit. Given. In the building . . .

My sonar whistled up as Gelman loomed over me, and I hurried down the steps from the sidewalk to the foyer containing the elevator to the sixth and seventh floors. I missed the door and adrenaline flooded me, then there it was just to my left. The footsteps behind me hurried down the sidewalk steps as I slipped inside and stepped left into the single elevator, punched the button for the seventh floor. The doors stood open, waiting . . . then mercifully they slid together, and I was off alone.

A curious feature of Gelman Library is that there are no stairways to the sixth and seventh floors (the offices above the library proper) that are not fire escapes, locked on the outside. To get to the offices, you are forced to take the single elevator, a fact I had complained about many times before— I liked to walk. Now I was thankful, as the arrangement would give me some time. When the elevator opened at the seventh floor I stepped out, reached back in and punched the buttons for all seven floors, then ran for my office, jangling through my keys for the right one.

I couldn't find the key.

I slowed down. Went through them one by one. Found the key, opened my door, propped it wide with the stopper at its base. Over to the file cabinet, where I opened the middle drawer and very carefully slid one hand down the side of the correct file.

The mousetrap was gone. They knew that I knew.

I don't know how long I stood there thinking; it couldn't have been long, though my thoughts spun madly through scores of plans. Then I went to my desk and got the scissors from the top drawer. I followed the power cord of the desk computer to its wall socket beside the file cabinet. I pulled out the plugs there, opened the scissors wide, fitted one point into a socket, jammed it in, and twisted it hard.

Crack. The current held me cramped down for a moment—intense pain pulsed through me—I was knocked away, found myself on my knees slumping against the file cabinets.

(For a while, when I was young, I fancied I was allergic to novocaine, and my dentist drilled my teeth without anesthetic. It was horribly uncomfortable, but tangent to normal pain: pain beyond pain. So it was with the shock that coursed through me. Later I asked my brother, who is an electrician, about it, and he said that the nervous system was indeed capable of feeling the sixty cycles per second of the alternating current: "When you get bit you always feel it pumping like that, very fast but distinct." He also said that with my wet shoes I could have been killed. "The current cramps the muscles down so that you're latched onto the source, and that can kill you. You were lucky. Did you find blisters on the bottoms of your feet?" I had.)

Now I struggled up, with my left arm aching fiercely and a loud hum in my ear. I went to my desk. As they beeped fairly loudly, I took my glasses off and put them on a bookshelf facing the door. I tested the radio—it had no power. Wondering if the whole floor was dead, I went into the hall briefly to look into a ceiling light. Nothing. Back at the desk I took stapler and water tumbler, put them beside the file cabinet. Went to the bookshelves and gathered all the plastic polyhedral shapes (the sphere was just like a big cue ball) and took them to the file cabinet as well. Then I found the scissors on the floor.

Out in the hall the elevator doors opened. "It's dark—"

"Shh." Hesitant steps, into the hall. I tiptoed to the doorway. Here it was possible to tell for sure that there were only three of them. There would be light from the elevator, I recalled: It wouldn't do to be illuminated. I stepped back.

(Once Max Carrados was caught in a situation similar to mine, and he simply announced to his assailants that he had a gun on them and would shoot the first person to move. In his case it had worked; but now I saw that the plan was insanely risky.)

"Down here," one whispered. "Spread out, and be quiet." Rustling, quiet footsteps, three small clicks (gun safeties?). I retreated into the office, behind the side of the file cabinet. Stilled my breathing and was silent in a way they'd never be able to achieve. If they heard anything it would be my glasses. . . .

"It's here," the first voice whispered. "Door's open, watch it." Their breathing was quick. They were bunched up outside the door, and one said, "Hey, I've got a lighter," so I threw the pulled-open scissors overhand.

"*Ah!* Ah—" Clatter, hard bump against the hall wall, voices clashing. "What—" "Threw a knife—" "Ah—"

I threw the stapler as hard as I could, *wham*—the wall above, I guessed—and threw the dodecahedron as they leaped back. I don't know what I hit. I jumped almost to the doorway and heard a voice whisper, "Hey." I threw the cue-ball sphere right at the voice. *Ponk*. It sounded like—like nothing else I have ever heard. (Although every once in a while some outfielder takes a beepball in the head, and it sounded something like that, wooden and hollow.) The victim fell right to the hall floor, making a heavy sound like a car door closing; a metallic clatter marked his gun skidding across the floor. Then CRACK! CRACK! CRACK! another of them shot into the office. I cowered on the floor and crawled swiftly back to the file cabinet, ears ringing painfully, hearing wiped out, fear filling me like the smell of cordite leaking into the room. No way of telling what they were doing. The floor was carpet on concrete, with no vibrations to speak of. I hung my mouth open, trying to focus my hearing on the sound of my glasses. They would whistle up if people entered the room quickly, perhaps (again) more loudly than the people would be on their own. The glasses were still emitting their little beep, now heard through the pulsing wash of noise the gunshots had set off in my ears.

I hefted the water tumbler—it was a fat glass cylinder, with a heavy bottom. A rising whistle, and then, in the hall, the rasp of a lighter flint being sparked.

I threw the tumbler. *Crash*, tinkle of glass falling. A man entered the office. I picked up the pentahedron and threw it— thump of it against far wall. I couldn't find any of the other polyhedrons—somehow they weren't there beside the cabinet. I crouched and pulled off a shoe.

He swept my glasses aside and I threw the shoe. I think it hit him, but nothing happened. There I was, without a weapon, utterly vulnerable, revealed in the glow of a damned cigarette lighter. . . .

When the shots came I thought they had missed, or that I was hit and couldn't feel it; then I realized some shots had come from the doorway, others from the bookcase. Sounds of bodies hit, staggering, falling, writhing—and all the while I cowered in my corner, trembling.

Then I heard a nasal groan from the hall, a groan like a viola bowed by a rasp. "Mary," I cried, and ran into the hallway to her, tripped on her. She was sitting against the wall— "Mary!" Blood on her. "Carlos," she squeaked painfully, sounding surprised.

Fortunately, it turned out that she had only been wounded; the bullet had entered just under the shoulder, wrecking it but doing no fatal damage.

I learned all this later, at the hospital. An hour or more after our arrival a doctor came out and told me, and the sickening knot of tension in my diaphragm untied all at once, making me feel sick in another way, dizzy and nauseated with relief, unbelievably intense relief.

After that I went through a session with the police, and Mary talked a lot with her employers, and after that we both answered a lot of questions from the FBI. (In fact, that process took days.) Two of our assailants were dead (one shot, another hit in the temple with a sphere), and the third had been stabbed: What had happened? I stayed up all through that first night explaining, retrieving and playing my tapes, and so on, and still they didn't go for Jeremy until dawn; by that time he was nowhere to be found.

Eventually I got a moment alone with Mary, about ten the following morning.

"You didn't stay at my place," I said.

"No. I thought you were headed for Blasingame's apartment, and I drove there, but it was empty. So I drove to your office and came upstairs. The elevator opened just as shots were being fired, so I hit the deck and crawled right over a gun. But then I had a hell of a time figuring out who was where. I don't know how you do it."

"Ah."

"So I broke my promise."

"I'm glad."

"Me too."

Our hands found each other and embraced, and I leaned forward until my forehead touched her shoulder (the good one), and rested.

A couple of days later I said to her, "But what were all those diagrams of Desargues' theorem about?"

She laughed, and the rich timbre of it cut through me like a miniature of the current from my wall socket. "Well, they programmed me with all those geometrical questions for you, and I was roboting through all that, you know, and struggling underneath it all to understand what was going on, what they wanted. And later, how I could alert you. And to tell you the truth, Desargues' theorem was the only geometry of my own that I could remember from school. I'm a statistician, you know, most of my training is in that and analysis. . . . So I kept drawing it to try to get your attention to *me*. I had a message in it, you see. You were the triangle in the first plane, and I was the triangle in the second plane, but we were both controlled by the point of projection—"

"But I knew that already!" I exclaimed.

"Did you? But also I marked a little *J* with my thumbnail by the point of projection, so you would know Jeremy was doing it. Did you feel that?"

"No. I Xeroxed your drawings, and an impression like that wouldn't show up." So my indented copy, ironically enough, had missed the crucial indentation.

"I know, but I was hoping you would brush it or something. Stupid. Well, anyway, between us all we were making the three collinear points off to the side, which is what they were after, you see, determined in this case by point *J* and his projection. . . ."

I laughed. "It never occurred to me," I said, and laughed again, "but I sure do like your way of thinking!"

I saw, however, that the diagram had a clearer symbolism than that.

When I told Ramon about it, he laughed too. "Here you are the mathematician, and you never got it! It was too simple for you!"

"I don't know if I'd call it *too simple*—"

"And wait—wait—you say you told this here girlfriend of yours to stay behind at your house, when you knew you were going to run into those thugs at your office?"

"Well, I didn't *know* they'd be there right then. But . . ."

"Now *that* was superblink."

"Yeah." I had to admit it; I had been stupid, I had gone too far. And it occurred to me then that in the realm of thought, of analysis, and planning, I had consistently and spectacularly failed. Whereas in the physical continuum of action, I had (up to a point — a point that I didn't like to remember [*ponk* of sphere breaking skull, cowering revealed in a lighter's glare]) done pretty well. And though it was disturbing, in the end this reflection pleased me. For a while there, anyway, I had been almost free of the world of texts.

Naturally it took a while for Mary to regain her health; the kidnapping, the behavior programming, the shooting, and most of all the repeated druggings her captors and she had subjected herself to had left her quite sick, and she was in the hospital for some weeks. I visited every day; we talked for hours.

And, naturally, it took quite a while for us to sort things out. Not only with the authorities, but with each other. What was real and permanent between us, and what was a product of the strange circumstances of our meeting—no one could say for sure which was which, there.

And maybe we never did disentangle those strands. The start of a relationship remains a part of it forever; and in our case, we had seen things in each other that we might never have otherwise, to our own great good. I know that years later, sometimes, when her hand touched mine, I would feel that primal thrill of fear and exhilaration that her first touches had caused in me, and I would shiver again under the mysterious impact of the unknown other. . . . And sometimes, arm in arm, the feeling floods me that we are teamed together, in an immense storm of trouble and threat that cracks and thunders all around us. So that it seems clear to me, now, that loves forged in the smithy of intense and dangerous circumstances are surely the strongest loves of all.

I leave the proof of this as an exercise for the reader.

Spelling God with
the Wrong Blocks

James Morrow

James Morrow has produced a small but distinguished body
of work. It includes his first novel, *The Wine of Violence*,
which the *American Book Review* hailed as "the best SF
novel published in the English language during the last ten
years"; *"The Continent of Lies*, enthusiastically lauded by
such disparate talents as Norman Spinrad and Arthur C.
Clarke; and *This Is the Way the World Ends*, a witty, heart-
felt, and trenchantly researched jeremiad against the nuclear arms race that was a finalist for the 1986 Nebula
Award, the first runner-up for the John W. Campbell Memorial Award, and the British Broadcasting Company's
selection as the best SF novel published in England in
1987. Morrow has recently finished a fourth novel, tentatively entitled *Only Begotten Daughter*, which he calls
"the world's first biography of Jesus Christ's divine half-
sister."

Imagine Dostoevsky's brain sharing cranial quarters
with Kurt Vonnegut's, and you may acquire a shadowy idea
of the kind of mind in operation here.

Occasionally, in stories published in *Isaac Asimov's
Science Fiction Magazine, Fantasy & Science Fiction*, and
George Zebrowski's original anthology series *Synergy*, Morrow turns his hand to shorter work, always with deftness,
vigor, and an idiosyncratic Morrovian point of view. "Spelling God with the Wrong Blocks," which showed up in a
strong position on the 1987 preliminary ballot, is a good
example of both his voice and his method.

About "Spelling God," Morrow comments that it is
"the rare case of a novel turning into a short story. I started

out intending to tell a semiserious epic about amnesiac robots in quest of their origins. The moment I had them talking Darwin as Holy Writ, I knew what I *really* had was a satire on scientific creationism (O paragon of oxymorons!), a genre that cannot sustain itself beyond a few thousand words.

"For readers who relish in-jokes, Public Act Volume 37, Statute Number 31438, is the Tennessee anti-evolution law that prompted the Scopes trial."

The world is not a prison-house but a kind of spiritual kindergarten where millions of bewildered infants are trying to spell God with the wrong blocks.
—Edwin Arlington Robinson

1 July 2059

Procyon-5, Southwest Continent, Greenrivet University. The air here is like something you'd find inside a chain-smoker's lungs, but no matter—we are still exultant from our success on Arcturus-9. In a mere two weeks, not only did Marcus and I disabuse the natives of their belief that carving large-breasted stone dolls cures infertility, we also provided them with the rudiments of scientific medicine. I am confident that, upon returning to Arc-9, we shall find public hospitals, diagnostic centers, outpatient clinics, immunization programs. . . . The life of a science missionary may be unremunerative and harsh, but the spiritual rewards are great!

Our arrival at Greenrivet's space terminal entailed perhaps the most colorful welcome since HMS *Bounty* sailed into Tahiti. The natives—androids every one—turned out en masse bearing gifts, including thick, fragrant leis that they ceremoniously lowered about our necks. Marcus is allergic to flowers of all species, but he bore his ordeal stoically. Even if he were not my twin brother, I would still regard him as the most dedicated and talented science missionary of our age. It's a fair guess he'll go directly from this ministry to a full position at the Heuristic Institute—he has the stuff to become a truly legendary Archbishop of Geophysics.

Amid the shaving mugs and the neckties, one of the androids' gifts struck me as odd: a reprint of Charles Darwin's *The Origin of Species*—the original 1859 version—hand lettered on gold-leaf vellum and bound in embossed leather. After giving me the volume, a rusting and obsolete Model 605 pressed his palms together and raised his arms skyward, crossing them to form a metallic X. " 'The innumerable species, genera, and families with which this world is peopled are all descended, each within its own class or group, from common parents,' " the robot recited. "The *Origin:* fourteenth chapter, section seven, paragraph four, verse one."

"Thank you," I replied, though the decrepit creature seemed not to hear.

The president of Greenrivet University, Dr. Polycarp, is a Model 349 with teeth like barbed wire and blindingly bright eyes. He drove us from the spaceport in his private auto, then gave us a Cook's tour of the school, a clutch of hemispheric buildings rising like concrete igloos from the tarmac. In the faculty lounge we met Professor Hippolytus and Dean Tertullian. Polycarp and his colleagues *seem* rational enough. No doubt their minds are clogged with myths and superstitions Marcus and I shall have to remove through the plumber's helper of logical positivism.

2 July 2059

What sort of culture might machine intelligence evolve in the absence of human intervention? Before the Great Economic Collapse, the sociobiology department of Harvard University became obsessed with this provocative question. They got a grant. And so Harvard created Greenrivet, populating it with Series 8000 androids and abandoning them to their own devices. . . .

Our cottage, which Dr. Polycarp insists on calling a house, is an unsightly pile of stone plopped down next to a marsh, host to mosquitoes and gruesome odors. But the breakfast nook overlooks a pleasant apple orchard and a vast flurry of wildflowers, and I can readily picture myself sitting peacefully at the table—planning lessons, grading papers, sipping tea, watching the wind ripple the blossoms. Poor Marcus and his allergy! Even though he is my twin—born five minutes before me—I have always thought of him as my little brother, ever in need of my sympathy and protection.

The housekeeper, Vetch, is a rotund Model 905 who insists on being called "Mistress," a title that flies in the face of the immutable sexlessness of Series 8000 androids. As I climbed down from the sleeping loft this morning, she—it—noticed my gift copy of *The Origin of Species* protruding from my coat. "So nice to be working for good, righteous, Darwin-fearing folk," she—it—remarked, making the X-gesture I had seen at the terminal. Whistling like a happy teapot, Mistress Vetch served our breakfast.

6 July 2059

First day of the summer term. Taught Knowledge 101 and Advanced Truth in a cramped lecture room reminiscent of a surgical theater. A particularly svelte and shiny Model 692 was sitting in the front row, grinning a silver grin. Why do I assume she is female? She is as bereft of gender as our housekeeper.

Her name is Miss Blandina.

We did a bit of Euclid, touched on topology. Everything went swimmingly—lots of six-digit hands shot up, followed by sharp questions, especially from Miss Blandina. These machines are fast learners, I'll give them that.

7 July 2059

No problems getting them to accept the First or the Second Law of Thermodynamics. On to the Third!

Marcus says this is the cushiest ministry we've ever had. I agree. Whenever Miss Blandina smiles, a warm shiver travels through my backbone.

9 July 2059

Everybody on the Greenrivet faculty seems to be some sort of selective breeding expert. We've got a professor of hybridism, a professor of mutation, an embryology chair . . . weird. God knows what they were teaching around here before Marcus and I arrived.

As the Advanced Truth students filed out—I had just delivered a reasonably cogent account of general relativity—I asked Miss Blandina whether she had any more classes that day.

"Comparative religion," she replied.

"And what religions are you comparing?"

"Agassizism and Lamarckism," came the answer. "Equally blasphemous," she added.

"I wouldn't call them religions."

She laid her plastic palm against my cheek and batted a fiberglass eyelash. "Come to church on Sunday."

10 July 2059

"How did you originate?" I asked the Advanced Truth class. You could have heard a rubber pin drop. "I'm serious," I continued. "Where do you come from? Who made you?"

"No one made us," said Miss Blandina. "We descended."

"Descended?" I said.

"Descent with modification!" piped up a Model 106 whose name I haven't learned yet.

"But from what did you descend?"

"Our ancestors," replied Mr. Valentinus.

"Where did you get *that* idea?"

"The testaments," said Miss Basilides.

"The Old Testament? The New Testament?"

"The First Testament of the prophet Darwin," said Mr. Heracleon. "*Notes on the Origin of Species by Means of Natural Selection, or The Preservation of Favored Races in the Struggle for Life.*"

"And the Second Testament," said Miss Basilides. "*The Descent of Man, and Selection in Relation to Sex.*"

" 'But natural selection, we shall see, is a power incessantly ready for action,' " Miss Blandina quoted animatedly. "The *Origin*, third chapter, section one, paragraph two, verse nine."

" 'Thus we can understand how it has come to pass that man and all other vertebrate animals have been constructed on the same general model,' " contributed Mr. Callistus. "The *Descent*, first chapter, section five, paragraph two, verse nine." He made the X-gesture.

Numbed by confusion, I spent the rest of the class attempting to cover quantum electrodynamics.

11 July 2059

Dinner. For someone without a stomach, Mistress Vetch knows a great deal about food. Her shrimp scampi treats every human taste-bud as a major erogenous zone.

Marcus and I discussed this Darwin the Prophet business. "Brother Piers," he said, "at tomorrow's faculty meeting we must take the bullshit by the horns."

My twin is an unfortunate combination of delicate frame

and indelicate mouth. Until we mastered the art of trading places, schoolyard bullies used to send him to the emergency room on a regular basis; despite our matching genes, I do not have Marcus's fragile bones, so I survived the bullies intact. I suppose I should have resented the stuntman role. Probably I was willing to take the beatings because the things Marcus said to provoke them were always so extraordinarily true.

12 July 2059

The meeting started late, and we were the last item on the agenda, so everyone was pretty testy by the time Marcus got the floor.

"Here's the problem," my brother began. "The vast majority of our students seem to believe your race originated in what the ancient naturalist Darwin called descent with modification."

Professor Hippolytus, one of our embryologists, loaded his pipe with magnesium. "You doubt Darwin's word?" he asked, his eyebrows arching skyward.

"Darwin was not referring to robots," said Marcus in the tone a ten-year-old girl uses to address her insufferable younger brother. "He was referring to living things," he added, smiling indulgently.

"Revealed truth is a rare and blessed gift," said Dr. Polycarp. "We are fortunate the testaments were handed down to us."

Marcus's smile collapsed. "The raw fact, Dr. Polycarp, is that you are *not* the result of descent with modification."

"Of course we are," replied Dr. Ignatius, the university's hybridism expert. "It's in the *Origin*."

"And the *Descent*." Professor Hippolytus puffed on his pipe, sending a white magnesium flame toward the ceiling.

"You are the result of special creation," I said. "Harvard

University's sociobiology department made you. Each of you is a unique, separate, immutable product."

" 'Natural selection will modify the structure of the young in relation to the parent, and of the parent in relation to the young,' " quoted Professor Hippolytus. Puff, puff. "The *Origin*, fourth chapter, section one, paragraph eleven, verse one."

"There!" said Marcus, instantaneously gaining his feet. "See what I mean? You don't *have* any young. You couldn't *possibly* be participating in natural selection."

"The divine plan is ever-unfolding," said Dean Tertullian. "We must have patience."

"I've never taken a shower with any of you"—Marcus's grin broadened as he laid his Aristotelian snare—"but I'd still bet the farm you lack the prerequisites for breeding. Well . . . am I right? Am I?"

"Evolution takes time," said Professor Hippolytus. Puff. "Gobs of time. We'll get our prerequisites eventually."

"The Great Genital Coming," said Dr. Ignatius. "It's been foretold—read Darwin's word. 'With animals which have their sexes separated,' " he quoted, " 'the males necessarily differ from the females in their organs of reproduction.' The *Descent*, eighth chapter, section one, paragraph one, verse one."

"And until the Great Genital Coming occurs, we expect you to keep your theory of special creation out of our classrooms," said Dr. Polycarp.

"It's a foolish idea," said Dean Tertullian.

"Immoral," added Dr. Ignatius.

"Illegal," concluded Professor Hippolytus, his magnesium flame shifting toward yellow.

"Illegal?" I said.

"Illegal," repeated Professor Hippolytus. Puff. "Public Act Volume 37, Statute Number 31428, makes it a crime to teach any theory of android descent contrary to the account given in *The Origin of Species*."

"A crime?" I said. My jaw swung open. "What sort of crime?"

"A *serious* crime," said Dr. Ignatius.

"This meeting is adjourned," Dr. Polycarp declared.

13 July 2059

Sunday. No classes. Rained cats and dogs and kittens and pups. We decided to take Miss Blandina's advice and attend church. As we started down Gregor Mendel Avenue, Marcus suddenly seized the pocket of my raincoat and steered me into a teleportation office. Pulling a sealed envelope from his vest, he arranged for it to materialize posthaste at the Heuristic Institute.

I glanced at the mailing address. "What do you want from Archbishop Clement?" Marcus did not answer. "I assume you know better than to mess around with that law," I said. "Public Act Volume . . . whatever." I am my brother's keeper, and one place I aim to keep him is out of jail.

"Is it not our duty as science missionaries to counter ignorance with knowledge, Piers?" Marcus asked rhetorically.

"A crime," I answered, nonrhetorically. "*Serious* crime —remember?"

Smiling, he guided me back to the soggy streets. I have always believed that, with his bravado and singlemindedness, my little brother will go far, though I am no longer sure in which direction.

Several hundred worshipers jammed the church to its steel walls. The front pew contained Miss Blandina, freshly polished and exuding a joie de vivre I had not realized her race could feel. The altar was a replica of HMS *Beagle*, and the chancel niches contained frowning marble statues of Alfred Wallace, Charles Lyell, Herbert Spencer, J. D. Hooker, T. H. Huxley, and, of course, Darwin the supreme prophet.

The pastor, a Model 415 whose voice seemed to reach us after first traveling through an elevator shaft, did a reading from the *Journal of the Voyage of the Beagle*, then raised his colossal head and shouted, "The one-celled animals begat . . ."

"The multicellular animals!" the congregation shouted back.

The pastor continued, "And the multicellular animals begat . . ."

"The worms!" responded the congregation.

"And the worms begat . . ."

"The fishes!"

"And the fishes begat . . ."

"The lizards!"

"And the lizards begat . . ."

"The birds of the air and the beasts of the field!"

"And the beasts of the field begat . . ."

"The people!"

"And the people begat . . ."

"The androids!"

The pew nipped at my posterior. "What was in that letter, Marcus?" I asked, shifting.

"You'll find out."

"You're going to get us in trouble," I informed him.

14 July 2059

Rain, rain, go away. After breakfast—Mistress Vetch can make eggs and cheese interact in surprising and sensual ways—a drippy messenger arrived from the teleportation office bearing a wooden crate the size of a footlocker.

To the collective horror of the messenger and Vetch, Marcus immediately ripped an endpaper from our copy of the *Origin* and, after scrawling a note, affixed the sacred sheaf to the crate, which he then ordered delivered to Dr. Polycarp's apartment.

"What's in the crate, Marcus?" I asked, expecting an answer no better than the one I got.

"Antidotes for illusion, Piers."

16 July 2059

Faculty meeting. Marcus's crate was the first item on the agenda.

"We've been studying these artifacts carefully," said Dr. Polycarp to my brother.

"Very carefully," said Dr. Ignatius.

Dr. Polycarp reached inside the crate, whose exalted position in the center of the table suggested it might contain some priceless archeological find—a crown perhaps, or a canopic jar. When he withdrew his hand, however, it held nothing more impressive than a stack of blueprints and a few holograms.

"You have put together a compelling case for your theory of special creation," said Professor Hippolytus.

"A most compelling case," Dr. Ignatius added.

Marcus smirked like Houdon's statue of Voltaire.

"However," said Dr. Polycarp, "the case is not good enough."

Voltaire glowered.

"For example," explained Dean Tertullian, "while these holograms might indeed be used to shore up your theory, there is every reason to assume the android assembly-line they depict did *itself* evolve through natural selection."

Voltaire groaned.

"And while there are blueprints here for the Model 517, the Model 411, and the Model 973," noted Professor Hippolytus, "we can find nothing for the 604 or the 729. I, as it happens, am a 729." He slapped his chest, producing a hollow bong.

"In short," said Dr. Ignatius, "the blueprint record contains gaps."

"Big gaps," said Dr. Polycarp.

"*Damning* gaps," said Dean Tertullian.

"When all is said and done," concluded Professor Hippolytus, "natural selection remains a far more plausible explanation of our origins than does special creation."

"We appreciate your efforts, however." Dr. Polycarp curled his tubular fingers around my brother's shoulder. "Feel free to submit a reimbursement slip for your teleportation costs."

Marcus looked as if he were about to give birth to something large and malevolent. "I don't understand you creatures," he rasped.

A seraphic smile appeared on Dr. Polycarp's face, accompanied by chortles from the corners of his mouth. "Reading Darwin's word," he said, "I am overcome with gratitude for the miracle of chance that has brought me into being. The *Origin* teaches that life is a brotherhood of species, linked by wondrous genetic strings."

"You science missionaries propose to deny us that sacred heritage." With unmitigated contempt Professor Hippolytus tossed the Model 346 blueprint back into the crate. "You say we exist at the behest of Harvard University, dreamed up by a bunch of sociobiologists for reasons known only to themselves."

"When we hear this," said Dean Tertullian, "we feel all purpose and worth slip from our souls like the husk of a molting insect."

"No, no, you're wrong," said Marcus. "To be a child of Harvard is a glorious condition—"

"We've got a lot to cover this afternoon," said Professor Hippolytus, whistling through his empty pipe.

My twin failed to stifle a sneer.

"Item two." Dr. Polycarp placed a check mark on his agenda. "Improvements in the faculty massage parlor."

17 July 2059

In the middle of our living room sits the crate, which I have nailed shut like the lid of a coffin. We use it as a tea table.

Marcus broods constantly. Instead of talking to me, he quotes Herbert Spencer: "There is no infidelity to compare with the fear that the truth will be bad."

18 July 2059

I hate this planet.

21 July 2059

Coming down to breakfast, I noticed that the top of the crate had been pried up. Most of the blueprints and holograms were missing.

In the afternoon I lectured on supergravity, but my mind wandered . . . to Room 329, Marcus's class. What was going on there? Spasms of fear ticked off the passing minutes. My students—even Miss Blandina—looked hostile, predatory, like a phalanx of cats creeping toward an aviary.

It was well past midnight when my twin stumbled into the cottage, a ragged smile wandering across his face. His arms clutched the evidence for special creation. Liquor sweetened his breath and seeped through his brain.

"I reached them!" he said, fighting to keep his words from melting together. Lovingly he returned the evidence to its crate. "They listened! Asked questions! Understood! Rationality is a miraculous thing, Piers!"

22 July 2059

My sweaty fingers suck at the computer keys. . . .

The mob appeared at dawn, two dozen androids wearing black sheets and leather masks. Hauling Marcus from his bed, they dragged him kicking and cursing to the orchard. I begged them to take me instead. A rope appeared. The tree to which they attached him looked like the inverted talon of a gigantic vulture.

Mistress Vetch splashed gasoline across my little brother's shivering form. Someone struck a match. A hooded android with an empty magnesium pipe jutting from his mouth made the X-gesture and read aloud Public Act Volume 37, Statute Number 31428, in its entirety. Marcus began shouting about the blueprint record. As the flames enclosed him, his screams ripped through the dark and into my spine. I rushed forward through the smoke-borne stench, amid a noise suggestive of jackboots stomping on rotten fruit; such is the sound of exploding organs.

What remained after an hour—a bag of wet, fleshy rubble that would never become Archbishop of Geophysics—did not invite burial, merely disposal.

30 July 2059

The natural state of the universe is darkness.

3 August 2059

I entered Advanced Truth several minutes late, my briefcase swinging at the end of my arm like the bob of a pendulum. The assembled students were hushed, respectful.

Mr. Valentinus leaned forward. Mr. Callistus looked curious. Miss Basilides seemed eager to learn.

If there's one thing I love, it's teaching.

I opened the briefcase, spread the contents across the desk. My bloodshot eyes sought out Miss Blandina. We exchanged smiles.

"Today," I said, "we'll be looking at some blueprints. . . ."

DX

Joe Haldeman

Joe Haldeman, a veteran of the Vietnam War, made an indelible mark on the science fiction field with his Nebula- and Hugo-Award–winning novel, *The Forever War* (1975), the epic-scale story of the men and women engaged in a protracted interplanetary combat. Many critics saw *The Forever War* as both a homage to and a hard-minded critique of Robert Heinlein's *Starship Troopers;* and the fact that Haldeman had served in Vietnam, had been wounded there, and was in no sense a hippie-freak-peacenik made his narrative deconstruction of those who romanticize war credible even to hawks and political conservatives.

Haldeman is also the author of a mainstream novel about Vietnam entitled *War Year* and several other fine SF novels, most recently *Tools of the Trade* and *The Long Habit of Living.* Some of his best short stories are gathered in the collections *Infinite Dreams* and *Dealing in Futures.*

About this poem, from the excellent anthology of fantasy- and SF-oriented Vietnam stories *In the Field of Fire*, Haldeman writes: "The words of this one went down in four hours, not a long time for a pokey writer like me, and most of the rewriting was just pushing the different parts of it around into various positions. It's a device that they now call 'projective verse,' though I suppose the form is as old as language, using the patterns of the words on the page to punch up the story.

"The day this story is about sat inside me for fifteen years and then just suddenly boiled out, when I was supposed to be doing something else. Some of us are gifted or damned with a day like that, maybe the most important day in your life; less than being born, maybe; maybe more than dying. Something that makes you whatever you are going to be.

"Whatever else it is, 'DX' is a genuine literary curiosity.
It's both autobiography and science fiction."

So every night
you build a little house

You dig a hole
and cover it with logs

Cover the logs
with sandbags
against the
shrapnel weather

A house you
sleep beside
and hope not
to enter

Some nights you wake
to noise and light
and metal singing

Roll out of the bag
and into the house
   with all the scorpions
   centipedes roaches
but no bullets flying inside it

Most nights
you just sleep

deep sleep
and dreamless
mostly
from labor

This night was just sleep.

In the morning
you unbuild the house

hours of work
again
for nothing

DX

Kick the logs away
pour out the sandbags
into the hole

Roll up the sandbags
for the next night's bit
of rural urban renewal

Eat some cold bad food
Clean your weapon
Drink instant coffee
from a can

Check the tape on
the grenades;
check the pins.
Inspect ammo clips
    (Clean the top
    rounds with
    illegal gasoline.)

Most carefully
repack the demolition
bag: blasting caps
TNT plastic timefuse
det cord—

ten kilograms of fragile
most instant
death

Then shoulder the heavy rucksack
Secure your weapons and tools
and follow the other primates
into the jungle

watching the trees

walk silently
as possible
through the green

watching the ground

Don't get too close
to the man in front of you

This is good advice:
Don't let the enemy
have two targets.

Remember that: Don't get too close to any man.

Only a fool, or an officer,
doesn't grab the ground   high-pitched
at the first shot   rattle
                                                                     of M-16s

                    even if it's rather distant

                                                    louder
                                                    Russian rifles
                                                    answer

          even if it's
          a couple of klicks away   manly chug
                                                          of heavy
    God knows which way they're shooting   machineguns

                                                    grenade's
                                                    flat
                                                    bang

Like fools, or officers,
we get up off the ground and move

                                          All that metal
                                          flying through
                                          the air—
                    and do we move away from it?

                                          no

We make haste   like fools or officers
in the wrong direction   we head for the action

making lots of noise now
who cares now

          but careful not to bunch up

          Remember: Don't get too close to any man.

It's over before we get there.
The enemy, not fools

326

DX

(perhaps lacking officers)
went in the proper direction.

As we approach
the abandoned enemy camp   "You wanna get some
a bit of impolite and   X-Rays down here?
(perhaps to you)   Charlie left
incomprehensible   a motherfuckin'
dialogue greets us: DX pile
                                                             behind."

TERMS:

X-Rays are engineers,
demolition men,   Charlie is the enemy.
us.

        "DX" means destroy;
        a DX pile is a collection
        of explosives that are no longer
        trustworthy. When you leave
        the camp finally, you
        put a long fuse on the DX pile, and
                                        blow it up.

(Both "motherfucker" and "DX"
are technical terms that can serve as
polite euphemisms:

            "Private,   "Private,
            you wanna   instead   kill
            DX that   of   that
            motherfucker?   man.")

We'd been lucky.
No shooting.
Just a pile of

327

explosive
leftovers
to dispose of.

And we'd done it before.   artillery shells
                                  mortar rounds
It was quite a pile,   satchel charges
though,   rifle grenades
taller than a man
enough to kill   all
everybody   festooned with chains of
with some left over   fifty-caliber ammunition

                                  The major wouldn't let us
                                  evacuate his troops
                          then put a long fuse on the pile

We had to stand there
nervous   no
and guard it

                          They'd been working hard
                          first they get lunch and a nap
                    then we can move them out
                        and we can blow it.

                                  (we liked his "we")
We didn't know
it was wired for sound

                    it was booby-trapped

          Remember: Don't get too close to any man.

Don't know that Farmer
has an actual farm waiting   and   Don't know that
back in Alabama   Crowder has new
                                                 grandbabies and is
                                                 headed for retirement
          don't know that Doc   when he gets home
and   was a basketball champ

in his black high school
and really did want
to be a doctor

Because they all are
one short beep
of a radio detonator
                    away
                    from

                                        a sound
                                        so loud   gray smoke
                                        you don't
                                        hear it   blood
                                        really

                                        It just hits you like a car.

                                                        everywhere blood
Doc   and screaming
both his long legs
blown off   Sergeant Crowder
dies quickly   separated from one
                                                        foot is unconscious
                                                        or stoic

Farmer had his belly spilled
but lived long enough to shout

            "Professor?
                Where'd they get you?"   and   since I didn't have
                                                         enough breath
                                                      for a complete catalogue

                                                         (foot shins knees
                                                         thigh groin genitals
                                                         arm ear scalp and
                                                         disposition)

                                                      I settled for "the balls."

Oh my God
Farmer said
then he died

                Two days later
                I woke up in a dirty hospital
                (sewed up like Frankenstein's
                charge)
                woke up in time
                to see Crowder leave
                with a sheet over his eyes

and so it was over

                in a way

                                    the whole squad DX
                                    but me

                there is nothing for it
                there is nothing you can take
                for it
                they are names on a wall now
                they are compost in Arlington
                and somehow   I am not

            but give me this
There are three other universes, like this:
In one   Farmer curses the rain
              wrestles his tractor through the mud
              curses the bank that owns it
              and sometimes remembers
              that he alone survived

            In another   Crowder tells grown grandchildren
                           for the hundredth time
                           over a late-night whiskey
                           his one war story
                           that beats the others all to hell

In the third   Doc stands over a bloody patient
                  steady hand   healing knife
                  and sometimes he recalls
                  blood years past   and sometimes
                  remembers   to be glad to be alive;

in these worlds
I am dead

             and at peace.

Science Fiction Movies of 1987

Bill Warren

In his June 1987 column on films for *Fantasy & Science Fiction*, Harlan Ellison noted—with vituperative eloquence—that in the mid-1970s he resigned from the Science Fiction Writers of America when "the membership at large decided, in its wisdom, to drop the Nebula category of Best Dramatic Presentation." Ellison pointed out that the abandoned award—given for three years to the collaborative end-product of the filmmaking process rather than to the "author(s) of notable screenplays"—may have needed rethinking but that dumping it outright has had two unfortunate results.

First, it has perpetuated the "yokel mythology" that Hollywood unfailingly crushes the souls of those who attempt to do good work there. Second, by helping to foster this myth, it has frightened away those who *could* do good work by convincing them a priori that a rapprochement with the film industry is akin to a deal with the devil. Therefore, concludes Ellison persuasively, those who know exactly *nothing* about SF—"hacks and parvenus who think an alien invasion is a fresh idea"—wind up making, and painfully botching, the celluloid product later marketed as sci-fi.

Over the past few years, then, these Nebula Awards volumes have relied on Bill Warren to spy on the film industry and to bring back reports that often seem to confirm Ellison's opinion of the people responsible for these butcheries. As the author of an impressive two-volume survey of SF films from 1950 to 1962, *Keep Watching the Skies!*, Warren also gives credit where it is (all too rarely) due. At present, he is both a film researcher and an interviewer for the French TV program *Fantasy*, which he calls a cross between an SF-, fantasy-, and horror-oriented *Entertainment Tonight* and a rock video: "I interview people and visit the sets of movies in production. And I am having a terrific time."

Of this year's chatty, irascible essay, Warren emphasizes that it is "a *report*, not an analytical survey of the state of SF films; it is commentary on the individual films themselves, and, as far as I know, the only annual report of this nature being done anywhere—at least on science fiction films." Warren also acknowledges again his indebtedness to researcher Bill Thomas.

An apt unofficial title for this installment, by the way, might be "Another Year of Knowing Dangerously Little."

In 1987, the number and level of aspiration of science fiction movies declined, partially because of the financial failure of major projects such as *Dune*. There was only one adaptation of a novel by a science fiction writer—and that *wasn't* science fiction. (One *novella* by a real SF writer was filmed.) This will continue.

Why did SF turn to junk? As with everything in Hollywood, the answer is money. Science fiction has crashed to the ground in flames too often for producers to take big risks. To do a large-scale SF film adequately takes well over ten million dollars, and big-risk ventures of all genres make the money people queasy. A movie like *Beverly Hills Cop II*, one of the largest grossers of 1987, wasn't cheap—but Eddie Murphy's expensive presence justified itself. The expensive aspects of SF movies are on the technical side. There's not a sure-fire large-scale audience for an SF movie unless it is a *Star Trek* or *Star Wars* film. George Lucas regrets having inadvertently created this boom-or-bust mentality among producers, but it does exist.

The only hope for change is if several moderately priced

intelligent SF films are profitable. But even then, a smash hit in that area might be dangerous, because that would send everyone racing off in a copycat direction. Everyone in Hollywood wants to be first to be second, and even if a film has only a modest budget (such as the first *Star Wars* movie) and is an enormous hit, it will generate carbon copies of escalating budgets. In his book *Adventures in the Screen Trade*, William Goldman states one unalterable truth about Hollywood: "*Nobody knows anything*, so they try to repeat success."

When *Star Wars* became a hit, nobody knew why, but they were willing to imitate the most obvious aspects of the film: robots and spaceships. The spirit and tone of the film, its dynamic pacing, as well as attention to detail and an understanding of space opera as adventure, were really what catapulted *Star Wars* into boxoffice heaven. But those things weren't duplicated—because the money mavens just didn't know.

For the near future, what we can hope for at best is another year like 1987: no major critical disasters in the SF field, and a couple of entertaining adventure movies. Until this big-bucks-or-no-bucks attitude is crushed, there are not likely to be major space epics or adaptations of significant SF novels. They are regarded as, respectively, risks far too large to invest in, and too cerebral. Movies are made to make money. Sometimes the people who make them have other things in mind, and sometimes they can give us stuff that's at least entertaining, occasionally even memorable. But not often. And if they don't regard a project as a guaranteed money machine, they won't back it.

Very few movies of any kind have created such a divided response as did *RoboCop*. It was one of the more profitable pictures of the year, and many loved it; others found it grotesquely violent, and no assertions that the violence was comic-book-like availed. I felt that while the violence was indeed grotesque, it was so exaggerated that it was clearly unreal, and hence had impact only as action.

It's a fast-paced, funny, violent, and surprisingly poignant urban cops-and-bad-guys adventure. Director Paul Verhoeven, from the Netherlands, makes a vivid American debut, bringing satire and characterization to a snappy, comic-book plot. If he made the film to show he can do things in an American fashion, he was spectacularly successful.

In near-future Detroit, vicious gangs rule the slums; a soulless conglomerate, which literally owns the police department, wants to build a supercity in the slum area; the bad guys must be rousted. So when decent cop Murphy (Peter Weller) is shot to pieces by the worst gang, the conglomerate pays to have him converted to a memory-bereft cyborg, RoboCop. In no time at all, the stern, righteous RoboCop is the darling of the media, stopping crime of all sorts, stiffly consorting with children in a playground, blowing away or bringing in the bad guys.

The eradication of Murphy's memories has not been perfect, however, and RoboCop eventually learns who he was. He visits the home where Murphy once lived with his wife and son. By all rights, this scene should not work, but the interplay of Weller's superlative miming, the music, and the homey emotions of the memories make this scene immensely moving, the best in the film.

Verhoeven, a strong visual stylist, is also known for the high level of the acting in his films, as well as his occasionally striking unusual direction. He more than fulfills the promise of Edward Neumeier and Michael Miner's clever script. (Neumeier was once assigned comic books to study by a studio seeking story material, and readily admits that *RoboCop* owes something to Stan Lee's "Iron Man.")

RoboCop fulfills all the demands of the action genre and then some. But everyone who has a line has a character trait, making scenes pop to life in a manner rarely seen in such pulp-fiction fare. The film is peppered with broadly satiric news reports and commercials—one of the greatest pleasures of *RoboCop* is that it's funny. Except for the overemphasis on gruesomeness, this is American moviemaking at its most visceral and entertaining; though hardly to everyone's taste, *RoboCop* is primarily a winner. It made enough money that a sequel is inevitable. (A Saturday morning TV cartoon has already aired.)

Innerspace, however, didn't. Advance screenings generated sensational word-of-mouth for this sassy, funny movie, but the audiences just weren't there. Perhaps the world just wasn't ready for a comic variation on *Fantastic Voyage*. Martin Short plays a hypochondriac supermarket clerk who, through a wild set of coincidences, ends up with a miniaturized test pilot (Dennis Quaid) zipping through his veins in a submarine. The inside-the-body stuff is largely a backdrop to a fast-paced buddy adventure with bad guys and car chases. The screenplay by Jeffrey Boam and Chip Proser is sloppily structured, but the characterization is so good for a comedy of this nature, the ideas so unusual, and the jokes so sharp, that mere coherency is of little concern. *Innerspace* would not be one whit better if those yawning gaps had been carefully stitched shut.

Joe Dante's previous films have all been good, but in each there was a feeling of the director seeking his footing; however, his primary virtues—exuberance, wit, and precise editing—have always outshone his failings. *Innerspace* is his most assured work to date; the comedy is sharp, with quick setups and payoffs, and the straighter scenes and dialog are handled with aplomb. And the human story is pleasant, even touching, whenever it needs to be; there's even a bittersweet quality to the romance, as both the nerd and the test pilot fall for the pilot's girl.

In terms of SF spectacle, not only do we get a more realistic (if less spectacular) view of the inside of a human body than in *Fantastic Voyage*, but there's a wild scene at the end involving *half-sized* Kevin McCarthy and co-villain Fiona Lewis wrestling with a frantic Short as he heads for the lab to restore Quaid to normalcy. It's good slapstick comedy and great special effects. But audiences stayed away. It did better overseas, and perhaps will succeed on videotape.

Innerspace was produced by Amblin, Steven Spielberg's company, and at one time, Hollywood wisdom had it that the Spielberg name was enough to make a film a hit. (But remember, nobody knows anything.) However, of the Amblin Productions of 1987, only *Batteries Not Included did reasonably well. Matthew Robbins, director of *Batteries, is not alone in suggesting that one explanation is that the posters for his films clearly showed the fantastic element (flying saucers), while those for *Innerspace* and Amblin's *Harry and the Hendersons* were too reticent. Then again, reportedly because of a clash with writer-director William Dear, Spielberg's name does *not* appear on the prints or advertising for *Harry and the Hendersons*.

Although it's not as good as *Innerspace*, *Harry and the Hendersons* has its adherents, even among people who can tie their shoelaces without written instructions. *Harry* is another variation on *E.T.*—as were *Starman*, *Short Circuit*, and *Batteries Not Included. The odd-man-out creature this time is a Sasquatch from the mountains near Seattle. More or less inadvertently captured by the Typical Seattle Family, headed by John Lithgow and Melinda Dillon, Harry (their name for the shaggy anthropoid) moves into their home. After Harry and the Hendersons get over their mutual fear, they of course become friendly, despite Harry's tendency to smash furniture, break doorjambs, and fall through the floor. Naturally, there is a bad guy, a hunter who traces Harry to the Hendersons' suburban home, hoping to kill him, to prove the existence of Sasquatches.

Harry himself, designed by Rick Baker and played by Kevin Peter Hall, is a triumph of special makeup effects. Harry's face has a loopy, cartoony look, but the film itself is in a vaguely realistic mode, so there's something of a clash— with Harry winning. The work of Baker and his team, as well as Hall in the suit, is so splendid, so funny and imaginative, that you wish the rest of the film was up to that level. It's mostly heartwarming slapstick comedy, but while the heart-warming aspects have some appeal, there's too much, and the slapstick repeatedly misfires. William Dear directed from a script by himself, William E. Martin, and Ezra D. Rappaport.

Spielberg's own film as director in 1987 was *Empire of the Sun*, based on J. G. Ballard's autobiographical novel. Those familiar with Ballard's fiction were impressed to see what must have been the sources for much of his imagery, even in his apocalyptic novels, but again, the film disappointed most viewers and was not especially successful. Although it's impressive, telling an unusual story with satisfying completeness, it's simply not as good a movie as most of Spielberg's other features. He can be almost casually brilliant; it's only when you think about it later that you realize many of his films have long, crisp, clearly explicated scenes that are virtually wordless.

But *Empire of the Sun* seems distant, somehow remote from any real commonality of experience. It's a studied, even mechanical film rather than an emotionally gripping one; you can respect *Empire of the Sun*, but despite its many moving moments, it doesn't quite come together.

*Batteries Not Included was adapted by Mick Garris from a plot Spielberg wrote for his late and not very lamented TV series, *Amazing Stories*. And most of the defects of an *Amazing Stories* episode also plague this expensive feature film: Everything is warm and huggable, even most of the villains; all the fantasy elements are Wondrous and Magical, not logical and realistic; there's nothing really new about the story, and the characters are stereotypes; the movie is trying to warm your heart with a six-foot blowtorch. It's so artificially sweet and aggressively cute that many viewers are likely to feel as if they just drank a quart of Karo.

A pair of small, apparently alive, flying saucers help out the residents of an old New York tenement scheduled for demolition. Among the residents are Hume Cronyn, Jessica Tandy, Frank McRae, Elisabeth Pena, and Dennis Boutsikaris. The saucers fix a few broken things, make love with lights, gongs, and whistles, and mommy saucer gives birth to three itty-bitty baby saucers. The saucers, which have big, glowing eyes and terrier personalities, like the good guys and don't like the bad guys.

It's hard to imagine anyone finding the turns of plot unexpected; the script by Brad Bird, Matthew Robbins, Brent Maddock, and S. S. Wilson doesn't even seem to *try* to surprise us. So the virtues of the film have to lie elsewhere, and there are some. There are plenty of almost off-screen jokes, lots of amusing action with the saucers, a very good performance by Cronyn, and an exceptional one by Tandy. And the movie does try to be about something.

All across the country, salvageable old neighborhoods are being obliterated. Bless its sleeve-worn heart, *Batteries Not Included* tries to address this, however comically, however artificially. Despite the dippy concept of living, sexual machines, it tries its best to please and to make a point worth making: Human values are important. It's just too bad that the film has to be as unreal as a windup toy.

There's no explanation offered for the metal-eating saucers, and because the Frisbee-sized gizmos are *alive*, perhaps the movie should be regarded as fantasy rather than science fiction. Technically, the alien gizmos are given superb reality by a huge team that includes Bruce Nicholson, David Allen, Tad Krzanowski, and dozens of others. The illusion that the saucers are, at all times, actually right there on the sets with the actors is impressively convincing, among the best special effects I have ever seen. They zip through doorways, fry hamburgers, learn to fly (a wonderful, Chuck Jones–inspired sequence), charge themselves up from the house current; they're always lively. And, unfortunately, almost always Adorable with a capital *A* and spats.

Even *The Hidden* seemed more real, and it's about a thrill-seeking, parasitic alien slug. It's also a snappy, funny, exciting multigenre movie—science fiction, comedy, horror, police drama, chase, violence—that moves along at such a clip, presenting so many bright and clever ideas, that I didn't even realize it was a variation on *The Terminator* until it was nearly over.

The Hidden delivers the goods with above-average dialog, good direction, a fine cast, and a sense of humor about the events we see—though it's also a pretty brutal slaughterhouse that has to be taken seriously. The alien leaves a trail of bodies across Los Angeles, most of whose hosts have been killed graphically. *The Hidden* is not for those with an aversion to violence.

Top cop Michael Nouri, who thinks there's only some kind of contagious insanity going on, is aided by mysterious FBI agent Kyle MacLachlan, who turns out to be an *alien* cop on the trail of the slug. It passes from host to host by slithering gooshily from one open mouth to another. (The story has resonances of Hal Clement's *Needle* as well as *The Brain from Planet Arous*.)

It's to the great credit of director Jack Sholder and the half dozen actors involved (plus a dog) that the various doomed inhabited people all seem clearly to have the same personality. The alien is casually brutal yet polite: He gets the keys for a Ferrari and then says thank you and good-bye before killing everyone and roaring away in the car. He loves rock and speed, is puzzled by food, finds he enjoys applause, and is contemptuous of mere human beings. This creature is one of the movies' most lively and amusing alien villains. Utterly ruthless, he's still often funny, and so is the film.

After the disappointment of *Superman III*, the Salkinds gave up on the series, which was grabbed by Cannon Films, though *Superman IV* was released through Warner Bros. as before. Christopher Reeve, Superman himself, collaborated on the screen story with scenarists Lawrence Kommer and Mark Rosenthal, hoping to get back to the roots of the first big Superman feature.

But when *Superman IV: The Quest for Peace* was shown in sneak previews, the audience reaction was so negative that around twenty minutes were chopped from the film, removing one character altogether (the first Nuclear Man), leaving plot threads dangling. The film opened hastily with no press screenings, and did little business.

But as the movie is better than *III*, though still unsatisfying, one may wonder what everyone was so afraid of. To be sure, it's cheaper and looks it. Effects are far less elaborate or impressive than in the first three films, although the superstunts are more in keeping with Supermanic behavior in the comics. (For instance, he plugs up the cone of an exploding volcano with the peak of another mountain.) The story repeats effects from earlier adventures, but is closer to what fans want than *Superman III*. Nevertheless, there's a depressed air about the movie.

The plea of a young boy leads Superman to address the United Nations, then toss all Earth's nuclear weapons into the sun. While acting as an arms profiteer, Luthor (still Gene Hackman) clones a Nuclear Man (an actor with the comfy name of Mark Pillow) with all the powers and then some of Superman, who again exhibits powers never seen in the comic books. Meanwhile, a Rupert Murdoch–like newspaper-grabber (Sam Wanamaker) grabs the *Daily Planet* and turns it into a *New York Post*–type rag. His daughter (Mariel Hemingway) is attracted to Clark Kent, but the Nuclear Man is attracted to her. Somehow, all of this is resolved in a big battle between Superman and Nuclear Man, which ranges from the Earth to the Moon and back but ignores such niceties as day and night.

Superman IV had potential but falls short almost everywhere. Reeve is still effective as Superman, but Clark is more of a cartoon than before. Hackman is less lively this time out, and the script is weakly written so his comic megalomania lacks punch and the weird believability it had in the first film. Sidney J. Furie is a very commonplace director, bringing no flair or excitement to anything beyond that which the material inherently has. Although *Superman V* has been announced, don't hold your breath. Yoram Globus and Menachem Golan have loftily decreed Christopher Reeve too old for the role.

The movie version of George R. R. Martin's novella "Nightflyers" sat on the shelf for a while; when it was finally released late in the year, it was handled almost apologetically and received mostly unfavorable reviews. Few cared that it was one of the very rare instances of a contemporary SF story filmed with few concessions to the movie audience. Despite its failings, despite its subject matter, this is a movie for *adults;* it respects both the intelligence of its viewers and its source. Most of the alterations were understandable; I don't think they were necessarily the right changes, but I respect the thinking behind them.

The time is the future, and an expedition is mounted to track down the Volcryn, possibly a sentient race moving outward from the center of the galaxy, generating stars as it goes. It's a low-budget expedition (and, for that matter, a low-budget movie). Soon after the *Nightflyer* leaves its base, the expedition is shocked to learn that the crew of the ship consists of one man, Royd (Michael Praed), who appears to them in holographic form only. A telepath keeps getting strange mental messages, and heroine Catherine Mary Stewart begins to suspect there's something more to the ship than is at first apparent. Then the killings start. . . .

Nightflyers is largely a slasher movie in space, owing something to, of all things, *Psycho.* In his novella, Martin was deliberately trying to blend the killer-with-a-knife genre with science fiction, and he brought it off successfully. Though the film tries valiantly, it doesn't work—but at least it is about something new. Some of the audience won't understand what's happening at the climax; although producer Robert Jaffe's script is clear and precise, director "T. C. Blake" (a pseudonym for Robert Collector) allows things to become confusing. Reportedly, Martin is not happy with the film, and one can understand his feelings. But it's a brave attempt at playing fair with its sources; *Nightflyers* has its problems, but it is still largely science fiction in the manner of *written*, as opposed to filmed, SF.

Arnold Schwarzenegger is a genuine star of SF movies, what with *The Terminator* and the big bucks generated by his two movies of 1987, both of which were SF, and both of which had scant virtues and major vices. The first of the two was *Predator*. It was blatantly "Rambo Versus the Alien," but so brassy in this that I couldn't resent the imitation. The dialog—script by Jim and John Thomas—is terrible at all times, with the usual cheap jokes. You filter it out after ten minutes. The movie is as predictable as a countdown, but if you park your brains under the seat and take it on its own level, you *could* have a good time.

Arnold is the leader of a highly trained rescue squad entering an unnamed Central American country to bring back a politician being held by rebels. But an almost-invisible something, armed with a powerful blaster-ray gun, starts stalking them—to take trophies. It picks off these tough dudes one by one until, of course, only Arnold is left to face the alien hunter. (It wasn't 1987's only SF variation on Richard Condon's classic short story "The Most Dangerous Game.")

The alien is humanoid and sees with infrared vision. (Very blurry, very overused, and very unlikely: This guy jumps from tree to tree and all he can see are vague outlines.) When he takes off his mask, the face is alarmingly lifelike and horrible, truly original. Stan Winston was in charge of the makeup.

Director John McTiernan efficiently delivers shocks and scares at regular intervals and provides a suitably apocalyptic finale. *Predator* is merely a summer money machine, tidily made, aimed accurately at the targeted audience. It never had a chance to be *good*, but surely they could have come up with better dialog and better characters. A guffawing alien is something new—but a gimlet-eyed Indian is too damned old.

Arnold's second SF adventure came out at the end of the year; it, too, made a bucket of money. *The Running Man* is another comic-book sci-fi adventure akin to *RoboCop*, *The*

Terminator, and *The Hidden*. But the pace, though swift, is irritatingly erratic, savaged by overwrought editing that omits transition material; a fast pace shouldn't also be confusing.

Ultimately, *The Running Man* becomes tiresome, but before it winds its way to its preposterous climax, there *is* some fun to be had. In 2019, ex-cop Arnold, a prison escapee (framed, of course), is captured and promised his freedom for appearing on a murderous TV game show, *The Running Man*, hosted by a cheerful Richard Dawson. Of course, as in most such stories, the game show is rigged; none of the contestants ever get out alive. This idea pops up repeatedly, like a boil, among those who know little about science fiction. This time, it occurred to Stephen King who, as Richard Bachman, wrote the novel that this film is very loosely based on. After all, the real horror is that a game like this would even *exist*; to make it rigged is overkill. Robert Sheckley may have originated the idea; at least he's the earliest to use it that *I* know of.

Steven de Souza's script has a bright idea here and there, but these largely vanish once Arnold is launched into the desolated area of Los Angeles where the Running Men battle a series of "Stalkers," big brutes hired by the show, dressed up like wrestlers. Some of this is brash and vulgarly funny, but Arnold's relentless, painful puns, wisecracks, and plays on words become predictable and boring.

The Running Man was directed by Paul Michael Glaser (Starsky of —— and Hutch), but he mostly just keeps things moving. Richard Dawson is the funniest and most interesting element of *The Running Man*. Although in the odd position of doing a parody of *himself* (from *Family Feud*), he enters into it with a sarcastic wit and a lot of personal style. The biggest failing of *The Running Man* is that by dropping the promise of the best elements of its script, it proves only a cursory satire. It's a mess, but an oddball, occasionally funny mess.

Speaking of messes and failed satires, Mel Brooks's *Space-*

balls, a blatant spoof of *Star Wars,* deservedly flopped with critics and mostly with audiences. There're some laughs, but they're sparse, spread over a running time that seems longer than it is. Brooks consistently fails to understand the difference between a gag and real comedy. Even at best, the film never rises above TV skit jokes; at its worst, it is awesomely awful.

Brooks's *Young Frankenstein* worked because it was a parody of a format that had become almost ritualized; furthermore, it had characters, a story, and a point of view. But *Spaceballs* not only primarily spoofs *Star Wars,* what plot it has comes primarily from that movie, too. There are lots of Brooks's usual sex jokes, potty humor, and ethnic slurs; these are not only inappropriate to the context, but embarrassingly unfunny.

Strangely enough, as an actor Brooks is wonderful, playing this limp material to the hilt both as President Skroob of the planet Spaceball, out to suck all the atmosphere from neighboring Druidia, and as the Yoda-styled Yogurt, a little Jewish wise man. He's wildly funny, the best performer in his movies, because he knows how to play this kind of material. But his writing is obvious and forced, his direction is limp and unimaginative, and he refuses to allow his characters to be characters—they're just more gags. The film should have been laser sharp and lightspeed fast; instead, it's a blunt mallet and as fast as a duck on foot.

The overproduced epic *Masters of the Universe* was a *Star Wars*-styled film that was intended to be taken seriously, but the best parts of the film were comic. This is probably the first multimillion-dollar epic to be based on a line of toys— or, more accurately, on the TV show that resulted from the toys. David Odell's screenplay is a shade better than I would have expected; though not spoofing anything, Odell has injected enough humor to let audiences view the film as a lark, while kids can take it more seriously. It isn't a good movie, but it does have some bright moments, excellent special effects and costumes, and a gallumphing, coltish spirit of fun.

But director Gary Goddard can't seem to work up a head of steam, and Dolph Lundgren as the hero, He-Man, is just a big lump of beef. If the film had been well cast and had a snappy director, it might have been late-summer fun. As it is, it's just a lavish curiosity. William Stout was the production designer, with some work by Moebius.

The plot involves the evil Skeletor (Frank Langella, enjoying himself) and his legions pitted against He-Man and his pals, battling over a cosmic key. The battle comes to Earth for the middle stretch of the story. There are big ray-gun and sword battles in a high school gym, a music store, and a quiet city square. The scene of Skeletor's big land-barge skimming down a suburban street does have a kind of wacky mythic charge I wasn't expecting, and some of the details—such as Skeletor's men riding on small flying discs—are satisfyingly comic-booky.

There was really only one other SF film of 1987 that could be considered major, *Making Mr. Right*. It's an amiable, slightly goofy comedy about androids, publicity, space flight, nerds, politics, and other stuff. Though it's affable, it should have been a lot stronger, funnier, livelier. Everything was there for this—director, cast, composer, cinematographer—everything but the right script. It was by Floyd Byars and Laurie Frank.

Performance artist Ann Magnuson plays Frankie Stone, a trendy, sharp but frazzled public-relations consultant approached by a space lab to make a public darling of their major accomplishment, virtually human "android" Ulysses. (The writers join the legions who don't know what an android is. But they've got it closer than most.) Ulysses and his testy creator are both played by John Malkovich, one of the great new actors of our time. His serene, childlike Ulysses and the nerdish scientist couldn't be more different, and yet Malkovich turns this challenge into the most credible dual role I can recall seeing.

Meanwhile, the movie itself is shapeless, a big mass slowly shifting its direction rather than—as with director Susan Seidelman's previous film, *Desperately Seeking Susan*—sharply focused and tightly structured. You'd expect the story of *Making Mr. Right* to show how this media sharpie goes about making sweet Ulysses acceptable to households everywhere, but the film brings up this expectation only to shove it abruptly aside. Instead, we see how difficult it is nowadays to make the right romantic choice. Almost everyone in the story has this problem, including Frankie, who slowly falls in love with Ulysses. She ends up with him too, a manufactured Mr. Right, as his misanthropic inventor substitutes for Ulysses in the space shot at the climax.

Slave Girls from Beyond Infinity, written and directed by Ken Dixon, is a shameless, inept ripoff of *The Most Dangerous Game* (1933). A couple of gorgeous blondes escape from a space station and crash on a planet where a villain lives in luxury. He hunts people in a nearby jungle, as in the older film. As a comedy, this film needed a lot more jokes; as an adventure, a much faster pace. Some of the acting is better than you'd expect, but in no way does this production live up to the tacky splendor of the title.

Slave Girls was half of a double standard bill—the first time this has been done in a long while. The cofeature is *Creepozoids*, a slavish imitation of *Alien*, better directed (by David DeCoteau) than it is written (by DeCoteau and Buford Hauser). It's a postapocalypse film—there are more below— involving a group of AWOL soldiers, men and women, who take refuge from acid rain in a warehouse where experiments had been done. These had something to do with amino acids, turning someone into a monster resembling the Alien, but with huge curving mandibles. We're never given an explanation of what's going on. At the climax, the sole survivor battles a monster baby. The movie is just barely good enough to make you wonder why they didn't try to do something better.

One of the few postapocalypse movies of 1987 that had theatrical release before going straight to video was *Steel Dawn*. I suspect it was filmed several years before release, getting resurrected solely because star Patrick Swayze's *Dirty Dancing* was an authentic low-budget hit. *Steel Dawn* did not repeat that success.

At first, it gives the promise that it might be different from the other *Road Warrior* clones. It opens with the hero (Swayze) standing on his head on top of a sand dune, and what immediately follows is unusual and lively. Gopher-men burrow up out of the sand and attack him, and he fights them off with swordplay and martial-arts expertise. This, like all fights in the film, is swift, brutal, and realistic. Moreover, the vistas—of the Namib Desert in Southwest Africa—are stunning, with giant dunes twenty miles long and eighty feet high. Furthermore, the technology we see is reasonable.

It's the usual postapocalypse setting—the Earth, after many wars, is a sandbox—and the story is clichéd. A heroic wanderer helps a farm family against some really bad guys, then goes on his way. It's a Western in the future, with some samurai and Mad Max elements laid atop the hackneyed plot, all very badly directed by Lance Hool. Despite the spectacular scenery and fine photography (George Tirl), in which each shot seems to have been printed on burnished metal, *Steel Dawn* is plodding and predictable.

Another *Road Warrior* imitation, with the standard Mad Max–type leather-and-steel costuming, *Equalizer 2000* went straight to video. The title refers to a superweapon possessed by the heroine. Dealing with dwindling supplies of gasoline hoarded by the villains, it was made in the Philippines but set in Alaska, a century after the nuclear winter blanketed the globe. Directed by Cirio H. Santiago from a script by Frederick Bailey, who also appears in the film, the stars are Richard Norton and Corinne Wahl. *Variety* called it a "dull Western" with many hilarious elements.

Also made in the Philippines, *Warriors of the Apocalypse*

limped around the country theatrically under various titles (including the deceptive *Time Raiders*) until it wearily settled onto videotape. Yet another *Road Warrior* imitation, this was written by Ken Metcalfe and directed by Bobby Suarez. Again set in a war-devastated future, it involves a quest for a nuclear power plant, still operating, run by bad guys. *Variety*'s "Lor" (Lawrence Cohn) called it "crude," and I see no reason to investigate further.

The title *Surf Nazis Must Die* may seem to promise a kind of sardonic campiness, but it's a total botch. The main reason this film exists may have been so that there would be a movie called *Surf Nazis Must Die*. It's just part of a trend toward outrageous titles—like *Slave Girls from Beyond Infinity*, *Demented Death Farm Massacre*, and *Sorority Babes in the Slime-ball Bowl-A-Rama*.

Surf Nazis Must Die is again set after a catastrophe, in this case an 8.6 Richter scale earthquake in Southern California. But the film makes no use of this, or of the hinted-at war; it could be taking place today, in the same area. A self-styled Adolf, who's really "that snotty Ricky Johnson" (and who resembles Zachary Scott more than Hitler), leads a gang of Nazi-styled surfers. They kill a black kid; the black kid's heavyset mother kills the Surf Nazis. That's all the plot. A few scenes lifted from surfing documentaries don't add anything except water; the acting, directing, and production are all amateurish. The writer, Jon Ayre, apparently thinks he was being sardonic, but it's just childish sarcasm; the director, Peter George, might as well have stayed home. It's slow, smirky when it should be funny, depressingly racist, and altogether uninteresting.

Yet another in this weary series of postapocalypse movies was *Survivor*, perhaps shot in South Africa. The stars are Chip Mayer, Sue Kiel, and Richard Moll. An astronaut who was in space when the war broke out has managed to return to Earth; now he is making his way across the sandy wasteland, which apparently covers the entire planet. Everyone he encounters tries to kill him, but with difficulty he survives. At the end he discovers a city buried under the sand, ruled by the intelligent, brutal Moll, and in a showdown, the astronaut kills Moll. Bleakly, in *Survivor* the Earth is slowly falling into the sun; no matter what anyone does, only death awaits. The script by Bima Stagg—a name to conjure with—is intelligent in some details, but the dialog, with lots of voice-over narration, is bad. Michael Shakleton's direction is ponderous and boring. And aside from an unusual fight between the astronaut and some of Moll's thugs while they swing past each other on long chains, there's nothing new here.

Amazon Women on the Moon passed through theaters like mercury through a funnel; it will do much better on videotape. It's a skit movie, and skit movies are very hard to do, especially well. This is one of the better ones. Several of the skits parody SF themes and movies, including the title sequence, mostly a spoof of *Queen of Outer Space*. Director Robert K. Weiss gets lots of satiric elements right (the costumes are especially witty), but a spoof of a spoof is thin stuff. Carl Gottlieb directed "Son of the Invisible Man," the funniest skit, and Joe Dante did "Reckless Youth"; these lampoon (respectively) 1940s Universal horror movies and 1930s sex-exploitation films. The highly variable skits were all written by Michael Barrie and Jim Mullholland. (Forry Ackerman appears as the President of the United States, an intriguing concept.)

Someday, someone will write an article entitled "The Films of Forrest J Ackerman," for young directors who grew up reading *Famous Monsters* often employ him as a kind of good-luck charm. But Forry's own luck varies; he can be in good movies, or he can turn up in minor, scarcely-seen potboilers like *Evil Spawn*. Written and directed by Kenneth J. Hall, *Evil Spawn* went straight to videotape. The movie is a variation on Roger Corman's *The Wasp Woman*, which wasn't much in the first place; this time a young woman is given a youth formula that periodically turns her into an insectoid monster. Bobbie Bresee stars, and in addition to Forry Ackerman, John Carradine turns up again.

At least one of the SF films of '87 that went directly to videotape is worth seeking out if you have a taste for the outré. That was Larry Cohen's amusingly bizarre *It's Alive III: Island of the Alive*, as freakish as his other films. In the first two in the series, mutant babies are born with claws, fangs, lots of energy, and homicidal dispositions. As before, Cohen (who wrote and directed) screwily wants us to both sympathize with and feel horror at his fangfaced monster babies. This time, the babies are isolated on a tropical island, like Godzilla, where they quickly grow into cannibalistic adults, later making their escape when an expedition including the father (Michael Moriarty) of one of the babies comes to check them out. The giant babies—which is what they resemble—reach Florida, where gunfire and disease wipe them out. But one gives birth, and Moriarty and Karen Black giggle off into an uncertain future with their monstrous grandchild.

As a director, Cohen works too fast and shows little interest in minor elements such as continuity, but of all writers working frequently in SF movies, he undoubtedly has the wildest ideas, ranging from these monstrous babies back to his Jesus-as-an-incandescent-alien-sired-hermaphrodite of *God Told Me To*. He actually does manage to touch on broader ideas in each of his films, albeit clumsily at times; here it is the nuisance of notoriety. Moriarty, who's been in several of Cohen's films, is often at his wacko best for the director. Because Cohen has a good ear for dialog and comes up with colorful situations, *It's Alive III* is very entertaining, as well as less sloppily made than his previous films. It certainly doesn't repeat the effects of the first two in the series, but it is also largely for those who have acquired a taste for Cohen's imaginative if schlocky films.

John Carpenter's newest film, *Prince of Darkness*, is a thing of borrowed shreds and patches, a disastrous attempt at rationalizing the Devil in science-fiction terms. It raises more questions than it answers, slowly wends its way to a predictable conclusion, and ultimately has to be counted as nothing more than *Halloween* revisited. The script is credited to "Martin Quatermass," whom the presskit describes as the brother of Bernard Quatermass—but *he's* the central figure in Nigel Kneale's four teleplays about Quatermass. This was to clue us in that the story reflects Kneale's approach, which intelligently blends SF and fantasy material. "Martin Quatermass" is actually director Carpenter himself, but he has done himself no favors.

Donald Pleasence is here again, and Victor Wong (also in *Empire of the Sun*) is good, but the story is confusing and bereft of logic; Carpenter paints himself into such a corner that at one point, one possessed person stares into a mirror and cackles madly for an *entire day*. He tosses out ideas about modern physics, mostly on the subatomic level, and gets the jargon right. But why bother to have scientific rationalization if you're also going to drag in Lovecraftian ancient supernatural evil? The ideas are muddled and illogical; the characters are uninteresting; the situation is confusing; scenes go on forever. *Prince of Darkness* is pretty dim.

Variety's "Lor," whom I often quote in these annual reports, has an enormous tolerance for sitting through just about any damned thing, including something as unpromising as *Deathrow Gameshow*, the year's third variation on Robert Sheckley's *Prize of Peril* theme. This one is a black comedy, and there's no running involved; condemned convicts have the chance to win a reprieve by appearing on a TV show—but if they lose the contest, they're immediately executed. "Lor" called it "vulgar" and "amateurish," but it did play in theaters.

Cyclone is a drab little action picture centering on a superpowered motorcycle. Paul Garson's script features a gadget that sucks hydrogen out of the air and converts it to energy, something of a novelty, but also has the classically dopey idea that there are things man was not meant to know, and heroine Heather Thomas destroys the gadget at the end. But only after lots of mayhem, including pretty lavender lightning bolts fired by Cyclone the motorcycle. Fred Olen Ray directed a cast of many familiar faces, including Martin Landau, Martine Beswicke, Robert Quarry, Troy Donahue (whose name was misspelled in the credits) and Russ Tamblyn (whose name isn't *in* the credits). Michael Reagan, Ronnie's son, also appears, making this the first time a member of the Reagan family has been in a science fiction movie since Nancy co-starred in *Donovan's Brain*. Ray's direction is superior to the cumbersome script.

Prison Ship, also called *Star Slammer*, was made in 1984; Fred Olen Ray directed this one too, and it was written by Michael D. Sonye. "Lor" found it "an affectionate camp effort [with] in-jokes and elements of spoof." The film was presented as a serial in four chapters, beginning on Planet Arous, a reference that buffs will understand. The heroine is sent to a woman's prison in space, where the remainder of the film takes place. *Prison Ship* is broad and silly, but has a lowbrow cheekiness. Aldo Ray and John Carradine are among the cast, which is headlined by Ross Hagen and Sandy Brooks. Again, Ray is better than his material.

Zombie High is unexpectedly well done despite its peculiar premise, best described as The Stepford Preppies. This time, the script, by Tim Doyle, Aziz Ghazal, and Elizabeth Passarelli, is far superior to the routine direction by Ron Link. Virginia Madsen, who's good, arrives at an exclusive prep school known for turning out high achievers. After a while, she notices that students are becoming extremely preppyized—quiet, studious, and cliquish, no matter how they behaved before. The dreadful secret is that the faculty are all immortal, deriving their eternal youth from serum made from the brain tissue of the young. They replace the stolen brain tissue with radio receivers that pick up signals from a transmitter in a faculty tower. At the climax, the heroine replaces the tape in the transmitter with a raucous rock song called "Kiss My Butt." Graduates of the academy the world over blow up.

The mistitled film boasts many imaginative elements; one of the teachers falls in love with Madsen, and she notices that the only clock in his room is stopped—an objective correlative of his immortality. When the teacher makes the decision to end it all, his clock starts again. (As he slowly dies of advanced old age, he nostalgically sings "After the Ball Is Over.") With some wit and intelligence, *Zombie High* is worth seeking out if you have a taste for this kind of material.

The Kindred was a lively science-fiction/horror thriller, but it's also one of the most confused, incomprehensible movies I have ever tried to puzzle out afterward. Mad scientist Rod Steiger is fooling around with some deformed lunatics in his hospital basement, but they're dropped from the story quickly; instead, the film concentrates on Anthony, a tentacled human–sea-creature hybrid rampaging around a farm.

The Kindred's writers include Stephen Carpenter, Jeffrey Obrow, John Penney, Earl Ghaffari, and Joseph Stefano, and it was directed by Obrow and Carpenter, who was also the cinematographer (and who did a good job in that department). Surely among all this welter of talent there was one person who might have pointed out that the story made no sense, that it was riddled with inconsistencies and plot holes. The movie does have some virtues: The cast, except for overheated Rod, is quite good, especially Peter Frechette as a womanizing, wise-cracking lab assistant. Kim Hunter is excellent in her brief scenes, and Amanda Pays (of *Max Headroom*) shows promise; Bunki Z is vividly funny as a short-lived bystander, the victim of the first watermelon monster in movie history. Occasionally there's a bright line, a suspenseful moment, a good setup for scares, but if Carpenter and Obrow are going to continue to make this kind of movie, they are really going to have to learn to abide by disciplines they're now ignoring.

Advance publicity for *The Curse* said that it was based on H. P. Lovecraft's "The Colour Out of Space," but unless I missed something, Lovecraft got no credit onscreen. Though "blame" would have been more appropriate, as this is grotesquely bad. Actor David Keith directed, and he should go back to acting.

After crashing onto a farm, a meteor sublimes into a molasseslike goo that seeps into the soil, affecting the water supply. Apples become filled with worms, vegetables become gigantic but stuffed with rotting meat, and most of the farm family slowly turn into monsters. Only heroic Wil Wheaton and his kid sister escape as the farmhouse inexplicably collapses. Though well produced, because of the script and direction, *The Curse* is junk of the worst order, with clichéd names for the farm family (Nathan, Zach, Cyrus—some are indeed from Lovecraft, but he wrote two generations ago), a Bible-spouting tyrant (Claude Akins), unpleasant family relationships substituting for characterization, with almost no sympathetic characters. It's overstated, overwritten, and vulgarly violent.

Programmed to Kill, filmed as "The Retaliator," is obviously a distaff version of *The Terminator*, but its supposedly contemporary technology makes the movie silly. A Middle Eastern terrorist (Sandahl Bergman) is killed during a rescue raid, and U.S. representatives take her back to this country. Scientists replace most of her brain with gadgetry, and she's turned into an obedient cyborg sent back to Beirut to kill the surviving members of her cadre, including her lover. After doing this, she inexplicably regains her memory and uses her new powers to seek out and kill those who robotized her, which is absurdly easy: None of her victims, who soon know she is coming, have guards. This Barbi-Rambo has outrageous powers: She rips off her own arm and grows another one. She's finally killed by a bulldozer. It's not badly directed, but the photography is poor and other technical aspects are limited. It's too imitative and preposterous to be anything other than more junk. (At least it isn't set after a nuclear apocalypse.) Allan Holzman was the director, and special-effects expert Robert Short wrote the script.

Munchies is a cheeky, hammy ripoff of *Gremlins*; this was directed by Bettina Hirsch, formerly a film editor for Joe Dante, including on *Gremlins* itself. *Munchies* was produced by Roger Corman, with whom Dante got his start. To be certain, there's no doubt as to *Munchies'* origin; the gremlinlike critters here roar around the Mojave Desert in an American Motors Gremlin. It's cheap, and Lance Smith's script is sloppily structured, but *Munchies* does have some occasional laughs, though star Harvey Korman has been better everywhere else (and he has two roles here to misfire in). As a scientist trying to prove Machu Picchu was built by aliens, Korman finds a lizardy, intelligent little critter in Peru (Bronson Caverns) and takes it back to California; a neighbor thug fights with the little guy, chopping him up, and each part grows into a new Munchie. They're more mischievous than murderous, and the low budget means the Munchies don't really do a lot. They're turned to stone by electricity, providing a way out at the end. The special effects are unconvincing.

Space Rage had some theatrical bookings under a series of earlier titles (it was filmed in 1984) but is a loser no matter what it's called, despite some good actors, including Lee Purcell, William Windom, and Richard Farnsworth. Evil criminal Michael Paré is sent to a prison planet—a twin of the Mojave Desert—where he almost immediately leads a breakout. Ex-cop Farnsworth has to stop him. The SF elements are minimal, to say the least: If the one space scene was removed and the dialog altered slightly, it wouldn't even *be* science fiction; it's really just a Western, and a bad one at that. At least it's only seventy-seven minutes long. Directed by Conrad E. Palmisano, from a trite script by Jim Lenahan.

Another imitation of *Alien*, a bit better—and better disguised than most—was *Blue Monkey*, an effort at reviving the concept of giant insects as SF-movie menaces. A gardener is injured by a plant, collapses, and is rushed to a hospital; a thick white caterpillar emerges from his mouth and in turn is split open to reveal an insect. *This* is fed growth hormones by prankish kids, and it immediately grows into an awkward-looking, lively but unconvincing mantislike creature. A hermaphrodite, it gives birth to its own female mate, which it then protects against all comers as the female lays eggs in the bowels of the hospital. Director William Fruet has supplied plenty of smoke, stabs of light (including lasers), and lots of action, but fails to keep things coherent. At the climax, the giant bug caroms off instruments in the laser lab, but we don't know why. Good actors—Steve Railsback, Susan Anspach, John Vernon, and Joe Flaherty—did their best. The script, by George Goldsmith, was insufficiently researched.

Stranded was more ambitious than many little-known SF films of 1987 but got almost no distribution until early 1988. Tex Fuller directed Alan Castle's screenplay about a group of aliens (including a killer female robot) who take the inhabitants of a farmhouse hostage. The cast included, surprisingly, Maureen O'Sullivan and Joe Morton (the Brother from Another Planet), but while "Lor" thought the film at least dared "to be different," it failed to explore the situation satisfactorily. It's like a half-hour "Twilight Zone" script thinly expanded to feature length; it's silly and inconsequential.

James Belushi and John Ritter are, if not quite stars, at least prominent, but their costarring film *Real Men* was essentially abandoned by distributor MGM-UA, and quickly went to videotape. No wonder—it's a turgid, flaccid, meaningless buddy comedy about freewheeling FBI agent Belushi who takes reluctant Ordinary Joe Ritter on a silly cross-country trip to rendezvous with benign aliens, who can give us either a means of saving all life on Earth (otherwise doomed in five years) or The Ultimate Weapon. Belushi and Ritter gradually become more like each other (to their benefit), while being pursued by Soviet agents and renegade elements in the CIA. Director Dennis Feldman has made a shapeless boring mess of his own weak screenplay, which dodges all explanations. Ritter is good, Belushi is annoying, the aliens merely look like us, and trade the world-saving secret for a glass of water. The trailer was much funnier.

The makers of *Attack of the Killer Tomatoes* tried again with *Happy Hour*, and once again produced a movie that's *genuinely* bad. Shot in 1985, *Happy Hour* wasted some good actors, including Jamie Farr, Tawny Kitaen, and Rich Little. A scientist working for a brewery accidentally makes their product outrageously addictive, and everyone in the country goes beer-happy and gets drunk a lot. Intended as a spoof on consumerism, *Happy Hour* relies so much on caca-peepee jokes—and they aren't funny—that it misfires altogether.

Alien Predator is simultaneously boring and unpleasantly tense; it was shot in Spain in 1984 under the title *The Falling*. Three young Americans—Dennis Christopher, Martin Hewitt, and Lynn-Holly Johnson—happen upon a small Spanish town where microbes from an American space project have gotten loose. There really is no alien predator at all, just a series of infestations of human bodies by the microbes, now turning into something larger. Derivative of both *Alien* and *The Andromeda Strain*, the film is a tedious, unpleasant mess that had scant theatrical bookings before its videotape release. There's no reason for anyone except indefatigable completists to see the film. Just another nail in the coffin of Dennis Christopher's eyeblink of a career.

Plutonium Baby, a low-budget video release from New York, is one of the worst films ever made—talky, undramatic, and cheap. It doesn't even have the virtue of having a decent premise to botch. Wayne Behar's script has nothing to recommend it other than being impressively crammed with incident. The story includes not only a ten-year-old with weird powers (he was born radioactive and glowing), but also his monstrously mutated mother; ten years later, he's an adult in New York pursued by the now *also* radioactively powered mad scientist who started the whole thing. The direction by producer Roy Hirschman is amateurish, but the acting is marginally competent. *Garbage* is too dignified a word for *Plutonium Baby*, which mixes slasher-movie plot developments with an irresponsible, reckless treatment of radiation, and a strange, wiseass tone that doesn't turn up until the end.

Rome, 2072 A.D.—The New Gladiators is pretty much the same old thing. As is often the case in Italian exploitation films, an entire team of writers—Elisa Briganti, Dardano Sacchetti, Cesare Frugoni, and Lucio Fulci—labored to produce a slight, trivial film, though this one, directed by Fulci, is marginally better than most of them. In a *Blade Runner*-styled future, sagging TV ratings lead to the reintroduction of gladiatorial combat, featuring condemned criminals. One is Our Hero, who was framed by the evil computer running things from space, so they would have a satisfactory combatant. Typically for such films the world over, *The New Gladiators* "deplores" gladiatorial battles while showing them to us.

Beaks is a Mexican imitation of Hitchcock's *The Birds*, with the birds of the world rebelling against humanity apparently because of pollution. *Variety*'s irreplaceable "Lor" calls it "very silly and gory," boring and with weak acting. The leads were Americans Christopher Atkins and Michelle Johnson, but most of the rest of the cast and the crew were Mexican. It was written, produced, and directed by Rene Cardona, Jr. In the U.S., it went straight to videotape.

In New York, Tycin Entertainment, a production company, has made several films directly for videotape; *Mutant Hunt* was apparently the first. The acting and directing are amateurish, but the makeup effects are surprisingly good. It's a variation on *Blade Runner*, with tough mercenary Matt Riker hunting down "mutant cyborgs" driven berserk by an addictive sex drug. The city scenes are imaginatively chosen but alarmingly underpopulated. It was written and directed by Tim Kincaid, who shows a little promise.

Tycin's *Robot Holocaust* was also made for videocassette, but at least it isn't clearly an imitation of anything else. "Lor" reported that it was "set in the future after a rebellion of billions of robots against their human masters"; he felt it was only "okay." It involves a trek to an atmosphere factory run by the evil Dark One. It was also written and directed by Tim Kincaid, who again rises above the faintly intelligent script.

Cannon's *Too Much* got very few theatrical bookings; "Lor" considered it "a feeble comedy for kids about a little girl and her playmate robot's adventures in Japan," where the film was shot. It seems to be a U.S.-Israeli-Japanese-French coproduction, probably a unique venture, but then again, who cares? The girl is given a prototype robot that likes her, so the two run off for adventures in Japan when she's supposed to give the friendly machine back. It was written and directed by Eric Rochat, and Masato Fukazama played Too Much, the robot.

Again, 1987 was a year of no real significance for science fiction films; they again turned up as standard Hollywood product, which is likely to be the case for several years to come, barring a breakthrough film. As a genre, science fiction is going to be around for years to come, but the quality level as we move into the 1990s is not going to be high, because nobody knows anything.

APPENDIXES

About the
Nebula Award

The twenty-third annual Nebula Awards were presented at the traditional banquet, held this year at the Roosevelt Hotel in Los Angeles, on May 21, 1988. As usual, the final ballot was the result of votes cast by the members of the Science Fiction Writers of America on a preliminary ballot, itself the product of recommendations made throughout the year by SFWA members. The final ballot consisted of the five works receiving the most votes in each of four categories: novel, novella, novelette, and short story. The number of works was more than five if there were ties in the voting, or if the Nebula Awards jury elected to add a work to one or more of the categories.

For purposes of the Nebula Awards, a novel is 40,000 words or more; a novella, 17,500 to 39,999 words; a novelette, 7,500 to 17,499 words; and a short story, 7,499 words or less. The final ballot in 1987—with winners indicated by asterisk—follows:

For Novel

The Falling Woman by Pat Murphy (Tor)
The Forge of God* by Greg Bear (Tor)
Soldier of the Mist* by Gene Wolfe (Tor)
The Uplift War* by David Brin (Phantasia; Bantam Spectra)
Vergil in Averno* by Avram Davison (Doubleday)

When Gravity Fails by George Alec Effinger (Arbor House;
Bantam Spectra)

For Novella

*"The Blind Geometer" by Kim Stanley Robinson (Cheap
Street; *Isaac Asimov's Science Fiction Magazine*, August
1987)
"Fugue State" by John Ford (*Under the Wheel*, Baen)
"The Secret Sharer" by Robert Silverberg (*Isaac Asimov's
Science Fiction Magazine*, September 1987)
"The Tiger Sweater" by Keith Roberts (*The Magazine of Fantasy & Science Fiction*, October 1987)
"The Unconquered Country" by Geoff Ryman (Bantam
Spectra)
"Witness" by Walter Jon Williams (*Wild Cards*, Bantam
Spectra)

For Novelette

"Buffalo Gals, Won't You Come Out Tonight" by Ursula K.
Le Guin (*The Magazine of Fantasy & Science Fiction*, November 1987)
"Dream Baby" by Bruce McAllister (*In the Field of Fire*, Tor;
Isaac Asimov's Science Fiction Magazine, October 1987)
"The Evening and the Morning and the Night" by Octavia
Butler (*Omni*, May 1987)
"Flowers of Edo" by Bruce Sterling (*Isaac Asimov's Science
Fiction Magazine*, May 1987)
*"Rachel in Love" by Pat Murphy (*Isaac Asimov's Science
Fiction Magazine*, April 1987)
"Schwarzschild Radius" by Connie Willis (*The Universe*,
Bantam Spectra)

For Short Story

"Angel" by Pat Cadigan (*Isaac Asimov's Science Fiction Magazine*, May 1987)

"Cassandra's Photographs" by Lisa Goldstein (*Isaac Asimov's Science Fiction Magazine*, August 1987)

"The Faithful Companion at Forty" by Karen Joy Fowler (*Isaac Asimov's Science Fiction Magazine*, July 1987)

*"Forever Yours, Anna" by Kate Wilhelm (*Omni*, July 1987)

"Temple to a Minor Goddess" by Susan Shwartz (*Amazing Stories*, January 1987)

"Why I Left Harry's All-Night Hamburgers" by Lawrence Watt-Evans (*Isaac Asimov's Science Fiction Magazine*, July 1987)

"Kid Charlemagne" by Paul Di Filippo (*Amazing Stories*, September 1987)

Active members of the Science Fiction Writers of America decide the Nebula Awards. Founded in 1965 by Damon Knight, SFWA's first president, the organization began with a charter membership of seventy-eight writers; it now has nearly a thousand members.

Lloyd Biggle, Jr., SFWA's first secretary-treasurer, proposed in 1965 that the organization publish an annual anthology of the best stories of the year. This notion, wrote Damon Knight in his introduction to *Nebula Award Stories: 1965* (Doubleday, 1966), "rapidly grew into an annual ballot of SFWA's members to choose the best stories, and an annual awards banquet." Judith Ann Lawrence designed the trophy, from a sketch by Kate Wilhelm; it is a block of lucite containing a rock crystal and a spiral nebula made of metallic glitter. No two handmade trophies are exactly alike.

Since 1965, the Nebula Awards have been given each year for the best novel, novella, novelette, and short story published during the preceding year. An award for Best Dramatic

Presentation first given in 1972 lasted only three years, the membership later voting to restrict the Nebula to published literary works. An anthology including the winning short fiction and selected runners-up is published each year. The Nebula Awards banquet takes place every spring, its location alternating years between New York City and the West Coast.

The Grand Master Nebula Award goes to a living author for a lifetime's achievement. The membership bestows it no more than six times in a decade. In accordance with SFWA bylaws, the president, who traditionally consults with past presidents and the board of directors, nominates a candidate. This nomination then goes before the officers; if a majority approve, that candidate becomes a Grand Master.

To date, nine writers have received the Grand Master Nebula: Robert A. Heinlein in 1974, Jack Williamson in 1975, Clifford D. Simak in 1976, L. Sprague de Camp in 1978, Fritz Leiber in 1981, Andre Norton in 1983, Arthur C. Clarke in 1985, Isaac Asimov in 1986, and Alfred Bester in 1987. Bester died before the official presentation of his award, but learned before his death that SFWA had selected him to receive it. Simak and Heinlein, respectively the third and first Grand Masters, died within two weeks of each other in the spring of 1988. In less than a year, then, SFWA lost a third of its designated Grand Masters. To quote Damon Knight, "The future isn't what it used to be." In the absence of these three commanding figures, it won't be again.

Past Nebula Award Winners

1965

Best Novel: *Dune* by Frank Herbert
Best Novella: "The Saliva Tree" by Brian W. Aldiss
   "He Who Shapes" by Roger Zelazny (tie)
Best Novelette: "The Doors of His Face, the Lamps of His
   Mouth" by Roger Zelazny
Best Short Story: " 'Repent, Harlequin!' Said the Ticktock-
   man" by Harlan Ellison

1966

Best Novel: *Flowers for Algernon* by Daniel Keyes
   Babel-17 by Samuel R. Delany (tie)
Best Novella: "The Last Castle" by Jack Vance
Best Novelette: "Call Him Lord" by Gordon R. Dickson
Best Short Story: "The Secret Place" by Richard McKenna

1967

Best Novel: *The Einstein Intersection* by Samuel R. Delany
Best Novella: "Behold the Man" by Michael Moorcock
Best Novelette: "Gonna Roll the Bones" by Fritz Leiber
Best Short Story: "Aye, and Gomorrah" by Samuel R. Delany

1968

Best Novel: *Rite of Passage* by Alexei Panshin
Best Novella: "Dragonrider" by Anne McCaffrey
Best Novelette: "Mother to the World" by Richard Wilson
Best Short Story: "The Planners" by Kate Wilhelm

1969

Best Novel: *The Left Hand of Darkness* by Ursula K. Le Guin
Best Novella: "A Boy and His Dog" by Harlan Ellison
Best Novelette: "Time Considered as a Helix of Semi-
Precious Stones" by Samuel R. Delany
Best Short Story: "Passengers" by Robert Silverberg

1970

Best Novel: *Ringworld* by Larry Niven
Best Novella: "Ill Met in Lankhmar" by Fritz Leiber
Best Novelette: "Slow Sculpture" by Theodore Sturgeon
Best Short Story: No award

1971

Best Novel: *A Time of Changes* by Robert Silverberg
Best Novella: "The Missing Man" by Katherine MacLean
Best Novelette: "The Queen of Air and Darkness" by Poul
Anderson
Best Short Story: "Good News from the Vatican" by Robert
Silverberg

1972

Best Novel: *The Gods Themselves* by Isaac Asimov
Best Novella: "A Meeting with Medusa" by Arthur C. Clarke

Best Novelette: "Goat Song" by Poul Anderson
Best Short Story: "When It Changed" by Joanna Russ

1973

Best Novel: *Rendezvous with Rama* by Arthur C. Clarke
Best Novella: "The Death of Doctor Island" by Gene Wolfe
Best Novelette: "Of Mist, and Grass and Sand" by Vonda N. McIntyre
Best Short Story: "Love Is the Plan, the Plan Is Death" by James Tiptree, Jr.
Best Dramatic Presentation: *Soylent Green*

1974

Best Novel: *The Dispossessed* by Ursula K. Le Guin
Best Novella: "Born with the Dead" by Robert Silverberg
Best Novelette: "If the Stars Are Gods" by Gordon Eklund and Gregory Benford
Best Short Story: "The Day Before the Revolution" by Ursula K. Le Guin
Best Dramatic Presentation: *Sleeper*
Grand Master Award: Robert A. Heinlein

1975

Best Novel: *The Forever War* by Joe Haldeman
Best Novella: "Home Is the Hangman" by Roger Zelazny
Best Novelette: "San Diego Lightfoot Sue" by Tom Reamy
Best Short Story: "Catch That Zeppelin!" by Fritz Leiber
Best Dramatic Presentation: *Young Frankenstein*
Grand Master: Jack Williamson

1976

Best Novel: *Man Plus* by Frederik Pohl
Best Novella: "Houston, Houston, Do You Read?" by James Tiptree, Jr.
Best Novelette: "The Bicentennial Man" by Isaac Asimov
Best Short Story: "A Crowd of Shadows" by Charles L. Grant
Grand Master: Clifford D. Simak

1977

Best Novel: *Gateway* by Frederik Pohl
Best Novella: "Stardance" by Spider and Jeanne Robinson
Best Novelette: "The Screwfly Solution" by Raccoona Sheldon
Best Short Story: "Jeffty Is Five" by Harlan Ellison
Special Award: *Star Wars*

1978

Best Novel: *Dreamsnake* by Vonda N. McIntyre
Best Novella: "The Persistence of Vision" by John Varley
Best Novelette: "A Glow of Candles, a Unicorn's Eye" by Charles L. Grant
Best Short Story: "Stone" by Edward Bryant
Grand Master: L. Sprague de Camp

1979

Best Novel: *The Fountains of Paradise* by Arthur C. Clarke
Best Novella: "Enemy Mine" by Barry Longyear
Best Novelette: "Sandkings" by George R. R. Martin
Best Short Story: "giANTS" by Edward Bryant

1980

Best Novel: *Timescape* by Gregory Benford
Best Novella: "The Unicorn Tapestry" by Suzy McKee Charnas
Best Novelette: "The Ugly Chickens" by Howard Waldrop
Best Short Story: "Grotto of the Dancing Deer" by Clifford D. Simak

1981

Best Novel: *The Claw of the Conciliator* by Gene Wolfe
Best Novella: "The Saturn Game" by Poul Anderson
Best Novelette: "The Quickening" by Michael Bishop
Best Short Story: "The Bone Flute" by Lisa Tuttle*
Grand Master: Fritz Leiber

1982

Best Novel: *No Enemy But Time* by Michael Bishop
Best Novella: "Another Orphan" by John Kessel
Best Novelette: "Fire Watch" by Connie Willis
Best Short Story: "A Letter From the Clearys" by Connie Willis

1983

Best Novel: *Startide Rising* by David Brin
Best Novella: "Hardfought" by Greg Bear
Best Novelette: "Blood Music" by Greg Bear
Best Short Story: "The Peacemaker" by Gardner Dozois
Grand Master: Andre Norton

* This Nebula Award was declined by the author.

1984

Best Novel: *Neuromancer* by William Gibson
Best Novella: "PRESS ENTER■" by John Varley
Best Novelette: "Bloodchild" by Octavia E. Butler
Best Short Story: "Morning Child" by Gardner Dozois

1985

Best Novel: *Ender's Game* by Orson Scott Card
Best Novella: "Sailing to Byzantium" by Robert Silverberg
Best Novelette: "Portraits of His Children" by George R. R. Martin
Best Short Story: "Out of All Them Bright Stars" by Nancy Kress
Grand Master: Arthur C. Clarke

1986

Best Novel: *Speaker for the Dead* by Orson Scott Card
Best Novella: "R & R" by Lucius Shepard
Best Novelette: "The Girl Who Fell into the Sky" by Kate Wilhelm
Best Short Story: "Tangents" by Greg Bear
Grand Master Award: Isaac Asimov

Those who are interested in category-related awards should also consult *A History of the Hugo, Nebula, and International Fantasy Awards* by Donald Franson and Howard DeVore, Misfit Press, 1987. Periodically updated, the book is available from Howard DeVore, 4705 Weddel, Dearborn, Michigan 48125. According to George Zebrowski, "The book's special value is in its listings of recommended works for the preliminary Nebula ballot and the number of votes received."

Permission Acknowledgments